RISKIN

ALSO BY STEPHANIE HARTE

Tangled Lives

RISKING IT ALL

Stephanie Harte

An Aria Book

This edition first published in the United Kingdom in 2020 by Aria,
an imprint of Head of Zeus Ltd

A CIP catalogue record for this book is available
from the British Library.

ISBN: 9781035905485

Typeset by Siliconchips Services Ltd UK

Aria
c/o Head of Zeus
First Floor East
5–8 Hardwick Street
London EC1R 4RG

www.ariafiction.com

In loving memory of Grace Christie

19.11.99-11.2.17

My much-loved niece, deeply missed,
forever in my heart.

RISKING IT ALL

Stephanie Harte

1

Gemma

As long as I live, I'll never forget Bank Holiday Monday, August 31, the day my world turned upside down. Returning to our flat after a fourteen-hour shift, I put my key in the lock, and as I did, my eyes were drawn to a red smear on the white woodwork. A shiver ran down my spine as I closed the door behind me. I could see Nathan in the kitchen running water into the sink.

'Is everything OK?' I slipped my arm around his waist and went to kiss his cheek. That was when I noticed the blood pouring from his nose, dripping rhythmically onto the stainless steel before swirling down the drain.

'How was work?' Nathan asked as he cleaned himself up.

'Never mind that, what's happened to you?' I felt my heartbeat quicken.

'It's nothing; it's just a nosebleed.' Nathan brushed aside the issue of his mashed-up face.

Peering over Nathan's broad shoulder, I studied his profile. 'It's more than a nosebleed. Do you think it's broken?'

'I doubt it.'

'You look terrible.' I let out a long breath.

'You should see the other guy.' Nathan laughed.

It wasn't funny. I shook my head, frustrated by his attitude. It was obvious he'd been in a fight. 'Aren't you going to tell me what happened?' Folding my arms across my chest, I eyed him suspiciously while I waited for his reply.

'Let's just say my latest business deal didn't quite go to plan!' Nathan smiled. 'Honestly, Gemma, don't look so worried. I'm all right. The blood makes it look worse than it is.' Nathan paused and examined the dried stains on the front of his white T-shirt.

While I took in the extent of his injuries, my hand ran up and down his back. Apart from his bleeding nose, Nathan had multiple cuts on the left side of his face, and his eye socket was swollen and bruised. He'd been beaten to a pulp.

'Why don't you pour us some wine? I could do with a drink.'

I was halfway down my glass of Shiraz when Nathan sat down next to me on the sofa. Leaning forward, he kissed me on the cheek and then took hold of my hand. He pushed my brown hair out of the way, pulled me towards him, and kissed the side of my neck. The familiar smell of Davidoff's Cool Water filled my nostrils. I wanted to know what had happened to him, so I pulled away and shifted in my seat to create some distance between us.

'I think you'd better tell me what's going on.' As I spoke, I looked Nathan dead in the eye.

'Listen, Gemma, I can't go into details. I don't want to involve you.'

'I'm your wife, so I'm already involved.' Moving closer towards him, I squeezed Nathan's hand. 'Please tell me what happened.' I bit down hard on the side of my lip while I waited for him to speak.

Nathan lowered his dark eyes to avoid my gaze. 'Somebody I know was selling cheap laptops...' Nathan paused.

My heart sank. 'That doesn't explain what happened to your face. Please tell me the truth,' I said to fill the awkward silence.

'I didn't have enough cash for the deal, so I borrowed some money from a guy called Alfie.'

'Alfie Watson?'

'Yeah.'

I let go of Nathan's hand. Suddenly, everything had become clear. Just the mention of that man's name made angry vibes radiate from me.

'Oh for God's sake, Nathan, why the hell did you do that?' I felt fury flash across my face.

'I needed the money quickly. The deal was too good to pass up.'

Nathan's judgement was somewhat impaired when it came to making financial decisions. His business ventures were never successful and always ended in disaster.

Turning my palms up, I threw my hands in the air. 'I can't believe you were stupid enough to take a loan from Alfie Watson.'

Nathan shrugged his shoulders and ignored my comment.

'Have you lost your mind?' I was so angry; steam was almost coming out of my ears.

'No, Gemma, I haven't.' Nathan threw me the wounded look he'd perfected over the years, having used it a thousand times before. 'I don't know why you're overreacting like this.'

'I'm not overreacting. Look what he's done to you.'

Nathan and I had just experienced first-hand the way Alfie liked to carry out business. The man was a gangster. I touched the side of my husband's face with my fingertips, but he turned away from me and suddenly stood up. Nathan went quiet for a moment. I wondered what he was thinking about as he watched me without blinking.

'I brought this on myself.'

My eyes widened, and my mouth fell open in disbelief. I stared at Nathan, stunned that he was trying to justify Alfie's behaviour. But he was wasting his time; I was having none of it.

'How did you come to that conclusion?' I couldn't control the sarcasm in my voice.

'I provoked him by missing my first repayment.'

I knew this was how people got trapped in a spiral of debt. 'And that gave Alfie the right to kick the shit out of you, did it?' I put my hands on my hips and glared at my husband.

'I can see you're annoyed with me.'

I let out a loud sigh.

'I'm sorry, I messed up.' Nathan cast his eyes towards the floor.

If someone had given me a pound every time I'd heard

him say that, I'd be a millionaire by now, and then we wouldn't be in this situation.

'There's no telling what Alfie will do if we don't have the money when he comes back to collect it. Doesn't that worry you?'

'It'll be OK. I just need to sell the laptops.'

2

Gemma

I was woken in the early hours of the morning when Alfie and his four henchmen appeared in our flat. Adrenaline coursed through my veins when I saw the outline of their figures in the bedroom doorway. Terrified by their intrusion, I shook Nathan awake.

'Alfie's here. How did he get in?' I whispered.

Nathan threw me a sheepish look. 'I forgot to mention Alfie made me give him my key.'

My eyes sprung open. How could he forget to tell me something like that? Alfie was the first to enter our room. He stood at the foot of our bed, smoking a cigarette, watching us in silence.

'Don't look so worried. We're not here to hurt you,' Alfie said, as he sat down on the mattress.

But one of the men undermined his assurance. He stood in the shadows catching a baseball bat in his huge hand as he swung it backwards and forwards. Tunnel vision made me focus on it, and I blocked out every other sight and sound in the room.

Nathan put his arm around my trembling shoulder, and I edged closer to him. 'Please leave Gemma out of this.'

'Ah, isn't that sweet?' Alfie said, flashing a brilliant white smile. But almost instantly, his smile faded.

Alfie stood up, and I saw something shiny in his hand. Something silver glinted in the darkness. My eyes were glued to him as he approached me. When he got closer, my breathing became laboured. The light bounced off the blade when Alfie placed the knife against my throat. Dry-mouthed fear took over me. Holding the weapon in one hand, he stubbed out his cigarette on my bedside cabinet with the other. Pulling the quilt off me, he ran his free hand up and down my arm. His touch made me shudder, and I felt the contents of my stomach rise. I thought I was going to throw up.

'You're a lucky man, Nathan. You're married to a beautiful woman. It would be a real shame if something happened to change her good looks.' Alfie smirked.

'Please, leave her alone. This has got nothing to do with Gemma.'

'If you don't hand over five grand by six o'clock tomorrow evening we'll need to renegotiate our deal.' Alfie smiled.

'Five grand? I only borrowed five hundred from you.'

'I know you did, but you have a very bad credit history, Nathan, and lending money to someone like yourself is risky for my company.'

'You'll get your money back. I gave you my word.'

'And in the meantime, I'm making sure I'm properly

compensated.' Alfie winked then smooth down his slicked-back hair that wasn't out of place. 'Gentlemen, if you're ready we'll call it a night.' Alfie put the knife back inside his jacket, turned to his backup team and gestured towards the door. 'I'll be in touch,' he said over his shoulder before walking out of our flat with his men in tow.

'Are you OK?' Nathan asked, pulling me into his arms.

Overcome by terror, I was unable to speak and sat trembling in the bed. We stayed very still under the quilt, our eyes wide open, holding on to each other as Alfie's footsteps echoed down the stairs.

'Shush, it's all right, they've gone now.' Nathan stroked my hair and kissed the top of my head.

'Are you sure?'

Nathan nodded.

My mind began racing, as I replayed what had just happened. That was the most terrifying thing that had happened to me. I thought Alfie was going to kill me. But then I realised this was just a warning. If Alfie had wanted me dead, I wouldn't be breathing now. I began to sob, shaken up by the whole experience.

'Don't cry. Everything's going to be all right.'

I collapsed into my husband's arms with tears streaming down my face. Suddenly, I pulled away from Nathan and looked him in the eye. 'How does Alfie know where we live?'

Nathan shrugged his shoulders. 'I don't know.'

'What if he comes back?' After tonight, I'm not sure I'll ever feel safe in my home again.

'He won't. I'll give Alfie the money tomorrow, and then he'll leave us alone.' Nathan weaved his fingers into my long brown hair.

'Where are you going to get five thousand pounds from?'

'Don't worry. I'll get it. Now, let's get some sleep.'

Even though I was mentally drained and physically exhausted, sleep was the last thing on my mind. As I tried to drift off, the recurring vision of tonight's visit played over and over again. It was on a loop inside my head. I was scared to close my eyes. Every time I did, I could see Alfie's face.

Nathan pulled me towards him and wrapped his arms around me. That was the last thing I remember before I fell into a fretful sleep. When I jolted awake, covered in sweat, Nathan lay beside me, staring at the ceiling.

'It's OK, you've just had a bad dream.' Nathan stroked my cheek before planting a kiss on the tip of my nose.

'No, it's not OK. What will Alfie do to us if you can't pay back the money?' Turning onto my side, I stared at my husband.

'He's not going to do anything because I'm going to pay back every penny.' Nathan avoided making eye contact with me and continued to stare at the ceiling.

'But how are you going to raise five thousand pounds in such a short space of time?' I slid my hand onto his bare chest to get his attention.

'I'll think of something.'

'After you pay him back, promise me you'll never get involved with Alfie again.' I studied Nathan's face for a reaction.

'I won't.' Nathan turned towards me and looked deeply into my eyes. 'I'm sorry I put you in danger. If I'd known what Alfie was capable of, I'd never have borrowed the money from him in the first place.'

'Are you sure you'll be able to raise that amount of cash by tomorrow?'

'Yes.'

Although I was furious with Nathan for getting us into this situation, he'd somehow convinced me the ordeal would soon be over, and at this point, I had no reason not to believe him.

3

Nathan ?

Nathan pushed open the door of Mamma Donatella's Italian restaurant. Rosa looked up from setting the table as her son approached her, and a huge smile spread across her face.

'Can I ask you a favour?'

'Of course.' Rosa reached up, placed her hands on the sides of Nathan's face and planted two kisses on his cheeks. 'What happened to you? Did you get in a fight?'

Nathan ignored his mother's questions and got straight to the point. 'Can you lend me some money?'

Rosa shook her head before walking across to the counter. Picking up her handbag, she took out her purse. 'You're thirty-two years old, Nathan, but sometimes you still act like a little boy. How much do you want this time?' she asked, taking out a twenty-pound note.

'I need a bit more than that.'

Rosa looked in her purse again. 'That's all I've got on me.'

Nathan bit his lip and walked over to where she was standing. 'Can I borrow five grand?'

Rosa looked into the troubled face of her son. 'That's a lot of money. Why do you need so much?'

'For a business deal,' Nathan replied, running his knuckles under his chin.

'I'm sorry, Nathan, I haven't got that sort of money.' Rosa went back to laying the tables.

'Can you borrow it from Donatella?' Nathan hoped his mother wouldn't notice the desperation in his voice.

Rosa stopped what she was doing and looked up at her son. Her eyes narrowed as she peered at him. 'You want me to borrow five thousand pounds from my sister?'

'Yes.'

'I can't do that.' Rosa shook her head.

'Please, Mum, I wouldn't ask you if I had another option.'

Rosa let out a long breath. 'OK I'll try, but I'm not making any promises.'

'Can you get the money today?' Nathan crossed the room and stood next to his mother.

'I don't know. Anyway, what's the rush?' Rosa paused and fixed Nathan with an interrogating stare.

'Today's the deadline for the deal.' Nathan shoved his hands into the front pockets of his jeans.

'Aren't you going to tell me what the deal is?'

Why was she asking so many questions? 'It's just a bit of business.' Nathan rolled his eyes, irritated by the constant barrage.

Rosa looked up at her son and folded her arms across her chest. 'I think I have a right to know what you'll be spending the money on. I'm sorry, Nathan, but if you don't tell me what it's for, I'm not going to ask Donatella to lend it to you.'

Nathan thought for a moment. He didn't want his mother to know he owed the money to a gangster. But she wasn't about to back down, so he decided to bite the bullet and come clean. It would be too stressful trying to hide the truth from her. 'I need it to pay off Alfie Watson.' Nathan braced himself for her response.

At first, Rosa froze at the mention of Alfie's name. Then she threw her hands up and started shouting at her only child. 'For goodness' sake, Nathan. Why did you borrow money from him? That family are nothing but trouble.'

Nathan lowered his eyes and looked out from under his thick dark lashes as Rosa glared at him. She didn't need to tell him something he was fully aware of, but that wouldn't stop her. Nathan let out a long sigh. He wasn't in the mood for one of her lectures, but he'd have to bite his tongue if he wanted her help.

'Is that how you got the black eye?' Rosa's expression softened, and she squeezed her son's hand.

'You've missed your vocation. You should have been a detective.' Nathan managed a half-smile. He'd never been able to fool his mother. She always got to the bottom of things.

'You might be a grown man, but I'm going to give you some advice whether you like it or not.'

Here we go again, Nathan thought, knowing he was about to take a reluctant ride on the merry-go-round that was powered by Rosa's nagging. The topic occasionally varied, but the dialogue never changed. It was draining. Even though he knew her words of wisdom stemmed from genuine concern, he didn't want to hear them. But if he didn't let her vent, he'd have a situation on his hands. There was no point trying to silence his mother when she was about to give him a piece of her mind.

'Once you pay back the money, stay away from the Watsons. They're dangerous.'

'I will.'

'If I do this for you, I want you to do me a favour.' Rosa obviously wasn't going to miss the opportunity to strike a bargain.

'What's that?' Nathan knew there would be a price to pay for Rosa's generosity.

'This is the last time I'm bailing you out. Do you understand?' Rosa wagged her finger.

'Yes.' Nathan threw his arms around Rosa's small, curvy frame and hugged her tightly. She had raised him alone, and they were extremely close. 'Thanks, Mum.'

Rosa pulled away and looked her son in the eye. 'It's about time you got yourself a proper job.'

Nathan shook his head. 'I've got a proper job.' He considered himself an entrepreneur, and no amount of Rosa's pestering was going to turn him into a corporate suit.

Rosa had worked hard over the years to make ends meet. There was no doubt that had caused her a great deal of stress and had given her sleepless nights. Nathan knew Rosa had done her best for him. It couldn't have been easy raising a child on her own, but he'd hated being the poor kid at school. It was just another thing that made him stand out from his cruel classmates. Most of them had two parents and siblings and lived in large houses. He resented having to live in a small rented flat with his mum because his father had abandoned them, and having to wear supermarket trainers when everyone else had designer ones was such a humiliating experience, it left him with a deep-seated obsession for money and material things.

Because of his humble beginnings, Nathan was determined to overcome any obstacles that would stop him from realising his dream to be financially successful. He was convinced money was the key to happiness, and although Rosa had tried to instil a good work ethic in him from an early age, he was more interested in get-rich-quick schemes. He wasn't going to work long hours, seven days a week for a pittance like his mum. Nathan didn't want the type of risk-free job that came with a big salary and a shiny Apple MacBook. That was too safe an option.

4

Gemma

This wasn't the first time Nathan had got us into trouble. He had a history of making terrible financial decisions, but borrowing money from a man like Alfie Watson was the worst one so far. Everyone knew Alfie. His reputation as a dangerous, trigger-happy gangster and head of a notorious crime gang preceded him.

Why hadn't Nathan texted me to say he'd given Alfie the money back? Questions flooded my mind. I was all over the place and found it impossible to concentrate at work. It didn't help that business was always slow at the restaurant when it was wet outside. The day dragged on, and I spent most of it clock-watching. With nothing to do apart from stare at the rain pelting against the glass, I peered out of the steamed-up windows of Mamma Donatella's while the only two customers nursed their cold cappuccinos.

'At this rate, they could still be here when we open for lunch tomorrow,' Bernardo said under his breath. 'You look exhausted, Gemma.'

'I didn't sleep well last night.' That was an understatement. I'd tossed and turned and felt so unsettled after Alfie's unexpected visit.

'Why don't you go home? We're not busy. I'll see you in the morning,' Bernardo said.

After grabbing an umbrella from the stand near the entrance, I made the short journey home. Since the bank repossessed our home, following another of Nathan's failed business deals, his aunt and uncle had let us live in the flat above the restaurant. It was a sparsely furnished one-bedroomed property, but we were in no position to be ungrateful and knew we were lucky to have it.

The first thing I noticed when I opened the front door and entered the hall was the mess. My heart sank. Surely we hadn't been burgled in broad daylight? Broken glass littered the floor and crunched under my feet as I walked across to where the phone dangled. It had been ripped from the wall. The small table that used to stand below it was now smashed to pieces. I glanced into the kitchen. The contents of all the cupboards were turned upside down and lay scattered over the floor, with broken crockery everywhere. An overturned bookshelf blocked the living room doorway. Lifting it up, I stepped over the books strewn across the entrance. Then I spotted Nathan in the far corner of the room, tied to a chair with a black sack over his head.

'Oh my God!' I dropped down on my knees by his side and quickly removed the bag. He had a cloth in his mouth that prevented him from speaking. 'Are you OK?'

'Can you untie me?' Nathan croaked. His mouth had dried out.

I tried to free Nathan's hands, but he was bound so

tightly I couldn't loosen the knot. Gasping for breath, he began to cough.

'Let me get you some water.'

Sifting through the debris on the kitchen floor, I managed to find an unbroken plastic tumbler. Filling it with cold tap water, I rushed back to Nathan's side and held it up to his lips. Then I managed to untie his wrists that were secured with rope behind the back of the chair. His ankles were bound to the wooden legs with duct tape.

'No prizes for guessing who did this to you. You did give Alfie the money, didn't you?' So many questions were spinning around in my head.

'I gave him five grand,' Nathan replied, rubbing his wrists.

'So what's the problem? I don't understand.' My eyebrows knitted together in a frown, none of this made any sense to me.

'Alfie's changed his mind; he's decided I owe ten grand now.' Nathan lowered his head and let out a defeated sigh.

I felt anger radiate from me. His interest rates were extortionate. There must be something we could do. We couldn't let Alfie get away with this. 'Can't we go to the police?'

'No way.' Nathan shook his head.

I reached forward and touched my husband's arm with my fingertips. Nathan looked away and rubbed the back of his neck. We had to report this.

'You could have Alfie arrested for what he's done to you.'

Nathan turned around and glared at me. 'If I get Alfie nicked, what do you think he'd do to us?'

I shrugged my shoulders.

'Trust me, Gemma, we can't go running to the cops. We

don't want to upset him any more than we already have. Otherwise, he'll do more than just threaten us.'

My eyes widened. 'So you'd call being beaten up, gagged and tied to a chair in your own home a threat, would you?'

'I didn't keep my side of the deal. This is the way things work in his world. He's just giving me a warning.'

If that was the case, I dreaded to think what Alfie was capable of. This wasn't a bit of low-level intimidation. What the hell had Nathan got us into? We'd been in some scrapes before, but nothing on this level and I had to admit I was scared to death. Nathan had been my partner for all of my adult life, and I couldn't imagine ever being without him. I loved him with all my heart, but being married to a man who liked to push the self-destruct button wasn't easy. I buried my head in my hands as my tears began flowing freely.

'Don't cry, Gemma.' Nathan threw his arms around my shoulders and pulled me towards him.

What were we going to do? I couldn't believe a loan for five hundred pounds had turned into a debt of ten grand in a matter of days. That was some interest rate. But that was how men like Alfie made a living. He didn't have a conscience. I stepped back from Nathan and wiped my tears away on the back of my hand. Looking around the room at the devastation, it was clear to see we were in way over our heads.

'If I don't give Alfie another five grand by tomorrow, I'll have to face the consequences.'

It wasn't a closely guarded secret that men like Alfie smiled with pleasure when they inflicted pain on their victims.

Nathan laughed off the threat. His defence mechanism was kicking in, but it wasn't funny. It suddenly struck me that possessions are replaceable, people are not. Nathan's life was in danger. I couldn't bear the thought of something happening to him over a stupid debt. Nathan was the love of my life, and even though he drove me insane sometimes, I wouldn't want to face the future without him.

Alfie Watson was not a person to be messed with. He wanted his money back, and he'd use any means to get it. But we had no way of raising the money, so what were we going to do? When we lost our home, the creditors took everything and left us penniless. The few belongings we'd managed to replace were now smashed to pieces, so selling them wasn't going to be an option.

Nathan and I locked eyes and stood in silence, trying to take in the enormity of the situation. Although Nathan was putting on a front, I could tell he was as scared as I was. Nathan slipped his arms around my waist and kissed the side of my neck. I put my hands on his biceps to create some distance between us.

'What will happen tomorrow when we haven't got the money?'

5

Nathan

Alfie didn't believe in ringing the doorbell. Just after midnight, he let himself into our flat when Gemma and I were in bed. Maybe it was just my unsociable nature, but I didn't like people showing up unexpectedly. I'd hoped he might have a change of heart and not come after me for the rest of the money. The amount he was expecting me to repay on a five hundred pound loan was ridiculous.

'Have you got my money?' Alfie asked.

'No.'

'That's very disappointing, and I had such high hopes for you.' Alfie shook his head.

'I'll get the other five grand. But I'm going to need more time.' Throwing back the covers, I got out of bed and stood in front of Alfie, in my Calvin Klein boxer shorts.

'That's one thing I can't give you. How old are you, Nathan?'

Alfie looked me straight in the eye before taking a long

drag on his cigarette. Then the bastard exhaled the smoke straight into my face.

'Thirty-two.'

'You're only three years younger than me, and you haven't got a pot to piss in.'

Out of the corner of my eye, I could see Gemma watching me as my expression changed. I was fuming; Alfie had hit a nerve. I'd spent my whole life trying to shake off the poverty label without much success. I just hoped I could control my temper. I couldn't afford to escalate the situation. Dropping his cigarette onto the floor, Alfie ground it out with his leather shoe. His disregard for our flat made my blood boil. When his men trashed it yesterday while Gemma was at work, they'd destroyed most of our possessions, ripping up clothing and smashing anything breakable. I could see she'd found the experience traumatic. It was the second time she'd lost everything and that was hard for her to accept.

'I'm a generous man, so I'm going to give you the opportunity to put things right between us,' Alfie said.

'What do you want me to do?' I asked the question, but I was dreading the answer.

'You won't be doing anything. You just need to take a seat.' Alfie smirked.

Gemma and I exchanged a glance, and a puzzled expression spread over her face. Alfie laughed and looked over his shoulder to where the other men were standing.

'Knuckles, bring Gemma over here.'

My mouth fell open in horror. I tried to think straight, but my mind was all over the place. I glared at Alfie with wide eyes. What was he playing at?

The huge guy who had been wielding the baseball bat

last night approached the bed. He pulled the covers off Gemma, breaking her nail as she tried in vain to cling to them. Grabbing her by her wrist, he pulled her to her feet.

'Get your hands off her,' I shouted, scrambling over the bed. I shoved Knuckles in the chest with the palm of my hand to get him away from my terrified wife. But the blow didn't move him. The man was built like a brick shithouse.

'Nathan, if you take another step, Frankie will blow your fucking head off,' Alfie said. The man produced a gun from inside his suit jacket before stepping behind me with the weapon drawn.

Nothing could have prepared me for the spectrum of emotions I experienced while I waited for Alfie to decide Gemma's fate. At first, I felt numb. I couldn't believe this was happening to us. Then I felt fear and utter helplessness. I wanted to protect my wife from Alfie, but I was powerless to stop him while the barrel of a gun was digging into the back of my skull. I hoped Alfie wasn't going to rape her. I'd always thought masked men in dark alleyways assaulted women. But that was before I entered Alfie Watson's seedy world. This man had walked into my home, and now he was threatening the most important person in my life. I didn't care what happened to me, just as long as he didn't hurt Gemma.

Alfie stood in front of her, immaculately dressed in a dark navy three-piece suit. Knuckles was still holding her wrist. She struggled against him to break his grip. Alfie's eyes scanned over my wife, and that's when my anger kicked in. It was time he realised, I wasn't going to let him do anything to her without me putting up a fight. In a fit of rage, I lunged towards him, but Alfie's minder grabbed my arm and wrenched it behind my back before my fist had time to connect with his face. Gemma managed to slap Alfie herself, catching him square on the jaw. I had to suppress a smile when I saw the red mark it left on his skin.

Alfie began to laugh. 'It's OK, Knuckles, you can let her go now. You're feisty, aren't you? I'm impressed.'

'I'm not trying to impress you.' Gemma looked Alfie straight in the eye, with thinly veiled contempt.

'Ouch, Gemma, you really know how to hurt a man's feelings.'

Alfie clutched his heart as if her words had wounded him before he moved towards her and picked up a lock of her long brown hair. He held it up to his nose and inhaled deeply. It freaked her out, and I saw her flinch.

'Relax, Gemma, I'm not going to hurt you. I just wanted to get a closer look at you. Now let's get back to business. Your husband owes me a lot of money.'

'I know he does, but you've made it impossible for him to pay it back,' Gemma said, unable to hide the anger in her voice.

'I gave Nathan a deadline, but he's failed to meet it. I'm going to offer you an alternative. Would you like to know what it is?'

Gemma nodded.

'If you visit a jewellery shop for me, you can clear Nathan's debt.'

'What's the catch?' Gemma asked, narrowing her eyes.

'Are you always this suspicious?' Alfie laughed. 'There's no catch, I just want you to do a bit of shopping for me.'

'Let me get this straight, if I agree, you'll write off the debt. Is that what you're saying?'

'Yes, that's right. So, talk to me, Gemma, do we have a deal?' Alfie held his hand out towards Gemma.

Gemma looked over at me, and after a moment's contemplation, I spoke. 'I can't let Gemma do that.'

'You don't have another alternative, Nathan,' Alfie replied.

'Let me go instead of her.'

'No.' Alfie shook his head. 'What's your problem, Nathan? I only want her to go shopping for fuck's sake.'

6

Gemma

Nathan and I spent the next week on tenterhooks. On the one hand, we were delighted not to have heard from Alfie, but on the other, we were stuck in a state of constant uncertainty, not knowing when he would come back into our lives. We should have realised we wouldn't have to wait too long.

Alfie paid us a visit in the early hours of the morning, gaining entrance to our flat in the usual manner. There was nothing more terrifying than someone opening your front door while you were asleep in bed. But this was how Alfie set the scene. He instilled fear in you without uttering a word. He had a reputation as a gangland boss to uphold and did whatever he wanted, whenever he wanted. It would have been stupid of us to expect Alfie to call at a reasonable hour and wait for us to let him in.

'I hope I haven't disturbed you.' Alfie's voice sounded menacing in the darkness.

Nathan switched on the bedside lamp. I rubbed sleep from my eyes and attempted to adjust to the unwelcome light.

'It's two o'clock in the morning,' Nathan said.

Alfie pulled back the sleeve of his charcoal grey suit and checked the time on his designer watch. 'I won't keep you long. I just want to make arrangements for my shopping date with Gemma. I'll send a car to pick you up at midday. You'll be going to an expensive shop, so you'll need to dress the part. Make sure you wear something nice, but not too distinctive.'

What did Alfie mean by that? 'No trackies and trainers then,' I replied.

Alfie arched an eyebrow. 'Wear something classy. I want you to look sophisticated.'

A black Mercedes-Benz S-Class Saloon pulled up outside Mamma Donatella's just before twelve.

'Nathan, the car's here. Do I look all right?' I was wearing a black pencil dress and tailored jacket with black barely there high-heeled sandals that fastened with an ankle strap.

'You look incredible, absolutely stunning.' Nathan smiled, pulled me towards him and kissed my cheek. 'Are you OK, Gemma? You're shaking.'

'Am I?' I was terrified and fixed Nathan with a panicked stare.

Nathan wrapped his strong arms around me and held me tightly. 'You don't have to go through with this. I'll go and tell Alfie the deal's off.'

'No, it's OK. I don't know why I'm so nervous. I'm only going shopping.' I pulled away and gave Nathan a half-smile. I needed to get downstairs before I talked myself out of it.

The tinted window lowered as Nathan and I approached the car. 'You've chosen your outfit well. Black is always a good option when you want to blend in.' Alfie let a slow smile spread across his face.

His comments had done nothing to put my mind at ease. I felt more nervous than ever.

Dressed in a dark suit, Alfie's driver stepped out onto the pavement. He walked around to the back passenger door, opened it and waited.

Nathan squeezed my hand, then kissed me on the cheek. He got in the car and took a seat on the cream leather upholstery next to Alfie. 'I can't let Gemma go on her own.' Nathan ran his hand around the back of his neck.

'I'm not surprised you don't want to part with your lovely wife, but we had a deal. You're not coming with us.'

Their eyes locked, and I forced my feet to move. Taking a deep breath, I stood next to the open doorway, tugged on Nathan's arm, and he turned around to face me. 'I'll be back before you know it.'

Nathan got out of the car, threw his arms around me and looked me in the eye. 'Are you sure you want to go through with this?'

I nodded. 'I'd better go.'

'Look after her,' Nathan said when I got in the car.

I didn't take my eyes away from Nathan's until the electric window closed. When the Mercedes pulled away, I glanced over my shoulder. Nathan stood on the edge of the pavement with his head in his hands. So it wasn't just me who thought this was a bad idea then. I stared straight ahead of me. The sooner this was over with, the better. Alfie didn't say a word. He remained tight-lipped for the whole of the awkward journey. You could have cut the atmosphere in the car with a knife.

'Should I park here, Alfie?' the driver said, slowing down outside De Beers Diamonds in Hatton Garden, London's jewellery quarter.

'No, Tommy, drive on for a bit, then park up. I need to give Gemma her instructions.'

My mind went into overdrive, and I balled my hands in my lap. 'So what do you want me to buy?'

'I think you've misunderstood the situation.' Alfie grinned.

Now I was totally confused, so my eyes searched Alfie's for an explanation. 'I thought you wanted me to go shopping?'

'I do, but you're not going to buy anything. You're going to steal it.' Alfie watched my face for a reaction.

I knew there'd be a catch. 'I'm sorry, but I'm not prepared to do that,' I replied, channelling my inner ice queen.

'Do I need to remind you that we had an agreement?' Alfie smirked.

I bit down hard on the pad of my thumb while I considered my options. Alfie laughed. As far as he was concerned, we'd made a deal, and that was binding. Being the boss, he got to dictate the terms; it didn't matter to him if they were fair or not.

'It's too late to pull out.'

Staring into space, I agonised over my decision. 'I can't go through with it.'

'Gemma, I've been more than patient with you, but now I want my money back. If you decide not to do the job, there will be serious repercussions. Do you understand?'

'Yes.' I tried to appear confident, but there was no denying the wobble in my voice when I spoke. At the back of my mind, I knew if I didn't do what Alfie asked, I could end up with a bullet in my head.

'When somebody disappoints me, there are always unpleasant consequences. You don't want to disappoint me, do you?'

Alfie's threatening words were going round and round in my head. 'No, but I can't...'

Alfie interrupted me before I could finish what I was saying. He put his finger under my chin and tilted my face upwards. 'You're such a beautiful young woman; it would be such a shame if something happened to change that, wouldn't it?'

My breathing quickened, and my hands suddenly felt hot and clammy as Alfie's words rang loud and clear in my ears. If I'd thought things were bad before, something told me they were about to get even worse.

Alfie had a reputation for shooting first and asking questions later, so if I didn't go along with his plan, who knew what would happen. Whether I liked it or not, I was about to become his personal shopper; I didn't have a choice in the matter.

'I've never done anything like this before. What if I lose my nerve?' I said, letting out a resigned sigh.

'You won't.'

Alfie turned his blue eyes on me. I could see he wasn't about to change his mind. There was no point stalling any longer. I was just delaying the inevitable. A vision of myself wearing the traditional burglar's dress code of stripy top and a mask, with a bag marked SWAG slung over my shoulder, suddenly popped into my mind.

'I suppose you'd better tell me what you want me to steal then.' I didn't want to do this, but what else could I do? Alfie had complete control of the situation.

'You're going to take a diamond ring.' Alfie smiled.

My eyes grew wide. 'How am I going to get away with that?'

'You're going to switch it.'

'I won't be able to do it.' I was a nervous wreck. I'd never get away with it.

'That's a pity because you've run out of options. Your debt is still outstanding, and the interest on it grows very rapidly. The longer you delay, the more you're going to owe.'

I closed my eyes and took a deep breath. As I tried to psych myself up, I realised I was damned if I did, damned if I didn't. Whichever choice I made, the outcome would be negative. Alfie got out of the car and opened the boot. When he returned, he was carrying a large gift box. He handed it to me and told me to open it. Inside the box was a black Hermès Birkin bag.

'That must have cost a fortune,' I said.

'It did, but you can't play the part of a wealthy woman if you don't have the right props. You'll find everything you need in there. Put the jewellery on and familiarise yourself with the contents of the purse.'

I unzipped the bag and opened the magnetic clasp of the black leather purse. It was stuffed full of fifty-pound notes. 'I'm confused.' Narrowing my eyes, I stared at Alfie. 'Why do I need all this money? I thought you wanted me to steal the ring.'

'I do, but the staff need to believe you can afford to pay for it.'

The purse also contained exclusive credit cards. Taking one out, I examined it. So I was Emma Jones, was I? After removing my jewellery, I slipped on the platinum Rolex, diamond-encrusted wedding ring and huge solitaire from the jewellery wrap.

'Look inside the pouch. That's the ring you're going to switch.' Alfie sank back into the leather seat and watched me over his shoulder.

'Is this really a fake?' I asked when I took the full band eternity ring out of the velvet cover. It didn't look like a lump of glass mounted in metal. Alfie smirked while I turned the ring around in my hand. I watched the light bounce off it. It was so convincing. What if I got them mixed up? My temples were pulsating in time with my heartbeat, and I could feel a tension headache starting.

Alfie turned to face me. 'You're going to walk confidently into the store and use your charm on the employees. Spin them a line about being a bored, wealthy housewife. If they think you have an endless amount of money to spend, they'll be tripping over themselves to serve you.'

I could feel the perspiration break out on my upper lip, but resisted the urge to wipe it away. What if they didn't believe me?

'You only get one chance to make a first impression. People always judge you on your appearance when they're sizing you up, so it's good to have a polished exterior,' Alfie said.

I glanced at him, not a hair out of place, and dressed in an expensive suit. He clearly liked to practise what he preached. To the outside world, Alfie looked like a smart businessman, not a criminal.

'You want the person who serves you to see inside your purse at the first opportunity, so they realise it's bulging with cash.'

Taking a deep breath, I tried to regain control of my racing pulse. My head was pounding, making it difficult for me to concentrate.

'Ask the assistant if you can try on several items of jewellery at once,' Alfie explained. 'Make sure you pick a variety of items from different trays. That will make it harder for them to keep track of what they've got out of the cabinets. The object of the exercise is to confuse the person serving you.' As Alfie spoke, he smoothed back his blond hair.

I didn't know how I was going to remember all of this. Lifting my fingers to my temples, I began massaging the sides of my head.

'Don't stress yourself out, Gemma. You'll be fine once you're inside. There's a lot riding on this.' Alfie smirked.

No pressure then, I thought as doubt filled my mind.

'Your mobile will ring every ten minutes or so, to give you a reason to keep opening your bag. When you feel the time is right, select a ring that looks like the copy, try it on and switch it with the fake one when the assistant isn't looking.' Alfie flashed me a smile.

What if there wasn't a ring that looked like it? I had a horrible feeling I was going to mess this up. I covered my mouth with shaking fingers. Suddenly overcome by a wave of nausea, I wasn't sure I could go through with this. I couldn't imagine stealing the ring would be as easy as that. I looked down at my trembling hands and wondered how I was going to be able to pull this off.

'What if I get caught?'

Alfie fixed me with a blue stare, but he declined to answer my question. His silence put me on edge and did nothing to calm my anxiety.

7

Gemma

I took a deep breath and exhaled loudly. It was time to get this over with. I couldn't put it off any longer. Stepping out of the car in the centre of London's diamond district was overwhelming. With my heart pounding in my chest, I approached the impressive glass-fronted building, trying to appear confident. Pushing open the heavy door, I stepped into the luxurious double-height showroom and crossed the room to the mirrored display cases. The ultra-modern shop was enormous, and my heels echoed ominously on the dark wood floor.

'Hello, my name's Chris,' the sales assistant said.

I looked up into the eyes of the young man dressed in a smart suit and smiled, willing myself to stay calm. 'Hello,' I replied.

'Would you like some help?' Chris asked, tilting his head to the side.

'Yes, please.'

'Are you looking for anything in particular?' Chris's

casual tone struck the right balance between being helpful and not too pushy.

'Not really, just something that catches my eye.'

Chandeliers hung high above the cabinets full of jewels and watch collections. Everything looked incredible as the light bounced around. Following Alfie's instructions, I put the Birkin bag down on the counter, took out my purse and opened it so Chris could see the contents. While pretending to look for something inside it, my eyes scanned the room to locate the security cameras. There were several above the cabinets and one at the entrance.

'Let me know if you'd like a closer look at anything.'

That was my cue. The sooner I made the switch, the sooner I could get out of here. 'Could I try that on, please?'

'Of course.' Chris unlocked the glass case containing an incredible sapphire and diamond bracelet. He opened up the clasp and placed it on my wrist.

I twisted my arm around, admiring the way the stones sparkled. 'It's beautiful. Could I try that ring on as well?'

'I'll have to put the bracelet back first. We're only allowed to get one item out at a time.'

'Oh, that's a shame,' I replied, pasting a dejected expression onto my face.

Chris looked over his shoulder to see if anyone was watching us. 'I'm not meant to do this, but as my manager's on his lunch break, I suppose I could bend the rules on this occasion.'

'Thank you; I'd really appreciate that.'

'If you'd like to follow me.' Chris beamed and began walking to the corner of the showroom, near the entrance. 'I shouldn't be telling you this, but there's a blind spot in the camera field just here, so nobody will be able to see what we're doing.'

That's convenient, I thought, giving him the biggest smile I could muster, while my stomach twisted into a knot.

Chris was going out of his way to be helpful, and I was about to take advantage of that. I didn't want to play the evil villain, but I didn't have another option. A pang of guilt hit me when I looked into his young, trusting eyes. I had to get a grip. This wasn't the right time to lose my nerve and start examining my conscience. My mobile suddenly began to ring in my bag and interrupted my train of thought.

'You're doing great,' Alfie said as if sensing my hesitation.

He hung up before I had a chance to reply, but knowing he was watching my every move didn't put me at ease, it scared the life out of me.

Chris took the pieces I'd selected out of the cabinets. While standing feet from the assistant, I slipped the jewellery on and off. Then I spotted an eternity ring very similar to the one Alfie had given me and asked to try it on. I thought I'd given the game away when I had trouble placing it on my finger. My hands were trembling so badly. Surely Chris must have noticed.

I jumped when my mobile began ringing. 'Excuse me a minute.'

'Of course,' Chris replied, turning away momentarily to give me some privacy.

I reached into my bag, and once my hands were out of sight, I swapped the real diamond with the fake one before answering the call.

'See you soon,' Alfie said before the line went dead.

I had the ring, but I still needed to get it out of the shop without anybody realising. My eyes darted around the room to see if anyone was watching me, but all the other staff were busy with their own customers.

'Are you having trouble deciding?' Chris asked when I placed the fake eternity band back in the tray.

'Is it that obvious?' I replied, trying to keep my voice steady and not let my nerves get the better of me. 'I'm torn between the sapphire and diamond bracelet I first tried on and this.' I pointed to an enormous ruby ring on a different tray from the eternity band.

'You've got good taste,' Chris flattered, delighted at the prospect of selling one of the expensive items he'd shown me.

'What time are you closing today?' I asked, glancing at my platinum Rolex. I hoped he wouldn't notice the perspiration that had broken out on my upper lip.

'Six o'clock.' Chris's voice was full of disappointment.

'In that case, I'll come back later with my husband. I'd like him to help me make the final decision.'

'OK.' Chris began putting all the high-value items of jewellery away, realising the sale had fallen through.

'I'll be back soon. Thank you for all your help.'

'You're welcome.' Chris managed a half-smile.

I took that as my cue to leave and turned away from the counter. Willing myself not to panic or do anything that might arouse suspicion, I began making my way towards the entrance. My palms were sweating, and my legs felt like jelly, but I kept putting one foot in front of the other until I reached the glass doors. Just as I was about to walk out, a man's voice stopped me in my tracks.

'Excuse me, madam,' the security guard said.

I struggled to remain calm. My natural instinct was to run, but instead, I turned towards the huge man while my heart attempted to break through my ribcage. 'Is something the matter?' I asked, drawing in a deep breath. I held it while I waited for him to respond. At that moment, I didn't trust myself to breathe normally. If I started to hyperventilate, I'd look as guilty as I felt.

The guard gestured towards Chris, who was rushing to where I was standing. The world seemed to have slowed down around me as waves of panic washed over me. He must have noticed I'd switched the ring, I thought. This was the moment I'd been dreading. I knew I'd never be able to get away with it and now I'd been caught red-handed.

'Here, take this,' Chris said, beaming from ear to ear as he passed me his card. 'Just in case I'm on a break when you come back. If I'm not on the shop floor, phone me, and I'll come back to serve you.' His hazel eyes lit up at the prospect of making some hefty commission on the sale.

'Thanks,' I replied, doing my best to force the words out of my dry throat as I took the card from him.

'Let me get that for you, madam,' the security guard said as he opened the glass door.

Relief flooded my body, and I drew in shallow breaths as I attempted to slow down my racing heart. Walking out into the bright sunshine and freedom, I gripped the handle of the bag so hard my knuckles turned white.

Tommy opened the passenger door as soon as I stepped out of the store. Slumping onto the cream leather seat, I stared straight ahead at the walnut dashboard and realised that my life would never be the same again.

'I love it when things go according to plan.' A smug

expression spread over Alfie's face. 'You don't look very happy, Gemma.'

'That's because I feel like shit.'

I threw Alfie a filthy look before I dropped my head in my hands. As my chest began to tighten, I concentrated on my breathing. Inhale. Exhale. Inhale. Exhale. Sitting up straight again, I focused my eyes on Alfie's.

Alfie laughed. 'Come on, Gemma, give us a smile.'

Strangely enough, I didn't think I could manage that. This had been the worst day of my life so far, and I had a fair few to choose from.

'You should be proud of yourself. What you just did takes a lot of guts, you know?'

'It was a horrible experience. If you must know, I was terrified.'

'It didn't show. You carried yourself like a true professional. Anyone would think you'd done this a hundred times before.'

'I can assure you I haven't.' I didn't try to hide the angry tone in my voice.

'Then you're a natural. You've been blessed with good looks and a persuasive tongue. Those qualities are essential for this kind of work.'

My eyebrows shot up to my hairline. How dare Alfie say that? Turning away, I broke eye contact. Right now, the last thing I wanted to do was engage in conversation with him.

'Don't get the hump, Gemma.'

I didn't bother to answer him. My silence said it all. I couldn't hide the fact that I was seething. I wouldn't have stolen the ring if I'd had another choice. It struck me how differently we viewed the situation. I felt guilty and full of shame, whereas he was like an excited puppy. As my mind began to wander, I thought about his upbringing and what might have made him turn to a life of crime. But he'd been born into the Watson dynasty, so choosing a different profession was never going to be an option for him.

8

Gemma

My parents taught me the importance of doing the right thing from an early age, even if everyone else wasn't. Throughout my childhood, they'd drummed into me that honesty was the best policy. With the proverbial message ringing in my ears, I knew they'd be disgusted with me for what I'd just done. But they probably wouldn't be surprised. Suffice to say, I was the black sheep of the family and had always been a big disappointment to them.

I was only seventeen when I met Nathan on the beach at Southend. My friends and I had travelled there on a day trip from London. We'd hit it off instantly; we'd both had difficult childhoods, but for very different reasons, so we shared common ground. I fell under the spell of his Latin good looks, and he changed my life. We became inseparable. My parents hit the roof when I dropped out of school without completing my A levels and moved in with him.

They accused me of being a difficult teenager. Apparently,

I was too young to be in such a serious relationship. My family fiercely objected. They felt I was rushing into things and was doing it to spite them. But I wasn't trying to hurt them. I was falling in love. It was a powerful thing and something I'd never experienced before. Nathan was like a breath of fresh air. He showed me what love was supposed to feel like. Since I could remember, I'd dreamt of meeting someone who would love me for me.

My parents wouldn't give Nathan a chance. They thought our relationship was a recipe for disaster, and it would all end in tears. The more they tried to interfere, the further away they pushed me. Nathan and I didn't feel like we were too young to be in a serious relationship, so I took no notice of them. We were in our own little bubble surrounded by the excitement of our brand-new love. We didn't need anything or anyone else.

As I contemplated our current situation, it crossed my mind that if I'd taken their advice and married a wealthy businessman like Rebecca, my perfect younger sister, had done I might not be in this position now. I considered the fact that my parents might have been right when they said Nathan was no good for me and we wouldn't last the test of time. But my stubborn streak wouldn't let me believe it. In my eyes, feeling loved was far more important than money. I'd rather have Nathan in my life than Rebecca's shiny new car and four-storey house any day.

Marriage was something that had to be worked at, and sometimes it could be hard. Nathan and I have had our fair share of problems in the past, but we'd always got through them. So I wouldn't just throw the towel in the minute the going got tough. But right now, we needed to have a serious chat about our future. It was long overdue. The reckless decisions my husband kept making affected both of us, and at the moment, his selfish behaviour was taking its toll on our relationship. Being married to a man with an addiction was draining.

9

Gemma

When we pulled up outside Mamma Donatella's, Nathan flew out of the restaurant door and stood by the side of the blacked-out Mercedes.

'Can I go now?' I asked, giving Alfie a sideways glance.

I faked a polite smile and counted the minutes until I could get out of the car. I could see Nathan pacing backwards and forwards on the pavement out of the corner of my eye and couldn't wait to be reunited with him.

'Nathan looks like he's getting bored waiting for us. Aren't you going to invite me up? We need to discuss the deal we made.'

Alfie gestured to where my husband was standing, looking troubled, presumably to coax me into giving him the right answer. Not for the first time, I felt pressured into doing something I didn't want to do. Against my better judgement, I took the coward's way out and said what he wanted to hear.

'Would you like to come up for a drink?'

'I thought you'd never ask.' Alfie laughed. He leant towards the front seat. 'Open the door for Mrs Stone, will you?'

Tommy stepped out of the car and released me from the upholstered prison I'd been held captive in. Nathan rushed over, and I tumbled into his strong arms. The feeling of them around me, holding me tight, made me feel safe at last.

'Gemma's invited me up for a drink,' Alfie said.

Nathan's brown eyes searched mine. He studied me with a questioning gaze, wondering why I would have suggested that.

Alfie stretched out on our leather sofa with a tumbler of neat Jack Daniel's in his hand. Poised and confident, he looked like a celebrity about to answer questions on a chat show. In complete contrast, Nathan and I sat opposite watching him, fidgeting like two naughty school children outside the headmaster's office.

'Let's get down to business, shall we?' Alfie said after a long, uncomfortable pause.

I stirred in my chair, placed my hands in my lap and took a deep breath, dreading what he was about to say.

'Show Nathan the ring.'

Taking the five-carat diamond eternity band out of the velvet pouch, I handed it to Nathan, and he held the sparkling ring up to the light.

'The job wasn't an easy one, but Gemma did very well. She followed my instructions to the letter.' Alfie swirled his drink around before twisting the glass in his hands, watching our reaction.

Nathan squeezed my hand and smiled at me. 'It's a relief to know our loan is paid off now.'

Alfie laughed. 'Whatever made you think that?'

With fury bubbling up inside me, I got to my feet. 'You said if I got the ring, our debt would be clear. I should have known we couldn't trust you.' I spat out the words before turning my back on him, so I didn't have to see the smug look on his face.

Nathan had realised I was about to blow my top. He could tell I'd reached my tolerance limit. 'Calm down, Gemma.'

That was the worst thing he could have said to me. It was like pouring petrol on a fire. 'Don't tell me to calm down. It's your fault we're in this situation.'

Nathan and I both had a tendency to be fiery, and I lashed out at him in a knee-jerk reaction before remembering we had company. I stole a glance at Alfie out of the corner of my eye. The way he sat grinning, clearly delighted that he'd been able to play Nathan and me off against each other, almost made me lose control, and I was tempted to let him have it. But then I remembered how he felt about people being disrespectful, and I decided maybe this wasn't the right time. Don't take the bait. Just ignore him, I told myself, but that was going to be easier said than done.

'I'm sure you appreciate I'm a very busy man,' Alfie said.

'Yes, we know that.' Nathan stared at me from beneath his long, dark lashes.

Sensing Alfie's blue eyes watching me, I turned to face him, and although I tried not to, I threw him a dirty look before I could stop myself.

'Do you remember how long we spent in the car before you went into De Beers?'

'Yes,' I replied, glaring at him.

'It took me ages to convince you to go through with

your part of the deal, and time is money, so the debt automatically increased.'

That wasn't fair. He never told me that would happen if I didn't go in straight away. I had to hold back angry tears that threatened to spring into my eyes. I was infuriated by the injustice of it all.

'You should have realised the clock was ticking... tick, tock, tick, tock.' Alfie laughed again. He was playing games with us.

I crossed my arms and studied Alfie. I wondered how much we still owed him, but before I asked the question, I had a horrible feeling I already knew the answer. Something told me he would never let us pay off this debt. This was turning into a living nightmare, and there was no way out of it.

Alfie finished his drink, then wiped his lips on the back of his hand. He leant back on the sofa and crossed his long legs at the ankles while maintaining eye contact with me. 'Are you angry with me, Gemma?' he asked with a smile on his face.

Nathan's eyes darted towards me and his brows creased together. I'd seen that look before and knew he was silently telling me to keep quiet before I said something we'd both regret. But I couldn't help myself. I had a tendency to say whatever came into my mind, and didn't always think before I spoke.

'Angry isn't a strong enough word to describe how I'm feeling,' I said through gritted teeth. I couldn't hide the look of disgust on my face.

Alfie straightened himself in the chair. 'For what it's worth, I really enjoyed working with you.'

What the hell was he talking about? A blind rage swept over me. 'I wouldn't go so far as to say that. You sat in the safety of the car while I went into De Beers and stole the ring. I was the one taking all the risk.' Inside I was seething, so it was impossible for me to hide the acidic tone of my voice.

'What do you mean you stole the ring?' Nathan asked.

His question was left unanswered as Alfie fixed me with a death stare. It would appear my outburst had hit a nerve. I wondered how much he was going to take from me before he made me pay for my rudeness.

'You shouldn't have said that.'

'Why not?' My words came out sharply.

'Because you've offended me.' Alfie smiled, but the usual twinkle in his blue eyes was missing.

'What a shame.'

Nathan tilted his head to one side and looked at me with wide eyes. 'Gemma, shut up before you make things worse.'

Alfie's lips stretched into a wider smile as he watched me without blinking. 'The way you speak to me fascinates me, Gemma. Normally, people are too frightened of the consequences to be as disrespectful as you are.'

Nathan shook his head at me, and I felt myself cringe. I'd managed to do it again. Why did I always say the wrong thing? I should have thought about what might happen if Alfie took offence at what I'd said, and suddenly wished I'd been less blunt. But it was too late to take it back.

'It's interesting that you think my role was easy,' Alfie continued. 'Just because I wasn't physically in the shop, doesn't mean I was any less involved.'

Silence hung heavy between us. I stared at Alfie with a look of pure hatred. 'I'm afraid I don't agree with you. You were less involved because you didn't get your hands dirty.'

'What are you two talking about?' Nathan asked. As

he tried to work out what was going on, his head sprang backwards and forwards between Alfie and me like he was watching the final on Wimbledon Centre Court.

'When I got the ring for Alfie today, I didn't pay for it. I switched it for a fake.'

Nathan stood in front of me with his mouth opening and closing like a human goldfish. He obviously wanted to say something, but he was lost for words.

Alfie looked down and swirled the drink in his glass before downing it. 'Get me another drink, Nathan.'

Nathan stood in the doorway, gripping Alfie's glass of Jack Daniel's tightly in his hand. A worried look spread across his face as he watched Alfie walk towards me and stand too close for comfort.

Alfie leant forward, and his lips brushed my ear. When his breath hit the bare skin on my neck, it made me shiver. 'You're a smart girl, Gemma, and that's why I want you to join the firm.'

'Here's your drink,' Nathan said.

Alfie pulled away and took the tumbler from Nathan.

'I know you want Gemma to work for you, but that doesn't seem fair. It was my debt, so I should be the one to repay it.' Nathan took hold of my hand and squeezed my fingers.

Alfie's forehead creased. 'You're hardly in a position to name your terms.'

'I appreciate that, but...'

Alfie cut him off with the palm of his hand. 'If you want to pay off your debt, Gemma needs to join the team.'

'Can't I take her place?' Nathan asked. The frustration in his voice was obvious.

'No. You don't have the right set of skills. The easiest way to put this is, Gemma's face fits, and yours doesn't. You get the picture, don't you?' Alfie smirked. The look he gave Nathan said a lot more than his words.

A flash of anger spread across my face. Nathan's borrowing had got us into trouble before, but nothing on this scale. If Alfie hadn't blackmailed me, I'd never have agreed to go into De Beers. My mind kept replaying the scene over and over. I realised I'd been incredibly lucky to steal from such a big organisation and not get caught. But as far as I was concerned, it was a one-off.

'I'm sorry, Alfie, but I can't work for you again. If I'd messed up today, I would have been arrested and sent to prison, wouldn't I?' Folding my arms across my chest, I waited for Alfie's reply.

'But you didn't mess up, did you? You kept a cool head, made the swap and walked right out the front door of one of the largest companies in the international diamond trade. That's pure class, Gemma.'

The debt had spiralled out of control at an alarming rate. How could we ever pay Alfie back when he kept changing the amount we owed? Being given the runaround was getting on my nerves.

Alfie sucked in air through his teeth. 'Now you two sit tight, and I'll be in touch when Terry's valued the ring.'

'Who's Terry?' I asked. My imagination began running riot.

Alfie finished his drink and, without answering my question, walked out of our flat.

IO

Nathan

I clasped my fingers behind my head and stared at my wife. 'When the Mercedes drove away with you inside, I was terrified I'd never see you again.' Stepping towards her, I wrapped my arms around her and kissed her soft lips before she rested her face on my chest.

I felt guilty that I'd let her down. I wished I'd never borrowed that money now. I had no idea Alfie was going to make her steal the ring. Knowing that Gemma had become involved in this because of me was difficult to accept. I didn't know what I would do if anything happened to her. I loved Gemma more than anything. She could have any man she wanted, but she'd chosen me. Knowing that was the best feeling in the world.

Gemma took a step backwards and stared at me with her beautiful green eyes. She had never been good at hiding her feelings. Her emotions were always written all over her face. She broke eye contact when her eyes filled with tears. She tried to blink them away before I noticed.

'Please don't cry. I'm sorry I got us into this. I promise I'm going to sort it out.' I reached forward and touched my wife's arm.

'Do you think Alfie will kill us if we can't pay him back?' Gemma asked, dabbing her eyes on the back of her hand.

'No.' I shook my head to reinforce my words.

'How can you be so sure?'

'He won't get his money back if he does, will he?' I smiled, hoping to put her mind at rest, but I knew Gemma could see through me.

Gemma and I were playing the waiting game. Only Alfie knew when he'd venture into the sanctity of our home next. The only thing that was certain was that he would visit us again when we least expected it. Having that thought at the back of my mind would keep me awake at night.

Alfie rarely ventured out without his heavies. There was always somebody shadowing him, watching his back. But in recent days, his habits had changed. He'd still arrive unannounced, but at a reasonable hour without his minders in tow. Thankfully, so far, all of his visits had been social. We hadn't discussed business since the day Gemma stole the ring. Instead, we'd make small talk while he sipped Jack Daniel's on the sofa of our living room. Then after he'd had a couple of drinks, he'd leave.

'I've got a question for you, Nathan. How do you intend to keep yourself financially afloat?' Alfie asked, out of the blue, when he came to see us today.

His question blindsided me. I hadn't got any new projects in the pipeline but decided to keep that to myself. 'I'm sure something will turn up soon.' I gave Alfie a lacklustre smile, but I could tell he was sceptical about what I'd just said.

'I can see you're a confident man, and that's great, but confidence won't pay your bills.' Alfie stretched out his legs and crossed them at the ankles. 'You call yourself an entrepreneur, but you're not very good at making money, are you?'

'I have my moments.'

I clenched my jaw and got to my feet. Alfie's comment annoyed me. What did the success rate of my business ventures have to do with him? Admittedly some of the deals I'd made in the past had turned into disasters, but others had been profitable. I'd made mistakes. I was happy to hold my hands up to that. At least I wasn't afraid to fail. Fear of failure is the main reason people don't take chances. I was optimistic that things would pick up.

'You're skint; you haven't got a pot to piss in, and I want my money back. So where are you going to get it from?'

Alfie's face adopted a smug smile, and I felt myself squirm in my seat. I cast my eyes towards the floor so I wouldn't have to look at him gloating.

'Terry has a price for the ring, which brings me to the purpose of my visit.' Alfie took a sip of his drink.

Now he had my undivided attention. 'How much did he offer you?' I asked, staring him straight in the eye.

'Four thousand, and your share is ten per cent.'

'You're having a fucking laugh, aren't you?' I could feel the rage building inside me. 'You put Gemma through hell for four hundred pounds!' I couldn't believe what I was hearing. The valuation was far worse than I'd expected. I couldn't bring myself to look at my wife. I knew she'd be devastated.

Alfie lit a cigarette and wisps of smoke swirled into the room from the smouldering tip. Then his face broke into a slow smile. 'Life sucks, doesn't it, Nathan? But you're the one who put Gemma in this position, not me.'

I glared at Alfie. This didn't make any sense. It was an expensive ring, not something that came out of a cracker.

'The assistant in the shop told me it cost twenty thousand pounds,' Gemma said. I could see she was still reeling from what Alfie had just told us.

'I'm sure it did. A ring of that quality would cost a fortune if you were to buy it, but you stole it, so now it's only worth a fraction of its previous value,' Alfie said, explaining the finer details of jewellery theft to us. 'It's unfortunate, but that's the way it is.'

'So what was the point of making Gemma steal it?' I asked.

'Terry will pay cash for the ring, and then you'll be four hundred pounds better off than you were this morning, so everyone's a winner.'

The only winners were Alfie and Terry. They stood to make a fortune out of this deal.

'I'll take the money Gemma earned off your debt, so that leaves fourteen thousand six hundred to repay.' Alfie stood up and smoothed down his slicked-back hair.

I had to resist the urge to wipe the smile off his smug face. Every time we thought we'd repaid the money, Alfie changed the amount we owed. I could see Gemma out of the corner of my eye; she looked stressed out and weighed down by the whole situation.

'Can't you freeze the interest to give us a chance to clear the debt?' Gemma asked with an undertone of desperation creeping into her voice.

'That's not the way my business operates. You didn't borrow the money from a bank.' Alfie smirked.

Gemma's beautiful face fell into a scowl. How kind of Alfie to draw our attention to the small print of the contract, I thought. 'So where do we go from here?' I asked without much enthusiasm. My optimism had been flattened by the large dose of reality Alfie had just given me.

He stubbed out his cigarette on the floor, put down his glass and walked out of the flat without saying another word. He didn't need to. By cutting short the conversation, he'd spoken volumes. I watched him close the door in silence, and had to accept our fate with resigned indifference.

11

Gemma

Alfie had firmly established himself as an alpha male. Walking with a self-assured swagger, he'd greet you with a firm handshake while looking you directly in the eye. Everything about him exuded power and confidence. From the sharp suits he always dressed in, to the way he carried himself. Alfie could be charismatic, but he could also be terrifying. By his own admission, the speed at which his personality could change was what scared people the most. We were in way over our heads, and that terrified me.

I thought back to another devastating time when Nathan lost everything we owned trying to save a failed business. It was my worst nightmare, and I wasn't sure we'd make it out the other side. I'm ashamed to say I almost gave up on him. But despite the dark days, we didn't split up, and in time things got better. Even though it was tough, I'm so glad I never gave up on our marriage. Nathan meant everything to me. I loved him with all my heart. He'd faced abandonment before, and I knew how badly that affected him. Growing up without a father to love and care for him scarred him deeply, so I could never put him through the pain again.

Rosa was a fantastic mother, and there's no denying Nathan was smothered with affection, but due to their circumstances, he learned from an early age to take care of number one. It didn't excuse his reckless behaviour, but because I knew this, it helped me to understand why he acted the way he did. Facing a financial struggle on a daily basis left its mark on him.

Our childhoods couldn't have been more different. I grew up in Richmond and never wanted for anything. But no amount of material possessions could replace the amazing feeling of being loved and cherished. When I met Nathan, I experienced for the first time what it felt like to be worth something to someone. Even though our upbringings were poles apart, we were like kindred spirits in many ways.

When we lost our home and all our possessions, Nathan's aunt and uncle, Donatella and Bernardo, took pity on us. They didn't want to see us homeless and destitute, so they offered us jobs in their Italian restaurant and allowed us to live in the flat above it. Having no children of their own, they treated Nathan more like a son than a nephew. We were lucky to have jobs and a place to live, rent-free, for as long as we needed it, but the opportunity didn't come without more sacrifice on my part. I had to give up my dream position as a personal assistant, to the director of a fashion house in the West End of London, because I couldn't afford to commute from our new home in Southend-on-Sea, Essex. I found the move traumatic. But there was no point dwelling on the past and everything we'd lost. We had to focus on the future and believe that, in time, things would get better.

I should have insisted that Nathan took the job Donatella offered him, instead of turning his nose up at it. I didn't like waiting tables either, but one of us had to try and keep some money coming in. I wish I'd put my foot down, but I was too soft with him. In fact, we were all guilty of that. Nathan had such a lovely way about him, he had the whole family wrapped around his little finger.

I suddenly realised it was time to accept the inevitable. We we're never going to be able to clear our debt if I didn't agree to work for Alfie. Although Nathan had promised he'd think of something, and believe me, I wanted to have faith in him, he hadn't managed to come up with a solution. Every time he started a new venture, he'd insist that this time things would be different and nothing bad would happen.

Unfortunately, the story always seemed to end the same way. Nathan's get-rich-quick schemes had a habit of failing miserably. Then he'd feel compelled to try and recover the money he'd lost by taking chances on risky deals. He'd developed an uncontrollable urge to be reckless, even though his destructive behaviour was taking its toll on us. On more than one occasion recently, I'd thought about leaving him. Walking away, before I got any more involved, felt like the obvious thing to do. But I'd invested so much time and energy in our relationship, I couldn't bring myself to go through with it.

12

Gemma

When I returned home from my shift and found Alfie and his men waiting for me, I stared at them with huge eyes. The emotional impact of strangers entering my personal space uninvited was something I would never get used to. It was stressing me out. I wondered if I'd ever feel safe in this flat again.

'What the hell is going on?' I said when I saw what they'd done to Nathan. They'd beaten him up again, and Knuckles was aiming a handgun at his knee. 'Please, don't hurt him,' I said, covering my mouth. I wanted to scream, but what good would that have done?

'I'm OK, Gemma,' Nathan replied.

'I'm glad you're back,' Alfie said. 'I was just having a little discussion with your husband about loyalty and respect. It's never a good idea to piss off people with connections.'

It wasn't so much the words Alfie had just spoken, but the tone in which he delivered them that sent a chill through my body. His message was loud and clear. If we knew what was good for us, we shouldn't mess him about. Inside, my mind was in turmoil, but I had to keep calm.

'My patience is starting to wear thin now. Do you think I'm stupid, Gemma?'

'Of course not.'

'Don't take me for a fool then.'

Alfie took a step towards me, and I felt my pulse quicken. In the blink of an eye, he could turn into a violent thug. It's true to say, he got a kick out of hurting people and I hoped I wasn't the next in line. Although I was crumbling inside, I straightened my posture and composed myself.

'When I've been generous enough to lend a person money, I sometimes find it's necessary to provide a little reminder if they don't give it back. There's more at stake here than just the debt, you know?'

I looked straight into Alfie's blue eyes, hoping to appeal to his better nature, if he had one. But I knew he hadn't; the man was pure evil. 'We fully intend to pay back every penny we owe.'

'That's good to know because this is the first rung on the intimidation ladder.' Alfie flashed his straight, white smile in my direction.

If that was the case, we were in serious trouble. Whether we liked it or not, we were going to have to cooperate. I didn't want to find out what the next rung was like.

'I don't want to inflict suffering if I don't need to. A gunshot wound to the knee is pretty much the maximum amount of pain a person can tolerate. So I usually reserve that as a last resort.'

Emotions were running high. I couldn't afford to say the wrong thing. As I thought about how to respond, I decided that maybe my best option was to keep quiet.

'Now let's get back to business. How are you two going to pay back my money?' Alfie asked, pulling the sleeves of his suit jacket back over his wrists.

'Do you still want me to join the firm?' I cast my eyes downwards, dreading his answer.

I saw Alfie smirk out of the corner of my eye. 'Now that's a silly question. So does this mean you're accepting the position?'

'I suppose so.' I tried to keep the begrudging tone out of my voice, but it wasn't easy.

'Would you like to go shopping for me again?

My stomach turned over at the thought. 'Do I have a choice?'

'Of course, you have a choice, Gemma.' Alfie's face broke into a huge smile. 'I wouldn't dream of making you do anything against your will. That's not my style. I'm a gentleman.'

I struggled to suppress the laugh that wanted to escape from my lips. In a matter of minutes, Alfie had transformed himself back from a ruthless underworld boss to a suave charmer. His behaviour was erratic and unpredictable. I had to admit, not knowing what he might do next was keeping me awake at night.

'Just so we understand each other, stealing is not my style. I haven't agreed to work for you because I want to, but because you're holding a gun to my husband's head.'

'Nobody's holding a gun to Nathan's head. Knuckles is aiming at his kneecap,' Alfie replied, arching an eyebrow. He wasn't smiling any longer.

I clenched my lips together to keep me from saying something I'd regret. All I could hear was my anxious breath as silence hung in the air between us. My heart pounded in my chest as the tension in the room intensified.

Alfie and his men didn't need to use weapons; just their presence was enough to make you feel the danger. Even though they hadn't fired a single shot, I knew they'd think nothing of taking Nathan's life. In Alfie's line of work, he used this heavy-handed approach on a daily basis.

Nathan and I were desperate to escape from Alfie's clutches, but he wasn't ready to let us go yet. Instead, he'd now enlisted me as a gang member, and if we wanted to get out of this nightmare alive, we'd have to do what he said.

I would never understand why Nathan decided to borrow money from a criminal. He'd made a stupid choice, and now we were drowning in debt, so we'd have to suffer the consequences. It would have been easy to hold it against him, but there was no point, so I shoved the bitter thought aside. We were in this together, for better, for worse. We'd signed up to that when we got married and tempting as it was to turn my back on all of this and walk away, I wouldn't do that to Nathan. We'd lost everything before. I had never forgotten how awful that felt. My stomach still twisted into knots at the memory.

But we came out the other side and were doing well until Alfie Watson came into our lives. Although it was difficult to imagine at the moment, I had to believe that one day we'd be free of him.

13

Gemma

Nathan stood in the living room, dressed in a T-shirt and jeans, taking the cork out of a bottle of Chianti when I arrived back from work. He'd laid the table with white crockery and candles, and my stomach rumbled as I breathed in the aroma of Mediterranean cooking that filled the room. Being brought up in an Italian family, he was an excellent cook. He'd learnt from an early age to be proficient in the kitchen. I posed no serious competition for him. Nathan pulled a chair out for me, and when I sat down, he began massaging the tops of my shoulders with his strong hands.

'This is a nice surprise. What have I done to deserve this?'

'I just wanted you to know how much I love you.' Nathan poured me a large glass of wine before stooping to kiss me.

'I love you too.'

Nathan ran his fingers through his thick, dark hair, and his T-shirt rose up a little, exposing his muscular stomach. 'I know I can be selfish and sometimes take you for granted.'

Pain contorted his face as he looked at me. 'I'm sorry you got dragged into this. I've let you down again. Most women would have walked away from me years ago.' Nathan shook his head and let out a long sigh.

'Well, I'm not most women, so I'm not going anywhere.'

I stood up, looked into my gorgeous husband's face and wrapped my arms around his waist. Nathan made me feel special, and after years of living with self-doubt, for that, I would be eternally grateful. He had managed to restore my self-esteem and in my book that counted for a lot. I would always have his back. It was the least I could do.

'I'm lucky to have you, but I don't deserve you. You've had to give up everything for me.'

Nathan cast his eyes towards the floor. He looked like a broken man, so I squeezed his hand. There must be something I could say to help him shake off the sadness. A depressive state of mind could be contagious. I hated seeing him like this and wanted to bring him back from the very dark place he was currently visiting.

Admittedly, borrowing money from a shady character like Alfie Watson hadn't been one of his best ideas, but that was no reason to walk away from him. Nathan and I loved each other, and the trials we'd battled through together had only made our relationship stronger.

'I promise I'm going to get us out of this.'

'I know you will. No matter how bad we think our problems are, there's somebody out there worse off than us.'

Nathan pulled me close and rested his chin on the top of my head. I wasn't sure I believed what I'd just said, but I hoped my words might cheer him up. Nathan's blue mood didn't need lowering any further.

★

Halfway through our candlelit dinner, just as Nathan's spirits were lifted, we were rudely interrupted. Alfie opened our front door and walked in like he owned the place. The man had a nerve letting himself into our flat whenever he felt like it. His intrusion was a problem, and I was tempted to say something. But I'd better be careful how I approached it. Alfie was highly unpredictable; he possessed a loose-cannon personality trait. The last thing I wanted to do was to escalate the situation, so I decided to say nothing.

He swaggered into the living room and sat down next to me. My heart started to race, pounding against my ribcage like it was attempting to break free. Staring straight ahead of me, I put down my knife and fork and pushed my plate away.

Nathan cleared his throat and glared at Alfie from across the table. 'To what do we owe the unexpected pleasure of your company?' Nathan's words were laced with sarcasm.

I winced, wondering how Alfie would react.

'Do you treat all your guests like this?' Alfie laughed.

'Only the ones I don't like,' Nathan replied in a venomous tone.

Alfie arched an unimpressed eyebrow and took a long drag on his cigarette. Everything went quiet. With only the sound of my heartbeat filling my ears, tension hung heavy in the air while we waited for his response.

'I'm not sure I like the way you just spoke to me, Nathan.' Alfie paused and looked down as if considering his next words. 'You have a serious attitude problem,' he continued.

Nathan and I glanced at each other. He took a deep breath and let it out slowly as he tried to remain calm.

'What do you want, Alfie? I'm sure you didn't come here to analyse my personality, did you?'

'There you go again.' Alfie shook his head and locked eyes with Nathan. 'Maybe your mother should have spent less time waiting tables and more time teaching you some manners.'

Nathan's nostrils flared, and his face reddened. Alfie had dared to insult his beloved Rosa, and it was all he could do to control his temper. After his dad left, she'd had no choice but to work long hours to try and keep a roof over their heads. Alfie smirked, delighted that he'd been able to get under Nathan's skin. They stared at one another as if trying to look deep into each other's subconscious mind.

Alfie turned towards me. 'You haven't offered me a drink, Gemma. The service isn't very good in here tonight.'

I got up from the table and went to get him a Jack Daniel's. Nathan pushed his chair back and suddenly stood up. He dug his fingers into the table as a surge of anger washed over him. He couldn't take any more. Alfie had now been offensive to both the women in his life in the same visit.

'Don't speak to my wife like that.'

Alfie leered, lifting his eyes to meet mine when I handed him the glass.

'Here you go.'

'Thank you, Gemma.' Alfie flashed me a smile.

'You're welcome.' I wanted to add: I hope you choke on it, but thought better of it.

'Now, why don't you take a seat? We've got business to discuss.' Alfie patted the chair with his free hand. When he saw the look of horror on my face, he threw his head back and roared with laughter.

'What business?' Nathan asked as we exchanged looks.

'This doesn't involve you,' Alfie said, before fixing his blue eyes on me.

'I want you to switch a watch for me. Just do the same as you did last time. The simple plans always work the best.' Alfie beamed.

I began digging my nails into my palms as I looked at Alfie without any emotion. I forced my fingers to unclench, then started knotting them into my dress instead. 'You must think I've got nerves of steel...'

Alfie interrupted me before I could protest any further. 'Terry's made an impressive replica. The only difference between the two is the price. The fake is worth about ten quid, whereas the real one retails at one hundred and thirty-five thousand pounds.'

I stared at Alfie with eyes like saucers. He looked away and stared down at his drink, mesmerised by the moving liquid as he swirled the contents around the glass.

'Gemma's not working for you again. It's too dangerous,' Nathan said.

Lifting his head up, Alfie narrowed his eyes. 'That's not your decision to make.'

'I've had enough of this shit,' Nathan yelled, squaring up to Alfie. Lunging forward, he grabbed him by the throat with one hand while the other balled into a fist.

I was shocked by Nathan's outburst. 'For God's sake, calm down,' I said, yanking his hand away and stepping between them.

'You shouldn't have done that,' Alfie said. Smoothing down his charcoal grey suit, he opened the single button.

I didn't know what had come over Nathan, but there was

no telling what Alfie would do to him now. He was not the sort of man you wanted to fall out with. Alfie didn't try to hide his anger – Nathan had well and truly pissed him off. Fixing Nathan with an icy stare, he pulled back the front of his jacket just enough to reveal the end of a gun, sitting in the waistband of his trousers.

I held my breath, but panic tore through me when Alfie calmly pulled the gun out and pointed it at Nathan. My heart raced. What would Alfie do next? Would he shoot Nathan, or was he just making a point? Fear gripped me, but I knew if I didn't intervene, things weren't going to end well.

'Please don't do this,' I said, looking into Alfie's eyes.

'Give me one reason why I shouldn't,' Alfie replied.

My mind went blank, and I couldn't think of anything to say. I'd never felt so scared in my entire life and hoped Alfie wouldn't pull the trigger while we were making eye contact. I wouldn't wish this experience on my worst enemy. Resisting the urge to fall to pieces, I tried to think logically instead. Forcing myself to face my fear head-on, I took a deep breath to calm my nerves and stepped closer to Alfie. Reaching up, I put my hand on the barrel of the gun to stop him from shooting.

'Please, put the gun away.'

Alfie laughed. He had a reputation for being cold-hearted and took pleasure from other people's suffering. I wanted to drop to my knees and beg, but this wasn't the right time to show weakness.

'If you ever pull a stunt like that again, I'll jam this barrel so far down your fucking throat, I'll be able to see what you had for breakfast. Do you understand me?' Alfie said before he lowered the gun.

Nathan nodded.

'I'm sorry, I didn't hear what you said?' Alfie cupped his hand to his ear.

'Yes, I understand,' Nathan said through clenched teeth.

'You should count yourself lucky; I'm not in the habit of giving people second chances,' Alfie said, putting the gun back in his waistband and fastening his jacket. 'Be ready at two o'clock tomorrow, Gemma.'

Tossing his cigarette onto the floor, Alfie crushed it under his shoe before heading to the door. I waited until he was out of earshot before I gave Nathan a piece of my mind.

'What the hell were you thinking of?' I shouted, throwing my hands in the air. Nathan held his hands out in front of him as he tried to pacify me. 'I thought he was going to shoot you.'

My emotions finally got the better of me, and I covered my eyes with the palms of my hands as I tried to stop the tears running down my cheeks. It was no use, and I began weeping like a baby.

'I'm sorry, Gemma. Please don't cry.' Nathan reached out to me.

14

Nathan

I knew I shouldn't have lost my head with Alfie, but something inside me snapped. I couldn't help myself. I hated the sense of being controlled. Alfie had taken over mine and Gemma's lives, and there was nothing I could do to stop him. The frustration I was feeling boiled over into anger. I didn't care what Alfie did to me, but Gemma's safety had to come first. She was the most important person in the world to me, and I would protect her with my life, but right now, Alfie wouldn't let me, and that was eating me up inside.

Being the product of a broken home, I'd had to grow up fast and learn to be independent. Nobody would be there to pick me up and kiss me better if I fell. That was a tough lesson for a child to learn, but it was the way things were, so I had to get over it.

There was never a good time for your parents to divorce, but knowing my dad left my mum for another woman when I was a baby had a profound effect on me. It wasn't so much the fact that they'd split up, but the fact that he didn't have any contact with me since the day he left that I found hard to accept. I felt that he'd abandoned me and I hated him for that.

It was a sad fact of life that low-income children had a hard time getting ahead. Believing that the past determines your future was something I found hard to shake off. Nothing knocked your confidence more than having to wear cheap, ill-fitting clothes when everyone else in your class had designer gear. The other kids used to tease me about it. That psychologically scarred me. There was no better driving force than poverty. I developed an overwhelming desire to be rich, but look where that had got me.

There had to be a way to get us out of this situation. It wasn't fair that Gemma had become involved in the mess I'd created. I was the one who had borrowed the money.

15

Gemma

When the Mercedes pulled up at the kerb, I breathed a sigh of relief. I couldn't wait to put some space between myself and Alfie. Slipping his hand inside his suit jacket, he took out a velvet pouch containing the replica watch and gave it to me.

As I made my way towards Harrods, my heels clicked on the pavement. Concentrating on the rhythmic sound, I tried desperately to encourage a sense of calm to wash over me. Holding my head high, I walked into the entrance and made my way to The Fine Watch Room, located on the ground floor of the seven-storey building. Black marble, glass and minimalist display cabinets stretched out before me.

As I casually began browsing, I could see this wasn't going to be an easy job. The shop's centrepiece, made up of a trio of counters, displayed the best watches. The diamond-encrusted lion that Alfie wanted was beneath the glass. How was I going to get away with this? There were highly visible security devices located immediately overhead. I'd have to try and make the switch while the cameras were rolling.

'Good afternoon,' the sales assistant said.

'Good afternoon,' I replied.

'My name is Susan. Is there anything, in particular, you're looking for?'

Aware that I only had one opportunity to get Alfie's lion out of the cabinet, I couldn't afford to mess this up. 'I'd like a new watch; I'm bored of this one.' I gestured to the platinum Rolex on my wrist, feeling myself cringe as I acted out the part of a woman with a bottomless bank balance.

Although Susan smiled politely, I got the distinct impression she wasn't too keen on me. Realising charm alone was unlikely to work on Susan, I'd have to try a different approach, and think of another way to get her onside. That in itself was going to be challenging; she didn't look like she'd be prepared to bend the rules for anyone.

'Do you only wear platinum?' Susan asked, scanning her eyes over my jewellery.

'No, I'm a bit of a magpie really. I like anything that glitters.' I smiled, hoping to break down the barrier between us.

'Do you have a budget in mind?' Susan looked at me with a blank, expressionless face.

'Not really. I'm lucky enough to be married to a very wealthy man who also happens to be incredibly generous. So, if I see something I like, he'll let me buy it,' I said, hoping I hadn't gone overboard.

This mature lady had no doubt seen it all before. I was just another one of those annoying customers, with more money than sense. 'Would you like to try some of the watches on?'

'Yes, please.'

After unlocking the cabinet, Susan took out a small, elegant ladies' watch with delicate flowers on its face. 'This is a beautiful timepiece from Boodles. It's made from eighteen-carat white gold,' she said, holding it out for me to take.

'Ooh, it's stunning, isn't it?' I removed my Rolex and slipped the other watch onto my wrist.

'It's part of their new range, the Blossom collection. I don't know whether you are familiar with it.'

'Yes, I am.' I'd never heard of it before in my life, but Susan didn't need to know that, I decided.

'The bezel and blossoms are made up of round brilliant-cut diamonds totalling almost two carats,' Susan pointed out. As a rare smile spread across her face, it softened her stern features.

'It is a beautiful watch.' Holding it away from my body, I began admiring it from every angle. The mobile inside my Hermès bag started ringing. 'Please, excuse me a moment.'

Susan forced out a strained smile and waited impatiently for me to finish my call. Her attitude was starting to irritate me. While I spoke to Alfie, I wondered if she treated all her customers this way or only the ones who were about to spend thousands of pounds. She didn't have a nice way about her, and if I had genuinely been about to buy something, I would have taken my custom elsewhere.

'It has an alligator strap, and the dial is made of white mother of pearl.' Susan continued with her sales pitch the moment my call ended.

'How much is it?'

'It's twenty-two thousand five hundred pounds.' Susan's steely grey eyes bored into mine, to judge my reaction.

My upper lip beaded with perspiration, so I willed myself to focus on the job in hand. 'I thought it would be more than that,' I replied in as light a tone as I could manage, hoping to convince the human lie detector in front of me, that money wasn't an object.

Spurred on by the fact that the price was of no concern to me, and thinking only of the commission she was about to earn, Susan began selecting increasingly more expensive items for me to try on.

Eventually, she took Alfie's watch out of the display cabinet. 'If you want something unusual, this is an exquisite timepiece made by Chanel.'

She demonstrated how the diamond-encrusted head of the lion slid to one side, to reveal the hidden dial, before handing it to me.

'That's incredible.'

'The Lion Vénitien is a very clever design, incorporating a watch and a bracelet in one piece.'

Susan's miserable face stopped puckering for a moment when I slipped the feline bracelet onto my wrist.

'I've never seen anything like this before.' That wasn't strictly true. The one Terry had made looked remarkably similar to the untrained eye.

'The watch is crafted from white gold, with a mother-of-pearl dial and adorned with five hundred brilliant-cut diamonds.' Susan looked delighted, and she beamed from ear to ear, thinking she'd hit the jackpot.

I'd left my bag on the floor, so when my mobile began ringing again, I ducked down below the cabinet to answer it. I pretended I was having trouble locating my phone, in my cavernous bag, to give myself some time. Sliding the black satin strap over my hand, I switched the watches. Turning my back on Susan, I walked away from the counter briefly.

Holding the mobile in my hand, I went back to where Susan was waiting. 'I'm sorry about that; my husband wanted to know what was taking me so long! Men are so impatient, aren't they?'

Susan nodded in agreement. But I could tell by her hostile body language that she'd like nothing better than to see the back of me. After she'd persuaded me to part with a huge sum of money, that is.

'I'm finding it difficult to choose between them. They're all beautiful. How much is this one?' I asked, with the fake on my wrist.

Susan didn't seem to notice the fact that I'd switched the watches. She was distracted by the pound signs that were rolling around her eyes.

'Let me just check.'

Who was she trying to kid? Susan knew exactly how much it cost. I thought my acting had been good, but she was giving me a run for my money with her Oscar-winning performance.

'It's slightly more expensive. It's one hundred and thirty-five thousand pounds.' The words rolled off Susan's tongue with ease.

I jumped when the mobile vibrated in my hand. 'Oh no, it's my husband again, he's waiting for me at the Oyster Bar,' I said, switching the phone off. 'I'll have to come back after we've had lunch.'

Slipping the watch off my hand, I handed it back to Susan, who looked at me with thinly veiled contempt in her eyes.

'Enjoy your meal,' she said in a sarcastic tone, and only just managed not to snarl her lip when she spoke.

As I made my way out of the exit, each breath was a struggle. My heart was pounding so hard and loud it felt as though it was going to beat its way out of my chest. Overcome with emotion, I battled to keep my unquenchable tears within when I took a seat in the car.

For a moment, Alfie didn't speak but stared at me while he lit a cigarette. 'Are you all right?'

I nodded my head and tried to regain composure, but I lost the fight. The floodgates opened, and I began weeping bitter, angry tears.

Alfie adjusted his tie, shifted in his seat, then threw me an uncomfortable look. 'What's up, Gemma? Did something go wrong?'

Embarrassed by my behaviour, my eyes darted everywhere and anywhere. I wanted to avoid looking directly at Alfie until I could take a tissue out of my bag and dry my eyes. 'No, everything went to plan.' My voice sounded breathless.

Glancing sideways, I could see Alfie had fixed me with a steely glare, so I forced myself to look up from my lap. When I did, I met Tommy's eyes. He was watching me in the rear-view mirror.

'Have you got the watch?' Alfie turned towards me in his seat.

'Yes.'

'So what are you wailing about?'

'I was terrified I was going to get caught. There were cameras everywhere.'

'Of course there were, it's a high-profile store, Gemma. But nothing's missing, is it? As long as the staff weren't suspicious of you, they won't bother checking the footage or, more importantly, their stock. Don't stress about it; companies don't keep the images long before the system automatically overwrites them.' Alfie turned away and looked out of the blacked-out window.

'I hope you're right about that.'

'I am. That's the beauty of the switch. We get to steal things right under the store's nose without them noticing. They won't even realise they've been hit.' Alfie brought his eyes back to mine. 'You're an excellent thief, Gemma,' Alfie said, after an uncomfortable pause.

'Is that meant to be a compliment?'

'Of course. Sleight of hand is not an easy thing to master. You should be proud of yourself.'

How could I be? I'd been pushed way past my comfort zone. Stealing wasn't exciting; it scared me to death. I suddenly felt drained, and my body began to tremble, as I experienced the after-effects of the adrenaline rush. I attempted to shake off my fatigue, but my strength had been sapped. I couldn't seem to lose the feeling of exhaustion.

I'm the type of person who listens carefully to their conscience, and it was telling me that stealing was wrong whatever the circumstances. Slumping in my seat, I paused for a moment, trying to find a response. But I couldn't think of anything appropriate to say. Alfie's words played over and over in my mind. Taking the watch from my bag, I handed it to him. It was exquisite, and I watched him as he held it up to the light. Suddenly he began to laugh.

'You've even got the perfect name for a jewel thief, Gem Stone.'

I shook my head in disbelief. How dare Alfie say that to me? His comment enraged me. I knew I should ignore it, but I felt the need to defend myself. 'I'm not a thief.'

Alfie raised an eyebrow. 'I'm sorry if I've offended you, but what would you call a person that walks into a shop and charms the sales assistant out of thousands of pounds' worth of diamonds then?'

It was obvious Alfie was deliberately trying to antagonise me. His blue eyes watched me as my posture stiffened. He seemed to be taking great delight in winding me up, and that made me feel uneasy.

'I'm only doing this because you're blackmailing me. Not because I want to,' I said, turning to face Alfie. I couldn't hide the look of distaste in my glare.

'That's a very serious accusation, Gemma.'

The smug look on Alfie's face was making anger build up inside me. He was close to making me lose my temper, but I knew that would be a mistake. I'd have to bite my tongue instead. The atmosphere in the car was tense. Alfie and I had reached a stalemate.

'You have the right combination for this line of work; that's why you've been so successful. You're beautiful as well as being light-fingered.' Alfie seemed determined to draw a response out of me. He just wouldn't let it go.

'I wasn't going to let you in on my secret, but seeing as you're so fascinated by my talent, I'll come clean and admit that I am in fact a descendant of The Artful Dodger.' I hoped my comment would convey my boredom and put an end to this conversation.

Alfie began to laugh. 'That wouldn't surprise me in the slightest. You're a feisty character, aren't you, Gemma?'

Alfie wasn't the first person to say I had a spirited side. My mother told me on many occasions that my fiery personality had been getting me into trouble since the day I was born.

16

Gemma

Alfie was exploiting us, and he knew it. We were trapped in a never-ending cycle of fabricated debt, and there was no way out for the foreseeable future.

Alfie put his hand inside the pocket of his black pinstriped suit and pulled out two British passports. 'Now your probation period is over, and you're officially on the team, we're going to be taking a trip to France,' Alfie said, before taking a seat on our leather sofa.

Nathan and I both looked at each other. 'Why do you want us to go to France?' I asked, meeting Alfie's gaze for a brief moment.

A huge smile curved his lips. 'For a business trip. You've got new passports with new identities.' Alfie opened the cover and showed us the details.

Nathan rubbed his knuckles under his chin, and a look of concern spread across his face. I'd never seen him like this before. He usually managed to look as if he was on top of the world when everything was crumbling around him. He'd always been an expert at hiding his feelings, until now.

'Why do we need new passports?' I asked.

'I would have thought that was obvious.' A smile spread across Alfie's face. Then he laughed, fixing me with his blue eyes. 'What you're about to do isn't exactly legal, so it's better if you assume a new identity.'

For me, that was the light-bulb moment. Alfie now officially owned us. He'd changed our names and was about to turn us into fugitives, making us travel on forged documents. We were being sucked deeper into the criminal underworld we knew nothing about. But why did we need to go to France? I had a horrible feeling that instead of sightseeing, I'd be shoplifting. A picture was forming in my mind: Alfie was going to turn me into an international thief, and there was absolutely nothing I could do about it.

'I'll be in touch as soon as I've made the arrangements,' Alfie said, getting to his feet. 'Bring enough clothes for about a week. You'll need both smart and casual things.'

Nathan hadn't said a word all the time Alfie had been here. I wondered what he was thinking. I was having trouble taking it all in. It was one thing working for Alfie in London, but now he wanted us to go to France.

'What am I going to tell my mum? She knows we're skint, so she'll know something's up when I tell her we're going away.'

'I'm amazed that's all you're worried about,' I replied, shaking my head from side to side.

'You've seen my mum lose her temper before. You know it's not a pretty sight.'

'Your mum's temper is the least of our worries.' I couldn't help rolling my eyes. Rosa might be a passionate Italian, prone to being theatrical when showing her feelings, but she was hardly in the same league as Alfie Watson. 'Hasn't it occurred to you that Alfie must be planning a bigger job this time?'

Nathan shrugged his shoulders.

If he wasn't, he wouldn't be going to the trouble of taking the whole team across the Channel, would he? I didn't want to think about what he'd got lined up for me this time. I was going to end up with a criminal record by the time we'd paid off this debt. My eyes misted over as I tried to digest that thought. Nathan put his finger under my chin and tilted my face towards his. He wiped away the tears that had begun to fall, before planting a kiss on the top of my head. Then he pulled me towards him and put his strong arms around me. I buried my face into his chest as my tears flowed freely.

'I wish you'd never got dragged into this. I'd gladly take your place. You know that, don't you?'

I pulled away and stared at my husband. 'We both know Alfie won't let you do that.'

'I'm going to talk to him and see if he'll let us swap places.' Nathan pulled me towards him and placed his hands on my waist.

'There's no point; he'll never agree to it.' I let out a sigh.

'Hopefully, this will be the last job,' Nathan said in an optimistic tone.

'It won't be. We'll never be free of him. You're deluding yourself if you think otherwise.' Acid coated my words.

Nathan and I looked at each other. He knew I was right; there was no way out of this impossible situation. For a brief moment, I considered contacting my parents and asking them to lend us the money to clear the debt. They could afford to, but my pride wouldn't allow me to stoop that low. They would have been delighted if they knew Nathan and I were in trouble. It would be a case of we told you so, and I wouldn't give them the satisfaction.

17

Nathan ?

'If you're in trouble, don't keep it from me.' Rosa's brown eyes searched her son's for the answer to her question. She wanted to know what was going on.

'Everything's fine, honestly,' Nathan snapped, then immediately felt bad, so he forced himself to smile.

Rosa put her hands on her hips and looked up at her only child. Guilt began gnawing away at Nathan, but he was determined to hide the truth from his mum.

'I know there's something you're not telling me. I can sense it.'

'It's nothing.' Nathan shrugged his shoulders.

'If it's nothing, why are you on edge all the time?' Rosa's face softened as she reached forward and touched her son's arm. She clearly knew he was lying. 'Do you think I haven't noticed how strangely you've been acting recently?'

Nathan's eyes widened. 'I don't know what you're talking about. I haven't been acting strangely.'

Rosa threw him a look, and Nathan let out a loud sigh

before sliding his hands into the front pockets of his jeans. He knew Rosa wouldn't stop until she got to the bottom of this.

'You're behaving like a caged animal. What's wrong with you?' Rosa's fingertips scrunched together, and she began waving her hands in front of his face.

Nathan declined to answer and started biting the skin on the side of his nail.

'If you're not going to tell me, I'll have to work it out for myself.' Rosa fixed Nathan with an interrogating stare, and after a long pause, she continued to speak. 'I can only think of two reasons why you'd be acting like this.'

'OK, Sherlock, tell me what you've concluded,' Nathan said in a disrespectful tone of voice.

Rosa gave her son a disapproving look. 'The most obvious reason is Gemma. She's been on edge as well recently. Have you two had a fight?'

'Gemma and I are fine, Mum,' Nathan replied, unable to hide the irritation in his voice.

'So it must be Alfie Watson who's causing the problem. Did you pay him back the money?'

Rosa waited patiently for Nathan's reply, but instead of answering, he turned his back on her. He couldn't look her in the eye and blatantly lie to her, but he couldn't tell her the truth either.

Rosa stepped in front of her son. 'Nathan, I asked you a question. Did you pay Alfie back?'

'Not exactly,' Nathan muttered, turning his face away.

'What do you mean?' Rosa asked. She looked into her son's face and attempted to make eye contact with him.

'We tried to, but Alfie's interest rates are so high we're having trouble keeping up with them.'

Rosa threw her arms in the air and started screaming obscenities in Italian. Her hand gestures went into overdrive as she tried to express herself.

'I told you to stay away from Alfie Watson, but you never listen to me, do you?' Rosa shook her head and began wagging her finger at her son.

Nathan let out a long breath and folded his arms across his chest. Then he turned his back on his mum. Deep down, he knew she was trying to help, but she was talking to him like he was still a child, and that made anger boil up inside him. But the last thing he wanted was to fall out with her, so he bit his tongue and let her vent.

'That man is crazy.' Rosa stepped in front of Nathan, fixed him with a glare and began tapping the side of her head with her index finger. 'There's no telling what he could do to you. Your life means nothing to him.'

'He won't get his money back if I'm dead, will he?' Nathan flashed his mother a defiant smile.

'Less of the attitude, Nathan. You'll end up living in constant fear if you don't stay away from that man.' Rosa locked eyes with her son. 'I could shake you. When are you going to learn?' Rosa raised her voice and waved her hands wildly in front of her son's face. 'You'll end up just like your father.'

Nathan rolled his eyes. 'I'm in debt, Mum, I'm not a womaniser.' Now she'd really lost the plot. What the hell was she talking about?

'It would break my heart if you turned out like Gareth,' Rosa rambled on.

'I won't. I'd never cheat on Gemma.'

Rosa stepped back and looked up at her son. 'Why did you keep this business with Alfie from me?'

Nathan inhaled a deep breath. 'I didn't want to worry you.'

'Even though you're a grown man, I'm still your mum, so it's my job to worry about you.'

'You don't need to. I can take care of myself.'

'Alfie Watson is a dangerous man. It's not a good idea to owe him money.'

'I know, that's why I've got to do exactly what he tells me to.'

'Go to the police, Nathan, and tell them what's happened.' Rosa's eyes pleaded. For once, it seemed she desperately wanted her son to listen to her.

'I can't.' Nathan shook his head. 'If I do, Alfie will find out, and then none of us will be safe.'

'The police will protect us.' Rosa clasped her hands tightly together.

'No, Mum, it's too risky.' Nathan bit the side of his lip.

'So what are you going to do?'

'I can't tell you, but Gemma and I will be going away for a while.'

'Are you going into hiding?'

'No, but don't worry about us, we'll be OK.'

'Please tell me where you're going.' The olive-toned skin on Rosa's forehead puckered and her eyes filled with fear.

'I'm not sure myself. Alfie hasn't told us yet, but when we come back, this nightmare will be over.' Nathan bent down and kissed his mum's cheek before he left her with her thoughts.

18

Gemma

Alfie told us we'd be travelling to Paris on the Eurostar. I questioned why we weren't flying. Surely it would be easier. But apparently there are too many security checks, and Alfie had information from a reliable source, that border checks are particularly weak on this route.

Nathan and I stared at him in stunned silence. There were so many things I wanted to say, but unfortunately, I couldn't find the right words. So instead, I listened, almost in a trance, to what Alfie was telling us.

'After we arrive at St Pancras, we'll go through passport control twice,' Alfie said before inhaling deeply on his cigarette.

That seemed a bit strange. Then I remembered a trip I'd made with my family years ago and realised Alfie was right: French immigration control takes place at St Pancras, before you board the Eurostar, not when you arrive in Paris.

'What happens if we get stopped?' Nathan asked, biting the side of his lip.

'Trust me; you'll get through the checks. They're just a formality. The whole process takes about thirty seconds,' Alfie assured us.

Let's hope he was right. Our passports weren't genuine. The police were bound to notice. It crossed my mind that if we got caught at this stage, it would save us from whatever it was Alfie had lined up for us. But he was confident that the passports were of such a high standard that not even highly trained border officials would be able to spot they were false documents. His supplier placed a microchip in the back cover, and the inside pages were genuine with holograms all across them. Alfie boasted that the craftsmanship was excellent. He began grinning, and as he did, his blue eyes twinkled.

My stomach flipped at the sight of his smug smile. It shouldn't have come as a surprise to me that a man like Alfie, with his criminal connections, would know all about exploiting the security system. But his reassurance did little to calm my nerves. However he tried to sugar-coat it, Nathan and I would be travelling on forged British passports, under the names Emma and Ethan Jones, and that made me uncomfortable, to say the very least.

'So the fact that our fake passports are high quality is meant to put my mind at rest, is it?' I asked, locking eyes with Alfie. He ignored my concerns.

How could the inside pages be genuine? As I considered the possibilities, Alfie let me in on the secret. His source had a contact that worked for the Home Office. He didn't need to say any more. My eyes widened, but I shouldn't have been surprised. I should have realised he'd have friends in high places who could get him whatever he wanted.

'It only takes my guy three days to produce the documents. They're expensive but worth every penny. There's nothing money can't buy, Gemma.' Alfie winked.

What the hell was that supposed to mean? There were loads of things money couldn't buy. I knew that better than anyone. Money couldn't buy happiness or love or freedom for that matter.

'When are we leaving?' I asked, changing the subject.

'The day after tomorrow. Mummy dearest will be devastated. Rosa's such a controlling bitch; it's about time we cut the apron strings and set you free, Nathan.' Alfie straightened the lapels of his suit jacket.

I let out an involuntary groan and nudged Nathan with my elbow. 'Let it go,' I muttered under my breath before throwing him a look, warning him to shut his mouth. Alfie knew how to push Nathan's buttons, and the more he reacted to it, the more pleasure Alfie got from it.

'Did you say something, Gemma?' Alfie asked.

Just as I was about to reply, Nathan squared up to Alfie.

'You don't even know my mum, so I'd appreciate it if you kept your opinions to yourself.' Nathan's cheeks flushed, as he tried to keep his temper under control. He clenched his jaw, and as he did, the muscles in the side of his face twitched.

'I've known Rosa for years... but I'm not going to say how. Gentlemen, shall we?' Alfie gestured to the door. Then his face broke into a broad grin. He knew he'd got the upper hand.

19

Gemma

Alfie's blacked-out Mercedes pulled up outside Mamma Donatella's on that grey November morning. As we walked towards the car, I could sense his blue eyes watching me. When we got closer, Tommy stepped out and opened the back passenger door for us.

'Hello, Gemma, you're looking as beautiful as ever,' Alfie said when I took a seat next to him.

I was wearing skinny jeans, a pale grey jumper, white Converse trainers and a dark purple Puffa jacket to keep the autumn chill at bay. My hair was pinned up into a loose bun.

'Thank you,' I replied, forcing out a reluctant smile.

Rosa's worried face was pressed up against the window of the Italian restaurant when the car pulled away from the kerb. Nathan and I looked at each other as we watched her tiny frame fade into the distance. I wondered whether we'd ever see her again.

*

When we arrived at the check-in gate for the 12:24 train from St Pancras International, Alfie handed us our tickets. We scanned the barcodes and made our way to passport control. As we stood in the queue, I realised hiding my nerves was going to be a challenge. My heart was racing, and the pulse in my neck beat so strongly, it was bound to be visible. No matter how good the forgeries were, if I looked guilty, I'd give the game away. I had to get a grip.

Alfie leant towards me and whispered in my ear. 'They only ask questions if something doesn't look right. You've got nothing to worry about. Stay calm, and I'll see you on the train.'

I nodded and took a deep breath in through my nostrils. Nathan squeezed my hand and pulled me towards him. I looked up at his handsome face as the buzz of conversation hovered in the air around us. We didn't speak to each other while we stood at the yellow line waiting to be called. When the official beckoned me to the counter, my heartbeat went into overdrive.

'Good morning, madam, can I see your passport please?' the young man said.

'Good morning,' I replied, handing over the document. I hoped he wouldn't notice my trembling hands.

The official checked the photo, scanned my passport and gave it back to me. Then he gestured for me to move towards the French booth where a lady sat behind the counter.

'Good morning,' she said, calling me forward.

I handed over my documents. The lady looked at my photo then stamped the passport before giving it back to me.

'Thank you,' I said.

'Have a pleasant trip,' she replied.

That was it; I was through passport control with my made-to-order, fake British passport. I'd passed the security checks with frightening ease and was shocked that it had been that simple. It was scary to think how many career criminals and terrorists were exploiting the system. Within thirty seconds, Nathan had done the same, and he came to stand next to me.

'Let's go and find the Business Premier carriage,' Nathan said, taking hold of my hand.

Alfie had booked us seats at a table for two. We sat down, facing each other, and once we were on the move, a waiter brought over a bottle of champagne.

'On behalf of everyone on board, I'd like to offer you both our congratulations on your wedding anniversary,' he said.

Nathan and I looked at each other. It wasn't our anniversary, but we weren't about to say no to a free bottle of bubbly. Alfie must have arranged this. It was no doubt part of his elaborate plan.

The waiter placed the ice bucket down on the table and popped the cork. Filling the first glass, he handed it to me.

'Thank you,' I said.

I took the flute from his hand, but as I lifted the glass to my lips, I paused before I took a sip. Would Alfie add the cost of this champagne to our debt? Probably, but right now I didn't care about that. I needed a drink after what we'd been through. My nerves were shot to pieces.

20

Gemma

Alfie had booked us a room at the George V. The Four Seasons Hotel was right in the centre of Paris, steps from the Champs-Élysées. We weren't used to such five-star luxury, but Alfie was a man who enjoyed the finer things in life.

Nathan and I checked in, and a porter took us to an incredible room on the second floor. It was bright and spacious with cream-coloured walls, a thick, pale grey damask carpet and eighteenth-century-inspired furniture. An enormous bed stood on the far side, covered by an ivory silk bedspread and matching cushions.

'I trust you have everything you need to enjoy your stay,' the young man said in a smooth French accent. 'If not, please don't hesitate to contact reception.'

As soon as we were alone, Nathan checked out the walk-in wardrobe and marble bathroom with freestanding bath and twin sinks. I lay down on the bed and looked up at the magnificent crystal chandelier with large faceted droplets, suspended from an ornate plaster ceiling rose in the centre of the room. I wondered how long it would be before we were disturbed. A knock on the door followed as if someone had just read my mind.

Nathan crossed the room and opened the polished mahogany door. Alfie stood on the other side dressed in his trademark smart suit, flanked by Knuckles and Tommy.

'Aren't you going to invite us in?' Alfie said, and a smile spread across his face.

My heart sank at the sight of him. I reluctantly got to my feet when Nathan stepped to one side and allowed them in.

Alfie walked over to the large, airy windows, framed by full-length pewter curtains. 'What do you think of the room?' he asked while admiring the incredible view of the hotel gardens. 'I spared no expense.'

'I've stayed in worse.'

Nathan's barbed comment made me nervous. Why had he said that? Throwing an insult in Alfie's direction wasn't a smart thing to do, given his unpredictable nature. But as luck would have it, instead of reacting angrily to it, Alfie decided to ignore it and laughed it off.

'I'm glad you like it, but don't get too comfortable, we've got work to do. I'll meet you down in the lobby in fifteen minutes,' Alfie said, checking his watch before sauntering out of the door.

It was mild for November, I thought as we stepped out of the hotel and walked towards the Place de la Concorde. Alfie had told us to stay behind him and behave like tourists. So we did as instructed and took photos on our phones of the

STEPHANIE HARTE

street performers on the wide pavements of the Champs-Élysées. While we were taking a selfie in front of the Arc de Triomphe, I began thinking about what Alfie had planned for us. At that moment, he turned his head and looked over his shoulder towards us. Not for the first time, I wondered if he'd just read my mind. The thought of that put me on edge.

'We won't be doing any shopping today,' Alfie said, 'but I'll show you where you'll be going tomorrow.'

Up until that point, I'd been enjoying our time in Paris. But the good feelings I'd had suddenly disappeared while we strolled through the Jardin des Tuileries. The season's last foliage looked beautiful bathed in an amber glow as the afternoon sunlight filtered through it. But even that couldn't take my mind off tomorrow's job, no matter how much I tried to block it from my head. Nathan could sense my apprehension and took hold of my hand. We passed the Louvre, and walked in silence along the banks of the river Seine, towards the Opéra quarter.

Alfie stopped outside a building on the Place Vendôme, one of the city's most famous and beautiful neoclassical squares. 'This is Boucheron's flagship store. It's where they keep all the best pieces.'

Nathan and I looked at each other. Then I turned away from him and stared through the window of the impressive shop front with ornate columns, crystal chandeliers, and potted orchids, to familiarise myself with the interior.

Nathan and I didn't normally eat four-course dinners in fancy restaurants, served by waiters dressed in tailcoats, but tonight, that's exactly what we did. Le Cinq had three

Michelin stars, but it wasn't the food I was thinking about when I looked around the marble-floored room filled with palm trees. The place was incredible. We were finishing our coffee when a text message came through on the mobile Alfie had given me earlier.

I take it you've enjoyed the best that money can buy.
Now it's time to go to your room.

I stood by the bedroom window mesmerised by thousands of twinkling fairy lights strung around the hotel gardens, while Nathan poured us each a glass of wine.

'Sorry to disturb your romantic evening,' Alfie said, letting himself into our room and pushing his way past Nathan. 'I need to run over the plan; then you should get some sleep.'

It was only nine o'clock. I hadn't been to bed that early since I was a child.

'When you go to Boucheron's tomorrow Nathan's going with you.'

Nathan and I looked at each other. I wondered why we were going together. The change of routine raised a lot of questions in my mind, but I couldn't think of a way to ask them, so I said nothing.

'Now listen carefully, you're going to swap this lump of glass for the ten-carat cushion-cut diamond solitaire they have for sale. It costs five hundred thousand euros because the quality of the diamond is so rare and unflawed,' Alfie said, handing me a ring with a large, single stone.

How did he expect me to switch that? They might not even let me try on a ring of that value, and even if they did, it was going to be protected by so much security, it would be impossible to steal.

'Both of you need to dress the part tomorrow, wear something smart. You know the routine by now, Gemma. You're an old hand at this.' Alfie laughed, implying I was some kind of career criminal.

'Why are both of us going shopping this time?'

'I thought you might appreciate some company as this is the biggest job yet. But if you'd prefer to go alone, that can be arranged...' Alfie smiled before he walked out of our room.

It was going to be a long night. I knew I wouldn't be able to get much sleep. All I could think about was tomorrow's job.

21

Gemma

Nathan and I walked into L'Orangerie as soon as it opened at 7.00am. We were shown to a table overlooking the marble courtyard, where vivid green ferns and dwarf orange trees contrasted with the black planters and furniture. Sitting in the early morning sunshine, in the art deco style glass and steel conservatory, I tried to calm my nerves by taking in the beautiful view.

'Bonjour, madame,' the waiter said.

'Bonjour.'

'Are you ready to order?'

'Yes, can I have a full American breakfast, please?'

'Certainly and what would you like, monsieur?'

'I'll have the same, please,' Nathan replied.

The waiter brought us our food along with freshly squeezed orange juice, assorted berries and a chocolate croissant, but I struggled to eat any of it. It looked delicious, but my nerves were affecting my appetite. I felt sick. The sooner this was over with, the better.

★

Nathan squeezed my hand as we stood on the pavement outside Boucheron. Once inside the luxurious interior, we made our way to an enormous display cabinet; its contents glittered under the light of the chandeliers. Almost instantly, a young man approached us.

'Can I help you?' he asked.

'Yes, I hope so. We're looking for something very specific,' Nathan replied, oozing confidence as he spoke.

'What did you have in mind, monsieur?'

'Unfortunately, my wife lost her engagement ring recently. She's understandably very upset about it, so I want to replace it.' Nathan took charge of the conversation as we'd agreed.

'I am sorry to hear that.'

'The ring was a ten-carat diamond set in platinum. Would you have anything like that available?' Nathan asked.

The sales assistant's eyes widened. He knew a ring like that cost a lot of money. 'I'm sure I'll be able to find something suitable for you,' he replied, barely disguising his smile.

'Thank you,' Nathan said, putting his arm around my shoulder.

The assistant opened the cabinet, protected by multiple surveillance domes, and took a beautiful ring from the display and handed it to me. 'How about this one, madame?'

I slipped it onto my finger and admired how it looked. 'I do like it, but for sentimental reasons, I'd prefer to get an exact replacement if possible.' I sighed, knowing that the setting was wrong. 'My ring was a solitaire; it didn't have diamonds surrounding it like this one.'

Placing the ring back in the cabinet, the assistant handed me another. 'Was it more like this one?'

'Yes, very similar,' I replied, locking eyes with Nathan. Now we had the ring Alfie wanted; we needed to make the swap.

It didn't take long for the store manager to realise a large sale was about to take place and he hurried over. He smiled and introduced himself to us.

'Excuse me one moment,' the manager said before turning towards the assistant serving us.

While they were having a brief conversation in French, I took the opportunity to switch the rings, but I couldn't locate the replica in my cavernous bag. I took a step back from the glass and tried to catch Nathan's eye so he'd know something was wrong.

'It's a beautiful ring, darling. It's just like the one you lost. But I think you should try some other rings on as well before you decide.'

I handed back the solitaire. Hopefully, another opportunity would present itself for me to try and switch the ring again.

'What about that one?' Nathan pointed to a large square-cut emerald ring.

'You have excellent taste, sir,' the manager said, muscling in on the sale. He tilted the exquisite platinum set ring, so that the halo of diamond pavé surrounding the main stone caught the light. 'All our gems are ethically sourced and certified for your peace of mind.'

Nathan pulled back the sleeve of his navy Armani suit and checked the time on his TAG Heuer watch. 'We're about to spend a lot of money, so I want to make sure you're happy. Why don't you decide which one you'd prefer over lunch?' Nathan smiled, but judging by the anxious-looking manager's face, he didn't agree. He was keen to close the sale.

I held the ring between my thumb and forefinger. My eyes lingered on it before I handed it back.

'Thank you for your help – we'll see you shortly,' Nathan said, shaking the manager by the hand.

My husband put his hand on the small of my back and guided me towards the door, oblivious to the fact that I'd just messed up the switch. Panic started to rise within me and stopped me thinking straight. My head began swimming as we stepped out of the store, and quickly lost ourselves in the crowd of people, walking along the wide pavement. My phone let out a muffled sound inside my bag. I unzipped it, took the mobile out and positioned it so Nathan could read the text as well. The message was from Alfie.

Keep walking straight ahead. There's a car waiting for you.

I wanted to run in the other direction, but Nathan caught hold of my hand, and we stepped up our pace until we reached a black BMW parked a short distance away. The back passenger door was already open, and Knuckles leant against the side of the car looking casual in jeans and a baseball cap. I let Nathan get in first because I didn't want to have to sit next to Alfie. Knuckles closed the door behind us, got into the driver's seat and pulled out into the heavy traffic.

'How did it go?' Alfie asked.

'Like a dream.' Nathan grinned.

More like a nightmare, I thought. I sat slumped on the seat, next to my husband, silently wondering how I was going to break the news to Alfie. I felt physically sick. As I sat looking at the world go by, my breathing became so rapid, it fogged up the car window. In an attempt to calm myself down, I focused on the scenery. Staring through the murky layer on the glass, I hoped to divert my thoughts to something more pleasant.

'You're very quiet, Gemma,' Alfie said, stretching his arm along the back of the seat and squeezing my shoulder. I jumped as his fingers made contact with me.

22

Alfie

I took a packet of cigarettes from the inside pocket of my suit jacket. Tommy obligingly lit it for me, while I eyed Nathan. He was a complete waste of space. I should never have allowed him to get involved. It was obvious he'd cock up the job. The dopey bastard hadn't realised Gemma didn't make the switch until she eventually blurted it out. The Stones' incompetence had just cost me five hundred thousand euros, so Nathan was going to have to pay for that.

Knuckles pulled the BMW up outside Gare du Nord station. Johno and Frankie were tailing us as I thought we'd be transporting a valuable diamond and could do with the backup. We'd continue with our plan to get out of the country and say goodbye to Paris for the time being. It was too risky to attempt the switch again.

'Get rid of the cars and join us at the departure gate.'

★

I handed Gemma a Thalys ticket, and she eyed me suspiciously before she read what was written on it. She tried to hide it, but I could see by the look on her face that she was gutted. The arrival station was Bruxelles Midi and not London St Pancras as she'd hoped. She stared at the ticket in disbelief, realising that meant she wasn't going home. We'd be in Brussels in less than ninety minutes thanks to the high-speed train.

'Why are we going to Belgium?' Nathan asked, studying his ticket.

I didn't bother to reply. After the stunt he'd pulled earlier he was lucky I didn't give him a slap. I certainly didn't owe him an explanation.

We took our seats as the train pulled out of the station. Gemma and Nathan were sitting several rows ahead, opposite each other. I stared at Gemma as she looked out of the window, watching the scenery as it began to change. She looked drained. All the fight had gone out of her. I didn't like seeing her like that. The long face didn't suit her.

When we stepped onto the platform at Brussels, the station was packed with busy commuters. Myself, Frankie and Tommy led the way. Nathan and Gemma were sandwiched between us, Knuckles and Johno. I couldn't trust them not to try and do a runner.

As we neared the exit, I glanced over my shoulder, and I could see Gemma was looking anxious. She was no doubt scared of being stopped by border control. But she didn't need to worry, we were travelling in the Schengen area, so the barrier was open. We didn't have to show our passports and weren't subjected to any other security checks either. That's my kind of immigration system. By abolishing the internal borders between countries within the zone, it allowed people free and unrestricted movement. That gave criminals like me the opportunity to pass through unprotected borders, using false names and fake passports.

I'd always loved France. It was the gateway to the rest of Europe.

23

Gemma

Once we were outside the station, Alfie hailed a taxi, leaning through the open window so he could speak to the driver. The car pulled out into the rush hour traffic and made the short journey to the Hotel Metropole. We would be staying in another hotel in another city. There seemed to be a pattern emerging. This was going to be my life for the foreseeable future. You didn't have to be a genius to work that out.

The doorman came over to the taxi to help us with our luggage, before showing us into the reception area of the nineteenth-century hotel. I was glad to see it lived up to Alfie's high expectations. It was a work of art and oozed old-style opulence with its stained-glass ceiling panels and sweeping marble staircase. Glittering chandeliers hung above the teak-panelled room, which was lined with ornate pillars and adorned with gilded furniture.

After checking in at the biggest desk I'd ever seen, a young man in a red and grey uniform collected our luggage.

'Bonjour, if you would like to follow me, I'll take you to your room,' he said, in near-perfect English. He led us to the far side of the lobby, where we waited for the charming antique caged lift.

Our room was incredible. Champagne-coloured walls contrasted with dark blue carpet and furnishings. The enormous bed, covered with a navy velvet bedspread, looked tiny in the great expanse of the room. A full marble bathroom and dressing room adjoined it.

'I hope you have a pleasant stay,' the bellboy said.

'Thank you, I'm sure we will,' Nathan replied.

'As this hotel is the birthplace of the Black Russian cocktail, you might like to go to the Metropole bar to try one,' the young man said, drawing our attention to this interesting fact as he was leaving the room.

Once we were alone, Nathan collapsed back onto the bed. 'I could get used to living like this.'

I looked straight into my husband's dark brown eyes.

'What's up? Don't you like travelling around Europe, staying in first-class hotels?'

'I would, if we were on a proper break, but you've forgotten one tiny detail. We're on the run.'

'That's a bit melodramatic. Don't overreact, Gem. We're not on the run.' Nathan laughed.

'We will be when the police catch up with us.'

Before Nathan had a chance to reply, someone began pounding on the door. No prizes for guessing who that is, I thought.

Alfie strode into our room in his usual confident manner, only accompanied by his sidekick Knuckles. He'd left the rest of his entourage behind.

'Get us a drink will you, Nathan.' Alfie pointed towards the minibar.

'Jack Daniel's?' Nathan asked.

Alfie nodded. 'And you'd better bring one for Gemma – she looks like she could use a stiff one.' Alfie threw back his head and laughed.

'You have such a lovely way with words, Mr Watson,' I said. Alfie's biggest problem was that he mistook being an arsehole for being funny, but I decided maybe I should keep that to myself and not say it out loud.

'You're acting like a prude. Lighten up, Gemma. You know the sexually repressed librarian look doesn't suit you. You haven't got the figure for it.' Alfie glanced across at my husband to gauge his reaction.

The joke had gone too far, but Alfie either didn't realise or didn't care. Fury was boiling up inside me. I opened my mouth, intending to give him a piece of my mind, but something told me not to, and I managed to hold my tongue. I'd only give his schoolboy humour airtime by venting at him, so I decided to blank him instead.

Nathan, on the other hand, didn't hesitate. He must have sensed my anger; I wasn't very good at hiding it. 'Don't you dare speak to my wife like that.' He looked like he wanted to rip Alfie's head off.

'What are you going to do about it?'

Nathan couldn't take any more and lunged forward. Grabbing the lapels of Alfie's suit, he squared up to him. Knuckles pulled Nathan off, pushed him to the ground and pinned him face down on the floor.

Biting my tongue, I resisted the urge to cry out. I forced myself to stay still and keep quiet. I didn't want to make the situation any worse than it already was. But it was torture having to stand by and watch, knowing there was nothing I could do to help.

'You're a fucking hothead just like your mother, Nathan.' Alfie dusted off the front of his suit.

24

Gemma

I ran the shower until the room billowed with steam, then walked behind the glass screen of the wet room. I closed my eyes and stood under the steady flow. As soon as the warm water started running over my naked body, it began to wash away the stress of the day. I could feel myself beginning to unwind.

I didn't hear Nathan open the bathroom door but suddenly felt him cover the side of my neck with warm butterfly kisses. My whole body tingled. Nathan placed one hand on my stomach and pulled me back towards him.

'Mind if I join you?' Nathan whispered in my ear.

His hand wandered down my body, and he began kissing the other side of my neck, right behind my ear. It felt good when his strong body pressed mine against the cold, wet marble tiles.

Turning to face my husband, I wrapped my arms around his neck while keeping my back against the wall. He moved his mouth onto mine, and our lips touched, softly at first, and then our kiss became more passionate. My body ached for him as his strong fingers entwined in my hair.

Nathan held me close as we exchanged steamy kisses. Lifting one of my legs, he slid his hand along my thigh and gripped my buttock.

'I love you, Gemma. Don't ever forget that.'

'I love you too.'

Our eyes locked and he gently entered me. Nathan moved slowly at first, but then he began pushing deeper and faster. The muscles on his back tightened more with every thrust he made. Our bodies locked together as each wave of pleasure washed over us. Ecstasy built up inside my body until finally, my muscles tensed around him.

25

Gemma

We were staying just around the corner from the Grand Place, so Nathan and I decided to take a stroll around the beautiful gardens and historic buildings. It felt good to be out of the room, even if Frankie and Johno were tailing us, at a discreet distance.

I was finding it difficult to ignore the temptation of the chocolate-filled window displays as we walked along the traditional cobblestoned lanes. The heavenly aroma hit me as I opened the glass door of Godiva's. It was so strong I could almost taste it. I considered myself an expert when it came to chocolate, but I'd never seen anything like this before. I was almost drooling as I stared at the trays of individual chocolates, sat behind the glass cases.

Picking up some blond cigars, I began making my way around the shop. By the time I'd got halfway, chocolate-covered pretzels, nuts and biscuits had somehow found their way into my hands. Nathan pulled the plug on my shopping spree after I'd asked the assistant to fill the largest gold ballotin with a selection of gourmet truffles.

Nathan and I were watching TV when Alfie let himself into our room just before midnight. 'You two look like you're having fun.'

We both glanced in his direction but didn't get up. I was sitting between Nathan's thighs on the plush sofa leaning back against his broad chest. He had one arm draped over my shoulder as we shared a bottle of red wine.

Nathan put his glass down on the table, picked up the remote control and turned off the sound.

'I just came to tell you that we'll be moving on in the morning.'

I sat upright, swung my legs around and placed my feet on the floor. 'Where are we going?' I asked.

'To Antwerp – you need to be ready to leave at ten.'

Antwerp was Belgium's diamond district. No prizes for guessing why we're going there, I thought. We'd spent the last few days relaxing, eating waffles, and taking full advantage of the luxurious bathroom facilities. We'd sit at opposite ends of the enormous whirlpool bath, filled with scented bubbles, like a couple of bookends, gazing into each other's eyes, the way we used to when we first met.

I should have known Alfie would put an end to our enjoyment sooner or later. But I promised myself then and there that if we ever got out of this, the first thing I was going to do was treat us to a Jacuzzi bath. Every couple should have one.

26

Gemma

'That's the World Diamond Centre headquarters,' Alfie said, pointing out the Mercedes' window.

The heavy security presence on the street outside the building indicated its importance. I hoped he wasn't expecting me to steal something from in there.

'Most of the world's production of rough diamonds trade in Antwerp,' Alfie continued.

I didn't care how many diamonds passed through this city; I just wanted to know what he had planned for me next.

'Head to Willemdok, Knuckles.'

Alfie led the way to an incredible motor yacht berthed in the marina. Nathan and I stood on the sun-bleached decking admiring the ultra-modern, all-white exterior of the gleaming vessel. It must have cost a fortune. Living a life of crime obviously did pay after all.

Alfie climbed onto the deck and offered me his hand.

'Are we going somewhere on this?' I asked, hoping for once he'd give me a straight answer.

Alfie flashed me a knowing smile but declined to answer. 'Welcome on board the *Lady Nora*. She's a beauty, isn't she?'

She certainly was. This was the kind of toy the uber-rich owned. The *Lady Nora* was a status symbol.

'Knuckles, get the yacht ready to sail. We need to move her out of here and moor up somewhere else that isn't tidal.'

'We could berth her at Breskens instead. That marina's got immediate access to the North Sea,' Knuckles replied.

As we left the port of Antwerp, I wondered why we needed access to the North Sea. I was tempted to ask but didn't bother. There was no point. Alfie never answered my questions. That frustrated me beyond words. He had such a skill of avoiding them; if he fancied a career change, he could easily have become a politician.

I sat on deck, with the wind in my hair, watching the world go by. Huge container ships, barges and other yachts accompanied us as we cruised down the busy stretch of river, and even though it was noisy, it was strangely therapeutic.

'We'll moor here tonight, and tomorrow morning, you and Tommy are going back to Antwerp by speedboat,' Alfie said to Nathan. 'You get to stay on board and relax, Gemma.'

'Aren't I the lucky one?' I laughed, but it sounded forced even to my ears.

Why wasn't I going with them? Don't get me wrong, I

was delighted not to be, but the thought of staying behind on the yacht with Alfie filled me with dread. My mind was full of conflicting emotions.

'Let me give you a guided tour of the facilities.'

Alfie led Nathan and me below deck to the luxurious dining area. Traditional cherry wood surfaces and gleaming brass contrasted with the modern all-white interior.

I ran my fingers along the back of one of the leather chairs pushed under the large table that could seat ten.

'She's beautiful, isn't she? That's why I named her after my mother,' Alfie said, beaming with pride.

Alfie threw me with that comment. Was he about to reveal he had a caring, tender side to his personality? Maybe I'd misjudged him after all. But when I thought about it, the idea of this violent man having a mushy, sentimental side was ridiculous, and I almost laughed out loud. Men like Alfie didn't show their feelings. He'd see that as a weakness.

I was about to make a snide remark but stopped myself just in time. I remembered I was going to be on my own with him tomorrow, so it probably wasn't the best idea to get on the wrong side of him.

'There's plenty of room to accommodate all of us in the four staterooms,' Alfie continued. 'Mine's the one on the left.' Alfie gestured towards the back of the yacht, like a steward pointing out the emergency exits on a plane. 'You and Nathan take the one opposite.'

Alfie disappeared up the staircase as Nathan and I made our way along the corridor to the spacious cabin. We stopped in our tracks when we heard his muffled voice coming from the deck above us. Nathan and I strained to hear what he was saying. From what we could make out,

Tommy and Nathan were going back to Antwerp to carry out a bit of business while the rest of us would be staying on the yacht. Nathan and I looked at each other. We both knew that whatever business Alfie was planning to do, it wouldn't be legal.

27

Alfie

Don't you just love it when a plan comes together? The day Nathan came to me and asked to borrow money from the firm, I jumped at the chance. The Stones and the Watsons had old scores to settle, so I was delighted to kick-start the cycle of revenge. Nothing would give me greater pleasure. It had been a long time coming, but the dish was best served cold, wasn't it?

More than twenty years had passed, but I still couldn't forgive Rosa for what she'd done to my family. I'd carried the pain with me for such a long time and it had festered inside me like a cancer, spreading and multiplying through every cell of my body. It seemed only right that her precious son, Nathan, should be punished in return. Rosa loved him more than anything in the world. Making him suffer for something she did would be torture for her. Now it was my turn to destroy what she valued most in life.

The desire to get even with the Stones hadn't been forced upon me, it was a primal instinct. I had an unquenchable craving for revenge. It flowed through me like the blood in my veins. My negative feelings towards Rosa hadn't dissipated. They had intensified and become an obsession. Inflicting suffering on her was high up on my bucket list. I was fully committed to ruining her life. The first thought that came to mind every morning when I woke up was how I could make her pay.

One of my greatest pleasures in life was getting revenge on a person who had wronged me, so I'd become a bully at an early age and had honed my skills over the years. The process felt as normal as getting out of bed in the morning. Intimidation was a powerful tool. A threat often served as a form of protection. It ensured the person wouldn't try anything in the future without fear of retaliation.

I never expected to reel Nathan in so effortlessly. He'd walked right into the trap. Nobody in their right mind would ask me to lend them cash. He was like a lamb to the slaughter and more naive than I'd given him credit for. Nathan hadn't borrowed the money from a bank, so naturally, I was going to exploit him. Did he seriously think nothing bad would come of it?

The size of the debt was no longer relevant. Gemma and Nathan had broken the law on countless occasions. Now I had them right where I wanted them. They couldn't walk away from me because they needed the protection of the firm to keep them out of jail. Gemma had nothing to worry about. I wouldn't let her see the inside of a cell. I couldn't say the same for Nathan. I wouldn't have wanted to be in his shoes. I could be a nasty bastard when the mood took me. Everyone knew I had a vicious streak and I couldn't be held accountable if I was provoked by someone I didn't like.

Thanks to Nathan's stupidity, he'd got them trapped in a situation of his own making. No wonder their marriage was in trouble. My heart bled for him. As if!

28

Gemma

The calming sound of water lapping against the hull, and the gentle rocking motion of the boat lulled me into the most peaceful night's sleep I'd had in ages.

'It's time to get up,' Alfie said, hammering his fist on our door and waking me with a start.

A beautiful sunrise was seeping into our cabin, bathing our room in rosy light. I pulled back the curtain behind the bed and watched the golden sun edging its way over the horizon, casting pink and orange rays across the still water. What a breathtaking scene.

'We'll be out in a minute,' I replied, settling back down under the covers.

I nudged Nathan with my elbow. He pulled me towards him and wrapped his arms around me before planting a kiss on the top of my head.

'I'm not happy about leaving you here with Alfie,' Nathan said.

I wasn't delighted by the prospect either, but Nathan

had enough on his plate at the moment, without worrying about me.

Alfie threw open the door. 'What's taking you so long? You need to hurry up – we've got to catch the tide.'

After putting my coat on over my pyjamas, I stood on deck and watched the speedboat leave the marina with my husband on board. I'd be lying if I said Nathan's concerns about my safety weren't on my mind. I was apprehensive too, and given Alfie's track record, I was well within my rights to feel the way I did. As the boat faded into the distance, Nathan pulled up the collar of his jacket before he turned and waved to me. His dark hair was dishevelled, blowing wildly in the chilly morning air.

Tommy moored the boat at Willemdok marina. 'You see that building over there?' he said, pointing to the large red-brick construction on the riverbank. 'That's the Museum aan de Stroom, the one I was telling you about.'

'I remember, and the Diamond Pavilion's next to it,' Nathan replied, putting on a baseball cap and dark sunglasses.

'Make sure you're quick. We've got to get back out of the marina on this tide,' Tommy said, giving Nathan a handgun.

Nathan put the gun inside his jacket and walked calmly along the jetty and through the glass doors of the pavilion. He walked past a security guard and followed the sign directing him to an exhibition showcasing precious metals and jewels. Once inside the room, Nathan pulled out the gun, pointing it at the two members of staff setting up the display.

'Do exactly what I say, and nobody will get hurt. Put the jewellery in that case.'

Nathan passed a large black bag to the young man, who filled it. Taking the bag from his shaking hands, Nathan fled out of an emergency exit, running the short distance to the waiting boat. Once Nathan was on board, Tommy opened up the throttle and sped out of the marina. He weaved in and out between the other vessels while negotiating the river's many bridges and locks.

'You nailed it,' Tommy said, slapping Nathan on the shoulder.

29

Nathan

Thank God that was over. I'd been seriously dreading that job. After the fiasco in Boucheron with Gemma, I knew I couldn't afford to fuck it up. Alfie was gunning for me. He'd laid the blame firmly at my feet for the aborted switch, which was fine by me. It was bad enough that Gemma was involved in this. I didn't want her to suffer for our failed attempt.

We were at the mercy of a cold-blooded crime boss because of my stupidity. If I hadn't gone through with the robbery, there was a very real chance he was going to kill me. I knew how some gangsters operated and wondered if I'd lose a body part, have my teeth pulled out or be fed alive to a sty full of hungry pigs before our ordeal was over. Fear was a powerful driving force. It could make a person agree to do almost anything.

I had to admit I was nervous before my visit to the Diamond Pavilion, but once my adrenaline started pumping, I let the rush take over. I never realised stealing something could be so exciting. I racked my brain to find a logical explanation for why I'd found it so appealing, but there wasn't one. It wasn't as if I'd even get to keep the items I'd stolen, so it had to be for the thrill of it. I'd been completely seduced by the experience. It didn't even feel like I'd committed an offence. I was just working for Alfie, wasn't I?

Not knowing much about the personality traits of people who carry out violent crime, I couldn't be sure whether I fitted the typical profile of an armed robber, but my love of risk-taking and thrill-seeking helped me carry out the job. That was for certain. I'd had no intention of hurting those people, even though I was armed. But I had to admit, I found the fear of getting caught as exciting as winning a high-stakes poker game. Gemma always maintained I was an adrenaline junkie. She was right.

Even as a small child, I'd liked exciting games. I'd had no interest in doing jigsaws or being a bookworm, and if my mother was to be believed, I'd been a daredevil from the moment I became mobile. Cot diving was an everyday activity for me as soon as I could crawl. Pretty soon, I progressed to tree climbing and sliding down the stairs in a cardboard box. It was the danger element that made it so exhilarating.

As a result of my mum working long hours, I'd spent a lot of time unattended, which allowed me the freedom to hone the risk-taker within me. I developed a thrill for taking chances and loved to push the boundaries. I wasn't afraid to take myself out of my comfort zone. I saw it as a challenge. By the time I was a teenager, I was fearless, but my mum often accused me of being rebellious. I preferred to use the word 'independent'.

Thanks to the non-existent father figure in my life, I'd become the man of the house at an early age. It was a role I'd acquired by default after he rejected me. When I was a child, I hated the fact that my home life was different to that of my peers, but as I grew up, instead of blaming myself for my father's absence, I started blaming him. Holding on to the pain, anger, and resentment was toxic and I ended up hating my dad. He'd abandoned me when I was a baby, so I'd had to negotiate life's hurdles and make my way in the big wide world without him. That was a difficult lesson to learn.

30

Gemma

As soon as Tommy and Nathan arrived back, Knuckles expertly steered the yacht through the calm water of the harbour, and it glided out to open sea.

Nathan cupped my face in his hands, before kissing me passionately in full view of the others. Feeling self-conscious with all the pairs of eyes watching us, I pulled away, embarrassed by his public display of affection.

'If you can bear to put her down, I'd like to know how the job went,' Alfie said with a look of distaste on his face.

'It was a piece of cake,' Nathan bragged, holding up the case.

'Let's go below deck,' Alfie replied.

Nathan emptied out the contents of the bag. The stash of pink and yellow diamonds, emeralds, sapphires and rubies spilt across the large cherry wood table. Alfie picked up the gems and began inspecting them.

'You've done well. It takes balls to walk into a museum

in broad daylight and walk out with a case full of jewels.'
Alfie slapped Nathan on the back.

'It was easier than I thought it was going to be. I was
expecting there to be cameras following my every move and
security guards stalking the corridors. But the place was
deserted,' Nathan said, shaking his head in disbelief.

Even though the museum was open, tourists don't normally
visit that early in the morning, so the security was lax.

'I made my way to the room where a man and woman
were setting up the exhibition display. They didn't take
any notice when I walked into the room, so I went up to
them, pulled out a gun and told them to fill the bag with the
jewels. I left through the emergency exit a few minutes later.
I'd gone before anyone had time to raise the alarm.'

My mouth fell open in shock. The weight of Nathan's
news felt like it was going to crush me. How could he pull
a gun on two innocent people? Carrying out an armed
robbery was in a completely different league to anything
we'd done before. I didn't want to hear what Nathan had
to say. Right now, locking myself in my cabin seemed like a
good option, but I stood rooted to the spot. I felt compelled
to listen, even though I knew I wasn't going to like it. I
needed to know what had happened.

Nathan sat on the edge of the table with his arms
folded across his chest, telling us about the experience. His
revelations made me feel sick. I was disgusted that Alfie had
made him do something like that. He'd been put in such a
dangerous position. What if something had gone wrong? I
stood dumbstruck, letting the reality of the situation wash
over me.

'I was surprised how little security there was,' Nathan said.

The corners of Alfie's mouth tilted up in a smile. 'The temporary exhibitions are always like that. You'd think the organisers would have learnt by now: if they're going to put high-quality gems and diamonds like these on display, without anyone guarding them, they're going to attract their fair share of thieves.'

Alfie seemed keen to share his extensive knowledge of burglary with us. When executed correctly, a robbery only needed to take a matter of minutes. The longer you hung around, the more likely you were to get caught, he informed us. But I couldn't help noticing that he never seemed to be the one who got his hands dirty. That job was always left to somebody else.

'Is the jewellery insured?' I asked.

'Yes, which is just as well for the exhibition because once the stolen diamonds enter the supply chain, they'll be virtually impossible to trace.' Alfie beamed. 'If they're very high profile and too recognisable, Terry might have to re-cut the stones into smaller pieces. But then they'll be sold on, never to be seen again.'

31

Gemma

Alfie had given Nathan and me a glimpse into his very dangerous world. He had us dangling from a thread, and at this stage, there was no escape for us. I hated the idea of being on the run from the police until I was old and grey.

'The exhibition job was a big step for you. I know you're a risk-taker, but I wasn't sure you'd be able to do it. I shouldn't have doubted you. You're a chip off the old block.' Alfie congratulated Nathan on his meteoric rise in importance in the firm.

Nathan stared at Alfie while he contemplated his words.

'Private collectors approach Terry all the time looking for particular pieces. He's a gifted jeweller, so he provides me with very convincing copies. I steal the original item, give it to Terry, and he sells it to the buyer, job done.'

I couldn't believe what I was hearing. I hadn't realised I'd been stealing to order; I thought I'd just been mindlessly shoplifting. I glared at Alfie, then folded my arms across my chest. My disdain was obvious.

'Is something the matter, Gemma?'

I threw Alfie a look of contempt, and he smiled back at me. 'You didn't steal the jewellery, I did!'

Alfie shrugged his shoulders then dismissed me with a wave of his hand. 'That's just a small technicality. The bottom line is, the buyer knows the jewellery's stolen, but they don't give a shit.'

My body stiffened at his remark. I was so angry with him; I could almost feel steam coming out of my ears. I don't know what pissed me off more, the way Alfie waved his hand at me or his attitude. 'Of course they don't give a shit. It isn't their head on the block; it's mine.'

Nathan squeezed the top of my shoulder.

'You really need to learn to relax, Gemma, or you'll give yourself premature wrinkles.' Alfie winked.

I felt my cheeks flush as fury bubbled up inside me. I was tempted to slap him around the face, but he turned his back on me, picked up an exquisite pink diamond ring and held it up to the light.

'Luckily for us, they don't follow regulations closely in Tel Aviv, so I'll get Terry to try and shift some of this stuff. They never ask questions about the source of the stones, but the price on the black market isn't always good. If that's the case, we'll hold on to the gear. Diamonds make excellent underworld currency,' Alfie said as a slow smile curved his lips.

Not wanting to appear like the new kid on the block, Nathan nodded implying he knew exactly what Alfie was talking about, but he didn't have a clue. He was as puzzled as I was. We didn't have long to wait before we found out what underworld currency was. Since the crackdown on money laundering, instead of dealing in cash when buying and selling, criminals sometimes used diamonds. They could be transferred from person to person, almost entirely anonymously. It was the easiest way to move large amounts of money around the world because police sniffer dogs weren't able to detect the smell of diamonds.

Alfie flashed me another smile as he explained the process in great detail. He should consider writing a beginner's guide to the principles and practices, I thought. I'm sure *Illegal Diamond Trading For Dummies* would be hugely successful.

'It's probably a stupid question, but why do you want to move large amounts of money around?' Nathan asked, tilting his head to the side.

'You're right, it is a stupid question. I feel like I'm on fucking *Mastermind*.'

'Are you going to tell us?' I asked.

Alfie flashed me his white smile. 'You're a clever girl, Gemma. You should be able to work it out for yourself. Why do you think?'

'I have no idea,' I replied, locking eyes with Alfie.

'Drug distribution is an expensive business.' Alfie grinned.

My mouth fell open, and Alfie's words bombarded my brain as they swam around my head. I didn't think things could get any worse, but I was wrong. He'd just confirmed my worst nightmare. We were in so much trouble. A feeling of dread came over me. I was so stressed, I couldn't think straight. I tried to convince myself to stay calm. But I was on the verge of hysteria as several possible outcomes to our situation started to form in my mind.

The first was of Nathan and me, locked behind bars with no chance of parole, for the rest of our lives. The next involved us being chased from country to country, pursued by Interpol agents. But the one I didn't want to consider was having notched up criminal records as long as our arms, we ended up being gunned down and didn't survive this nightmare. The frightening thing was, that was a real possibility.

This wasn't how I'd imagined my future, and with my ever-diminishing fertility window constantly in my thoughts, I was determined it wasn't going to turn out like this. Not if I had anything to do with it. I'd never been a quitter, so I'd have to devise a strategy to break free. I wasn't going to let Alfie control us any more.

We didn't fit into this brutal environment. We needed to get as far away from Alfie as possible. Otherwise, we would spend the rest of our lives running scared. We must have paid off our debt by now. I hated having to work for Alfie. I was at war with myself over it. What we were doing was against the law, and it was playing on my conscience. I constantly felt guilty about what I'd done.

'I can't believe you pulled a gun on two innocent people and threatened to shoot them,' I said when we were alone in our cabin.

I was genuinely shocked that my husband was capable of behaving like that. Nathan didn't try to justify why he'd terrorised those people with a weapon. Instead, he stared at me like I was the one with the problem.

'What do you want me to say, Gemma? I didn't pull the trigger, did I?' Nathan fumed.

'Sounds like there's trouble in paradise.'

When I heard Alfie's voice, it made me see red. I flung

open our cabin door and glared at him. 'Didn't anyone ever tell you it's rude to eavesdrop?'

Alfie stared back at me, as a look of pure delight spread all over his face. 'I was hardly listening in; the whole yacht can hear your conversation. If you two don't pipe down, people will hear us coming before we get anywhere near Boulogne.' Alfie winked a blue eye at me.

Why were we going to France again? I thought Alfie had said we needed to stay away from there.

32

Gemma

You could cut the atmosphere in the cabin with a knife, so I turned away and looked out the window at the endless blue view as I tried to get my head around the situation. Nathan didn't like being given the silent treatment, but right now staying quiet was the best thing I could do. He was impossible to talk to when he was in a mood like this, so I'd realised over the years that sometimes my silence was more powerful than any words I could say to him. He knew I was angry with him. I felt he'd gone too far when he'd stolen the exhibition jewels. It scared me to think how easily he'd slipped into the role of an armed robber.

I'd never seen this side of my husband before, and I didn't like it. What the hell had got into him? The man I'd married was kind and generous and wouldn't hurt a fly. I felt an unexpected urge to cry and struggled to hold back my tears. I suddenly realised how isolated I'd become. I no longer had any contact with my family. Nathan and I had spent so many years wrapped up in each other that I'd lost touch with my friends as well. As I stared at the huge expanse of water before me, I'd never felt more alone.

Nathan meant everything to me, but the nightmare we were trapped in had put us under so much stress, it was driving a wedge between us. I was very aware that if I lost Nathan, I would have nobody left in my life that I truly cared about. The thought of being alone terrified me.

As a child, I was never deprived of material things. My parents were wealthy, and I came from a privileged background. But growing up without their love and affection made me constantly crave it. Despite being born into the same family, my sister and I were treated completely differently. I don't think she ever realised how toxic our parents were, mainly because she wasn't on the receiving end. When something went wrong, it was always my fault. I shouldered the blame for everything. Being the favourite, Rebecca could do no wrong. I always wanted to be idolised the same way. It wasn't much fun being second-best. The experience left me with low self-esteem, but since I'd met Nathan, I'd battled to overcome it. If the experience had taught me anything, it was to be resilient.

I'd closed the door on my relationship with my family years ago, and I had no desire to open it again. In fact, I'd rather go over Niagara Falls in a barrel than make contact with them. We hadn't just become estranged overnight; it was a gradual process. We'd never had a good relationship and the older I got, the more strained it became.

It went seriously downhill when I started going out with Nathan. They had no time for the man I adored. I shouldn't have been surprised. But I never thought they'd make me choose between them. I didn't want to be put in that position. We weren't close, but they were my parents. Giving me an ultimatum felt extremely manipulative. It showed me that they didn't care if I was happy or not, so it made the decision easier for me. It wasn't a tough choice. I chose Nathan and even though things are rocky between us at the moment, I don't regret it for a minute.

33

Gemma

When Alfie summoned us, Nathan and I made our way to the saloon. The social area of the yacht housed the dining table and a plush U-shaped white leather settee.

'The police have just released some CCTV of the theft at The Diamond Pavilion. They're hunting for the armed robber.' Alfie grinned.

My hands flew up to cover my mouth as I tried to take in what Alfie was telling us. Nathan stared into the middle distance with a blank expression on his face.

'Have you seen the footage?' I asked, hoping he wouldn't notice the panic creeping into my voice.

Holding my breath, I waited for Alfie to reply. Why was he stalling? There could only be one reason: the net was closing in on us.

'There's nothing to worry about; the image is grainy.'

'Can you see Nathan's face, and more importantly, can

he be identified from the footage?' My upper lip beaded with sweat.

'According to the police report, they are looking for a male suspect who threatened two staff members with a gun during the robbery. He's described as white and in his early twenties.'

'Early twenties,' Nathan repeated before his face broke into a huge grin. 'I'm thirty-two!'

'The only other information the police have is that the man fled the scene on foot. They've asked international diamond houses to be vigilant in case any of the items are offered for sale,' Alfie continued.

I knew this would happen sooner or later. It was only a matter of time. I bit down hard on the pad of my thumb and wondered if the police were looking for me. The shops I'd robbed had cameras running twenty-four hours a day. I felt on edge knowing there was footage of Nathan committing the robbery being circulated on TV.

'Don't look so worried, Gemma. All the cops have got is a poor quality clip that lasts a couple of seconds. That's why they're appealing to the public for help,' Alfie said.

'But the witnesses gave a description of Nathan.'

'I can't believe they thought I was in my early twenties! I must be doing something right.' Nathan's face broke into a huge beam then he ran his hand through his thick, dark hair. He was delighted by the compliment.

I shot him a disapproving look.

'Don't you just love the public?' Alfie laughed. 'Witnesses always get the facts wrong, and in this case, they got it very wrong. Anyway, the description they gave could fit half the population. The cops might as well be looking for a needle in a haystack.' Alfie winked, and a huge smile spread across his face.

Even though Alfie assured me that the police had nothing to go on, they were looking for a man ten years younger than Nathan, the colour drained from my face. This whole experience was stressing me out.

I pushed my chair back and stood up. 'I've had enough of this. When are you going to let us go home?' I asked, putting my hands on my hips.

'What do you make of that, gentlemen?' Alfie said to his henchmen. 'The way Gemma's talking you'd think I was physically restraining the two of them and holding them to ransom.'

The sound of Alfie's laughter echoed around the room. It sent a shiver down my spine. That was exactly what he was doing. We were living in a constant state of fear. It haunted me every time I thought about how much things had changed since he came into our lives.

'We must have cleared our debt by now,' I said.

Alfie narrowed his eyes. 'I've already explained this to you. You're part of the team now, so you're in this for the long haul. The debt is no longer relevant.'

I couldn't get Alfie's words out of my head. I didn't want to be part of the team. I wanted my life to go back to the way it used to be before he'd turned it into a nightmare, full of threats and violence.

'The Diamond Pavilion heist has given us a lot of collateral,' Alfie said.

I wondered what he meant by that but knew better than

to ask. 'Does that mean we can blow it all on cheap booze at the hypermarket?' I asked, and a sarcastic tone seeped into my words.

The look on Alfie's face told me I'd infuriated him, without him having to say a word. He pulled out one of the leather chairs. 'Sit down, Gemma,' he said before he took a seat at the opposite side of the table. Crossing his arms in front of his chest, he glared at me. As he continued to study me, my heart began pounding. Had I gone too far this time?

34

Alfie

Gemma continued to fascinate me. Not only was she stunningly beautiful with her long brown hair and green eyes, but she wasn't afraid to stand up to me. That was rare. Not many people were brave enough to do that. For the life of me, I couldn't work out what a strong woman like her saw in a loser like Nathan. She deserved better. I would gladly take her off his hands.

Now that the two of them worked for me, they would need to start over from scratch. Gemma and Nathan Stone were about to disappear off the grid. They wouldn't be returning to the UK for the foreseeable future. For the next stage of the journey, they'd be travelling on French passports.

'Why have you changed my name again?' Gemma asked when I handed her the document bearing the name Emma Martin.

'You'll blend in better if you have the same surname as half the French population.'

'We're coming into port,' Knuckles called.

I got to my feet and peered out of one of the many windows. I loved Boulogne. It was the only port on the Côte d'Opale with direct access to the sea, so if we needed to make a run for it in the middle of the night, we could get away and wouldn't have to wait for the tide. Knowing that meant I'd sleep soundly.

As we entered the marina, Knuckles guided the yacht into the berth, and the sound of the engine stopped.

Tommy looked up, then glanced over at me. 'Should I put the jewellery back in the bag now?'

'Yes, and put the paperwork in there as well.'

'What's the paperwork for?' Gemma asked.

'It's a bogus certificate for the shipment of stones. If the Port Authority decide to search us, we don't want them to think the jewellery isn't legitimate, do we?'

I flashed Gemma a smile before I started to make my way along the corridor, towards my room. When I reached the doorway, I turned and looked over my shoulder.

'I want you to dress up for dinner tonight, Gemma. Make sure you wear something classy and put red lipstick on. I like red lipstick,' I said as if we were going on a date.

La Plage was an expensive restaurant. Gemma deserved the best. When I saw the look on Nathan's face, it made me smile. I might go on the charm offensive later and really wind the wanker up.

35

Gemma

La Plage stood right on the seafront. Unsurprisingly, the beachside restaurant specialised in fish. As I looked at the unimposing exterior of the building, I couldn't understand why Alfie had been raving about it. It didn't look very impressive.

But once we were inside, my opinion changed, and I realised I should have reserved judgement. The interior couldn't have been more different. It was elegant and refined with soft music playing in the background and just the right level of lighting. The maître d' introduced himself as Pascal, and greeted us as if we were old friends. Following Alfie's request, we were shown to a spacious table, covered with a white linen tablecloth in the corner of the restaurant.

Alfie sat down with his back against the wall, facing the door. 'Gemma, come and sit next to me.'

I looked up at Nathan. He was furious, but thankfully instead of reacting, he didn't say a word and took a seat at the far end of the table.

The waiter handed us all menus. 'I'll be back in a moment to take your orders.'

Before the waiter had a chance to leave the table, Alfie took the liberty of ordering everybody's starter. He chose the house speciality: red mullet served on a bed of tomatoes and black olives from the restaurant's à la carte menu.

'Would you like to order some wine?' the waiter asked.

'Yes.' Alfie took the extensive list, which was as thick as a book, and selected a bottle of white Bordeaux with a hundred-euro price tag.

'That is an excellent vintage, and it will complement the fish.' Pascal nodded, clearly impressed that Alfie hadn't needed any advice.

The waiter brought out the wine and showed Alfie the label. He gestured his approval, so the waiter pulled the cork from the bottle. Alfie inspected it, and then the waiter poured a small amount into his glass for tasting.

'It's excellent. You'd better bring us another one – that won't go far between the seven of us,' Alfie said, looking around the table.

Our delicious starter was followed by a sharing platter of oysters, langoustines, dressed crab and lobster with tarte au chocolat and hazelnut ice cream to round off our meal. After we'd finished our coffee, Alfie ordered a bottle of Japanese malt whisky for the table. I never knew the Japanese made whisky, but then Nathan and I didn't normally dine in Michelin-starred restaurants. Now I understood why Alfie had been eager to bring us to La Plage. Although the restaurant was expensive, the quality of the food was incredible.

The waiter brought the bill over to the table and placed it down in front of Alfie. He didn't turn a hair at the price of the meal and produced a large fistful of euros from his wallet to settle it.

I found myself gazing at the huge pile of notes on the table. You would think he'd feel nervous carrying so much cash around. But I suppose Alfie didn't need to worry about anything with his guys watching his back.

'Wouldn't it be easier to pay by credit card?' I asked.

'It might be if I had one.' Alfie grinned.

'You haven't got a credit card?' My eyes widened. I couldn't imagine life without plastic. I was going to ask him why, but I had a pretty good idea I knew the reason. Alfie loved to be flash, and waving great wads of cash around so everyone could see how much money he had was one of the best ways.

'In my line of work, it's never a good idea to leave an electronic footprint behind.' Alfie locked eyes with me.

I raised my eyebrows. That wasn't what I was expecting him to say.

36

Gemma

It was just before seven and early morning sunlight poured through the cabin curtains. It woke me from my sleep. Shielding my eyes against the glare, I sat up in bed when I became aware of muffled voices outside on the deck. I could hear Alfie talking to a man with a French accent, but couldn't make out what they were saying.

'Wake up, Nathan, something's going on.'

Nathan yawned and opened one eye. 'What makes you think that?' He leant up on one elbow and fixed me with his eyes.

'I heard Alfie talking to a man on deck.'

Nathan turned his head towards the door. 'I can't hear anything.' The way Nathan eyed me left me in no doubt that he was sceptical about my theory.

'That's because he's gone now.'

'It was probably one of the guys.' Nathan stretched his neck to one side.

'The man had a French accent.'

Nathan stifled a laugh. 'No way. You'd never expect to find a man with a French accent in France, would you? You crack me up, Gemma.'

'It's not funny. Alfie's up to something. I know he is.'

'Maybe he was talking to one of the local fishermen. Go back to sleep.' Nathan ran his fingers up my arm then settled back down on the pillow and closed his eyes.

I touched Nathan's arm to get his attention, but he rolled over and ignored me. I was almost certain that Alfie was talking to one of his contacts. But I would keep that to myself. Nathan would only question what I'd based that assumption on and then accuse me of having an overactive imagination. If he thought about it logically, why would Alfie even be up at this time in the morning if he wasn't up to something? I was sure he wasn't just having a casual chat with a fisherman. That was my husband's opinion, and he was entitled to it, but I thought he was wrong. Although I had no proof, I had a gut feeling I was right about this. I got to my feet and walked over to the door.

'What are you doing?' Nathan suddenly looked over his shoulder.

'I want to find out what's going on.'

'Come back to bed, it's way too early to get up,' Nathan said, patting the sheet next to him.

It didn't matter what time it was, there was no way I was going to be able to get back to sleep. My mind was buzzing, so I decided to put it to work. Channelling my inner detective, I pulled on my jeans and a cream cable-knit jumper and went to join Alfie on deck, leaving Nathan in the cabin.

'You're up early, Gemma,' Alfie said, looking up from his mug of tea. 'Didn't you sleep well?'

'Who were you talking to?' I asked, hoping to catch him out, by putting him on the spot.

I took a seat opposite Alfie, and my eyes searched his. I was certain I'd know if he was lying to me, not just from his words, but from his body language as well.

'I was talking to Tommy,' Alfie replied, putting his mug down on the table and turning his back on me.

He definitely hadn't been talking to Tommy, unless, of course, Tommy had suddenly developed a strong French accent. I'd expected Alfie to lie. He was a pathological liar and couldn't help himself. But his reluctance to tell me the truth on this occasion only confirmed what I already thought. He'd just given me the proof I needed.

37

Gemma

Having spent three uneventful days moored in the harbour at Boulogne, I was beginning to think Nathan was right. Alfie was just taking some time out. He wasn't planning anything. My intuition appeared to be wrong, after all.

But as night fell, Alfie started behaving strangely. He kept peering out into the darkness as if he was looking for something or someone while he paced up and down the deck. I caught Nathan's eye and realised he'd noticed it too.

'Are you expecting somebody?' Nathan asked.

Alfie leant down and looked him in the eye. 'I don't think that's any of your fucking business, do you?'

Alfie's aggressive tone was a wake-up call. My pulse started pounding in my ears. I hoped things weren't about to kick off.

'You're right. It's none of my business. I didn't mean to pry, but you seem very agitated. I was just curious to know why.'

STEPHANIE HARTE

'Well, you know what they say, curiosity killed the cat,' Alfie replied. Pointing two fingers towards Nathan, he pretended to fire an imaginary gun.

We'd just received a very clear reminder that Alfie was a gangster and it was never a good idea to piss someone like him off. If we knew what was good for us, we'd pipe down and not antagonise him further. Otherwise, who knows what might happen?

Alfie flashed me a confident smile, and I looked over his shoulder to where Nathan was sitting. I fixed him with my eyes to show him I was terrified, and he gave me a reassuring smile.

'Don't worry. It's OK,' he mouthed.

But I wasn't so sure. Alfie's personality could change at the drop of a hat. One minute he'd charm the birds from the trees and the next he'd turn into a violent maniac. I couldn't figure him out. He was impossible to read, and I didn't mind admitting his unpredictable nature scared me to death.

Alfie looked at his Cartier watch. 'It's time you two went to bed,' he said, before walking to the back of the boat and scanning the darkness again.

It went without saying that Nathan and I did as Alfie asked. Leaving the others on deck, we made our way to our spacious room and took a seat on the end of the bed, having closed the door behind us.

I turned to face Nathan. 'What do you think's up with Alfie?'

'I haven't got a clue.' Nathan ran his hand along his chin, which was covered by a dapple of dark stubble. Then he knelt on the bed behind me, put his strong hands on my shoulders and began to massage my tense muscles. 'Try not to think about it.'

'I can't help it.' I bit down on the side of my lip. I'd tried to forget about it, but every time I pushed the thought out of my mind, it seemed to surface again.

'Let me see if I can take your mind off things.' Nathan slipped his hands around my waist and began to kiss the side of my neck.

As he kissed me, I felt a rush of excitement. He was doing a good job of distracting me and had almost succeeded when a motorised boat suddenly pulled up alongside the yacht. I sprang to my feet and moved towards the door.

'What are you doing, Gemma?'

'Shush,' I said over my shoulder.

When I pressed my ear against the cabin door, I could hear the sound of muffled voices coming from the back of the yacht. Desperate to find out what was going on, instinctively I reached for the handle.

'Don't go out there. Alfie told us to go to bed.' Nathan caught hold of my hand and tried to stop me.

'I know he did, but I can't. Stay here; I won't be long.' Throwing my arms around Nathan's neck, I reached up and kissed him on the cheek.

Opening the door, I stepped out into the hallway and made my way along the shadowy corridor. When I craned my neck from the bottom of the stairs, I could just about see the deck. The first person I noticed was Alfie. He was at the back of the boat with Tommy. Frankie and Johno were at the water's edge. They were talking to a dark-skinned man with curly hair, who was standing up in a small dinghy, which was tied up next to the *Lady Nora*.

After a brief conversation, Frankie handed him a packet. The man looked inside and, satisfied with the contents, he placed five large holdalls on the jetty beside them, before he motored out of the harbour.

Frankie and Johno passed Alfie and Tommy the bags then got back on the yacht. Turning around suddenly, Alfie caught me watching from the stairwell. He stared right into my face, and my heart skipped a beat.

'Oh shit!' I said under my breath. Terror filled me. I was like a startled rabbit caught in the headlights. I couldn't think of what to do, so I froze.

Pacing across the deck, Alfie launched himself down the steps two at a time.

'You can't follow a simple instruction, can you? I told you to go to bed, didn't I?' Alfie shouted.

Spying on Alfie didn't seem like such a good idea any more. So this was it, I was about to face my fears head-on. There was a very real chance I wouldn't live to see another day.

Nathan burst out of the cabin. But instead of his presence helping the situation, Alfie flipped at the sight of him. He head-butted my husband, making his nose bleed. Reaching forward with one hand, Alfie pinned Nathan to the wall by the throat. Nathan attempted to claw Alfie off, but Alfie tightened his grip, and as he did, fear washed over me.

'Look how vulnerable you are, Nathan,' Alfie said through clenched teeth.

Nathan's eyes burned with hatred when he glared at Alfie. As the scene unfolded, I began to tremble. I hoped Alfie wouldn't see me like this, but I couldn't stop my body reacting this way. It was my fault Nathan was in this situation. I should have stayed in the cabin.

'I know you're scared; I can see the fear in your face.' Alfie laughed.

Nathan tried to break free, but he couldn't move his head. Alfie's hold was too tight. I moved towards them and forced myself to look at Alfie with apologetic eyes.

'Please let Nathan go.'

Alfie turned towards me and flashed me a pearly white smile. 'He seems to have quietened down now. He's not even attempting to struggle any more.'

I was terrified. Nathan looked to be in severe pain. The pressure Alfie was applying to his neck was crushing his trachea. He'd tucked his chin down to try and stop his airway from constricting any further, but it was becoming hard for him to breathe.

'You know I have the power to decide whether your husband takes his next breath or not, don't you?' Alfie smirked. 'How does that make you feel?'

It made me feel incredibly vulnerable. Alfie was a psychotic gangster. It wouldn't be hard for him to take another person's life.

'I'm sorry I didn't listen to you.'

'That's all right, Gemma, I accept your apology.'

I fixed Alfie with a pleading look and finally, he loosened his fingers. The sudden release made Nathan stagger forwards. He gasped for breath, desperate to fill his lungs with air, like a diver with an empty tank ascending from the deep blue. I rushed to his side and threw my arms around him. I couldn't hold it together any longer. My eyes welled up, and I began to sob.

'By the way, I never intended to kill Nathan. I was just demonstrating that I could if I wanted to.'

38

Nathan

It went without saying that I was prepared to protect Gemma with my life, but I never actually thought I'd need to until tonight. I held her in my arms while she sobbed. I knew she felt guilty that Alfie had taken his anger out on me. It wasn't Gemma's fault, so there was no point making her feel worse than she already did. It was Alfie's inability to behave in a rational way that was to blame. I was relieved he hadn't hurt her. I would never have forgiven myself if something happened to her. We wouldn't be in this mess if it wasn't for me.

Growing up with an absent parent made me cherish the people who really mattered in life. I'd had first-hand experience of not being able to rely on the person who should have protected me, so I knew how essential it was to look after your nearest and dearest. I would always have Gemma's back. I was sure that was why she cut me some slack.

I'd spent my whole life learning to get along without my dad. He wasn't there for me when I was growing up, and that was painful and confusing. It cast a shadow over my life and relationships in a significant way until Gemma came along and put everything into perspective. Before that, I'd been scared to lay myself bare in case I was rejected again. I knew I wouldn't be able to cope with the pain, so I'd decided I was better off on my own.

Gemma constantly proved her love to me. Her loyalty made me feel secure and good about myself, so I put her on a pedestal. I wanted her to understand how important and special she was to me. She quickly became the centre of my world. But I battled not to suffocate her in our relationship due to my insecure feelings. Suppressing my jealousy and possessiveness was a constant challenge.

To get to the root of my problems, Gemma encouraged me to talk about the past and my non-existent relationship with my dad. I was eaten up by poisoned thoughts. When she told me about the issues she had with her family, it gave me the courage to open up and let her in. She was patient and didn't try to rush the process. Instead, she chipped away the hard exterior I'd built up over time. Gemma was a good listener and was genuinely concerned about my worries. By sharing our bad experiences, it made us bond as a couple.

When I met Gemma, I was in a pretty dark place. The absence of the man who was supposed to be there to help me through the trials of life had left its mark on me, even though my mum had done her best to take his place. She'd taught me things that my father should have and assumed a role she should never have had to take on. I adored her for that. But by overcompensating, she inadvertently accentuated the feeling that something was missing in my life. But thankfully, Gemma filled that void. That was one of the reasons I was overprotective towards her.

39

Gemma

Nathan held my hand and led me to where Alfie was waiting for us on deck. In the distance, I could see the lights from the other boats twinkling on the water. They looked beautiful, but I wasn't here to admire the view.

'Seeing as you were so desperate to know what was going on, why don't you take a look in the bag?'

I turned my face towards Nathan's. I wished I'd listened to him now and stayed in our room. Giving me a gentle smile, he squeezed my hand, offering me some reassurance.

'Come on, Gemma, what are you waiting for?' Alfie passed me a black holdall.

My fingers trembled as they closed around the handle. I wasn't sure I wanted to open it.

'Let's go below deck,' Alfie said.

Putting the bag down on the polished table, I unzipped it, aware that all eyes were on me. I drew in a breath as I looked inside. I couldn't say I was surprised to see polythene-wrapped packages. I'd suspected Alfie was a dealer for some time now.

'Do you know what that is?' Alfie asked.

I felt myself shudder and then swept my hair back over my shoulder, hoping to appear unfazed. 'Something illegal,' I managed to reply.

Alfie roared with laughter. 'That's right, Gemma.'

'Is it heroin?' Nathan rasped, stuffing his hands into the pockets of his jeans. His voice sounded hoarse. It was obvious that it was painful for him to speak.

'No, it's cocaine. In a major city like London, this will have an estimated street value of fifty thousand pounds a kilo,' Alfie said, patting the top of the bag before he smoothed back his blond hair with the palm of his hand.

That was a huge amount of money. But I was sure there must be easier ways to make a living.

'Drug trafficking can be dangerous, but it has its rewards.'

'I realise it's lucrative but what about the people whose lives you ruin?' I asked, shaking my head from side to side.

Nathan threw me a look, and I felt the mood shift.

'That's quite an accusation. How do I ruin people's lives?'

'You sell them addictive drugs.' I fixed Alfie with a glare.

'You're mistaken, Gemma, I'm not a dealer, I'm a distributor. I just provide the stock. But it's not as easy as you think. It can be hazardous sometimes.'

'Do you seriously think being an addict isn't dangerous?' I said, my voice laced with sarcasm. Alfie took a step towards me, and I backed away in case my comment made him see red. I remembered how quickly his mood changed earlier, and I didn't want his violent side to make another appearance.

'Listen, Gemma, do yourself a favour and stop lecturing me.'

I faced Alfie with the most apologetic smile I could manage, realising I'd better shut up before I pushed him too far. 'I'm sorry, I seem to be suffering from a bad case of verbal diarrhoea this evening.'

'You need to pack your bags,' Alfie said after he walked into our cabin the next morning with a huge grin on his face.

Were we finally going home? My eyes widened at the prospect, and I had to try and suppress a smile. 'How come?' I asked, clearing the croakiness from my throat.

'We're heading down to the south of France. You're going to love it. You might even get to rub shoulders with the rich and famous.'

I let out an involuntary groan and realised it was too late to attempt to hide my disappointment.

'Why do we need to pack? Aren't we going to sail?' Nathan asked.

'No, we're going to take the train instead.'

'How long will that take?' I asked.

'About ten hours.'

My mouth fell open. 'Wouldn't we be better off flying?' I asked, not relishing the idea of a long train journey.

'It's too risky. Why go through passport control if you don't need to?'

We arrived in Cannes just after seven-thirty that evening and checked in at the nearby Hôtel Barrière Le Majestic, a luxury hotel, overlooking the sea, on the Boulevard de la Croisette.

When I first saw our room, I thought it resembled a beach hut, albeit an elegant one, with its white wood-panelled walls. The soft furnishings were in calming shades of blue, and the furniture was made from bleached driftwood. The interior had a relaxed coastal charm about it.

Opening the large French windows, I stepped out onto the private balcony and stared into the darkness. Detaching myself from my immediate surroundings, I allowed the sound of the ocean to clear my mind as I gazed into the distance. Then my mobile received a text from Alfie, and it brought me back down to earth.

As it's late, we'll eat at the hotel's restaurant.

Nathan and I made our way to the Petite Maison de Nicole and were shown to a table for two, overlooking the pool. When our food arrived, it was superb, beautifully cooked and presented.

'That was delicious, but I'm glad we're not paying the bill,' I said, putting my knife and fork back on my plate. I couldn't help feeling seventy-five euros for the main course was a little excessive.

'Yeah, I know, but we might as well make the most of it. We'll never get to eat anywhere like this again,' Nathan replied, leaning towards me and planting a kiss on my lips.

When Nathan sat back in his chair, I glanced up and noticed Alfie observing me. My pulse began to quicken. His stare was relentless as he examined my every move, like a hunter watching his prey. How long was he going to keep looking at me? I wanted to stare him down, but the intensity of his eyes made me feel too uncomfortable, so I decided to look away. As soon as I did, he sent me a text.

Meet me in the lobby at ten o'clock.

Alfie sat in a leather chair, reading an English newspaper while he waited for me to arrive. As I made my way towards him, I felt fear. No, it was more than fear, I was completely terrified. Sheer panic coursed through my veins and made my heart pound wildly inside my chest. I started to hyperventilate as my terror intensified. I'd have to pull myself together. I didn't want to give Alfie the satisfaction of seeing me like this, but the thought of meeting him on my own was scaring the life out of me.

'Gemma,' Alfie said, putting the paper down on a side table. 'You're looking beautiful as ever.'

We stepped outside the hotel and walked along La Croisette's wide promenade, which stretched along the shore of the Mediterranean. Even on a cold winter's day like today, the sun shone brightly above us, in a cloudless blue sky, while the calm turquoise water lapped at the sand. The Côte d'Azur was beautiful. The whole place oozed class with its elegant restaurants, designer shops and jewellery boutiques but I was sure we weren't here for a holiday.

Alfie gestured for us to sit down on a bench. At that moment, a gentle breeze blew in from the sea and rustled the palm trees on the white sand beach in front of us.

'I've got a little job for you to do.' Alfie passed me a ring box, and his face broke into a huge grin.

I looked out to sea and wished I could be anywhere but here. Alfie had just ruined my morning.

'Oh, great!' I didn't bother trying to disguise the sound of disappointment in my voice.

The thought of carrying out another robbery made me feel sick to my stomach. Finally, curiosity got the better of me, and I opened the box.

'It's incredible, isn't it? Terry's outdone himself this time.' Alfie took the beautiful oval-shaped ring out of my hand. 'Remember it's the same routine as before. Once you've got the ring, come out of the store and turn left. I'll be waiting in a nearby car.'

'Is Nathan coming with me?' I turned towards Alfie.

'Not this time. It would be too risky at the moment.'

Now that Alfie had put Nathan's close call in my mind, I stood up, suddenly overcome with nerves. 'I don't want to do the job on my own.'

'Sit down, Gemma.'

When Alfie pulled out a cigarette from his inside pocket and lit it, my eyes were drawn to the handle of his gun. I knew I wouldn't be able to back out. I didn't have another option.

'Why have you suddenly got cold feet?'

I tried to think of something to say. But even if I came up with a litany of excuses, Alfie wouldn't listen to any of them. He didn't need to. He had me trapped. I inhaled a lungful of sea air as I attempted to regain composure, but I was fighting a losing battle.

'I'm scared I'll mess up this time.'

'You won't.' Alfie stood up, dropped the cigarette he was smoking and crushed it with his heel. 'Let's go.'

I know I have a tendency to overthink things, and that makes them seem scarier than they actually are, but I looked down at my hands as they trembled in my lap and I knew I couldn't go through with it this time. No matter what the consequences were.

I stood up and turned towards Alfie. Then took a step back to create some distance between us. He wasn't going to like what I was going to say. If I was going to get out of this situation, I'd have to stay calm and focus. As long as I didn't let Alfie get inside my head, he couldn't take control of me.

'I'm sorry, Alfie, but I can't go through with it.'

Alfie's nostrils flared as he studied my face. I could see he was angry. I just hoped he'd be able to control his temper. I had a horrible feeling I was about to find out whether the gun inside his jacket had a bullet with my name on. I felt a shiver run down my spine at the thought of that. Alfie's eyes bored into mine for what felt like the longest moment. Then he smiled, picked up a lock of my hair and stroked it between his thumb and forefinger before he tucked the strand behind my ear.

40

Gemma

Nathan had come up with a plan to solve all our problems. If he could win some money, when Alfie took us out to a casino tonight, he'd be able to clear our debt. I pointed out to him his idea had a fatal flaw. It wasn't going to help. We were part of Alfie's team now, and he'd already told us our debt was no longer relevant. I had a horrible feeling the evening wasn't going to end well. Nathan ignored my concerns. Nothing was going to dampen his enthusiasm. He was like an excited child at Christmas.

We'd moved hotels since I'd refused to carry out the latest robbery, but instead of leaving the country, we were now staying along the coast at the Hyatt Regency Nice Palais de la Méditerranée. The impressive building, in the heart of Nice, towered above the Bay of Angels.

To say our room was luxurious was an understatement. Nathan opened the door, and I stepped onto the thick gold-coloured carpet, which felt springy underfoot. I immediately noticed a vastness of blue sky and sea through the full-length glass sliding doors on the far side of the room. After walking to where a single white orchid stood on a black lacquered table in front of the windows, I looked out at the balcony and the panoramic view of the bay beyond. Nathan was more interested in the enormous bed and threw himself face down onto the gold satin sheets draped with a velvet throw.

'This is the life. I'd never get bored of this kind of luxury,' Nathan said, running his hands over the smooth bedding.

I let out a long sigh. I hated living on the edge like this; it didn't appeal to me at all. I found it stressful, and that was driving a wedge between us that he seemed oblivious to.

Nathan rolled over and propped himself up on one elbow. 'What's up, Gemma?'

'Nothing.' I shrugged my shoulders.

Nathan joined me at the window. He threw his arm around my waist and pulled me towards him, but I turned my head away to avoid his kiss.

'I'm going to have a bath,' I said, releasing myself from his embrace.

Opening the door to the black marble bathroom, I was delighted to see fluffy towels, a robe and slippers waiting for me. Nathan flashed me a cheeky smile and followed me into the bathroom. He was hanging around like a puppy did when it was hoping for a biscuit and a tummy rub, and it was getting on my nerves. I knew exactly what was on his mind, but I wasn't in the mood.

'Can I join you?'

'I'm shattered, Nathan.'

'OK, I can take a hint.' Nathan left me alone, but moments later, he called from outside the bathroom door. 'I won't be long; I'm going to have a Turkish bath.'

Thank God for that, I thought. I was glad to have some time on my own. Maybe relaxing in some warm bubbles would help me to unwind.

When Nathan returned, I was stretched out on the plush purple velvet sofa, snuggled in a towelling bathrobe, with a large glass of wine in one hand and OK magazine in the other.

'How was it?'

'Really good. After you rejected me, I worked up a sweat in the sauna and steam room instead.' Nathan turned down the corners of his mouth, feigning sadness.

I rolled my eyes.

'Lighten up, Gem, I'm only joking. But seriously, it was a great experience. The massage was incredible.' Nathan beamed.

I was glad he'd enjoyed it and could tell he was itching to tell me about it. It was so obvious he wanted to make me jealous.

'Was the therapist pretty?'

'Only if you like the sumo wrestler look.'

She couldn't have been that bad. I suddenly pictured a woman resembling a shot putter pumped full of steroids manhandling Nathan and had to bite down on my lip to try and suppress a smile.

'Honestly, Gem, I'm not joking, the guy was like an ape. He was huge and hairy.' Nathan laughed.

I raised an eyebrow. 'I thought you were going to say, a tiny waif-like creature had worked on the knots in your back, with her small, but incredibly strong fingers, before she walked up and down your spine.'

'That's what I was expecting as well. But instead, I got a rub-down from King Kong. I don't mind telling you when he lathered my body with this sudsy cloth, which looked a bit like a pillowcase, I nearly had to beg for mercy.'

The whole experience sounded delightful. I couldn't hold in my laughter any longer.

'The massage was brutal. It felt like he was grappling with each of my limbs in turn. Then he started scrubbing me with a scratchy thing. I've never seen anything like it; it was like a giant corn on the cob.'

'You mean a loofah?' I smiled.

'Is that what it's called? Well, anyway, I'm surprised I've got any skin left, after the amount that fell off! Anyone would think I was part reptile.'

I burst out laughing and then pulled a face. 'Nathan, that's disgusting.'

'Then, in case I wasn't clean enough, he gave me another lathering with the pillowcase thing and rinsed me off with freezing cold water! I was meant to have a massage with hot oil after that, but I couldn't face it.'

Nathan poured himself a glass of wine. He wasn't painting a very good picture. I wasn't sure I'd bother to go; it sounded horrendous.

'I feel squeaky clean now, and my complexion is positively glowing, don't you think?' Nathan laughed and turned his head so I could see his handsome profile.

The time we'd spent apart today had done us both some good. It had cleared the air between us. We weren't normally together all day, every day and I'd got to the point where I couldn't stand to be in the same room as my husband. That sounded terrible, but I was only human, and sometimes people needed to give each other space so that they could appreciate each other again.

I looked over at Nathan, stretched out on the bed, and felt guilty that I'd pushed him away now. I put my glass down and walked across the moss-like carpet. Lying down beside him, I ruffled his hair. Nathan stared at me for a moment before he took me in his arms and kissed me.

41

Gemma

Located on the ground floor of our hotel was one of Nice's most famous casinos. Within its walls, it housed three roulette tables, two hundred slot machines and five blackjack tables. Nathan was ecstatic. His eyes lit up and almost began spinning in time with the fruit machines when we stepped inside.

This was my first visit to a casino, and what struck me the moment we walked in was the noise: ringing bells and the sound of money tumbling from machines wasn't very relaxing. Not to mention the seizure-inducing flashing lights that blinded me when I looked in their direction. We'd been here less than five minutes, and I knew I wasn't going to enjoy the experience.

As I glanced around the interior, I couldn't help noticing how it had been cleverly designed to keep players inside, spending money. There was nothing in here to distract a person from gambling. The outside world had become non-existent. No windows or clocks were visible so you'd never be able to keep track of the time.

As I fought my way through crowds of gamblers, I felt like we were stuck in a giant maze, intentionally set up so we'd get lost in it. I had to remind myself we were here to have fun, but I had to confess, I found the whole place extremely unpleasant.

The presence of so much security made me uneasy. I hadn't expected the casino to be such a closely watched place, but there were security guards and camera domes all around me. I suppose it made sense really. With all that money at stake, people might be tempted to try and beat the system. No wonder cameras, laptops and other electronic devices had to be left outside.

'This is great, isn't it?' Nathan sat mesmerised tossing money into a one-arm bandit, as he sipped on a cocktail.

'Yeah, this is my kind of heaven.' The constant noise and undertone was giving me a headache.

I was surprised Nathan wasn't bothered by the surveillance, especially since he'd been caught on CCTV recently and was wanted by the police. But he was under the spell of the fruit machine, and nothing was going to distract him from that.

Having lost most of his money on the slot machines, Nathan decided to try his luck at blackjack. He took a seat at the green-felt table opposite a black-vested dealer. The dealer shuffled and placed two cards face up in front of Nathan. Then he put two more on the table in front of himself, one facing up, one facing down.

'Wish me luck, Gem.' Nathan kissed me, then the corners of his mouth lifted up when he looked at his hand.

'Good luck.' I crossed my fingers under the table.

Nathan had the ace of spades and the queen of hearts. One of the dealer's cards was the six of diamonds, but there was no way of knowing what the other was. Without any hesitation, Nathan put down a purple chip.

'Isn't that worth five hundred euros?' I asked, hoping that I was mistaken.

'Yes,' Nathan replied, smiling at me.

I inhaled sharply, as he confirmed what I'd feared. 'Why are you betting so much?'

Nathan leant towards me and whispered in my ear. 'It's OK, Gem, I've got twenty-one – that's a winning hand. There's no way the dealer can beat me.'

Seeing Nathan sat at the blackjack table in a trance-like state, hypnotised by the cards in his hands, made my stomach turn. I couldn't bear to look. It would have been bad enough if it was our money he was spending, but it wasn't, it was Alfie's, and that was only going to make our financial problems worse. The sad fact was Nathan didn't care; he was a risk-taker.

'Please don't bet as much as that.'

But Nathan wouldn't listen to me. He just couldn't help himself. I felt like grabbing the chip back off the table and dragging him out of the casino before he could spend any more. But it was too late. The dealer had already signalled that no more bets could be placed.

I'd seen enough; I didn't want to know the outcome of the game. I needed to get out of this place and go back to our room. Nathan didn't even bother to look up from his cards when I slipped away.

The casino was like a labyrinth of machines and tables

that all looked the same. I felt like I was trying to swim against the tide, in an endless sea of them, as I battled my way through the crowd, trying to find the exit. Alfie's piercing blue eyes picked me out in the swarm, so I gave him a black look before I walked out the door.

Having climbed the stairs to the first floor, I suddenly realised that Alfie was behind me. I made my way along the corridor, located the card that opened the door to my room and pushed it into the slot. Alfie's hand appeared on the door above mine, so I glared over my shoulder at him.

'What do you want?'

'Calling it a night so soon?' Alfie was standing so close to me, I could feel his breath on the side of my face. 'So you weren't tempted to have a gamble then?' Alfie smirked.

I drew in a deep breath and willed myself to stay calm, knowing he was hoping his comment was going to provoke a reaction. I almost convinced myself to let it go, but as I attempted to detach myself emotionally from the situation, something snapped inside me. I'd had enough of the way Alfie was controlling our lives. He was a bully. I decided the only way to deal with a man like him was to stand up to him.

'What the hell are you playing at, Alfie?' I wasn't in the mood to be messed with.

'Excuse me?' Alfie gestured for me to go inside. 'If I'm about to get one of your lectures, I'd rather you did it in private. I've got my reputation to think of,' Alfie said, and his face broke into a huge smile.

'Why did you take Nathan to the casino? You know what he's like with money,' I said through gritted teeth. Alfie knew Nathan would never be able to resist the temptation. He'd lined him up to fail.

'Lighten up, Gemma. He's just having a bit of fun. Is that such a terrible thing?' Alfie cocked his head to one side.

I didn't care what he said, Alfie was exploiting Nathan. He wouldn't finish playing tonight until he'd lost everything. Then we were going to owe even more money. Alfie knew damn well we had no way of paying it back.

Alfie traced a line with his thumb over my lips. Then he ran it down the front of my neck until it rested between my breasts.

'What makes you think you have the right to touch me?' I fumed, pushing his hand away. I stood frozen to the spot, trying to swallow the lump in my throat, wondering what he was going to do next.

Alfie wrapped his strong arms around my waist and pulled me towards him. He was so close to me, I could smell his aftershave. 'Because you owe me, Gemma.'

'But you said our debt was no longer relevant.' I tried to sound strong, but my voice gave away how scared I was.

'I didn't say I was writing it off. You still owe me.'

'It isn't even my debt. It's Nathan who owes you the money.' I glared at him and folded my arms across my chest.

Alfie bent his head down and whispered in my ear. 'But I don't want to sleep with Nathan. He's not my type.'

'Well, you can forget that idea. That's never going to happen.' Alfie made my skin crawl, and if he thought I'd have sex with him to clear the debt, he could think again.

'You know how to hurt a man's feelings, don't you?' Alfie clutched his heart then threw his head back and roared with laughter. 'I'm usually surrounded by people who say what they think I want to hear. But you don't give a shit; you just tell it like it is. That's one of the things I like about you.'

For a moment, I considered letting his comments go. Even though I knew that would be the sensible thing to do, I wasn't in the habit of backing down, and the words tumbled out of my mouth before I had a chance to stop them.

'It might surprise you to know this, but I don't care what you think about me. That's why I speak my mind.' I looked Alfie squarely in the eyes.

Alfie smirked. 'Nobody else would get away with talking to me the way you do. But it makes a refreshing change. It's a novelty. I like your spiky attitude.'

'You think I'm spiky because I have no desire to be the teacher's pet; it isn't something that interests me.'

'That's too bad because you already are. In my eyes, you can do no wrong.' Alfie flashed me a bright smile.

I'd never been in a situation like this before. There was no logical reason why Alfie was pursuing me. I couldn't work out what he was playing at. He'd told me he wouldn't accept this behaviour from anyone else. So I came to the conclusion that it was all about the chase. Hopefully, he'd get bored with it. But it was human nature to want what you couldn't have, and rich, powerful men like Alfie always liked to get their own way.

Alfie caught hold of my hand, led me across the room and sat on the edge of the bed. When he pulled me down onto his lap, I could feel he was hard, and my heart started racing.

Alfie took my hand and ran it over the front of his suit trousers. My lungs tightened at the thought of what was facing me. Alfie was a strong man, and physically, I was no match for him. I wanted to cry out, but what was the point? Nobody was going to come and help me.

'Fuck off, Alfie. I want you to get out of my room right now.' Heat flushed my face when I shouted at him. I tried to keep the palm of my free hand from rising, but my brain didn't want to co-operate. As the slap echoed through the room, I leapt to my feet and watched Alfie's reaction. He flinched when my hand made contact with his skin, leaving his cheek red and throbbing. What the hell had I just done? There was no way I was going to get away with that, I thought. The look of anger in his glare said it all.

Alfie touched his cheek with his fingertips. 'You're lucky I'm a gentleman.'

As I was about to speak, Alfie put his hand up to silence me.

'So I take it you're turning me down. Your rejection is breaking my heart.' Alfie laughed. 'That's a pity – you might have enjoyed it. I've never had any complaints before.'

Alfie grinned then fixed me with his intense blue stare. He got to his feet, poured himself a Jack Daniel's from the minibar and swallowed it in one gulp. I kept hoping Nathan would burst into the room any minute and save me, but Alfie and I both knew that was never going to happen. He was preoccupied with trying his luck on the slot machines and games tables. Nathan seriously thought he could win more than he lost. He firmly believed that the next roll of the dice would bring chips raining down from the sky. But in reality, he was haemorrhaging money that we didn't have while I was trapped in a bedroom with a sex-starved, horny gangster.

Alfie suddenly leant towards me and pressed his mouth on mine. I could taste the whisky on his lips. 'If you get lonely waiting for Nathan to come back, I'll be in my room.' Alfie backed me into the wall and ground himself against me, but then he pulled back and headed out of the door.

42

Gemma

Love was a complicated business. I couldn't help feeling let down by my husband. His selfish behaviour was hard to forgive. How could I respect someone who was so determined to put his own needs first, whatever the cost?

I'd experienced this before where strong positive and negative feelings towards Nathan were co-existing. At the moment, the negative was outweighing the positive, and I felt like giving up on my marriage. I hated to admit it, but I was losing hope that things would ever get better. I was bashing my head against a brick wall. The only thing that could change a person was themselves. If Nathan didn't want to change, then all of the effort I put into helping him was wasted.

Every relationship was unique and had its own set of challenges. Ours had reached a definite fork in the road. Instead of it making me happy, it was sucking the happiness out of me. Should I try and find the strength to let it go?

It was difficult to think about throwing away the hard

work I'd put into our relationship. Nathan and I had been through so much together. I would hate to think that had all been for nothing.

In the beginning, I think we were afraid to admit to each other how we felt, in case it was one-sided. The fear of opening up was important for us to conquer. It was the thing that was holding us back. We'd had to push ourselves through the discomfort and face the fear head-on. Once we realised the feelings were mutual, there was no stopping us.

We were both dysfunctional in our own way, so when we found ourselves in a loving relationship, it surprised us both. I realised I could help Nathan get over his insecurities by giving him lots of love and he did the same in return. I was a complex character; my personality was full of contradictions. Getting to the bottom of my issues would be a challenge for the most experienced psychiatrist. But not for Nathan. He understood me on every level. We were so different but in other ways so similar.

I sometimes found dealing with Nathan's insecurities emotionally draining, but I was hardly in a position to complain. He'd had to battle plenty of my demons over the years. Nathan could be selfish, but he was also fiercely protective of me, and the people who mattered in his life. He was a true white knight, even though I wasn't a typical damsel in distress. I was a woman with a finely tuned bullshit detector and was capable of looking out for myself. I'd happily speak my mind if I thought somebody had stepped out of line. But it gave him so much pleasure to fight my corner. I wasn't about to take that away from him.

By the time I met Nathan, he'd had plenty of experience. He'd taken on the role of protector from an early age, doing the things his dad would have done if he'd been around. Nobody else had ever looked out for me the way he did, and I appreciated it more than he knew.

I wasn't enjoying walking the path I was currently walking, and it was fair to say that after everything that had happened, our relationship was in a bad place. It was falling apart at the seams. Trying to decide what to do for the best was agony. We used to thrive in each other's company and believed that as long as we were together, we could face whatever life threw at us.

Surely it had to be better to attempt to repair our relationship no matter how bad it had become, rather than walk away without any conscious effort. I still loved my husband, so I didn't think I would ever be able to give up on him.

43

Gemma

I lay in the darkness with only my thoughts for company, while I waited for Nathan to get bored of the casino and come back to our room. I realised now I shouldn't have left without him, but I hadn't expected Alfie to follow me. I'd had a lucky escape. For a horrible moment, I'd thought he was going to rape me. But thankfully, that wasn't his style. He didn't want to force me to sleep with him, he wanted my consent, and that was something he was never going to get.

I must have cried myself to sleep. In the early hours of the morning, I woke with a start. Somebody was knocking on the door. I pulled the covers around me, thinking Alfie had come back, but then I heard Nathan calling my name outside our room. My toes sank into the deep carpet as I walked over to the door and let him in.

'Thanks, Gem, sorry if I woke you.' The smell of alcohol on his breath was overpowering.

'Please don't tell me you've been in the casino until now.' My throat was dry, and as I strained out the words, the pitch of my voice changed beyond recognition. It startled me; I sounded like Darth Vader's daughter.

Nathan didn't answer but gave me a drunken smile.

'Do you know what time it is?'

Nathan shrugged his shoulders.

'It's three o'clock in the morning.' I might have been half asleep, but I could feel anger rising within me.

'I'm sorry. I didn't realise it was so late.'

'Is that all you've got to say for yourself?' I fixed Nathan with a glare.

'I lost track of the time,' Nathan slurred. He held on to the doorframe, and his eyes began to close.

I stepped out of the way, and Nathan staggered into the room. Within minutes it smelled like a brewery. Lurching ahead, he made it across to the bed, before he launched himself fully clothed into it.

My heart sank when I saw the state of him. I know what Nathan's like when he's drunk. He spends money like water. He'd have been throwing it around like it was worthless.

'You're in no condition to talk about this now, but we're going to discuss this tomorrow.'

'OK, whatever you say, Gem.' The moment the words were out of Nathan's mouth, he fell into a deep sleep.

When he started to snore, I felt like putting the pillow over his head and suffocating him. Lying on my back, I stared up at the high ceiling, mulling over what had just happened. I was tempted to wake Nathan up and tell him that while he was in the casino getting steaming drunk, I was up here trying to fend off Alfie's advances. But what was the point?

★

'Good morning, Gemma,' Alfie said, approaching our table while we were having breakfast. 'You're looking as beautiful as ever.'

My pulse quickened at the sight of him. 'I think you need to get your eyes tested.' I was make-up free, dressed in grey trackies and a white long-sleeve T-shirt and my long brown hair was pulled into a messy bun.

'There's nothing wrong with my eyesight. The sea air must be agreeing with you. You look fresh-faced and relaxed.' Alfie flashed me a smile and looked over at the buffet table where fresh fruit and an assortment of pastries were laid out. 'How's the food?'

'It's great,' Nathan replied, tucking into his omelette.

'And the hangover?' Alfie laughed.

'I haven't got one. I slept well,' Nathan replied.

I was tempted to make a comment about his snoring keeping me awake for half the night, but I didn't want Alfie to pick up on the tension between us.

'I'll leave you to enjoy the rest of your breakfast, but when you've finished, go and pack your stuff; we're heading off again.'

I hadn't meant to sigh as loudly as I did, but it was too late to stop it now. I didn't look up from my plate because I could sense Alfie watching me.

44

Gemma

'If you don't go shopping again for me, I'll be forced to tell Nathan about the other night,' Alfie said.

But instead of replying, I suddenly started laughing. I didn't mean to, but Alfie made me so uncomfortable I couldn't help myself. The moment I felt anxious, I often reacted this way. Nerves were a funny thing, weren't they? They affected people in different ways.

'You've got to be joking,' I finally replied. I had to fight the sudden urge to slap him around the face.

Nothing had happened between us, but being a skilled manipulator, he knew there was a good chance this tactic would work. Nathan had a jealous streak, so if Alfie planted the seed of doubt, I wasn't sure who he'd believe. Alfie could be very persuasive when he wanted to be. I weighed up the pros and cons, and against my better judgement, I found myself agreeing to do the job.

*

Cartier's was just minutes away from our hotel on the Promenade des Anglais. I stood on the pavement outside the store on Avenue de Verdun, looking in the window before I plucked up the courage to enter the prestigious store. Something didn't feel right this time. I hoped my nerves weren't about to give me away. A loud, critical voice suddenly began talking in my head, telling me not to do it. I tried to ignore it, but it was persistent. Composing myself, I switched on automatic pilot and walked inside.

A sales assistant with an unfortunate hairline, male-patterned baldness at its best, approached me as soon as I walked in.

'Bonjour, madame,' he said, clasping his hands in front of his chest.

'Bonjour.'

'Is that an English accent I can detect?'

'Yes.' As I replied, the running commentary continued inside my head. Why was this happening to me? I needed to stay strong, and not listen to the voice speaking to me loud and clear. I knew it must belong to my anxiety. I wished it would shut up and let me get on with the job in hand.

'My mother was English. She grew up in London,' the assistant divulged. 'When I was a child, I used to visit my grandparents every summer.'

'How lovely,' I said, wondering how much of his life story he was going to tell me.

'Would you like some help or are you just browsing?'

'I'd like some help, please.' I looked at my watch. 'I don't have much time. I'm in a bit of a hurry.' Hopefully, he'd take the hint and cut out the small talk.

'In that case, how can I help you?'

'My mother loves big cats. She's obsessed with them, so I want to buy her a bracelet for a special birthday that's coming up,' I said, hoping my nerves weren't as evident as they felt.

'Well, you've come to the right place. Cartier has always been famous for its feline jewellery.'

'I know it's a tall order, but do you have anything similar to Wallis Simpson's panther bracelet?' I asked, giving him my best smile.

The assistant raised his eyebrows. 'You know the original one sold at auction for over five million euros.'

'That's a bit more than I was hoping to spend.' I laughed. 'But if I get change out of a million, I'll be happy.'

Getting down to business, the assistant took a magnificent piece of jewellery from the display. 'How about this?' He held the bracelet out in front of me. 'You'll notice the panther has joints along its entire length, which allows it to drape itself and encircle the wrist.'

'That's just what I'm looking for. How much is it?'

'Eight hundred thousand euros,' he replied, then quickly attempted to justify the hefty price tag. 'A Cartier panther bracelet is a thing of exquisite beauty. It's pave-set with onyx and eight hundred and thirty-three diamonds and it's made from eighteen-carat white gold,' he said, putting it on my wrist.

'It's beautiful. I love the colour of the eyes.'

'Yes, the emeralds are stunning, aren't they?'

My phone began to ring, so I slipped my hand inside my bag but had trouble unfastening the clasp. To avoid arousing suspicion, I had to abandon making the switch.

I held my wrist towards the assistant after taking the call, and he released the clasp.

Holding the bracelet in my hand, I admired it from every angle and waited for another opportunity to steal it. I suddenly had an idea and began rummaging through my bag. I pulled out my purse and put the bracelet on the counter in front of me.

'Oh no, I've forgotten my card,' I said, biting down on my lip. 'I must have left it back at the hotel. You do accept credit cards, don't you?'

'We accept some, but...'

'I've got an American Express Centurion card,' I said before he had time to finish his sentence, knowing he was probably concerned that my card's limit wouldn't be high enough to cover the purchase.

'In that case, yes, you can pay by credit card.'

The assistant was obviously familiar with this exclusive black card that didn't have a spending limit attached to it. It was the ultimate status symbol, available by invitation only to those people lucky enough to be too wealthy to carry cash.

I looked at my watch again to remind the assistant I was short of time. 'I'll have to go back and get it. I'll be back in ten minutes.'

I needed to make my escape and get outside. I couldn't wait to feel fresh air on my skin. So I forced myself to walk casually towards the glass doors, but it was harder than you can imagine. Each step was torture. I could feel my heart pounding in my chest and beads of sweat formed on my upper lip.

Once outside, I did as instructed and turned left. I heard footsteps coming up behind me, so I quickened my pace. Glancing over my shoulder, I saw a man heading straight towards me. Panic gripped me as he started to close the gap, and I had to stop myself from breaking into a run. To my relief, he overtook me and disappeared into the crowd without giving me a second look.

The blacked-out Mercedes glided out onto the wide boulevard as soon as I got in the car.

'We're going to Monaco,' Alfie said. 'Sit back and enjoy the ride.'

I stared out of the tinted glass watching the beach as it whipped past the window, while I waited for my heartbeat to return to normal.

Alfie leant forward to talk to Tommy. 'Even though the views of the Côte d'Azur are spectacular from the top road, you'd better avoid the Grande Corniche. I think it might be too hair-raising for Gemma in her current state.'

I suddenly pictured myself in a convertible, with the wind blowing through my hair, like Grace Kelly in *To Catch a Thief*.

'Which road do you want me to take?' Tommy asked.

'The middle one,' Alfie replied.

Tommy drove the Mercedes along the Moyenne Corniche, one of three roads carved into the mountainside high above the coastline. We sped along, the car hugging the rocks as it wound around the tight bends.

'Don't look so worried.' Alfie laughed.

I gave him a sideways glance but continued to grip the

door handle; my knuckles had turned white. Although the scenery was picturesque, I couldn't admire the view. My stomach was in my mouth. I felt like I was on a roller coaster ride for the entire forty-minute drive.

'Head straight to the hotel, Tommy,' Alfie said.

I hadn't realised we'd arrived in Monaco until Alfie said that. There was nothing to indicate we'd left France and crossed over the border. But when I looked more closely, as we drove through the spotlessly clean streets, I couldn't help noticing they were teeming with wealthy people and luxury cars. Ferraris, Lamborghinis and Porsches were everywhere.

'This is where millionaires and the international elite gather. It's the playground of choice for the rich and famous,' Alfie said.

How the other half live, I thought, taking in all the glitz and glamour.

The car came to a halt outside the Monte-Carlo Bay Hotel, a high-end beachfront resort. It had its very own lagoon, waterfalls and tropical gardens.

Our room was modern and spacious with white oak furnishings and sandstone floors. It faced the seafront, so I stepped out onto the balcony, to admire the sweeping views of the Mediterranean. I was somewhat disappointed. If I didn't know better, I'd think we were in Las Vegas. Monte Carlo wasn't at all what I'd expected. It was dominated by high-rise hotels and apartments. The concrete jungle was a million miles away from its sophisticated neighbour, the French Riviera.

Once we'd settled in, hopefully, we'd be able to get away from the skyscrapers for a while. It would be lovely to take the tourist trail and see some of the sights. Maybe we could wander around the old, narrow streets and beautiful buildings of the historic quarter for a while. We should make the most of it. We were never likely to come back to Monaco. It wasn't exactly a budget-friendly location. Before I had a chance to suggest this to Nathan, Alfie barged his way into our room. I should have known he'd have other plans for us.

'Meet me in the lobby in half an hour, and we'll go for cocktails.' He checked the time on his Rolex before he let himself out.

Crossing my arms in front of me, I let out a sigh.

'I thought we'd go to a casino after dinner. You can't stay in Monte Carlo and not visit one.' Alfie stretched back in his chair as he sipped a mojito in the Blue Gin Bar.

'Can't you?' My face was like thunder, and I threw Alfie a look, unimpressed by his suggestion.

Alfie flashed me a satisfied smile. 'I need to give Nathan a chance to win back the money he lost, don't I?'

'We both know that's not a good idea,' I said, shooting Alfie another filthy look. I knew my words would fall on deaf ears.

'Why are you looking at me like that? You're becoming so bitter and twisted.' Alfie laughed.

I raised an eyebrow. Did he blame me? If we went to the casino again tonight, I knew for certain that Nathan would end up owing more money. There was no chance of him winning anything. But Nathan had a theory that nearly winning money was almost as enjoyable as actually winning it. So he'd have a good time trying.

Taking Nathan to a casino pretty much guaranteed his spending would spiral out of control again. I felt like we were sinking in quicksand. His behaviour was wrecking both our lives. But my protests were being ignored as usual. Alfie was determined to exploit Nathan's weakness, and I wasn't going to be able to stop him. I might as well have been on another planet for all the notice he took of me.

After walking the short distance from our hotel to the Casino de Monte-Carlo, we stopped outside the building to admire the exterior. It looked incredible lit up against the dark night sky and was the epitome of opulence, with its marble atrium and onyx columns.

Once inside the gambler's paradise, Nathan ordered a scotch and coke and settled himself down at the blackjack table. He'd been drinking heavily this evening. That was a bad sign. It would interfere with his concentration and affect his ability to make decisions. Having said that, Nathan appeared to be off to a good start, winning several hands in a row. But even if he'd been sober, I knew his luck wouldn't last. That was the nature of the game: he'd never be able to beat the house.

'Fingers crossed,' Nathan said, flashing me a bright smile.

It would appear his words cursed his cards. With Nathan's winning streak well and truly over, you would think that would give him the incentive to stop gambling, wouldn't you? But he decided he might as well keep playing, to try and win the money back.

'Place your bets,' the croupier said, after Nathan took a seat at the roulette table.

Nathan put his chips on seven red, and the croupier spun the wheel. He threw the small white ball in the opposite direction, and it raced around the circular track.

'No more bets.'

All eyes fixed on the ball running around the circumference of the wheel. It eventually lost momentum and fell into a numbered pocket. I had to look away when the croupier took Nathan's pile of chips away. It had landed on twenty-two black.

'Oh shit,' Nathan said, gathering up the few he had left.

'Don't you think you should call it a night before you lose everything?' I asked.

'I'll have one last game,' Nathan replied, taking a seat at the poker table.

'I'm going to get a drink.'

I ordered an espresso martini, but before I had taken a sip of the cocktail, Nathan arrived at the bar next to me.

'That looks nice,' he said.

Staring at him with fury burning in my eyes, I knew there was only one reason why he'd left the gaming tables. 'So you've finally lost all the money, have you?'

45

Nathan was a grown man, but he acted like a spoilt child when things didn't go his way. Perhaps if Rosa had been stricter with him, instead of doting on him, he wouldn't be like this now. Part of me felt bad blaming her – I was closer to her than my own mother, but ultimately she had played an important role in shaping the man her son had become.

I suppose deep down, I was as bad. Nathan had a vulnerability about him that brought out my protective side. He found it difficult to open up to people and had always been a bit of a loner. I'd also struggled with this, so we were on common ground. Nathan and I had always been so happy together in our couple bubble, I didn't think we needed anybody else in our lives. Now I was questioning that.

When I met Nathan, he'd already experienced rejection on a huge scale. His father was someone he should have been able to rely on. But his absence from Nathan's life had made him fear abandonment, so I'd always made excuses for his behaviour. I couldn't deny his selfish streak ran deep.

Nathan knew I didn't want him to go to the casino, but he took no notice of my concerns and now look at what had happened. Just as I predicted, he'd gone and lost more money. Money we couldn't afford to lose. It was hard to know what to do for the best. As an outsider looking in, it would be easy to think I should just leave, and believe me, that idea had crossed my mind more than once over the years. But the bottom line was I didn't want to be the one to initiate a break-up knowing how Nathan felt about abandonment. I couldn't do that to him, and if I was totally honest, I was scared of being alone. I'd become isolated from my friends and had been estranged from my family for years.

My parents were wealthy, and so was my younger sister, Rebecca. I'd thought about picking up the phone and begging them to help us a million times since we first got involved with Alfie. But I couldn't tell them about the situation we were in. They would never understand. They'd only judge me, and anyway, I well and truly closed that door when I married Nathan. My parents made me choose between them and Nathan. When I chose Nathan, it didn't go down well. They said it would never last. I wanted to prove them wrong. That was one of the reasons I felt determined to make my relationship with my husband work. The truth of the matter was Nathan's gambling addiction and his entrepreneurial endeavours were a bad combination. I didn't want my parents to know about the problems that had caused us. I knew his reckless behaviour was a defence mechanism. Thankfully, he had other redeeming qualities.

In a lot of ways, I envied the relationship Nathan had with his family. He didn't realise how lucky he was. He had their full support. They all adored him. Whereas I'd never been able to talk to my parents about anything. The emotional bond just wasn't there. We'd never been close. I didn't wish any harm on my family, but I gave up caring about them a long time ago. These days, the only thing I shared with them was DNA.

46

Gemma

While Nathan was busy drowning his sorrows at the Blue Gin Bar, I tried to think of a way for us to get out of debt. I couldn't continue to live like this, under a plethora of different names, and constantly on the move. There must be another alternative. I was confident that in time, we'd be able to find a way out of this nightmare.

Right now, the most important thing to do was to keep positive and believe that we'd get through this. I didn't doubt we'd encounter many obstacles along the way. But we were responsible for what happened next in our lives, not Alfie, so instead of letting him control us, it was about time we did something about it. We'd have to stay strong and never give up. If we could do that, one day I was sure we'd be free of him, but that all seemed like a distant dream at the moment.

'Why did you go to the casino again? You knew how I felt

about it.' I decided to confront Nathan when he finally came back to our room.

Nathan stared at me and then sat on the edge of the bed. 'I wish you'd talk to me about it.'

Nathan's problem was like the elephant in the room. We both knew it existed but never discussed it because it made him feel uncomfortable. Enough was enough. If we were going to get out of this, I needed to understand what drove him to be so reckless with money.

'I'm trying to help you. Please talk to me.' I couldn't hide the anger that had seeped into my voice. I was frustrated that he was shutting me out.

'I don't know what you want me to say.' Nathan put his elbows on his knees and covered his face with his hands.

'Why can't you stay away from the casinos? Are you addicted to gambling?' I asked the question, but I already knew the answer.

Nathan let his hands drop, and he turned towards me with a furious look on his face, clearly outraged by my suggestion. 'Of course I'm not. Don't be so stupid.'

Denial was Nathan's way of dealing with a problem he didn't want to accept. It was a coping mechanism he always used. He kept his emotions bottled up and didn't like to talk about what was bothering him. But it was time he faced the facts: he was lying to himself, and until he was prepared to admit there was an issue, we wouldn't be able to get out of this no-win situation.

'So if you're not addicted, why do you keep going back?'

Nathan shrugged his shoulders. 'It's fun. I love the rush I get from it.' He stretched out his long legs, got to his feet and stood in front of me. Reaching out, he curled his fingers around mine. 'I'm sorry, Gem, I didn't mean to lose more money. I just got carried away...'

I couldn't believe he'd just said that. Pulling my hands away, I crossed my arms over my chest. He was completely unable to control his impulsive behaviour. 'You never think about the impact your actions will have, do you?'

Nathan looked at me from under his thick dark lashes. 'I thought I could win some cash, and that would have solved our financial problems.'

His words had a hollow ring to them; he'd said them so many times before. In order to achieve his goal of financial stability, Nathan had always taken big risks. But unfortunately, his desperation to succeed was stronger than his fear of failure.

'But you didn't win any, did you? The deck is always stacked against you. If you don't admit you've got a problem, you'll never be able to break the cycle.' I put my hands on my hips and glared at him as fury bubbled under the surface of my skin.

'You know I've never been good at talking about my problems.' Nathan stared at me with a thoughtful look on his face as he contemplated my words.

'That's a cop-out, Nathan, and you know it.' I bit down on my lip, while I considered what to say next.

I was tempted to tell him about the visit Alfie had paid me while I was alone in our bedroom in Nice. If he'd realised what I'd been through, while he was out spending money we didn't have, he might feel guilty. Maybe then he'd give up gambling for good. But realistically, I knew that was never going to happen. I couldn't compete with the lure of the casino.

Nathan knew nothing about the events of that night. But they played over and over on a continuous loop in my head. Although I wanted him to know, I wouldn't risk telling him. I couldn't afford for him to fly into a jealous rage and get into a fight with Alfie. The man was an unpredictable psycho, and who knew what he would do to us if we crossed him?

'I know I've got a problem and my gambling has caused us a lot of grief, so I'll try and give it up.'

Although Nathan had finally admitted what I already knew, his words were too little and had come too late. I picked up my bag and headed towards the door. 'I'm going out. Don't wait up,' I called over my shoulder as Nathan bowed his head and retreated into his own world.

47

Nathan

I was consumed by guilt for getting us into financial trouble. I'd been so stressed out recently, I was close to breaking point. Being in debt was a complete nightmare. It was something that haunted me and kept me awake at night. Alfie was playing a game that I could never win because the rules kept changing. He was making them up as he went along and I had no control over that.

I'd hated growing up poor. It was a miserable existence. My desire to be rich drove me to take risks. But if I didn't sort myself out, there was a very good chance I would lose the most important person in my life. I didn't want to face the future without Gemma by my side.

Why couldn't I stop being reckless with money? I wasn't sure I knew the answer. It was a bad habit, and habits can be hard to break. It didn't help that I was an adrenaline junkie, so I guess I was hooked on the thrill I got from it.

Gemma had told me before that she thought my impulsiveness was a defence mechanism. It was my way of venting the hurt and anger I felt as a result of my dad leaving. Maybe she was right. Perhaps I used gambling as a form of escapism, to get away from a situation I didn't like, instead of facing the issue head-on.

I knew I hid my true feelings and made out I wasn't bothered that my dad wasn't in my life, but I did that to cover up the insecurity it had left me with. Having said that, I was never tempted to find my father. His rejection led me to see him in a negative light. It affected my self-esteem. I resented him for not wanting to stick around and be a part of my life, and I was scared that if I tried to make contact with him, he might reject me for a second time. I wouldn't put myself through that. I'd toughened my exterior to protect myself from being hurt. It was a challenge for anyone to try and break down my barriers. But Gemma had succeeded, and I sometimes thought she knew me better than I knew myself.

What had I done? I'd pushed her so far this time that she'd turned her back on me. I'd have some serious grovelling to do if I was going to get her back onside. I'd always convinced myself that Only Child Syndrome was a myth even though the facts were glaring me in the face. I was selfish, attention-seeking and always wanted my own way. How the hell did Gemma put up with me? The woman deserved a medal.

I needed to quit gambling before it cost me everything. I'd have to learn to divert my desire for excitement in a different direction. But breaking the cycle was going to be very challenging. It was going to be embarrassing to admit I had a problem, but if I wanted to save my marriage, I'd have to do it.

48

Gemma

The Blue Gin Bar, as its name would suggest had a sophisticated all-blue interior, and served seventeen different types of gin. As it was located on the ground floor of our hotel, it seemed the obvious place for me to go. After looking at the drinks list, I decided to order a Flower Bubble. The menu promised the cocktail would take me on a journey of the senses. I hoped it was right.

The bartender added Hendrick's Gin, Grand Marnier, elderberry syrup and lime cordial to a shaker filled with ice. He shook the metal container vigorously in front of me while I watched mesmerised. Then he poured my drink into a Martini glass, topped it up with champagne and added an orange twist before handing it to me.

After walking away from the bar, I sank down in one of the plush blue velvet chairs facing the water and took a sip of the cocktail. It was divine. As I swallowed my drink, my eyes were drawn towards the twinkling lights of the boats moored in the distance. They reflected on the water like stars in a dark sky. I couldn't help noticing that even at this time of night, the view across the Mediterranean was stunning. I'd love nothing more than to be sailing away on one of those yachts right now; then I could leave all of this behind me, I thought as I stared out to sea.

Nathan's behaviour was draining. It was frustrating because the terrible decisions he made affected both of us. Failure to achieve financial success and his father's rejection had delivered a devastating blow to his confidence. He'd found it hard to overcome his inner critic. I understood that, and I had tried to support my husband through all of it. But Nathan struggled to shake off the feeling that he didn't deserve to find lasting love. He was scared I would inevitably leave him. I'd always promised myself I'd never do that, but I wasn't sure how much longer I could put up with things the way they were. Something needed to change.

'Gemma, what are you doing here?'

The sound of Alfie's voice behind me made me jump and brought me back to my surroundings. I dragged my eyes away from the yachts and turned to face him. I looked him in the eye, and my chest began pounding.

'I'm admiring the view,' I replied, before gazing back out the window.

'Not soul-searching then?'

Alfie had hit the nail on the head, but I wasn't about to admit that to him. 'What made you ask that?'

'You looked deep in thought.'

'Like I said, I'm admiring the view.'

'Where's Nathan?'

'He's in our room.' Alfie knew I wouldn't be in a bar on my own if everything was all right between us.

Alfie took Nathan's absence as his cue to join me. 'I'm surprised to see you ventured out without him.'

His comment infuriated me, and it took a lot of effort on my part not to storm out of the lounge, but that would only have made matters worse.

'We're not joined at the hip. Aren't I allowed to go out for a drink on my own if I feel like it?'

'Of course you are. Have you tried one of these before? It's called The Dean.' Alfie raised his glass in the air. 'It's Tanqueray gin, sweet vermouth, pink grapefruit liqueur and orange bitters.'

'It sounds nice.'

'Knock that back, and I'll get you one.' Alfie stood up, and a huge smile spread across his face.

So much for having some time alone, I thought. But at least Alfie was being charming. Let's hope he stayed that way.

Alfie reappeared with our drinks. 'Why's Nathan in your room?' he asked with a smile on his face.

I didn't want Alfie to know we'd had words, but even if I didn't admit it, it was obvious.

'Have you two had another argument?' Alfie studied my expression while he waited for my response.

'The way you're talking, anyone would think we argue all the time.' I couldn't disguise the anger in my tone.

'Don't be so touchy, I was only asking.' Alfie held his palm out towards me, in a passive gesture, before he settled back in his chair and crossed his legs at the ankles.

I watched Alfie from across the table. He was everything

Nathan wanted to be: rich, powerful and successful. But he was also ruthless. He knew exactly what he was doing when he took Nathan to the casino. My husband was never going to be able to leave while he still had chips in his hand. He enjoyed the thrill of the bet too much. Gambling was very addictive.

I leant forward and put my drink down on the glass table. Alfie smirked, and I felt my eyes glaze over with tears. Nathan was a risk-taker. He didn't like to play it safe. The desire to win became all-consuming, and nothing else mattered to him. Why couldn't he learn to quit while he was ahead? Because of his selfish behaviour, we were both caught up in this downward spiral. Would he ever be able to control his habit? I folded my arms tightly around my body and hugged myself for comfort.

Alfie leant back in the chair and opened the buttons on the front of his suit. Then picked up his glass and drained it. 'This situation must be frustrating for you,' he said.

Hearing that made the fight seep out of me. I exhaled a loud breath and my eyes filled with tears. I tried to blink them away before Alfie saw them.

'I don't like seeing you cry, Gemma.' Alfie handed me my glass. 'Finish your drink, and I'll get us another one.'

'I should go.' I could already feel the effects of the alcohol.

'Stay for one more drink.' Alfie didn't wait for me to reply before he walked over to the bar.

'How did you get involved in all of this?' I asked when Alfie returned with our drinks.

'That's a good question.' Alfie laughed.

I was suddenly intrigued to know more about the man who was controlling my future. 'Surely there must have been other paths you could have taken in life.'

'Not really. I grew up in this environment, so I'm comfortable with it.' Alfie ran his hand through his slicked-back blond hair.

My mouth fell open. 'How can you be comfortable being a member of the criminal underworld?'

'I run the family business, Gemma. We specialise in sales and distribution,' Alfie corrected.

'Call it what you want, but your line of work isn't legal, is it? Doesn't that bother you?' I questioned, feeling brave with the alcohol floating about in my system.

Alfie shrugged and took a sip of his drink. 'What bothers me is that at any time, my freedom could be taken away. My entire world could come crashing down around me in the blink of an eye.' Alfie stared through me.

'If that's how you feel, why don't you do something else?' My eyebrows knitted together.

'It's all I know.' Alfie sipped his drink and leant back in his chair. 'When my grandad Billy was young, he wanted to make some money, so he got a job working for the most successful person he knew.'

I had to stifle a laugh. 'Who did he work for, The Godfather?'

Alfie tilted his head to the side. 'No, but it's not a bad guess. The guy was the head of an organised crime family.'

'And they advised him to follow an unlawful path, did they?'

Alfie stared down at the floor for a few seconds. Then his blue eyes looked into mine. 'He worked for the guy for a few years before branching out on his own. Grandad started the family firm in the sixties. I guess in hindsight, he was influenced by the wrong person.' He paused before he started talking again. 'Well, now you know how the business started.'

'It's interesting that you call it a business.'

'Why wouldn't I? Some of what we do is legitimate.' Alfie straightened his posture.

Now, this I had to hear. I arched an eyebrow, intrigued by what Alfie was going to say.

'My dad owns a car parts company, a restaurant and a club. He uses the surplus cash to run the companies. It's a good way to lose a few hundred grand that would otherwise be burning a hole in his pocket,' Alfie said with a smug look on his face.

That did surprise me. I couldn't even begin to imagine what it must be like to have spare money like that. It suddenly occurred to me that Alfie obviously made a huge amount of money through questionable means. By getting mixed up in his business, Nathan and I were in way over our heads.

'And anyway, if we didn't appear to be above board, the taxman would be sniffing around.' Alfie winked.

I had to admit I'd enjoyed our chat this evening. I hadn't expected Alfie to be so open and unguarded. I'd seen a different side of him and actually felt relaxed in his company for once.

'That's enough about me, let's talk about you, Gemma,' Alfie said, crossing his arms over his chest.

Picking up my glass, I finished my drink. 'I'm tired, I'm going to head off now,' I said, getting to my feet.

'Let me walk you to your room.' Alfie stood up and straightened the lapels of his dark grey suit.

I knew there was no point refusing his offer.

'Have you ever watched the Monaco Grand Prix before?' Alfie asked as we waited for the lift.

'I've seen bits of it on TV.'

'It's got to be the race that every Formula One driver dreams of winning, don't you think?'

I couldn't help wondering where Alfie was going with this.

'It's always been my fantasy to drive up and down the winding hairpin bends in a sports car. I might rent a Ferrari tomorrow and take you on the ride of your life. Would you like that, Gemma?'

'I don't think Nathan would be too happy about it.'

'I wasn't planning on inviting him along.' Alfie laughed.

We stepped inside the lift, and he pressed the button to the fifth floor. I stared straight ahead, hoping to avoid any further conversation. Alfie slipped his hand around my waist. As I turned to look at him, he put his hands on my hips and backed me up against the side of the lift. I could see his Adam's apple moving as he rested his forehead against mine. Lowering his head, he gently kissed my lips. I don't know what came over me, but I'm guessing it had something to do with the alcohol. I should have pushed him away, but instead, I ran my hands up his chest and kissed him back. We intertwined fingers as we explored each other's mouths. When the lift came to an abrupt stop, we pulled apart before the doors opened.

'Come back to my room, Gemma.'

'I can't. I don't want to betray Nathan.'

'I think you already did.' Alfie smiled.

49

Gemma

I'd spent a restless night lying next to Nathan, watching his chest fall and rise as he slept, while I tried to figure out why I had kissed Alfie.

Throwing on some clothes, I decided I couldn't wait any longer. I needed to talk to Alfie right now before Nathan woke up, so I crept out of our room and into the brightly lit hallway. Before I knew it, I was standing outside Alfie's room, knocking gently on the door. Then I came to my senses. What the hell was I doing? Turning around, I began pacing back down the hall, hoping he wasn't awake.

'I'm glad to see you've changed your mind,' Alfie said. He'd spotted me as I'd retreated along the corridor.

I stopped in my tracks; there was no point trying to run away. It was too late for that. Alfie stood in the doorway, wearing just his black Armani boxer shorts. Silence hung between us while he waited for me to walk back. As I got closer, I ran my eyes over his muscular torso, and my heart began pounding. I'd never seen him in anything less than a suit before, so I had to force myself to look up from his smooth chest and meet his blue gaze.

'I haven't changed my mind, but I need to talk to you about something important. Can I come in?'

'Of course you can.'

Alfie stepped to one side and let me into his suite. There wasn't enough space for me to pass him, and my hand brushed the skin on his taut stomach. I felt my pulse quicken in response, but instinctively my fingers recoiled. That wasn't supposed to happen, I thought. *You've got to focus on why you came here,* I repeated to myself, over and over again. *Don't let yourself get distracted.*

'What happened last night was a mistake,' I said, looking Alfie straight in the eye.

'Whatever you say, Gemma.' Alfie smirked.

'I shouldn't have kissed you, and I want you to know it's never going to happen again. Do you understand?' I babbled, trying to get the words out as fast as possible before my nervous heartbeat gave me away.

'I understand.' Alfie nodded.

'It was a one-off.'

'OK, I get it. You've made yourself clear.' Alfie's words said one thing, but his smile said something different.

'I mean it. Nothing will ever happen between us again,' I repeated, as much for my sake as Alfie's.

'I heard what you said.' A slow smile lifted the corners of Alfie's lips. 'But I'm not sure I believe you.'

'Well, you should,' I replied, allowing myself one last subtle look at Alfie's semi-naked body.

'You don't sound very convincing, Gemma.'

When Alfie draped his arm around my shoulder, my

heart skipped a beat, and my pulse began to race. I knew I needed to calm myself down before he noticed. I didn't want to make a complete fool of myself. But no matter how hard I tried, I couldn't seem to control the butterflies in my stomach.

'I'd better go,' I said, realising the sooner I put some distance between us the better. I wasn't sure I could trust myself.

Alfie was a very good-looking man, but I didn't want to admit that I was attracted to him, because then I'd have to face up to what I'd done. At this moment in time, my emotional state was too fragile to handle the truth.

'Why don't you stay?' Alfie's eyes never left mine while he waited for me to respond.

'I can't.'

'That's a real shame.' Alfie slid his hands around my waist and leant down to kiss me.

I turned my face away before his lips made contact with mine. Clasping my hands together to stop myself fidgeting, I took a step closer to the door.

'Do I make you nervous, Gemma?'

'No, of course not.'

'Then why can't you look at me without turning red?' Alfie smirked.

Leaving his question unanswered, I headed back out of the door with his words ringing in my ears.

50

Gemma

'Let me give you some advice, Gemma. Never go on a job expecting to get caught. If you do, you'll line yourself up to fail, and failure isn't an option.'

Attempting to get on top of my nerves, I tried not to pace as I walked around the exotic gardens of the Place du Casino. The central square was bustling with tourists enjoying the scenery and glorious winter sunshine. I hoped I appeared as carefree as they did. Taking one last look at the palm trees and the azure blue sky above me, I made my way to the Chopard Boutique.

Stepping through the dark wood door of the tiny jewellery store, armed with nothing more than a smile and my designer handbag, I made my way to the counter. Gazing into the glass cabinet, I scanned the contents for the ring on my shopping list.

'Are you looking for anything in particular?' the sales assistant asked.

I looked up at the sound of her voice. 'I was admiring

that beautiful ring. Is it a sapphire?' I asked, giving her my best smile.

'It's actually a blue diamond,' the middle-aged lady informed me.

'Oh, I didn't know there was such a thing.' My eyes sprung open.

'They are one of the rarest gemstones. Would you like to try it on?'

'Yes, please.'

'The stone is mounted on an eighteen-carat white gold band and paved with diamonds,' the assistant said, handing it to me.

'It's beautiful. How much is it?'

I slipped the oval-cut ring on and off my finger. Then delved my hand into my bag while the assistant checked the price.

'It's nine hundred and fifty thousand euros, madame.' When she told me the price, it just tripped off her tongue. She was so used to serving customers with bottomless bank accounts.

'That's more than I was expecting. It is a lovely ring, but before I spend that amount of money, I'd like to have a think about it.' I handed her the replica before walking out of the door.

The Mercedes engine was running when I got in the car. Alfie usually always sat behind Tommy. For some reason, he'd swapped positions with Nathan and was in the middle seat, so I had no option but to sit next to him.

'How did it go?' Alfie asked, turning towards me.

I looked down at my hands, trembling in my lap and realised there was no need for me to go into details.

'You see, I told you she'd be fine.'

Alfie turned to look at my husband. While he did, he ran his hand up my thigh. Nathan didn't seem to notice, but if he did, he chose to ignore it. Instead, he stared out of the car window at the yachts lining the harbour.

'You shouldn't have sent Gemma in there. It was too risky,' Nathan replied, not looking in my direction.

'Would somebody like to tell me what's going on?' I asked, turning sideways in the chair so I could face them both. 'You're talking about me as if I'm not here.'

'It's no big deal,' Alfie replied, giving nothing away as usual.

'Well, I'd call it a big deal.' Nathan turned and looked Alfie straight in the eye. 'The police have released CCTV footage of you, Gemma.'

My heart was in my mouth as I processed his words, and all of a sudden, I had a horrible feeling in the pit of my stomach.

'Don't look so worried, Gemma,' Alfie said, flashing me a pearly white smile.

Adrenaline rushed through my body, sending my pulse racing and making the palms of my hands sweat. My nerves intensified when I realised they were waiting for me to speak. But my mouth was so dry, I found myself gasping for air instead when I attempted to clear my throat. Taking a deep breath, I tried not to give away how I was feeling, but I knew it would be difficult to stop my voice from wobbling.

'Where did the police get the footage from?'

'Cartier's,' Alfie replied.

'Oh shit!' I let my face fall into my hands.

Alfie pulled my hands away. 'It's OK, Gemma, there's nothing to worry about. Even though they've got footage of you looking at the expensive panther bracelet, they didn't see you take it.'

'So why have they released it?' I looked Alfie straight in the eye, hoping for once he'd give me an honest answer.

'If you don't tell her, I will,' Nathan said, raising his voice.

'It's your lucky day, Gemma, your knight in shining armour's arrived to save you.' Alfie laughed.

A flash of anger spread across Nathan's face.

I was so worried, I couldn't think straight and all Alfie could do was make stupid comments. 'Stop changing the subject and tell me what happened. I want to know the truth.'

'After you left the store, the manager decided to check the bracelet over and realised it was a fake. He knew you must have switched it. So he checked the CCTV images, but he still couldn't see the moment you took it, even after closely inspecting the tapes.' Alfie settled back in the chair and stared straight ahead.

It suddenly became apparent why Nathan hadn't wanted to make eye contact with me. Guilt was written all over his face. He knew there wasn't going to be a good outcome to this.

'What else did the report say?'

'The detective in charge of the case said a professional thief must have been responsible, seeing as the store was robbed in broad daylight, despite being protected by sophisticated security devices.' Alfie threw his head back and laughed.

'Oh my God.' I ran my fingers over my forehead, hoping to ease the throbbing in my temples.

'The detective said the woman had clearly done this before and feared this was no isolated incident. He reckons you might be responsible for similar unreported robberies and urged jewellers to check their stock for fake items, as they could have been targeted without being aware of it. He advised stores to routinely check expensive items after a customer has handled them to stop this from happening. If they did that, we'd be out of business.' Alfie laughed again.

The footage had opened a can of worms, and now my life felt like it was crumbling around me.

'The description the police have issued of you is surprisingly accurate.' Alfie interlaced his fingers behind his head and smirked.

'What's so funny about that?' Anger seeped into my words.

'We were meant to be travelling to Paris next, but it's too risky to go back over the border at the moment, so we'll take the scenic route and head to Italy instead,' Alfie replied, ignoring my question.

'But shouldn't I be in hiding if the police are looking for me?' I knotted my hands in my lap.

'There's a look of terror in your pretty green eyes. Do me a favour, don't blow this out of proportion.' Alfie patted my thigh with his hand.

'That's easy for you to say, but the police know what I look like. They've got footage of me on CCTV.' I bit down on the pad of my thumb.

'You haven't got a bounty on your head.' Alfie turned to face me. 'Trust me, Gemma, everything will be OK. We need to get out of Monaco and lie low for a while to give the dust time to settle.'

Alfie made it all sound so simple, but we lived in a world where everything could be monitored. It suddenly occurred to me that without even realising it, we left a trail of personal information behind us. Now I understood why he kept changing our names and had banned us from using our iPhones and social media accounts. He'd given us a vintage Nokia to use, no doubt because it was less easy to track than a modern mobile. But it came with a condition. The only PERSON we were allowed to contact from it was him. Although I couldn't deny I was scared, when I thought about it logically, Alfie had probably done this a thousand times before, so if anyone knew how to avoid detection, he would.

'Anyway, there's nothing the police can do to you,' Alfie said, breaking the silence. 'They didn't actually see you steal the bracelet and they won't be able to locate it. So what are they going to charge you with?'

'But they have footage proving I was looking at the bracelet. Surely that's enough evidence.'

'You're forgetting one vital thing. The police have got to catch you first, and I'm not about to let that happen.' Alfie reached for my hand and squeezed my fingers.

That almost coaxed a smile from me.

'You know most people assume crime is impossible to get away with,' Alfie said, turning towards me.

I looked at him with a puzzled expression on my face. 'Correct me if I'm wrong, but aren't we on the run from the police?'

'Technically, we are, but they'll never catch us. You've

got nothing to worry about, Gemma. We get away far more than we get caught. Whoever said crime doesn't pay, was mistaken.' Alfie laughed then handed me a black bag. He sat and watched me as I unzipped the top and peered at the contents. 'Choose one,' he said as I lifted out two hairpieces.

'So I'm going to have to change my appearance, am I?'

'Just for the moment. Would you prefer to be a redhead or a blonde? Blondes have more fun, don't they?' Alfie winked, and then his eyes fixed on my lips.

I looked across at Nathan. 'What do you think?' I'd only ever been a brunette, so I didn't know which one to go for.

Nathan shrugged. 'It's up to you.'

Knowing that Alfie was keen for me to wear the blonde wig, I opted to be a redhead instead. It wasn't easy to sweep my long hair up into a bun in the confines of the car, but I just about managed to, securing it in place with a couple of clips before I put on the hairpiece.

'You look fantastic. Even your own mother wouldn't recognise you,' Alfie said as peals of laughter escaped from his lips.

I doubt she would recognise me even without the disguise, I thought. I hadn't seen my mother for twelve years.

'Head to the station, Tommy, we need to update Gemma's passport photo before we board the train.'

Alfie stood outside the photo booth, feeding the machine with coins as I posed for shots with both of the hairpieces. I wondered if this simple disguise would be enough to fool the police. Only time would tell.

'When will my new passport be ready?'

'It shouldn't be too long. We only need to get the photos added; we've already got the document. Tommy will sort it out when we get to Milan.'

'What if I get stopped on the way?' A vision formed in my mind of armed officers searching the train, accompanied by sniffer dogs, looking for a female fugitive. 'The police sometimes do spot checks, don't they?'

'I've travelled through France, Italy, Germany and Belgium loads of times and have never been asked for my passport once,' Alfie said.

I hoped he was right. I couldn't help feeling uneasy about the situation. Even though there are no regular checks, it was a legal requirement to carry your passport to prove your identity when travelling from one country to another. What would happen when I couldn't produce mine? Would I be taken away and thrown in a cell? I'd have to push that thought from my head for now. There was no point worrying about something that hadn't happened.

Once we were on board the train from Monaco to Ventimiglia, I took my overnight bag into the toilet and changed out of the black suit I'd been wearing. I did a double-take when I saw the redhead in the mirror staring back at me.

Alfie was right: I looked completely different. I didn't even recognise myself. The wig had drastically altered my appearance. I'd thought it would take more than a simple change of hair colour to do that. No wonder every film that featured a criminal on the run has a scene where the fugitive does this. If I changed the style and colour frequently, I'd be able to keep disguising myself. Maybe this would work after all. The police were looking for a slim woman with long, dark brown hair of about five foot seven in her mid-twenties. I couldn't change my age, height and build, although the description was slightly wrong – I'm thirty and five foot eight. But by changing my hair colour, it would hopefully be enough to throw them off the trail. I had no choice but to trust Alfie. It remained to be seen if it was possible to slip through the net and avoid detection like he said it was.

I made my way back to our carriage and sat down next to Nathan. When he glanced around at me, at first, he looked startled.

'Sorry, Gem, I didn't recognise you for a minute.' He laughed.

I smiled at how easily I'd just fooled my husband. But then again it made perfect sense. A person's hair colour is one of the first things we notice about them. Another thing is eye colour. If I wanted to undergo a complete transformation, I might need to invest in some coloured contact lenses. Not many people have green eyes. Having the rarest colour in the population could be the thing that ends up giving me away.

The twenty-four-minute train journey took us past some stunning scenery as it travelled along the coastal line. Tall cypress trees clung by their exposed roots to the steep rocky slopes. Far below us, the pristine beach's only visitors were the waves that gently lapped the shore. In the distance, a solitary yacht sailed across the calm cobalt sea, leaving only a trail of white foam in its wake.

I stared at my reflection in the window and wondered

how it had come to this. You could cut the atmosphere with a knife as Nathan and I sat together, awkward in each other's company. I glanced at my watch while we communicated through our body language that we had nothing to say to each other. Something had definitely changed between us, and with no conversation to interfere with my thoughts, I began to question our future. Since Alfie had entered our lives, he'd made it impossible to predict how things would turn out. We didn't know what we'd be doing from one day to the next, and that only added to an already stressful situation.

I had to put my thoughts on hold while we changed trains at the Italian border town of Ventimiglia for the onward journey to Milan. It would be another two hours before we reached the city. I wasn't looking forward to sitting next to Nathan again, but if the ocean views continued to be as breathtaking as they had been, it might not be such a hardship after all.

The train pulled out of the station, and as it slowly gathered speed, it reminded me of a roller coaster, and that was the way I felt about my relationship with Nathan at the moment. One minute we were up and the next we were down. All relationships were filled with uncertainty at some point, weren't they? Life was complicated, and the longer a couple had been together, the more complicated it became.

I began to consider the pros and cons of us staying together; right now, the cons seemed to outnumber the pros. It shocked me to think about how quickly our marriage had started to fall to pieces. I'd always thought it was rock solid. I loved my husband, but was love enough?

When we arrived at Genoa on the Italian Riviera, the train's route changed course and headed away from the coast. We finally said goodbye to the sapphire sea, rugged cliffs and white sand beaches as we cut through the mountains instead. The train climbed further up the mountain, and the scenery got better and better. I gazed at the terracotta-roofed houses with pastel-coloured walls before watching them fade into the distance. When we left the villages far behind us, we lost the view altogether and spent the rest of the journey in a tunnel.

With nothing else to look at, my thoughts drifted back to Nathan. At one time, he used to make me feel all warm and fuzzy inside. But he'd let me down so many times over the years, I'd reached the point where I was questioning our future together. Good communication was the key to any successful relationship. But Nathan and I had stopped communicating with each other, and now my emotional pendulum was swaying from one extreme to the other.

51

Nathan

Gemma didn't deserve any of this. She had paid a terrible price for my stupidity. I'd messed up big time, and I didn't know how to put things right. She was furious with me and who could blame her?

Being an only child, I'd always craved attention and companionship. From an early age, I'd wanted to surround myself with surrogate siblings and be the most popular boy in the class, but I didn't have the money to back up the position. It was always the rich kids like Alfie, the ones who had everything, who everybody wanted to be friends with. I didn't have anything to offer my classmates and found I had little in common with them. Most of them didn't come from a single-parent family like I did, and the kids whose parents were divorced still had contact with both of them. I had to spend a lot of time with my aunt and uncle so my mum could take advantage of the free childcare, and as soon as I was old enough, I became a latchkey kid.

My dad got the blame for everything that went wrong

in my life. I spent much of my adolescence silently raging against him. I was filled with resentment and self-pity and was unwilling to talk about or try to deal with my issues on any level. I discovered denial was a fool-proof way to avoid my problems.

I sometimes wondered if things would have been different if my dad had been around, but any time I thought about trying to find him, my fear of rejection stopped me in my tracks. No wonder I was a loner and had trouble letting people in. To deal with the pain I'd experienced, I built a high wall around myself so that I wouldn't get hurt in the future.

But Gemma wasn't trying to hurt me. She was trying to support me. It was time to stop making excuses for myself. I couldn't continue to let my difficult start in life affect my future. My mum had done the best she could for me. I might not have had material possessions, but she smothered me with love and affection, and that counted for a lot.

Gemma was the strong one in our relationship, but it was time I stopped being weak. I needed to man up before she got fed up with me. My insecurities were more draining than a marathon, and nobody wanted to be saddled with an emotional drain, did they?

52

Gemma

'Up until now, the modus operandi you've been using has proved to be very successful, and let's face it, your success is my success,' Alfie said, with a sudden glint in his eye.

'I'll take that as a compliment, shall I?' I replied, raising my eyebrows.

Alfie nodded and sat down on the king-size bed in our hotel room. 'The sleight of hand technique isn't an easy thing to master. But then not everyone is as charming as you, Gemma. I'm sure that helps when you're trying to distract the staff.'

I heard Nathan let out a loud sigh, but I didn't dare look in his direction. Alfie's words were so cheesy, I felt the need to throw him a look, and only just managed not to roll my eyes. But I couldn't stop the involuntary groan that escaped from my lips.

'There's nothing to it. I just go into the shop, start playing my magic flute, and stare at the assistant with my psychedelic hypnotic gaze. Before I know it, they're in a trance and under my spell.' I didn't bother to try and keep the sarcastic tone out of my voice.

'You're a bit of a comedian, aren't you, Gemma?'

'I do try,' I replied, giving Alfie a half-smile.

'You can joke about it if you want, but because you looked the part, the staff never suspected you were going to steal anything. Everything about you is classy, so you have the perfect profile to carry out the switch.'

'I obviously wasn't as convincing as you think. Otherwise, the police wouldn't be looking for me, would they?'

'You had a good run.' Alfie shrugged.

'And now my luck's run out.'

I took off the shoulder-length auburn bob I'd been wearing and released my hair from the clips. Running my fingers through it, I allowed it to tumble down my back.

'I wouldn't say your luck's run out, but for the moment you need to change your appearance. The hair colour is a good start, but you need to dress differently as well.'

'How am I meant to do that?' I asked, unzipping my small case. 'This is all I've got with me.'

'We'll go shopping tomorrow,' Alfie said, getting to his feet.

'No way,' I replied, flashing Alfie my best 'don't mess with me' look. I wasn't going near another jewellery shop now the police were on to me.

Alfie laughed. 'I didn't mean that kind of shopping. We need to hit the high street and buy you some new clothes.'

'What if I get spotted?'

'You won't. Trust me, Gemma, I know what I'm talking about. By the time I've finished with your transformation, you could be within spitting distance of people who've known you all your life, and they won't realise it's you. The police won't be able to find you if you're that unrecognisable.'

53

Alfie

Gemma was far too beautiful to be wasting her time with a loser like Nathan. If she just said the word, I'd be happy to take her off his hands.

Not being able to be with Gemma was driving me insane. It was torture for me to be in the same room as her and not put my hands on her. I could look, but I couldn't touch. That wasn't something I was used to.

I'd never met a woman like Gemma before. She was having a powerful effect on me. I couldn't get enough of her. She was like a drug. Gemma was the most beautiful woman I had ever met, but it wasn't just her physical appearance, her personality kept drawing me towards her. I admired her strength. She refused to be silenced and wasn't afraid to speak her mind. Gemma stood up for herself and didn't hide behind Nathan's back. She was fearless, whereas he was the weak link in their relationship. I was going to use that to my advantage.

Gemma didn't play the victim or point the finger of blame at her husband even though she had good reason to. She carried herself with dignity and didn't let Nathan's fuck-ups break her spirit. She tackled the challenges they faced head-on. That told me a lot about her. She was too good for Nathan.

Gemma had a certain vibe about her that made me sit up and take notice. Logic told me I shouldn't waste time fantasising about a woman who wasn't available. I wasn't the type of guy to try and lure a married woman away from her husband. But Gemma was different. She was the woman of my dreams. There was something about her I couldn't quite put my finger on. There was something about the way she made me feel I couldn't quite explain.

Now that I'd experienced this kind of attraction for myself, I understood the obsession my dad had with Rosa. I'd been so bitter about it at the time. All I could focus on was my mum's despair, but I finally knew how he felt. He hadn't fallen in love with Rosa to hurt my mum. It was out of his control. He'd been powerless to stop it.

I never expected to find myself in the same position. Love triangles inevitably get messy. I would normally just walk away from a situation like this. There were easier paths to take. But Gemma was worth fighting for, so I wasn't going anywhere.

I'd suddenly found myself outside my comfort zone. People became vulnerable when they were romantically involved. They became attached and dependent on their partner. The idea of putting myself in that position was alien to me.

54

Gemma

I was fully aware that Alfie knew how to pick luxurious accommodation, but he had really spoiled us this time. Having a corner position, our spacious room at the Palazzo Parigi Milano featured two balconies with different perspectives. One of the bustling city, and the other, the hotel's beautiful garden.

'I'm going to check out the spa,' I said.

I knew we'd probably be moving on again soon, so I didn't want to miss out on the opportunity this time, especially as this spa offered treatments from around the world, in seven different therapeutic rooms. After what I'd been through, I deserved a bit of pampering, and if I was totally honest, the idea of having some space from Nathan was very appealing.

'You've been gone for ages.' Nathan stopped flicking through the channels and turned the TV off when I walked into the room.

He looked like a five-year-old child sulking because somebody had taken his sweets. The temptation to stick out my bottom lip and pretend to suck my thumb was overwhelming, but I managed to resist the urge.

'Have I?' I wondered why he was even bothered.

'For a minute, I thought you'd done a runner.' Nathan laughed.

If he'd known that recently I'd been considering doing exactly that, he might not find it so funny. I'd asked myself the question: was I just holding on to my marriage to Nathan out of habit or was I still in love with him? I wasn't convinced I knew the answer any more. Just because we'd been together a long time, it didn't mean we should stay together. I wasn't about to let Nathan get to me. I was too relaxed after my Balinese massage, so I reminded myself that he could only wind me up if I let him. It was obvious that nothing had changed between us since I'd gone out. We still had a very strained relationship.

'I'm bored out of my mind stuck inside this room,' Nathan said.

I wanted to point out that it was his fault we were in this situation, but I couldn't face having another blazing row, so I made the decision to ignore him instead. I know the only way to handle him when he's like this is to detach myself from him. So I walked across the room and stood in front of the window that looked out over the garden. Taking a deep breath, I closed my eyes and pretended to be admiring the view.

'Did you hear what I said, Gemma?'

'Yes.' I turned around to make eye contact with him.

'So why didn't you answer me?'

I shrugged my shoulders and stared at him. Nathan glared back at me.

'I've got a terrible headache. I think I'll go to bed.' I know I shouldn't have lied, but having spent a lovely afternoon in the spa, I wasn't in the mood to babysit my husband this evening. It was too emotionally draining.

'Suit yourself.' Nathan slammed the door behind him when he left the room.

Staring into the darkness, I lay in the foetal position, hugging my knees, as I tortured myself about the state of my marriage. Our relationship had reached a fork in the road. Waiting for it to get better was like waiting for it to snow in the desert. I had come to the conclusion, the longer I put up with Nathan's behaviour, the longer he'd keep doing it. If he wasn't going to change, maybe it was time to let him go.

When I finally closed my eyes, it was as if I was back in the lift with Alfie. The memory should have been unpleasant, but it wasn't. I had a horrible feeling I was falling for him. I couldn't believe this was happening. I really hadn't seen this coming. There was a fine line between love and hate. My mind was in turmoil. I knew I was going to have trouble sleeping tonight.

55

Gemma

The next morning, I woke after a night of troubled sleep. Feeling very uneasy, I left Nathan in our room and met Alfie outside the front of the hotel. I couldn't deny butterflies began to flutter in my stomach at the sight of him. Within a few minutes, we'd walked the short distance to the high-end fashion district.

'Prepare to be impressed,' Alfie said, adjusting the front of his blue suit jacket. 'This place is known as the golden square; it's one of the most expensive and exclusive shopping districts in Milan.'

'I've heard of it,' I replied, looking at the network of streets and chic boutiques. 'I know people who shop here all the time.'

'I never thought Rosa or Donatella would come all this way to buy a new pair of shoes.' Alfie smiled, then pulled a face.

'They don't,' I replied, smiling back at him.

'Don't tell me Gareth and Bernardo are the fashion gurus.' Alfie laughed, shaking his head.

I turned my head away and began considering what he'd just said. It surprised me that Alfie knew the names of Nathan's family members.

'Come on, Gemma, don't keep me in suspense,' Alfie prompted, after a lengthy pause.

'Before I worked at Mamma Donatella's, I used to work for a fashion house in the West End. A lot of my clothes were given to me as samples.'

'That explains why you always dress well. What did you do?'

'I was the director's personal assistant, but the buyers used to come here regularly.' I let out a long breath.

'Why did you give up a job like that to work in a restaurant waiting tables?' Alfie raised his eyebrows.

Touching the side of my neck self-consciously, I thought about the best way to answer. 'I didn't have a choice.'

'That's the story of your life, isn't it, Gemma?'

The look on my face made Alfie realise he'd hit a nerve and he raised his hands in defence, studying my expression while he waited for me to reply.

'You've obviously never had to give up anything you love before.' I forced myself to look Alfie dead in the eye.

'And you know that for a fact, do you?'

'If you had, you wouldn't be so insensitive. It was my dream job, Alfie. It broke my heart when I had to leave.' I tried to keep my voice steady, but it wasn't easy. Talking about the way my life used to be opened up old wounds and made me feel very emotional.

'I didn't mean to upset you. What can I say? Sometimes I can't help myself, being an arsehole comes naturally to me.'

I appreciated Alfie's attempt at an apology and suddenly felt the need to explain, but I hoped he wouldn't notice the tears forming in my eyes. 'When our home was repossessed, we had to go and live above the restaurant, and that was too far away for me to commute from.'

'You've had to sacrifice a lot for Nathan, so I'm going to buy you whatever you want.' Alfie winked, before guiding me into Versace's flagship store. 'It's about time somebody spoiled you.'

I opened the door of our room several hours later, weighed down by shopping bags, and did a double-take when I came face to face with a man who could have been Don Corleone's twin. My husband was sitting at the table opposite the smartly dressed gentleman with slicked-back hair and pencil-thin moustache.

Nathan turned towards me and smiled. 'This is my wife: Gemma.'

The man got up from his chair and walked across to where I was standing. 'Hello, Gemma. I'd like to introduce myself. My name is Mario Malva,' he said, holding his hand out towards me.

I put down my bags. 'Pleased to meet you, Mario,' I said, shaking his hand.

'Your wife has expensive taste, doesn't she?' Mario gestured to the sea of designer shopping bags surrounding me. 'Let's start the game. Judging by the way this lady buys shoes, you'll need to win some money if you want to put food on the table tonight.' Mario smiled and made his way back across the room, then slowly lowered his heavy frame into the seat in front of the window.

Mario's words echoed in my head. Even though we'd only just met, this stranger had formed his own conclusion of me. I was about to tell him that Alfie had paid for everything, but then again, why should I? I didn't need to justify myself to him. It was none of his business. I have to admit, his suggestion that I was a spendaholic had my insides boiling. That statement couldn't be further from the truth. But I wouldn't give him the satisfaction of reacting to it. Nathan was the reason we were in financial meltdown and by the looks of things, he was about to make matters worse than they already were.

'Are you going to tell me what's going on?'

Nathan turned to face me with guilty eyes. He could see I was furious.

'We're just going to play a few games of poker.' Nathan forced out a half-hearted smile.

'I don't think that's a good idea.'

'Why not? We're just going to play a friendly game.' Mario smiled, and the skin at the corners of his eyes crinkled up.

Staring into the middle distance, I tried to process what was happening. It was bad enough when Nathan was gambling in the casinos, but this was taking things to another level. The thought of them playing poker in my room turned my stomach. I needed to get away. All of a sudden, the air in the room felt stifling.

'I'm going out,' I said, unable to look in their direction. I thought my husband might come after me, but the lure of the card game was too strong.

*

Three hours later I walked back into our room, having spent the afternoon in the spa. Nathan was pacing up and down in front of the windows. His ear was pressed hard against the phone.

'I need to borrow some money...' Nathan suddenly realised I was there and fell silent for a minute. 'I can't talk now, I'll call you back later.'

'Who were you talking to?' I asked, fixing him with a stare.

'Alfie.'

Anger was building up inside me. There was so much I wanted to say, but none of my words would come out.

'I'm sorry, Gemma.' Nathan rushed towards me, reached out and took hold of my hands.

After filling my lungs with air, I let out a deep breath before I spoke. 'I take it you lost the game.' Pulling my hands away, I stepped away from Nathan. I didn't know whether to laugh or cry. 'Why do you keep doing this? For God's sake, Nathan, when are you going to grow up?' I scowled at him with contempt in my eyes.

'I had a straight flush – that's a winning hand,' Nathan said, knowing that his words would either calm or escalate the situation. Then he put his hands in the front pockets of his jeans and lowered his dark eyes to the floor.

'If that's the case, why didn't you win?' I fired out my words like they were bullets from a gun.

'Mario's cards were higher.' Nathan's words sucked the energy right out of the room.

'What a surprise.'

'I was unlucky, Gemma,' Nathan replied, running his fingers along the dark stubble on his chin.

How many times had I heard that before? Every time Nathan gambled, it always ended the same way. I couldn't understand why he kept chasing his losses; he was never going to win back any money, and the sooner he accepted that, the better.

'So how much did you lose this time?' My green eyes bored into his and Nathan began squirming.

'Only five thousand.'

'Oh, is that all.'

Nathan incorrectly misinterpreted my sarcastic comment. 'It's not too bad, is it? I bet you thought I was going to say a lot more.'

I knew deep down Nathan was never going to change. My mouth fell open as his words rang in my ears. 'I didn't think things could get any worse than they already were, but you've gone and done it again. What the hell is wrong with you?'

'I'm sorry, Gemma.'

Nathan feigned a wounded expression and held up his hands, but his apology was falling on deaf ears. His mindless behaviour was destroying our lives. 'Where are you going to get the money from?'

'I'm going to borrow it from Alfie. Mario's coming back in an hour to collect it.'

As the reality of the situation sank in, it made me feel cold and hollow. The room felt airless, and I was having trouble breathing. I'd have to take myself out of the equation. With my stomach churning, I turned on my heel and made my way towards the door. I wanted to get as far away from

Nathan as possible. I couldn't bear to look at him. I needed some space to try and clear my head.

'Gemma, wait, let's talk about this,' Nathan called when I left the room, slamming the door behind me.

I stopped to catch my breath with my back against the wall in the empty stairwell. Drying my eyes on the back of my hand, I knew I'd have to get my head out of the clouds and stop giving Nathan any more second chances. Otherwise, we were never going to get out of this nightmare. We were stuck on a hamster wheel going nowhere.

56

Nathan

I had a sinking feeling in my heart that I'd just lost the love of my life. Gemma was the kind of woman who only came around once in a lifetime. Had I just blown it by being selfish and stubborn? I didn't want to think about the future without her. I had to do something before it was too late.

Gemma gave everything she had to give to our marriage. No matter what I did, she was always there for me. I'd put her through so much over the years. If she left me, nobody else could ever fill the void. I would never find another woman to love me the way that she did.

Every time she tried to keep me on the straight and narrow, she met resistance from me. I don't know why I wouldn't accept her help – God knows I needed it. I knew Gemma only had my best interests at heart. It must have been a constant source of frustration for her when I didn't listen to her and carried on regardless.

I knew I had pushed her too far this time. She wasn't going to put up with my shit any longer. Who could blame her? I was a living nightmare where money was concerned. What the hell was the matter with me? I was a grown man, but I was behaving like a child, denying there was an issue.

It was obvious Gemma was going to leave me sooner or later if I didn't sort myself out. But I couldn't seem to help myself, my finger always seemed to gravitate to the self-destruct button. It was time I stared my demons in the face and stopped ignoring my problems.

My destructive behaviour had caused endless misery for my long-suffering wife. If I wasn't careful I would end up pushing her away. I couldn't let that happen. I hoped the thought of losing Gemma would give me the motivation I needed to change. I'd been burying my head in the sand for so long now, breaking the cycle wouldn't be easy. But I had to do it. It was time to take control of my life and sort myself out once and for all. This was something I had to do myself. Nobody could do it for me.

I remembered only too well the range of emotions I'd felt when I'd realised my dad wanted nothing to do with me or my mum. None of them were pleasant, but they didn't compare to the devastation I felt at this moment in time.

57

Gemma

There was something about the way Alfie exuded power and confidence that made him incredibly attractive. When he walked into a room with testosterone seeping from every pore, everyone noticed him. He was a leader, not a follower. That impressed me more than I cared to admit, and I found myself having to fight the urge to want to be with him.

Alfie walked across the polished floor of the bar with a confident swagger. I was sitting in an oyster-coloured velvet chair, next to the large wrought-iron windows, overlooking the garden and the Milanese skyline in the distance. As the sun began to set, it cast long shadows across the vast terrace and illuminated sculptures.

'I thought I might find you in here.' Alfie smiled.

Letting out a long sigh, I took a sip of my wine. 'Am I really that predictable?'

'No, but when you weren't in your room, I wondered if

you'd be drowning your sorrows.' Alfie pulled out the chair opposite me and sat down.

I looked down at my lap, hoping he wouldn't notice that I'd been crying, but it wasn't going to be easy to hide the way I was feeling. As I glanced up, our eyes met. Alfie leant back in his seat and studied me.

'Nathan has just introduced me to his new friend.'

'So you hadn't met Mario before?'

'No, but from what I've been able to find out, it appears Mr Malva is a professional poker player.'

Alfie stirred his cocktail, then took a sip.

What an incredible coincidence that a professional poker player just happened to bump into Nathan in our hotel while I was out. I knocked back the rest of my wine, then put the empty glass down on the table between us.

Alfie called the waiter over and ordered two Thai Martinis for us.

'Surely Nathan must have realised he wouldn't be able to beat a professional. Sometimes, I don't understand how his mind works.' I sighed, shaking my head in disbelief.

The waiter put the two Thai Martinis on the table before heading back to the bar.

'Drink up, Gemma.' Alfie handed me a glass.

'I've never had one of these before.' Taking a small sip, I was pleasantly surprised, the vodka, lime, lychee liqueur and ginger ale worked well together. 'It's lovely, thank you.'

'My pleasure.' Alfie smiled. 'I'm not making excuses for Nathan, but he probably didn't know what he was up against. I can't imagine Mario mentioned that he played poker for a living.'

Nathan knew how I felt about gambling. I'd made myself

very clear, and yet he still continued to do it. He'd allowed it to take over his life, despite the consequences.

'I don't know why I keep defending your husband's actions, but it's possible the game was fixed, especially if there was money involved.'

'How could it have been fixed?'

'Sometimes serious gamblers make sure the odds are stacked against the other player, so it's impossible for them to win.' Alfie laughed.

'Why is that funny?' I asked, holding out the palms of my hands.

'It's not even remotely amusing, but you're looking at me like I've got two heads!'

That was because I was struggling to take it all in. 'So you think Mario cheated, do you?'

'I can't say that for certain, but I'd be surprised if the game wasn't crooked. These so-called professionals pretend to be skilled with a pack of cards, but really they just swindle people out of money for a living.'

That sounded exactly like somebody else I knew. Alfie might not cheat at cards, but he wasn't averse to making money out of other people's misfortune either. Something Nathan and I were experiencing first-hand. I found it interesting that he thought he was different to the likes of Mario Malva. It was unsettling. His comment riled me, and I was tempted to point out the similarity between them but decided to hold my tongue for once.

'How do you think Nathan met Mario?' I asked, looking into Alfie's blue eyes.

'He's a guest at the hotel.'

So it was a chance meeting after all. Or was it? Something

at the back of my mind told me they hadn't met by accident. It was a bit of a coincidence that Mr Malva just happened to be staying in the same hotel as us.

'Apparently, Mario lives in Sicily with his family, and by all accounts, they're very wealthy and powerful, so we don't want to go upsetting them.'

I began digesting what Alfie had just told me. Nathan had a habit of falling in with the wrong crowd, and things were going from bad to worse. I took a deep breath. 'Does Nathan owe money to a Mafia boss?'

'Not any more.'

Flopping back in my chair, I stretched out my neck while thoughts of the trouble we were in whirred around in my mind. Thanks to my husband's reckless behaviour, the amount we owed Alfie was growing bigger with each passing day.

Alfie gestured to the waiter, who promptly arrived at our table. 'Two Thai Martinis,' he said, ordering us another round.

'Not for me, thanks. I'm going to turn in.' I had to stifle a yawn when I replied. I was already feeling the effects of the alcohol without having any more.

'Make that one Thai Martini then.'

Getting up from my seat, I left Alfie to enjoy his cocktail. Plied with too much alcohol, I carefully crossed the parquet floor. The sound of my heels echoed around the high-ceilinged room as I walked towards the lobby. I pressed the button for the lift, but it took an eternity to arrive. It stopped several times as it made its way down from the top floor. It would have been quicker to walk.

When I stepped out of the lift on the fourth floor, Alfie

was waiting for me. I didn't take my eyes off him as he approached me. Pulling me towards him, he kissed me deep and slow in the middle of the corridor.

Without saying a word, Alfie took my hand and led me towards his room. I tried to talk myself out of going with him. It was simple really, all I had to do was walk the other way. It wasn't too late. *Don't do this,* I said to myself. But some of the decisions I made were better than others, and with that in mind, I ignored my own advice.

Once we were outside Alfie's room, I waited for him to enter first before I followed him inside, as my heart pounded against my chest. Closing the door behind us, Alfie gently pushed me back against it and traced the side of my mouth with his thumb. His touch made my pulse quicken, and a rush of excitement flowed through my body when he weaved his fingers into my long brown hair. I knew I should pull away, but my resistance had deserted me.

What the hell was I doing? No matter how pissed off I was with Nathan, it didn't justify me behaving like this. I was married, so I shouldn't be in another man's hotel bedroom, should I? Alfie kissed me, and as I closed my eyes, a huge red flag popped up right in front of me, warning me to get out immediately and never come back. I knew I shouldn't ignore it.

Alfie took my hand and led me over to the bed. 'I want to make love to you,' he said, running his fingers down my neck.

'We shouldn't be doing this.'

'Why not? We're both consenting adults.' Alfie pulled me towards him; I could feel the warmth of his breath on my skin.

I forced myself to look into his eyes. Alfie's tall, broad-shouldered frame had me going weak at the knees. 'I'm married, Alfie, doesn't that bother you?'

Alfie slid his hand around my waist, then lowered it to cup my buttock. 'I want you so much, I can't think of anything else. You've probably realised by now that when I want something, I don't stop until I get it.'

I knew I should pull away, but something was stopping me. So instead of doing the sensible thing, and listening to what my conscience was telling me, I pushed the voice out of my head. I didn't want any guilty thoughts interfering with what was about to happen.

Alfie moved his hands all over my body before lowering me down onto the bed. Towering over me, he took off his suit jacket and tie and slowly began unbuttoning his crisp white shirt. I stared at the toned physique in front of me. That was the moment I knew for certain I was going to be unfaithful to my husband. Alfie took my hand, pulled me onto my feet and unzipped my dress, then slipped it off my shoulders. I reached my hands forward and undid his trousers.

While kissing the side of my neck, Alfie unclasped my bra. As I took in the features of his handsome face, his hand found its way inside my knickers. He slipped his fingers deep inside me, so I wrapped my arms around his neck and pulled him closer to me.

We knew we were on borrowed time, so Alfie took a condom from the bedside cabinet and put it on. He must have sensed my hesitation because he pushed himself inside me before I had a chance to change my mind. Fast and furious was the only way to describe what happened next. As his thrusts came harder and deeper, he tilted my hips up, and I wrapped my legs around his waist, arching my body against his. The fear of being caught was driving my passion. With every thrust he made, tension grew within us until we collapsed together in a tangled mass of limbs. Alfie buried his face in my neck, and I closed my eyes momentarily. I couldn't afford to fall asleep while he lay on top of me.

Alfie rolled onto his back and pulled me towards him. I lay with my head on his chest, listening to his breathing. I thought back to the hotel in Nice. I was sure he was going to rape me that night, but he didn't. I remember him telling me that wasn't his style. Who would have thought that a few months later, I'd be getting into his bed willingly? I definitely didn't see that coming. I never imagined in my wildest dreams anything like this would happen. Deep down, I knew nothing good would come of it.

Lying naked in a hotel bed with a man who wasn't my husband made me feel vulnerable all of a sudden, so I pulled the sheet up over my shoulders. As I lay there, staring into the darkness, I wondered why I hadn't been able to resist Alfie. I'd like to say I was scared to turn him down, but I knew that wasn't true. I was just making excuses.

'That was incredible, Gemma,' Alfie said, kissing the top of my head.

'I should go.' Glancing at the clock, I realised it was two in the morning.

'It's late. Why don't you stay?' Alfie wrapped both arms around me as he shifted onto his side.

'You know I can't.'

Holding the sheet over me, I sat up and gave Alfie one last kiss, then got out of bed. I needed to take a shower so I could remove all traces of him from my body. When I came out of the bathroom, I glanced over my shoulder. Alfie lay on his side, watching my every move.

'You could forget all about going back to your room and stay here with me instead.' Alfie patted the bed next to him.

I let out an exaggerated sigh. 'You know I can't.'

When I started to cross the room, Alfie threw back the sheet and followed me. As I reached to open the door, he put his hand out to stop me. Turning me around to face him, he put his arms around my waist and pressed his naked body against mine.

'Don't go, Gemma.' Alfie began kissing the side of my neck.

I had to go back to my husband's room and pretend this hadn't just happened.

58

Gemma

Lying in bed next to Nathan with my eyes closed, I tried to understand what had driven me to be unfaithful to him. I wasn't sure why I'd ended up sleeping with Alfie. I'd like to blame the alcohol, but I knew that wasn't the only reason.

I wasn't trying to justify my behaviour, but Nathan and I were in a bad place at the moment. I'd had enough of his selfish attitude. I couldn't put up with it any more, and when I make up my mind about something, I don't usually go back on it.

Nathan's gambling was out of control. He could not or would not stop. When it became more important to him than me, something inside me snapped. I wanted to get back at him. He'd hurt me. I think sleeping with Alfie was my way of getting revenge.

I'd never been tempted to cheat on my husband before. I adored him. He was my best friend and meant the world to me. When you were in love with somebody, it was easy to convince yourself there was nothing wrong with your relationship. But recently everything had changed. I couldn't trust him, and a marriage couldn't survive without trust, could it?

I opened my eyes the next morning and saw Nathan lying on his front with his arms pushed under the pillows, watching me. My heartbeat quickened, and now that alcohol wasn't fogging my brain I bitterly regretted sleeping with Alfie. It was like a light had gone on in my head. I realised I'd made a huge mistake. I should never have betrayed my husband no matter what he'd done. Especially not with the man who had turned us both into criminals.

'Good morning.' Nathan reached across and kissed my cheek.

'Morning,' I replied, clearing my throat, my mouth was so dry my voice sounded croaky.

'I'm sorry about yesterday, Gem. Do you forgive me?' A slow smile spread across Nathan's handsome face as he looked at me from under his lashes.

Consumed by guilt, I turned away, breaking eye contact. Nathan was asking for my forgiveness. If he only knew what had happened last night. But I couldn't let myself think about that now; he was waiting for me to answer his question. 'That depends...'

'Depends on what?' Nathan took hold of my hand.

I looked sideways at him and shrugged. 'I think you know...' Folding my arms across my chest, I stared into the middle distance.

Nathan ran his fingers through his thick, dark hair and

edged closer to me. 'Listen, Gemma, if it's any consolation, I didn't know Mario was a professional when I agreed to play poker with him. I honestly thought I'd beat him. Otherwise, I wouldn't have got involved.'

'You don't get it, do you?' I turned to face Nathan and paused, knowing anger was about to seep into my words. 'That's the whole problem: you always think you're going to win, but you never do.'

Nathan cast his eyes down; I could see he was upset.

'You've got to stop doing this. Every time you gamble, you lose money. We'll never get out of debt if you don't give up.'

'I promise I'll try.'

Nathan had a habit of making promises he never kept. But he'd been the most important person in my life for such a long time, I was scared to be without him, even if it meant putting up with his selfish behaviour.

'You've got no willpower, so you need to stay away from temptation,' I lectured. It was hypocritical of me to say that after the way I behaved last night.

Our conversation was interrupted when my phone lit up. It began buzzing on the bedside table as a new message came through, so I picked it up.

I miss you already. Come back to my room and let me show you how much.

Panic coursed through my veins as I stared at the screen. I was terrified Nathan would see it.

'Is it from Alfie?' Nathan asked, trying to look over my shoulder.

'Yes.' I hoped he wouldn't notice the anxious tone in my voice. Tensing my jaw, I turned off the phone and tossed it back onto the table.

'What did he say?'

'He wants to see me.'

'Why?' Nathan looked me in the eye.

I could feel my pulse quicken. 'He didn't say.' I threw back the covers and got out of bed, hoping that I'd delivered the lie convincingly enough so that Nathan wouldn't suspect anything.

'Do you want me to come with you?' Nathan got up and dragged his fingers through his hair.

'No, why don't you go and order our breakfast? I won't be long.'

Alfie threw open the door and pulled me into his arms, before burying his face in my hair. 'What took you so long?' he asked before kissing the side of my neck. 'Thanks for coming.'

'You say that like I had a choice in the matter. What the hell do you think you're doing?' I pushed him away.

Alfie looked at me with a puzzled expression on his face. 'What's wrong with you?'

'In future, don't send texts like that to my phone. Nathan could have seen it.' Inwardly I was seething.

'Do I look like I give a shit if Nathan finds out?' Alfie shouted, stepping closer to me. His voice was full of anger.

'Well, I do and next time you've got something to say to me, don't bother getting in my face.' I stared into Alfie's blue eyes.

Alfie took a step back from me. 'You didn't seem very worried about Nathan last night when you were writhing naked in my bed.'

Alfie's words sucked the air out of the room.

'Last night was a one-off. It was a mistake.' I forced myself to stay calm, but I was riled up by his comment and the smug look on his face.

Alfie smirked. 'You sound quite convincing. But I know you'll change your mind.'

Alfie was very sure of himself, which probably explained why I'd felt inexplicably drawn to him. His confidence was attractive, and he was a good-looking man, so you couldn't help but notice him the minute he entered the room. But I meant what I said. I was never going to sleep with him again. What I'd done was wrong. 'I was drunk and angry. I shouldn't have slept with you to get back at Nathan.'

'So you used me. Thanks for clearing that up.'

'I'm sorry.'

Alfie closed the gap between us. 'Your concern is very touching. I have to say you're a class act, Gemma.'

'Thanks for the compliment.' I couldn't stop the sarcasm from seeping into my tone. 'I have to go. Nathan's waiting.'

'Nathan's no threat to me. He's a piece of shit. You're not going anywhere.' Alfie pushed past me and blocked the door. 'I thought you were going to wrap those long legs around me again, not dump me.'

What I wouldn't give to turn back the clock. 'You need to forget that anything happened between us.' I struggled to keep my words steady.

'I can't do that. I love you, Gemma. Isn't it obvious?' Alfie threw his arms tightly around me and gave me a lingering hug.

I honestly had no idea he felt like that. In my mind, we'd just shared a drunken one-night stand. As Alfie's words penetrated my brain, I tried to make sense of them. But I couldn't think straight. What the hell had I done? I could feel panic rising within me, and I had to summon every bit of strength I had to be able to reply calmly.

I wriggled out of his embrace and looked him in the eye. 'I'm sorry, Alfie, but I love my husband.' I hoped I didn't sound as flustered as I felt.

Alfie's eyes bored into mine as he registered what I'd just said. Then he leant forward and whispered in my ear. 'But I wonder if he'd still love you if he knew what I did to you last night. You enjoyed every minute of it, so don't pretend you didn't.'

I fixed my eyes dead ahead and tried to swallow the huge lump that had suddenly appeared in my throat. Even though I wasn't looking at him, I knew Alfie was watching me. I could feel his blue eyes scanning every inch of my body. Eventually, Alfie stepped away from the door.

'I think we both know you will end up in my bed again. It's only a matter of time.'

'Don't bet on it. I can assure you I won't make the same mistake twice.' I pasted on a fake smile.

'We'll see.' Alfie winked.

Alfie delivered his reply in such a confident manner it immediately got my back up. But I needed to put an end to this conversation, and I didn't want him to know he'd bothered me. So I shrugged off his comment, stepped past him and walked along the corridor. As I made my way to the restaurant, his words began to get under my skin.

59

Alfie

It was funny how things turned out, wasn't it? If Gemma had shown any interest in me in the beginning, who knows what would have happened. I might not have pursued her at all. It was much more exciting to go after a woman who wasn't interested in you and turn that around. Nobody wanted an easy lay, did they? But I could hardly accuse Gemma of that.

When I'd got the long-awaited nod last night, and Gemma ended up in my bed, I thought all my Christmases had come at once. All the hard work had finally paid off. I'd been trying to woo her for months now and genuinely thought she'd fallen for me. How could I have read the situation so wrong? I was usually a good judge of character. Gemma obviously wasn't. Otherwise, she'd have seen through Nathan years ago. For the life of me, I couldn't understand how a loser like Nathan held on to a woman like Gemma. He was punching way above his weight.

Nathan stumbled from one disaster to another while

Gemma followed in his wake, picking up the pieces. He didn't appreciate her and took her for granted. I would have loved the opportunity to show her what life would be like with me. I would treat her like royalty, which is nothing less than she deserved. I'd give her the world if she'd let me.

Surely the quickest way to corrode a relationship was to neglect your partner, but Nathan did that to Gemma on a daily basis, and she was still prepared to stay with him. I couldn't get my head around that. The phrase *happy wife, happy life* was lost on their marriage. They should have been equally invested in their relationship. Neither of them should have been more important than the other. Nathan seemed to have lost sight of that. He never took her feelings into consideration when he made decisions without consulting her, and yet Gemma showed him unwavering loyalty.

I wasn't going to walk away from her that easily. After what happened last night, I knew she had feelings for me no matter how much she tried to deny it. She might not want to act on them at the moment because of Nathan. But it was only a matter of time until she questioned their future again. Nathan needed to sort himself out if he wanted to hold on to his wife.

I could respect Gemma's wishes and forget anything had happened between us, but I wasn't going to do that. Nothing worth having comes easy. If I persevered, I was sure in time I could win her over. I just needed to make her realise she would be better off cutting Nathan adrift. Every king needed a queen, and if I was able to convince Gemma to leave Nathan, I would never let her go. She had my heart for as long as she wanted it.

60

Gemma

'You were a long time,' Nathan said when I sat down at the table.

Before I had a chance to answer him, my phone buzzed in my hand as a text came through from Alfie.

You're going shopping this afternoon.

There was no way I was going to agree to that, so I sent my reply.

No, I'm not.

Would you like to reconsider?

No.

Then I'll have to tell Nathan about last night.

I knew Alfie would carry out his threat if I didn't do what he wanted. He might as well be holding a gun to my head.

Are you trying to blackmail me?

Meet me in the lobby in an hour.

'What's the matter, Gemma?' Nathan asked, reaching over the table to touch my hand.

I stopped staring at the phone and looked up at him. 'Alfie wants me to go shopping.'

'That's ridiculous. I hope you told him you wouldn't. The police are onto you,' Nathan said, studying my face for a reaction.

I let out a long breath. 'I know that, but you know what Alfie's like. He wouldn't take no for an answer.'

'We'll see about that,' Nathan said, pushing his chair back from the table and standing up.

'Wait,' I said, louder than I'd intended. 'I've already told him I'll do it.' Getting to my feet, I went to stand next to my husband.

Pulling my hair back over my shoulder, Nathan whispered into my ear. 'It's too dangerous, Gemma. I can't let you go through with this.'

'I'm going to wear a disguise.'

Nathan shook his head.

'We don't have a choice. I'm sure I don't need to remind you that we're up to our necks in debt. We're not in a position to refuse.'

I felt a pang of guilt as Nathan broke eye contact with me. I couldn't tell him the real reason I had to go through with it.

Alfie was waiting for me in the lobby, and as I approached him, I could feel him undressing me with his eyes. I suddenly wished I'd worn something else. When I stopped next to him, I began self-consciously pulling down the hem of the black and white patterned dress.

'You look nice. That dress was a good choice – it really hugs your curves.' Alfie nodded his approval.

I smoothed down the clingy fabric and felt the hairs on the back of my neck rise. It seemed to take forever to walk the short distance to the jewellery store. On reflection, a wiggle dress probably wasn't the smartest thing for me to wear. It hindered the movement of my legs, and I would be in trouble if I needed to make a quick getaway. Stopping close to Bulgari, Alfie pointed out the entrance.

Making my way inside the shop, I quickly located the item Alfie was after. The overzealous assistant with the hairiest knuckles I'd ever seen couldn't do enough to accommodate me.

'I hope you don't mind me asking, but do I know you from somewhere?' He grinned.

'No,' I replied. The assistant's question sent my heart rate soaring.

'It's just you look very familiar. Perhaps I've seen you in a movie.'

'I'm not an actress.' I laughed, flashing the assistant my best smile as my pulse pounded wildly under my skin. But that wasn't strictly true. At this moment, I was playing the part of a wealthy socialite, wasn't I?

'I understand. I hope my behaviour hasn't caused you

any embarrassment. Please be assured, you can rely on my discretion.' The assistant touched the side of his nose with a forefinger.

That was almost enough to make me lose the plot. If it hadn't been for Alfie's threat, I would have abandoned the shopping trip immediately. But instead, I had to continue to play the part until I had the twenty-five-carat diamond ring Alfie wanted in my possession.

I got into the Mercedes and shut the door behind me. 'I'm not doing that again, it's too dangerous.' I sat down next to Alfie and glared at him.

'Let me see the ring.'

Nathan sat behind Tommy with his arms folded across his chest, looking out of the tinted glass. He didn't even glance in my direction. I'd just risked everything to carry out another job. It was his fault I was an international jewel thief, and the fact that he didn't have the decency to acknowledge me made me see red. I was about to have words with him, but before I could, Alfie interrupted.

'This little beauty is worth one and a half million euros.' Alfie held the yellow diamond in his hand and inspected it from every angle.

'Let me guess, Terry will give us ten per cent of that,' I said with a bitter edge to my words.

'That's still a lot of money.' Alfie turned in his seat and patted my thigh.

I pushed his hand away and looked him straight in the eye. What the hell was he playing at? Nathan was sitting on the other side of him. He had overstepped the mark. Alfie smiled and studied my expression. I felt the colour rush to my cheeks, so I turned away to break eye contact from his intense blue stare.

'The assistant recognised me from somewhere, but luckily he couldn't put his finger on where he'd seen me before.'

Alfie's face broke into a grin. 'He probably thought you were a celebrity because he'd never expect you to be a thief.'

I shot Alfie a look. 'The man in the jeweller's was convinced he knew me. What if he puts two and two together?'

'Listen, Gemma, you've got nothing to worry about. In the last couple of days, your face has appeared on every TV channel, and he still couldn't place you.'

'Is that meant to reassure me?' I tried not to let my voice quaver when I replied.

'Of course it is. Even though your picture has been circulated by the police, you still managed to walk right out the door of a high-profile jeweller's with another ring today.' Alfie threw his head back and laughed.

'I'm glad you find it funny.' I clenched my teeth together to try and suppress the anger that was building inside me.

'It's more than funny, it's hilarious, Gemma. So much for the industry being on high alert.'

Even though Alfie had tried to convince me that I was still under the radar, I felt the police were getting closer to catching me. I could sense it. I glanced across at Nathan, but he was still staring out the window as the conversation carried on around him. I turned my head so I could look at Alfie. He was leaning back on the leather seat, smiling broadly, looking like a man without a care in the world. If only the same could be said about me. I was finding this line of work so stressful, it was becoming detrimental to my health.

61

Gemma

It had just started snowing in Milan when Tommy drove the car onto the motorway and headed north, away from the city. Staring into the distance, I sat in silence. My head was spinning. It was only a matter of time before the police caught me. Knowing I was on the verge of going to jail over something I'd been forced into doing was difficult for me to accept.

'For the rest of the journey, we're going to be travelling along narrow mountain roads. I'll need to put snow chains on the tyres,' Tommy said, looking over his shoulder at Alfie as soon as we left the motorway.

Tommy got out of the car. While he fitted the chains, nobody said a word. The only sound in the car was the engine idling. We were soon back on the road, and to try and take my mind off things, I looked at the spectacular mountain scenery of the Aosta Valley as it whipped past the window. Breathtaking views of the unspoilt landscape and snow-laden trees were around every corner.

We stopped for lunch at the Alpine resort of Courmayeur, at the foot of Mont Blanc. I was glad to be out of the car. Despite the cold and the fact that I wasn't dressed appropriately for the December weather, it was a pleasure to walk around the snow-covered cobbled streets of the old town.

'What's up?' Alfie said. 'You haven't said a word since we left Milan.' A muscle twitched in his jaw as he studied my reaction.

'I'm absolutely freezing. I need to go and put something warmer on.' I lowered my chin and wrapped my arms around myself to try and prevent my body heat from escaping.

Alfie had ordered stone-baked pizzas while I'd been changing into jeans, a jumper and a down-filled coat.

When I put my hand on the back of the chair, Nathan turned to face me and was about to say the seat was taken when he realised it was me. Managing a half-smile, I sat down at the table with the others and took a sip of red wine. I suppose it was reassuring to know that even my husband did a double-take when he saw me.

'What do you think of Courmayeur?' Alfie asked as we made our way back to the car.

'It's beautiful. Are we going to drive over the Alps?' I asked. Travelling across an unspoilt winter landscape like that is something I've always wanted to do. If I was going to be spending the foreseeable future locked behind bars, there was no better time to start crossing things off my bucket list.

'I'm afraid not,' Alfie replied.

I shouldn't have been surprised really. That's the story of my life at the moment: one disappointment after another.

As we approached the mouth of the tunnel in northwest Italy, the dramatic snow-covered peak of Mont Blanc looked spectacular set against a backdrop of clear blue sky. But when Tommy began driving through the mountain, we lost the incredible scenery. For thirty-five tedious minutes, the only view we had was one of fire extinguishers and emergency telephones. The journey couldn't end soon enough for my liking. It felt like we'd been stuck inside for hours.

'Have you ever been skiing, Gemma?' Alfie asked, turning to face me as we emerged in sun-washed Chamonix.

'No, the idea's never appealed to me.' I put my hand up to shield myself from a burst of late afternoon sunshine that suddenly hit me in the eye.

'I bet you'd enjoy the après-ski though.' Alfie winked, then flashed me a bright smile. 'Tommy, see if they've got any vacancies, will you?' Alfie leant forward in his seat and pointed towards the Hotel Mont Blanc in the centre of the town.

A tense atmosphere spread between us as Nathan stood in front of the full-length window of our junior suite that overlooked the pool and Mont Blanc. As he stared at the snow-covered mountains, I wondered if he could sense that I didn't want to be alone with him. Turning to face me, he silently studied me, then took a step towards me.

'You're angry with me, aren't you?' Nathan paused for a moment before reaching for my hand.

Immediately, a lump built up in my throat, and I found myself fighting the urge to burst into tears. My mouth clamped shut. There was no tactful way to answer that question. I couldn't tell him how I felt without us ending up in a fight. I remained tight-lipped for an uncomfortable amount of time. He knew me well enough to know I was giving him the silent treatment. But as frustration built up inside me, I couldn't hold it in any longer. 'I'm wanted by the police. How do you think I feel?'

Nathan released my hand and clasped his fingers at the back of his neck. 'I've been so stupid. I should have known something like this would happen. Everyone told me to stay away from Alfie, but I didn't listen.'

Nathan's dark eyes searched mine while he waited for me to speak, but I had nothing to say and felt suffocated by the silence. I had to get out of the room. I couldn't stay and watch Nathan's Oscar-winning self-pitying performance. Did he expect me to feel sorry for him after what he'd put me through?

When I stepped out into the corridor, tears sprang into my eyes and trickled down my cheeks. As I walked, my tears flowed freely, and I struggled to hold it together. I leant against the window in the lobby and watched a magical sight. Steam was rising from the bright blue outdoor pool, while snow fell all around it. I wondered what it would be like to swim in water as warm as a bath when the air around you was below zero.

'It's beautiful, isn't it?' Alfie said as he came to a stop beside me.

'Yes,' I replied, still gazing at the pool and the view of the alpine scenery beyond it. Mont Blanc looked spectacular bathed in shades of pink by the setting sun. The mountain seemed to possess hypnotic qualities. As I watched the colours change, for a moment, I almost forgot all my troubles.

'Why have you been crying?' When Alfie touched my cheek with his fingertips, he brought me out of my daydream. 'Nathan's upset you again, hasn't he? I've had enough of this. I'm going to sort him out.'

'Please don't.' I met Alfie's blue eyes with a panicked stare. I knew he was serious, and much as I was furious with Nathan, I didn't want to see him come to any harm.

Dinner had been pure torture tonight. An awkward atmosphere hung in the air. The whole time we were eating, Alfie was eyeballing Nathan, silently challenging him, looking for any opportunity to start a fight. Nathan responded by drinking himself into oblivion while the rest of us sat back and watched. This evening couldn't be over soon enough for me.

'I'm going to bed,' I said, pushing my chair back from the table.

'Wait for me, Gem,' Nathan slurred, stumbling to his feet.

I walked out of the restaurant, while behind me, Nathan was doing the drunken stagger of a man who'd had a few too many. Bundling him into the lift, I pressed the button for the third floor, then guided him along the corridor, to stop him from bumping into the walls. I opened our door and then helped my intoxicated husband get into bed. I wasn't happy. What a waste of an evening. But the only blessing was, as soon as his head hit the pillow, Nathan fell sound asleep.

A knock on the door made me jump, and I hurried to open it, in case it woke Nathan. Alfie stood in the corridor, holding a bottle of champagne and two long-stemmed glasses.

'Care to join me?' he asked, leaning against the doorframe.

My head said, 'no chance,' but that's not what came out of my mouth. 'OK.' I knew I shouldn't go to Alfie's room alone, but I wanted to get him as far away from Nathan as possible.

Once inside Alfie's suite, he popped the cork, poured a steady stream of tiny bubbles into a glass and handed it to me.

'I want to get to know you. Tell me about yourself, Gemma.'

Alfie ran a smooth finger under my jaw, and I flinched at his touch. Without taking his eyes off me, he took a seat in one of the plush velvet armchairs and relaxed into it. I sat down opposite him, bolt upright, feeling like I was about to be interviewed for a job.

'What do you want to know?'

'Everything. Start at the beginning. Where did you grow up?'

'London,' I replied, as I watched the bubbles in my glass race each other to the surface.

Alfie laughed. 'You don't give much away, do you? London's a big place. What part?'

'Richmond.'

'Very nice, so you grew up rubbing shoulders with Mick Jagger and the likes, did you?'

'Hardly.' I swallowed down my anxiety lump. I knew Alfie wanted the warts and all full-length version of my life, but I was struggling to suppress my nerves, so all I could give him was one-word answers. I kept having flashbacks to the night I'd slept with him.

'Daddy must have a few quid then?'

I shrugged and hoped he wouldn't probe any further.

'Come on, Gemma, what's the big secret? If you'd said you grew up in Tower Hamlets, I'd let it drop, but your family obviously have money. Tell me about them.'

I let out a long sigh. 'There's not much to tell.' I didn't want to go into details. If I told him about my childhood, it would sound like I was having a one-woman pity party, and I didn't want his sympathy.

'Are you an only child?'

'No… I have a sister,' I offered reluctantly.

Alfie straightened his posture. 'So tell me about her. Is she older or younger?'

'Rebecca's two years younger than me. She's married and has two perfect children.' I tried to keep my tone light when I handed over the information but felt like I'd just introduced myself at an alcoholics anonymous meeting.

Alfie laughed. 'Correct me if I'm wrong, but I'm sensing there's some underlying tension between you two. Don't tell me she's the golden child and your parents constantly compare you to each other.'

He'd hit the nail on the head, but I wasn't about to give him the satisfaction of knowing that. Rebecca had become a clone of my parents, and because I wasn't, they thought I was the black sheep of the family. But if you asked me, I was the only normal one. 'Sorry to disappoint you, but that's not the case.'

'So are you two close then?'

'Not really.' I didn't want to add that I hadn't seen her since I got engaged to Nathan twelve years ago when I was eighteen.

'Why not?' Alfie sipped his champagne and studied me like he was analysing me during a counselling session.

'There's no particular reason; we just don't see eye to eye.'

'Doesn't that bother you?'

'No.'

I used to regret the distance between us, but the emotional bond is missing, so you can't force it, can you? I turned my head away, desperate to break free of his interrogating stare. Alfie leant back in his chair and studied me for a moment while finishing the champagne in his glass.

'So if your family are wealthy…' Alfie continued, refilling both our drinks. I knew what was coming next before he even asked the question. 'Why haven't you asked for their help?'

'Because I didn't want to.'

Even in the depths of my despair, I wasn't tempted to reach out to my family. Severing the ties of the toxic relationship that brought me nothing but angst was the best thing I'd ever done. I'd never regretted my decision for one minute. The experience had been empowering, and no matter how desperate things had become recently, I knew that making peace with them wasn't the answer. Alfie's intrusion into my private life was irritating me. I couldn't wait for the probing questions to stop.

'Are you always this guarded?'

'I'm not guarded.'

'So let me in on the secret then. Tell me why you didn't ask Mummy and Daddy to bail you out. There must be more to it.'

I could tell him the real reason, but I knew I wasn't going to. I didn't want Alfie to know that my family cut me off because they were disappointed in my choice of partner. They didn't approve of Nathan and thought he was a liability. My parents told me that if I married him, they would write me out of their will. That was fine by me; I didn't want their money. I hadn't had any contact with them since that day, and I had no desire to rekindle our relationship. I was better off without them in my life.

'It's a long story.'

'Luckily for you, I've got time to hear it.'

I let out another sigh and sat in silence for several minutes, hoping he'd get the message. I didn't want to talk about it, but I could see Alfie wasn't going to let it drop.

'In all honesty, we didn't expect the debt to spiral out of control the way it did. When Nathan first borrowed the money, we didn't know you were going to keep increasing the interest rate. If you hadn't, we'd have paid off the debt by now. Anyway, I prefer to do things my way. If I allow someone to help me, it means I lose control of the situation.' My barrier was firmly back in place.

'I'm impressed that you don't go running to your parents to fix your problems. You're fiercely independent, aren't you?' Alfie's face broke into a grin.

'I suppose I am.' I shrugged my shoulders. 'I was taught to stand on my own two feet from an early age,' I admitted.

'I can see that.' Alfie nodded. 'You've been brought up on tough love.' Alfie crossed his arms and looked at me.

My eyes began to mist up when I thought about it. If only he knew how true that statement was. 'It hasn't done me any harm.' Hopefully, if I told myself that enough times, I'd start to believe it.

'That still doesn't explain why you didn't borrow the money from your parents in the beginning.'

Alfie was like a dog with a bone. He was never going to let this drop, but no matter how much he persisted, I wasn't going to tell him the truth. 'I'd never ask for their help because they'd see it as a sign of weakness.'

'You're not weak, Gemma; but you're stubborn. Look at the situation you're in because you were too proud to ask Daddy to open his wallet.'

'I'd rather be in this situation than ask for a handout.'

'I don't know what to say. I can't believe you've put yourself through all of this instead of just asking for your family's help. Poor little rich girl.' Alfie threw his head back and laughed.

I felt the hairs stand up on the back of my neck, so I pushed my chair back from the table and stood up. 'I would never stoop so low as to ask them for money.' The words tasted bitter. Sometimes I hide behind a bolshie exterior because I have a deep-seated fear of not being good enough. Other people's disapproval terrifies me. I have my parents to thank for that.

'I was only joking,' Alfie said. Reaching up, he covered my hand with his, realising he'd overstepped the mark.

I pulled my hand away and gave him the evil eye. After taking a deep breath, I sat back down and continued to speak. 'It was never an option to ask them for money, so do me a favour and just drop it.' I needed to steer him onto a different subject. I didn't want to have this conversation. 'I told you about my family, why don't you tell me about yours?'

Alfie wagged a finger at me and the corners of his mouth lifted. 'All in good time.'

Taking that as my cue to leave, I stood up from my seat and glanced at my watch. It was late. 'I should go.'

'What's the hurry?' Alfie said, taking another bottle of champagne out of the ice bucket and popping the cork.

Alfie was making me flustered, so I weaved my fingers through my hair and swept it back into a ponytail. Then I let it fall over my shoulders, hoping I'd appear relaxed. Alfie put the bottle down, pulled me towards him, and placed his hands on the table either side of me, pinning me in front of him.

'Are you sure I can't persuade you to stay?' he whispered in my ear.

Alfie's breath felt hot on my neck. He ran his fingers up my thigh. Panic gripped me with an iron fist when he slipped his hand under my dress and pulled my knickers down. It was all happening so quickly. One minute we were talking and the next he was taking my clothes off. It was time to leave.

I couldn't betray Nathan again, so I pushed him away as hard as I could before retrieving my underwear from the floor. I felt like a hooker. Alfie raised an eyebrow and studied me intently as if he was trying to see what was going on in my mind. I was all fingers and thumbs as I hurried to put my underwear back on. Alfie kept eye contact with me while he poured us both a drink. He gave me a lust-filled look as he handed me the glass.

'You asked me about my family earlier, what do you want to know?' Alfie said carrying on as if nothing had happened.

I didn't want to engage in small talk with Alfie, I wanted to go back to my room. But I knew if I didn't tread carefully, he'd make sure Nathan would find out that we'd slept together. So I pasted on a false smile and took a sip of my drink instead.

'Everything, but I'll settle for whatever you're willing to tell me.'

Alfie laughed. 'That's a good answer. Let's start with Rosa. My dad was in love with her. He never gave a shit about my mum the whole time they were married, because he was obsessed with Rosa.' Alfie knocked back the contents of his glass. 'He'd make us sit in the restaurant for hours on end when we were kids just so he could be near her.'

'Mamma Donatella's?' I asked, raising an eyebrow.

'Yeah, my dad owns the place.' Alfie refilled our champagne then sat down on the velvet chair.

'I always thought it belonged to Donatella and Bernardo.'

'No, it happens to be one of Jethro Watson's legitimate businesses.'

His answer brought another question to my mind. 'Does Nathan know your dad owns it?'

Alfie shrugged his shoulders. 'I doubt it.'

I smiled across at Alfie. 'You were so tight-lipped about how you knew Rosa. I thought there was going to be a mysterious dark secret behind it, not a simple case of infatuation.'

Alfie glanced up and met my eye. 'There's a bit more to the story than that.'

'Don't keep me in suspense then.' I was eager to hear more.

Alfie smiled. 'Maybe some other time.'

62

Gemma

Nathan was sitting up in bed, waiting for me when I open the door of our suite. My heart began pounding when I saw him. I thought he'd still be asleep.

'Where have you been?' Nathan asked in the tone of an angry father.

'I went for a walk.'

'Dressed like that! There's snow on the ground, Gemma.'

Realising the red satin cocktail dress and high court shoes I was wearing had exposed me as a liar, I had little option but to offer another explanation. I couldn't tell him where I'd been. 'If you must know I was having a drink with Alfie and Tommy,' I snapped, feeling the need to fabricate the truth. Hopefully, Nathan wouldn't be suspicious if he thought the three of us had been together.

'Until five o'clock in the morning?'

Nathan went silent. I was sure he didn't believe me. The way he stared at me with his sad, dark eyes made me nervous. Doubt was written all over his face. I lay down next to him and turned onto my side, so I didn't have to look at him. I knew I wouldn't be able to sleep; my mind was buzzing, replaying the conversation we'd just had. My gut instinct told me Nathan knew about Alfie. Why had I cheated on him? I might have been drunk, but what was I thinking of?

For a huge portion of my life, Nathan had been the only person who mattered to me. I was seventeen when we met, and within two months we'd moved in together, much to my parents' horror. He gave my self-esteem a much-needed transfusion, filling my heart with so much happiness, it lifted me up and made everything better.

I lay in the darkness, trying to sleep when the phone on the bedside table buzzed as a new message came through.

You and Nathan have got no future together. Come to my room. We need to talk x

'What does he want now?' Nathan asked.
'He didn't say, but he wants to see me.'

Hurry up, Gemma x

My feet dragged along the corridor as I made my way back to Alfie's room. I didn't want to go, but I was scared he'd tell Nathan about us if I didn't.

When Alfie opened his door, his eyes lit up at the sight of me. He pulled me into the room and tried to kiss the side of my neck. I swerved sideways and stepped back to put some distance between us.

I let out a long sigh. It was hard living a double life. I hated lying to my husband. My emotions were engaged in an internal battle. Would he forgive me if I came clean and told him I'd had a drunken one-night stand with Alfie? Deep down, I knew the answer. It would destroy him if he found out.

'Things would be a lot easier for you and me with Nathan out of the picture. Have you ever thought about leaving him?'

I stared at Alfie with wide eyes. I thought I'd made it clear that there was no us. I wasn't going to leave my husband for him. Nathan was my first serious boyfriend. We'd become so ingrained in each other over the years, as far as I was concerned – in spite of my recent doubts – splitting up wasn't an option. I just hoped if Nathan found out he would agree with me.

The pulse began pounding in my temple. I couldn't bear to think about losing the love of my life. It was true our marriage was in trouble, and I'd spent a worrying amount of time questioning our future before I'd ended up in Alfie's bed. But I knew now I'd slept with him in a moment of madness. I'd made a terrible mistake, and I bitterly regretted cheating on my husband. It had made me realise how important Nathan was to me, and the last thing I wanted was for us to go our separate ways.

'I can give you the best of everything; you'll never have to worry about money ever again.'

There was more to life than money. Everything was crystal clear in my mind now. I wanted to get my marriage back on track and stay with my husband. I didn't want to be with Alfie. The most frightening thing about all of this was I knew he was going to use the fact that we'd had sex as a weapon against me. Why had I been so stupid?

'I'll make sure you have an amazing life,' Alfie said.

I knew he was waiting for me to speak. The problem was I couldn't think of anything to say, so the silence dragged on. I needed some space to try and process my thoughts. I looked back at Alfie as I left his room, and he flashed me a pure white smile.

63

Gemma

Clearing my throat, I prepared to drop a bombshell. I had something on my mind, and I needed to get it off my chest. 'Have you got a minute?' I said when Alfie opened the door of his room later that day.

'Of course.'

'I just wanted to let you know that as of now I'm retiring from my life of crime. I'm not working for you again.' I wiped the palms of my hands on my dress while I waited for his reply.

'No problem.' Alfie placed his hand over mine.

I'd been dreading having this conversation with him, but his response surprised me. He'd taken the news better than I'd expected. He was obviously eager to please me.

Alfie gave me a lingering look and slid his hands around my waist. I wriggled out of his grasp and took up a new position out of arm's reach. Did this man never give up? I should have known he'd expect some kind of repayment.

'You know, the main reason I kept increasing Nathan's debt was so I could be near you.'

His comment got under my skin. Tensing my jaw, I searched for a suitable reply, but couldn't find the right words. There was nothing I could say to describe how I felt. As anger built up inside me, I struggled to contain it.

'You're mad at me now, aren't you?'

Alfie read the look on my face correctly. I'd never been good at hiding my feelings. As I went to answer him, he cut me off by raising the palm of his hand.

'Look at this from my point of view: if I'd let you pay back the money and you were free to go, you wouldn't have stayed, would you?' Alfie scanned my face for a reaction.

He was right; I would have gone home at the first opportunity. But thanks to him, that wasn't an option now. I was wanted by the police in multiple countries, so I'd never be able to return to my old life. The realisation of that made me feel hollow inside.

'In my line of work, life can be short. You have to make the most of every day because you never know when it might be over.'

'What a sobering thought.'

'Travelling the world, staying in the best hotels isn't everyone's cup of tea. It can be tough living a life of luxury, but I find it's one way to spend my money. Do you want kids?' Alfie asked, completely out of the blue.

I wanted nothing more than to be a mother, and although I was thirty now, I was no closer to fulfilling that dream. Perhaps I would be if I'd listened to my parents and married a wealthy businessman like they'd wanted me to. They were determined to control my choice of partner and turn me into a clone of themselves. Money breeds money, so they say. But I told them I would never marry for money; I'd only settle for love.

Rosa could see Nathan and I were infatuated with each other, so she let me move into their rented flat, around the corner from Mamma Donatella's, two months after we met. My parents were disgusted that she was allowing us to live together under her roof, and this made our strained relationship even worse. I'd naively thought if I put some distance between us, it might improve matters, but I couldn't have been more wrong. It made everything ten times worse.

When we got engaged on my eighteenth birthday, it was the final nail in the coffin. My parents were disappointed in my choice. They were convinced Nathan was a gold digger. They threatened to cut me off and write me out of their will if I went ahead with the wedding. They made it clear: I had to choose between them and Nathan. I chose Nathan. We married a year later. None of my family came to the wedding.

'Why the long pause?' Alfie studied me.

'Yes, I'd like a family,' I replied, hoping my eyes didn't tear over and give away how strongly I felt about it.

'So why haven't you started one?' Alfie arched his brow. 'You're not getting any younger.'

I bristled at his comment, well aware of the fact that women only have a small window of opportunity for these things. Having children was something I wanted more than anything.

Alfie stepped towards me. 'I can see how important this is to you. Why put it off?'

I wondered how it could be so obvious to Alfie, and yet, my husband had never noticed how much starting a family meant to me. I listened to my biological clock ticking while I wrapped my arms around myself for comfort. Although I didn't want Alfie to know my business, the words were out of my mouth before I could stop them.

'Nathan wants to wait. He thinks having children will be too much of a financial sacrifice at the moment.'

I regretted saying that to Alfie as soon as I'd finished the sentence. I knew it was a cop-out. The real reason we hadn't started a family had nothing to do with money, no matter what Nathan said. It was because my husband refused to grow up. He was still a child himself, and a spoilt one at that.

'And his failed business ventures make financial sense, do they?' Alfie shook his head. 'Look at all the things you've had to sacrifice for him, and he repays you by taking away your chance to be a mother.'

'I think it's a bit premature for me to grieve for the children I will never have.' I hope I sounded more convincing than I felt.

'Maybe it is. But you've got to admit Nathan's not treating you very well.'

That was none of his business. But he was right. I could see right through what he was up to. Stirring the pot came naturally to Alfie.

'Nathan's number-one priority should be to make you happy, not miserable.'

'I'm not miserable.'

'You've got a face like a slapped arse, Gemma.'

'And you've got such a lovely way with words, I can't

help being flattered by the compliment,' I replied, unable to hide my sarcastic tone.

'When you leave Nathan, you could start a family with me instead,' Alfie said as if we had a rosy future ahead of us.

Being skilled at manipulating a situation, Alfie wasted no time offering me what he knew I wanted more than anything. I looked him in the eye so he'd realise I was serious. 'You can forget that idea. I'm never going to leave Nathan.'

'You will,' Alfie said with an air of confidence.

64

Gemma

It felt like every time I turned on the TV, my description was being aired. Realising I was finding this unsettling, Alfie decided a change of tactics was in order.

'We're heading to Switzerland,' he said when we took our seats in the car. 'It's only an hour away from France, but it'll give us a base in a different country while the cops are sniffing around.'

The thought of the police closing in on us made my pulse race, but there was nothing I could do about it. My fate was in Alfie's hands.

The drive wasn't at all what I'd expected. Instead of us travelling along a high alpine pass, on a road winding between snow-capped mountains, we spent the entire time on the motorway. But when the Mercedes came to a stop by Lake Geneva, the journey soon became a distant memory.

I stood for a moment on the shore of the crystal-clear lake, nestled below the base of the Alps. I breathed in the crisp, clear air. As I watched the swans gliding on the smooth surface of the water, in the bright winter sunshine, I knew this was the kind of view that people wrote home about, and it made me think of Rosa. She would be so worried about us, but there was no way to put her mind at rest. It wasn't possible to contact her as Alfie had confiscated our phones before we left England, and even though he'd given me a mobile to use, he'd told me it was only so I could communicate with him. Every day he checked the handset to make sure no personal calls had been made from it.

'Come on, Gemma, we need to check in,' Alfie said, distracting me from my thoughts.

In complete contrast to our surroundings, La Reserve Hotel resembled a safari lodge. I felt like I was in an African game reserve as we approached the building. Flaming torches burned brightly on either side of the main entrance.

'I'm not sure I want to stay at this place,' Alfie said when we walked into the lobby, and he saw the interior.

'Why not? I love it,' I replied, running my hand over the life-sized elephant that stood by the reception desk.

'It's a bit tacky for a five-star hotel, don't you think?' Alfie continued.

I shrugged my shoulders. 'Like I said, I love it, but it's your call.'

The decor of the colonial-inspired interior certainly wasn't bland. It had loads of unusual, quirky details. Busy walls clashed with loud leopard-print carpeting and hanging from the ceiling were huge glass chandeliers adorned with multi-coloured parrots.

'What are you going to do while I'm working tonight?' Nathan asked, looking me straight in the eye.

'I don't know; I hadn't thought about it.' I turned away and took in the exotic faux-safari décor of our room to break eye contact.

'I'm sure Alfie will be happy to keep you company.'

I could see Nathan's reflection in the window. He clenched his jaw so tight, his cheek rippled.

'What's that supposed to mean?' I asked. Our eyes met for a split second before I turned away and began unpacking, so I didn't have to face him.

I could see Nathan watching me out of the corner of my eye and wondered if he'd guessed that something had happened between us.

'I hope you won't be bored while I'm out.'

'Don't worry about me. I'll find something to do.' I turned to face Nathan and forced myself to smile.

'You could always go to the hotel bar for a drink. I know how much you and Alfie enjoy doing that.'

I gave Nathan a filthy look. 'What's got into you?'

'Do you find him attractive?'

Nathan appeared to be transforming into the green-eyed monster before my very eyes. I knew it wouldn't be long before it reared its ugly head again. Jealousy is a challenging emotion to deal with, so I'd have to choose my words carefully.

'Of course I don't.' I kept my eyes down when I felt the colour rush to my cheeks and hoped it wasn't visible.

Nathan took hold of my hand, pulled me around to face him and his eyes searched mine. 'Tell me the truth, Gemma.'

'There's no reason for you to be jealous, I don't find Alfie attractive.'

Nathan stared at me while he thought about what I'd just said. I'm sure he wanted to believe me, but the look on his face told a different story. My guilt was getting the better of me as we stood watching each other, and for a brief moment, I considered confessing. But if I told the truth, Nathan would go through hell, and although I'd be relieved of the burden, it would be at the expense of his emotional well-being. The last thing I wanted to do was feed his insecurity, so I stayed silent. My heart pounded, as I waited for him to speak. Nathan didn't say another word. Instead, his eyes scanned my face as if it was the last time he was ever going to see me, and the thought of that chilled me to the bone.

65

?

Tommy drove Nathan and Johno from Geneva to Lyon so they could carry out a job for Alfie. He'd discovered through inside information, given to him by his French contact, Jean-Claude, that certain supermarkets funnel cash from their tills, along pneumatic suction tubes, into their safes.

Tommy and the others were scheduled to arrive at midnight. They were going to keep the supermarket under surveillance for approximately an hour, before attempting the break-in. Alfie had come up with a highly organised plan to remove the used banknotes from the safe.

'It's time to go,' Tommy said, checking up and down the street to make sure it was empty.

Wearing ski masks, Nathan and Johno entered the store through an emergency door at the back of the building. They quickly located the heavily armed room that housed the safe. Alfie had worked out it would be much easier to make a hole in the suction tube than in the vault, so Nathan and Johno drilled into the pipe, before attaching a strong vacuum to it. They sucked the money back out of the vault, bypassing all the impenetrable security devices that protected it.

'Let's get out of here,' Nathan said.

Less than ten minutes later, after filling two black holdalls with cash, Nathan and Johno were safely back in the car.

66

Gemma

Troubled by the conversation I'd had with Nathan earlier, I declined Alfie's offer to go for a drink in the bar, deciding to stay in our room instead. I had a lot on my mind and wanted to be alone while I thought things through. Also, it didn't seem right for me to be relaxing with a drink while Nathan was spending his evening breaking into a safe. As I lay on the enormous wooden bed, my phone buzzed. A new text had come through from Alfie.

> You don't know what you're missing. I'm drinking a Mai Tai out of an artificial cow horn!

His text made me smile, but I didn't reply. The last thing I wanted was for Nathan to come back and find Alfie in our room.

I must have fallen asleep but woke with a start when I

heard the bedroom door opening; it was almost four in the morning. I had a horrible feeling it was going to be Alfie, but to my relief, it was Nathan.

'Thank God you're back.' The hardwood floor felt cool under my bare feet as I crossed the room to where he was standing. Reaching up, I placed a kiss on his cheek. 'How did it go?'

'Really well, we walked away with sixty thousand euros in a matter of minutes, so Alfie's happy,' Nathan replied, as a contented smile spread across his face.

'You must be shattered.' Rubbing sleep from my eyes, I tried to stifle a yawn.

'I'm not tired at all. But you look exhausted; Gemma, you should go back to bed.'

'They've just reported the robbery on the news,' Nathan said when I woke later that morning.

Nathan was sprawled out on the luxurious red velvet sofa in the living room of our suite and seemed completely unfazed by what he'd just told me.

'Oh shit!' I clenched my hands in front of my mouth, then covered my lips with my fingertips.

'The manager discovered the break-in when he opened up this morning. There weren't any witnesses, but the CCTV cameras captured everything. They don't have a description of us though because we were wearing ski masks,' Nathan said, flicking through the channels with the remote control.

'I wish I'd seen the report.'

'You didn't miss much. It showed the CCTV footage and it said the police were appealing for information.'

I let out a long breath. 'Aren't you worried you're going to get caught?'

'No. They won't be able to identify us from the footage they've got.'

The hours dragged by with nothing to do apart from stare out of the window at the view of Lake Geneva and the snow-capped mountains beyond. Lying low was becoming hard work. To pass the time while Nathan slept, I decided to go for a wander around the Christmas Village, set up in the grounds of the hotel. Ordering warm waffles and hot chocolate from one of the wooden chalets, I took a seat on a luxurious sofa, covered with faux fur throws, next to the ice rink. Suddenly my phone buzzed as a new text came through from Alfie. My heart sank as I read it.

Pack up your stuff. We're leaving tonight.

'What are we waiting for?' I asked as we sat outside a supermarket in Geneva town centre.

'We're just going to withdraw some money, and then we'll hit the road.' Alfie smirked.

Tommy pulled back his sleeve and checked his watch. 'Are you two ready?'

Nathan and Johno nodded before putting on ski masks. They got out of the car and quickly disappeared behind the building. After what seemed like an eternity, they reappeared carrying two bulging rucksacks. As soon as they closed the door of the Mercedes, Tommy sped off towards the autobahn. Nathan settled back in his seat, pulled off his mask, and sat staring out of the window for most of the three-and-a-half-hour drive.

'If we cross the border from one of the minor roads we'll avoid going through customs,' Alfie said.

Tommy came off the autobahn and drove through a valley filled with pine trees. As we prepared to pass into Germany, I saw a sign at the side of the road.

'Did you see that notice,' I said.

'No,' Alfie replied.

'It said if we have goods to declare, we mustn't cross here.'

'What were you planning on declaring?' Alfie laughed.

'Oh for fuck's sake, there's a roving patrol up ahead,' Tommy said, having spotted it in the distance.

'What are the chances of that? You wouldn't think they'd bother doing random checks at four o'clock in the morning, would you?'

Alfie leant between the front seats so he could get a better look at the checkpoint. He seemed perfectly relaxed, like this was a minor inconvenience. He was so unbothered, anyone would think he'd taken the lid off the biscuit tin and found that somebody had eaten the last chocolate finger. I could feel myself going into meltdown the closer we got. What were we going to do?

'Do you want me to turn around?' Tommy asked.

'No, keep driving and see what happens,' Alfie replied. 'Jean-Claude has assured me that all you have to do is slow down so the guard can check if you have a vignette fixed to your windscreen. Then they'll wave you through without you having to stop.'

Tommy slowly drove the car forward. As we approached

the guard, he peered in the window, then gestured for us to pull over.

'Everyone stay calm. Unless we give the Swiss police good reason to suspect something, we'll be on our way in less than five minutes,' Alfie said.

I hoped he was right. My heart began pounding as the Mercedes came to a stop. When Tommy lowered the window, and the official scanned his eyes around the car's interior, I had to fight back tears and will myself to hold it together. But that was no small task. My mind was whirring as one thought played over and over. If Nathan hadn't been stupid enough to borrow money from an underworld boss in the first place, we wouldn't be mixed up in this now.

Alfie reached for my hand and gave it a squeeze. 'You need to lighten up, Gemma. You look like a dog that's been caught chewing a shoe.'

The guard wanted to know if we had anything to declare. I felt myself freeze. But Tommy didn't hesitate, he shook his head to indicate we had nothing and handed over our passports. I sat in the back, trying not to draw attention to myself, wondering if our time on the run was finally up.

The guard looked at our documents, then turned away from the window and spoke to his colleague in French. Even though I couldn't understand what they were saying, I knew they were suspicious. Otherwise, they would have just waved us through.

'I thought Jean-Claude said they never bother to stop tourists,' Tommy said.

'He did. He told me we'd get waved through. But he also said there wouldn't be any border checkpoint if we stuck to a minor road. I can hear him now. "Just drive over the bridge, Alfie, and you'll see a sign telling you that you've entered Germany." Wait till I get my hands on the fucker.'

Alfie laughed.

'Step out of the car, please.'

The words I'd been dreading were ringing in my ears.

Alfie leant forward in his seat. 'What's the problem, officer?'

'I need to carry out a search of your vehicle.'

Panic gripped me. If he went through my bags, he'd find the jewellery.

'You'll soon be on your way. This will only take a minute.'

Alfie put his hands either side of the driver's headrest and whispered, 'Step on it,' into Tommy's ear.

Tommy shoved the Mercedes into gear and sped away from the checkpoint with screeching tyres. Almost instantly, our car was followed by wailing sirens and flashing lights as the police took up the chase.

Tommy drove at high speed while attempting to outrun them. Turning a sharp corner too quickly, the car swerved and nearly collided with the barrier on the opposite side of the road. Tommy regained control, but when valley fog suddenly engulfed the Mercedes, he accidentally clipped a tree, damaging the front passenger wing. The impact spun the car and almost tipped it over in the process. The sirens intensified behind us. But Tommy managed to pick up speed again, and we crossed the German border into France. Relief swept over me, as the sound of the pursuit faded into the distance. I was sure we were going to get caught.

'Should I head to the nearest underground car park and ditch the Mercedes?' Tommy asked.

Alfie nodded, making eye contact with him in the rear-view mirror.

'Get the bags out of the boot and make sure we haven't left anything behind,' Alfie said after Tommy parked the car on the lowest level.

There couldn't have been a better place for us to disappear. Being December, vast crowds had flocked to Strasbourg to visit the mulled-wine-scented Christmas Market. It had taken over the streets of the old town, and we were able to blend in easily with the tourists as we strolled around. Medieval buildings and pastel-coloured half-timbered houses lined the riverbank. They looked like they could have come straight from the pages of the Hansel and Gretel fairy tale.

As daylight began to fade, we left the twinkling Christmas trees of the main square behind us and booked into the Hotel Cour du Corbeau. It was more discreet than Alfie's normal choice, tucked away down a picturesque side street. Our spacious room overlooked a courtyard decorated with tiny white fairy lights, but even though our surroundings were idyllic, I found it impossible to relax.

For me, the most stressful part of life on the run was knowing that the police were looking for us, whereas Alfie seemed to get a kick out of it.

'I want you to do a job tonight, Nathan,' Alfie said.

'Are you serious? Isn't it a bit soon?' I protested, speaking up before Nathan had a chance to say anything. I hoped Alfie would listen to me.

'We've been here for a week now; if the police had any new leads, they'd have already tracked us down. It's time to move on.'

The pictures of the robberies were still all over the news. I thought it was too risky, but Alfie didn't care. As far as he was concerned, the police wouldn't be able to identify anyone from the grainy CCTV tapes of masked men.

That night Tommy brought a car around to the hotel entrance to collect us. For a change, he was driving an Audi, and this time it was silver and not black. Alfie had told him to pick a different make and colour just in case.

Before we got on the road to Paris, Nathan and Johno drilled into the tube of the supermarket safe in Strasbourg. They emptied the contents, swollen by pre-Christmas spending, with such ease that Alfie told Tommy to make detours through Metz and Reims, so they could clean out their supermarkets too.

As we drove through the night, exhaustion started to set in. My eyes were just beginning to close when the sight of the sun rising over the river Seine made me blink and open them again. Alfie reached for my hand. His touch made me jump. I pulled my hand away. Nathan was asleep on the seat next to me.

'Come to my room later, Gemma.' Alfie smiled and took hold of my hand again. He placed it on his thigh near his groin.

My hand sprang back as though I'd just touched a hot pan, and my heart began to race. Alfie's brazen attitude was scaring me, and I looked at him with a panicked stare. What the hell was he doing? Nathan was sitting inches away from me.

'Why are you looking at me like that?' Alfie smiled.

I shook my head. 'You know why.'

I'd quietly mouthed my reply, so I didn't wake Nathan up, but I felt him stir beside me. I glanced at him over my shoulder. When I was sure he was still asleep, I turned back to face Alfie.

'Make sure you come and find me later. I want to tell you the rest of the story.' Alfie winked.

67

Gemma

The conversation I'd had earlier with Alfie played over and over in my mind. I couldn't deny I was curious to find out more about his connection with Nathan's family, but I didn't know if he could be trusted to keep his hands to himself.

Alfie was a smooth talker. There was no denying he was an attractive man, and if I was being totally honest about the situation, I was flattered by the interest he was showing me. He could be incredibly charismatic. Alfie Watson could charm the knickers off a nun if he wanted to!

I didn't understand why Alfie wouldn't respect my decision. I'd made it clear that nothing more would happen between us. I wouldn't cross the line again. I'd been pretty blunt about it. But he was a man on a mission, flexing his alpha male muscles. He wasn't going to give up easily. Perhaps it was his pride that wouldn't allow him to accept it was over. Men like Alfie weren't used to being knocked back. He'd freely admitted he loved the chase, but

I wasn't trying to play hard to get. It wasn't as though I was encouraging him, far from it. In fact, the more unpleasant I was to him, the more he seemed to enjoy it.

I loved my husband, and I should never have been unfaithful to him. The thought of what I'd done to Nathan turned my stomach. I still couldn't believe I'd gone against my values in the first place. I never thought I'd betray Nathan's trust. It was very out of character for me.

I should have seen the signs earlier. My unhappiness had put me in a vulnerable place, and I'd let Alfie take full advantage of that. But it couldn't happen again. I didn't realise I was going to cheat on Nathan until it was too late. At the time I'd blamed the alcohol, but I'd been making excuses because I didn't want to face up to the truth. I wished I could say with complete confidence that I wasn't falling for Alfie, but I couldn't.

I was confused. My head was all over the place. I was a married woman, and I had no intention of reversing my vows. Nathan was the missing puzzle piece in my life. He completed me. So why was I being drawn towards Alfie? I knew it was wrong, but I couldn't help it. Much as I loved Nathan, his weakness where money was concerned had driven a wedge between us. Nobody could accuse Alfie of being weak. Was it Nathan's lack of certain qualities that was driving me towards Alfie?

Although I'd done my best to hide it, recently I'd found myself mooning about Alfie. It was becoming a struggle to suppress my thoughts. Acknowledging the fact that I had started to develop feelings for him was the first step in dealing with the problem. I'd have to snuff them out, or they could easily destroy my marriage.

If I went to Alfie's room, I knew it was likely he'd have a different agenda in mind other than storytelling. My mind was made up. It was probably too risky to be on my own with him. It wasn't just Alfie I was worried about, I wasn't sure I could trust myself.

68

Gemma

Tommy brought the car to a stop outside the Shangri-La Hotel, situated in one of the most exclusive and historic neighbourhoods, right in the centre of Paris. Our duplex suite was set over two levels and had an incredible unobstructed view of the Eiffel Tower and the River Seine.

My main priority was to get some rest. I climbed into the huge bed fully clothed. The only thing on my mind was sleep, but Nathan had other ideas as he stripped off and got in beside me. He pulled me towards him, and his hands wandered all over my body. When I didn't respond, he began nuzzling my neck.

'What's up?' Nathan leant up on his elbow behind me and kissed the top of my head while he waited for me to speak.

'I'm exhausted. I've been awake all night.' I looked at him over my shoulder before I let my head drop back down on the pillow.

The look on his face said it all. My rejection had hurt him, and although I felt guilty, I was too tired to do anything about it. I hadn't given Nathan what he wanted, so he turned his back on me and started sulking. He was acting like an attention-seeking child.

When I woke several hours later, I was alone in our room. I rubbed the sleep from my eyes before getting out of bed. Going up to the second level of our suite, I walked over to the full-length windows, opened them and stepped out onto the terrace. The view of the Eiffel Tower and Paris, the City of Light, was spectacular. Noticing Alfie on the adjoining balcony, dressed in an expensive suit with a crystal tumbler in his hand, I turned to go back inside, but it was too late, he'd already seen me.

'Gemma,' Alfie called, standing up from his chair.

I turned to face him and looked him in the eye.

'Don't go, we need to talk.'

'About what?'

'It's story time.' Alfie smiled, before lifting the tumbler to his lips. He finished his drink and walked through the French doors, closing them behind him.

I was desperate to hear the next instalment, so I banished my previous concerns from my mind. Before I had a chance to knock on Alfie's door, he opened it. Pulling me inside, he shoved himself into me, slamming our bodies into the wall. Alfie bent his face towards mine, and the mellow scent of Jack Daniel's filled my nostrils. Cupping my face, he went to kiss me, but before he could, I put my hand on his chest and pushed him away. I gave Alfie an exasperated look before taking a step backwards. My intuition had been right.

'You've got to stop doing this. I told you before; I'm not

going to sleep with you again. You need to accept it,' I said, looking him straight in the eye. How many times did I have to tell him? Surely I wasn't sending him mixed messages, was I?

Alfie looked startled at the knockback. 'So why did you come to my room?'

'You said you wanted to tell me the rest of the story.'

'And you believed me?' Alfie laughed.

His comment made my blood boil with rage. But I didn't want to give him the satisfaction of provoking a reaction from me. I needed some space, so I twisted the handle and was about to leave the room when he pushed the door closed.

Alfie took hold of my hand and led me across to the cream-coloured three-piece suite. 'Take a seat while I fix us both a drink.'

'I don't want anything, thanks,' I replied as I leant back on the gold cushions. I didn't want alcohol fogging my brain.

Alfie turned towards me and raised his eyebrows. Then he refilled his glass before taking a seat next to me.

'Now where did I get to?' Alfie grinned. I saw his eyes slowly travel up my legs while he waited for me to reply.

'You told me Jethro was in love with Rosa.'

A muscle in Alfie's jaw twitched while he considered his next words. 'My dear old dad wanted to be with her so badly he made sure the robbery didn't go to plan. Dad tipped off the police and Gareth got caught and sent down.'

My mouth fell open after Alfie dropped the bombshell. I was shocked. It was all news to me. But I had a feeling I hadn't heard the half of it. I hoped Alfie would reveal the rest. 'You're going to have to rewind a bit. I don't know what you're talking about.'

Alfie settled back against the cushions and took a sip of his Jack Daniel's. 'Whoops! Did I let the cat out of the bag? I assumed you knew Nathan's dad had been in prison.'

'I had no idea.'

'He's been released now, but he served a long sentence.'

My mind whirred as I tried to take in all the information. I wondered if Nathan knew about this.

'With Gareth behind bars, my dad thought he'd be free to make a move on Rosa, but she wasn't having any of it. Obviously, he didn't take that too well – her rejection stung. I know how that feels.' Alfie laughed, then leant forward and whispered in my ear. 'I can't get you out of my head, so putting an end to our affair isn't an option.'

'We're not having an affair; we spent one night together.' I couldn't keep the frustration out of my voice.

I suddenly felt uncomfortable and needed to put an end to this conversation. Without saying another word, I stood up and walked across to the door. Turning the handle, I stepped out into the corridor and breathed a sigh of relief.

69

Alfie

Gemma was messing with my head. Things weren't going the way I'd planned them. That was something I wasn't accustomed to, and I didn't like it. I was normally an excellent manipulator, but she was making it quite a challenge for me to win her over. She was a hard nut to crack. That wasn't going to put me off though. In fact, the more unattainable she was, the more attractive that made her.

I'd underestimated the impact she was having on me. I couldn't get her off my mind. I was intrigued by Gemma. She was never going to get in the queue to stroke my ego, and I loved that about her. She didn't just go along with everything I said. She was a strong woman who knew her own mind. Gemma stood up to me, and I respected her for that. The problem was, it only made me want her more. I'd never met a woman like her. She was one of a kind.

Gemma was unavailable, and that made her incredibly attractive to me. She was like forbidden fruit. I was used to getting what I wanted, so I wasn't going to lust after her from afar. I wanted her to be mine. I wouldn't consider the possibility of letting Gemma go. I wasn't just physically attracted to her. I was falling in love with her. I never thought I'd find a woman I wanted to spend the rest of my life with, until I met her. The fact that she was married to somebody else was a minor inconvenience. Nathan wasn't going to stand in my way.

After we'd spent the night together, I knew I wasn't imagining it, there was chemistry between us. No matter how much Gemma tried to deny it, we shared a connection. Every time I made eye contact with her, it sent shockwaves through my body. It was obvious she felt it too. Although she tried to play it cool, she was always the first to look away, more often than not with a distinct flush to her cheeks. Gemma's words might be barbed, but her body language was sending me different signals. It was revealing what she was trying her best to hide. She was attracted to me, and that was the only encouragement I needed.

Gemma wouldn't allow herself to believe we had a future together out of misplaced loyalty to the loser she was married to. Everyone could see Gemma and Nathan's relationship was in trouble. Nathan only ever looked out for himself. If Gemma gave the situation some serious thought and stopped being stubborn for a minute, she'd realise she'd be much better off with me. For one thing, she'd never have to worry about money again.

If Gemma had been truly committed to Nathan, she would never have been unfaithful to him. We were meant to be together. I realised that when I first met her. It was time to take her away from Nathan. I knew that wouldn't happen overnight, but I was prepared to be patient and happy to invest my energy into the challenge. I never could resist one, so I would give it my undivided attention. I was used to running the show. It wasn't in my nature to shy away from difficult situations.

Gemma needed to understand, I wouldn't take no for an answer.

70

Gemma

So here I was, at my wit's end, sitting alone in our room, waiting for Nathan to come back. I hadn't turned my phone on since I'd been to Alfie's room. I stared at the dark screen and braced myself before I switched it on. When the phone lit up, I could see I'd missed several messages. I scrolled back through them until I came to the first one.

Stop playing games, Gemma. Come back to my room x

We were going round in circles, and I felt emotionally exhausted. Alfie wasn't going to let me go until he was good and ready. I should have realised he'd see this as a challenge. Even though I'd spelt it out in black and white, Alfie was ignoring me. He was so used to being in control; this situation was alien to him.

What's taking you so long? I'm still waiting… x

Alfie always called the shots and got his own way. He liked to be in charge and thought he could control everyone and everything, including me. But if there was one thing I knew about myself, it was that I was an independent woman, and I would never be with a man who kept telling me what to do. I thought about whether I should reply to his message but then decided to read the others.

You know you want me as much as I want you x

Alfie was infuriating. It was clear from the tone of his texts, he thought I was bluffing. How many times would I have to tell him I'd never sleep with him again before he believed me?

Please, Gemma x

I was shocked by Alfie's begging tone. But instead of finding his emotional appeal endearing, I found it deeply disturbing. His needy behaviour was giving me the creeps. At this stage, it would have been easier to get rid of a case of persistent athlete's foot than him.

If Alfie thought bombarding me with texts every couple of minutes would persuade me to change my mind, he was mistaken. In fact, every time I read another message, it only confirmed that I should never have got involved with him in the first place.

Have I done something to upset you? x

I didn't know what to do. Alfie hadn't been put off by the fact that I hadn't responded to any of his messages. I was very tempted to type back a response, but I decided not to in case he misinterpreted what I was trying to say.

You'll be sorry if you make me wait too long.

I couldn't help noticing he hadn't ended his text with a kiss this time, and it was obvious his patience was wearing thin.

Do I need to spell out what will happen if you choose Nathan over me?

The tone of Alfie's texts had changed from needy to threatening in an instant, and he was beginning to scare me now. I knew how suddenly he flipped when things didn't go his way.

Why would I choose Alfie over my husband? We'd only had a one-night stand. Even though Nathan and I were going through a rough patch, I had no intention of leaving him. I wanted to save my marriage more than anything, and nothing, not even Alfie Watson, was going to stand in my way.

It was clear from his messages, Alfie was deluded. I knew I should ignore him. Replying would only open up the lines of communication. But before I could stop myself, my fingers tapped out a reply, and I hit send.

Are you threatening me?

I don't mind admitting, I was scared to see his reply, so I

switched off the phone and put it down on the bedside table. I know I have a tendency to overthink everything, even positive things, until I manage to make them look negative, but I couldn't help myself. My anxious brain was on the lookout for danger. I knew I was probably being paranoid, but then again, in this case, I think I had good reason to be worried. Alfie's behaviour was so unpredictable, and as he lived in a world ruled by violence, there was no telling what he might do. My imagination began running riot.

When I heard the door open and saw Nathan standing in the entrance, looking like a broken man, a feeling of devastation came over me. I would never forget the look on his face as long as I lived. It was etched in my memory like the words on a headstone. I realised he'd learnt the full extent of my betrayal. He didn't need to say a word; it was obvious he knew about Alfie. Shame poured from my eyes, and the mask I'd been wearing all this time began to fray.

Nathan fixed me with a questioning glare. 'How could you do this to me?'

Nathan had a zero-tolerance policy when it came to cheating. He stared at me with a hollow expression on his face, waiting for an explanation. Seeing him like this made guilt eat away at me.

So Alfie's threat had become real. Bile rose in my stomach as I processed Nathan's words. Alfie had callously told him about us. What a spiteful thing to do. If he'd kept his mouth shut there was a good chance Nathan would never have found out. But Alfie knew I was serious about saving my marriage, so this was my payback. I would never forgive him for that.

In the past, I'd always thought I'd be honest with Nathan. But now that I was faced with the situation, I didn't know what to do for the best. If I came clean, I risked losing my husband, so I considered pretending nothing had happened, but only for a brief moment. My conscience had got the better of me. Nathan deserved to hear the truth. Fuelled by guilt, the critical voice in my head was trying to teach me an important lesson; I needed to listen to it this time. I knew it was right; there was no point trying to deny it. It was time for me to face up to what I'd done. But this was going to be torture.

'Your gambling put a huge strain on our relationship, but no matter what I said, you wouldn't stop, you just carried on regardless. We were in a downward spiral. You kept letting me down, and there was nothing I could do about it.'

'Apart from jump into bed with Alfie.' Nathan shook his head. 'So let me get this straight, you're saying it was my fault you had an affair with Alfie, are you?' I didn't need to read the look in Nathan's eyes to know he was furious. His tone of voice conveyed that very well as he tried to keep a lid on his volcanic temper.

'I didn't have an affair with Alfie. I slept with him in a moment of madness,' I blurted out. Nathan deserved an explanation, but if I didn't understand why I'd done it, how could I give him one? 'I'm not trying to put all the blame on you, but you have to take some of the responsibility.'

'Do I?'

'Yes, you do. I didn't think you cared about me any more. Do you know how that made me feel?'

'You can't even come up with a good reason for throwing our marriage away… I expected more from you. You've changed, Gemma. You're not the woman I married.'

'And you're not the man I married. I gave up everything for you, Nathan.'

At the time, I thought I'd made the right decision. I closed the door on my family when I chose to be with Nathan. Ours was a tale of true love that would last against all the odds. We didn't need anybody else in our lives; we had each other. I lowered my eyes and hoped he wouldn't notice the tears that were starting to form.

Nathan slammed the door behind him and paced over to the window where I was standing, stopping right in front of me. 'I'm disgusted with you, Gemma.' He fired the words straight into my face.

My heart began pounding, reflecting my emotional state. 'You're disgusted with me? You've put me through hell. All you're interested in is getting us further into debt, and you've put our lives at risk in the process.' As I rambled on, wallowing in self-pity, the words kept spilling from my mouth in an endless stream. I couldn't seem to stop them. He wasn't going to like what I was about to say, but I needed to get it off my chest. 'Infidelity is a symptom of an unhappy marriage, and believe me, Nathan, I'm unhappy.' It was true: if everything had been all right between us, I wouldn't have ended up in Alfie's bed.

'Nothing's ever your fault, is it? You're never prepared to take the blame for anything. You haven't even told me you're sorry for what you've done.' Nathan's jaw clenched as he said the words.

He was waiting for an apology. I knew he deserved that, but the stubborn voice inside my head wouldn't let me.

'It's bad enough that at the first sign of trouble, you jumped into bed with somebody else, but it's unforgivable that you're suggesting I pushed you into doing it. I didn't drive you into Alfie's arms no matter what you think.' Nathan's eyes flashed with fury.

'You believe what you want, but it's time you faced facts: you use the roll of the dice as an emotional crutch.'

Nathan shook his head; he had no words. The injustice of it all was too much for him to bear, and he started shaking. Seeing Nathan at his most vulnerable triggered something within me. I wanted to put my arms around him and tell him everything would be all right. But instead, I wrapped my arms around myself for comfort. I couldn't bring myself to move; I was frightened he'd push me away.

I lowered my head. I was too embarrassed to look my husband in the eye. It wasn't fair of me to put all the blame on Nathan. No matter what he'd done, he didn't deserve to be treated like this. But instead of listening to the voice of reason inside my head, I continued to hold him responsible.

'While we were falling apart, you weren't there for me. I didn't have anyone I could talk to. I was lonely, and all you were interested in was blowing money in the casinos.'

Nathan looked at me with contempt in his eyes as I tried to defend myself. Would it make him feel any better if I told him sleeping with Alfie hadn't been worth it?

Nathan broke down and covered his gorgeous face with his hands. It would have been easier if he'd screamed at me, and began throwing things around the room, but instead, he sobbed his heart out as he came to terms with my betrayal. Seeing the man I loved in pain like this was unbearable.

'Can you imagine what's going through my head right now?' Nathan's face contorted as he spoke. I knew I'd caused all his childhood insecurities to resurface.

'I'm sorry.' I finally said the words he'd been waiting to hear.

I reached out to touch my husband, but he pulled away. What did I expect? His reaction was perfectly normal. Nathan clasped his hands behind his head and glared at me. He had every right to be angry.

'Why did you do it? I'd never cheat on you.' Nathan shook his head in disbelief as his dark eyes bored into mine.

When I saw the heartbreak on his face, it cut me like a knife. I could feel his pain. Nothing I could say would change what I'd done. I just hoped the damage was reversible.

'Do you even feel guilty?' Nathan spat his bitter words at me. He was seething.

'Of course I do. If it's any consolation, I feel like shit.' I hung my head in shame. I couldn't bear to look at Nathan.

'You feel like shit. What do you think I feel like?' Nathan let out a loud sigh.

I lowered my eyes to the floor. Part of me was relieved that he knew, but now I had to face the fact that my marriage might not survive and I had nobody to blame but myself. If I lost Nathan, I'd lose everything, and that was the price I'd have to pay for one night with Alfie. I thought things were bad before, but I knew I'd just hit rock bottom.

'I just don't understand why you did it?' Tears formed in Nathan's eyes again as he studied my face.

'I made a stupid mistake.'

'I thought you loved me.'

'I do love you.' I was desperate to throw my arms around him and make everything all right.

Nathan shook his head. 'You've got a funny way of showing it.'

'I'm so sorry. I never meant to hurt you.' It took all my strength to look Nathan in the eye. I wanted him to know my apology was genuine.

'They always say you should trust your instincts. I wish I had now. I knew you found Alfie attractive, but I didn't think you'd actually sleep with him.' Nathan clasped his fingers behind his head and let out a long breath. 'I suppose in hindsight, it was obvious you were falling for him, but the spouse is always the last one to know their partner's having an affair, aren't they?'

'We're not having an affair.'

'That's not what Alfie said.'

'He's lying, Nathan.' I wish I'd told him the truth before Alfie gave my husband his greatly exaggerated version of events. I should have seen this coming.

As I took in my husband's words, one sentence played over and over in my head. Do I need to spell out what will happen if you choose Nathan over me? While Alfie held on to the belief that there was a remote possibility I'd leave Nathan for him, he didn't feel the need to say anything. But once he'd realised that wasn't going to happen, he had an overwhelming desire to get even with me. Alfie was out to cause trouble.

'When Alfie told me he was sleeping with you, he might as well have taken a shotgun and blown a hole right through me. You've both shattered my life into a million pieces.' A pained expression appeared on Nathan's face as if he'd just ripped a plaster off an open wound before it had a chance to heal.

'We're not sleeping together. We had a one-night stand.'

'I can't bear the thought of you with another man. Do you know how it makes me feel when I picture you in Alfie's bed?' Anger flashed across Nathan's face, and his nostrils flared.

I couldn't even begin to imagine how I'd feel if things were the other way around. But I was too choked up to speak, so instead, I shook my head and tried to hold back my tears. I had no right to cry; I'd brought this on myself. Wallowing in self-pity wasn't going to help me. I wasn't the victim in this situation, Nathan was.

I bit the side of my lip and looked towards the floor. As I did, warm, salty tears poured from my eyes; I couldn't hold them in any longer. When my eyes filled up, I tried to blink them away, but they kept coming, running down my cheeks in a steady stream. Unable to speak, I wanted Nathan to take me in his arms and comfort me, but when I looked up at him, he stared right through me and continued speaking.

'Alfie told me the sex was fantastic, the best he'd ever had. I should never have had to hear someone say that about my wife, Gemma.'

Like molten lava, fury began to simmer in my stomach. Why did Alfie want to torture Nathan with the gory details and cause him so much distress? He'd made the situation much worse than it needed to be and it didn't change the outcome. I wiped my tears away with the back of my hand and swallowed down the lump that had formed at the base of my throat. I was ashamed of what I'd done and desperately wanted to put things right between us. I stared into my husband's face, looking for a glimmer of hope. Maybe in time, he might be able to forgive me.

'I wish I could turn back the clock.'

'It's too late for that.' Nathan's words stung. They felt like a slap on the cheek.

'I owe you an explanation.'

Nathan put his hand up to silence me. He didn't want to hear my excuses. Nothing I could say could justify what I'd done.

71

Nathan

I couldn't believe Gemma had done this to me. I'd never made any secret of the fact that I despised my dad for what he'd done to Mum and me. He'd left us to set up home with another woman when I was a baby. He walked out the door and never made contact with either of us again. As the years went on, I became bitter, and my attitude towards my dad worsened. I hated him for cutting me out of his life and would never forgive him. Gemma knew how I felt about cheating, and yet, she still did it.

I'd always thought being abandoned by your father was the ultimate betrayal. That was before I realised my wife was having an affair. How could she do this to me? I'd trusted her, and this was how she repaid me. I never thought she could be so disloyal.

Before I met Gemma, I was so guarded I wasn't sure I would ever allow anyone to get close to me. I'd built high walls around myself to keep everyone out. It was going to take a very special person to bring them down. Gemma was that person. At least I'd thought she was, until Alfie filled me in on what was going on behind my back.

Sometimes you click with a person and find it easy to tell them things you wouldn't normally share with someone you'd just met. People like that are rare, so you treasure them the most, but they could also be the ones who ended up hurting you more than you ever thought was possible. I'd been left blindsided by something I never thought would happen. Gemma had betrayed me. The woman I married would never have treated me like this.

In the past, there had been times when Gemma and I had found ourselves in a dark tunnel. But by sticking together, we eventually found our way towards the light and out the other side. Something terrible had happened to our relationship for us to be in this situation.

Forgiveness didn't come easily to me. I didn't know if Gemma and I would be able to get past a betrayal of this size. It wasn't a small bump on the matrimonial highway. We were going to have to navigate around a pothole of gargantuan proportions, the size of an extinct volcano. The road ahead would be tough and full of pitfalls. I wasn't sure we were strong enough to make it.

Trust can be broken in an instant, but it takes a long time to rebuild it. All the insecurities that had been plaguing me for so long had suddenly resurfaced. My jealous streak had gone into overdrive. Why had my wife fallen out of love with me?

At a time like this, I would normally have confided in my mum. But that wasn't going to be possible. She had experienced the same thing with my dad, and we were very close, so I would have loved the opportunity to talk things over with her. Mum loved Gemma like a daughter. She would be devastated if we split up.

If I ever brought up the subject of my dad, Mum would close down the conversation immediately. She never spoke about him and refused to discuss what had happened between them. On the rare occasion that I asked a question, she'd become incredibly distressed, so I stopped asking. I hated seeing her upset.

Now that I was in the same position, I realised how she'd felt. It was less painful to block the person out of your thoughts completely than try to understand the reasons your marriage fell apart. Gemma had just squeezed the life out of my beating heart.

72

Gemma

Alfie and I had crossed a line, and nothing would ever be the same again. I only had to look at Nathan to know his emotional wounds were still very raw. I'd been married since I was nineteen, most of my adult life, so my love for Nathan wasn't one-dimensional. It spread in different directions like the branches of a tree. I found the thought of losing my husband devastating. After the way I'd behaved, he might not consider giving our marriage another go. Who could blame him?

As far as I could see, the only way to move forward was to lay all my cards on the table. Although I couldn't justify why I'd slept with Alfie, I owed it to Nathan to try and explain what had led me to cheat in the first place. I wanted him to know the truth, but it was hard to find the right words.

'Every time you gambled, you lost money. We were sinking deeper into debt, but that never seemed to put you off,' I began.

Nathan looked at me like I had two heads. He didn't say

a word, but I could tell by the look on his face, I hadn't answered any of his questions, so I forced myself to carry on.

'You were convinced the next time you gambled, you'd get lucky, but you never did, did you?' I rambled on; I needed to get this off my chest without being sidetracked. If I stopped now, I might not have the strength to continue. 'I kept hoping you'd come to your senses.'

Nathan ran his fingers through his thick, dark hair and looked into the middle distance before he brought his eyes back to mine. 'Thanks for the lecture, Gemma. But I think you're missing the point. You were meant to be explaining how you ended up in Alfie's bed. How long has the affair been going on?'

'I slept with Alfie once. I'd hardly call that an affair.' Before Nathan had a chance to reply, I continued to talk, but the more I spoke, the more my voice wobbled. 'When I came back to our room, and you were playing cards with Mario, the little hope I'd been clinging to that you wouldn't gamble again was well and truly snuffed out.'

Nathan remained quiet, but a muscle twitched in his jaw as he studied my face. I could see he was trying to make sense of the situation. His silence made me nervous and raised a lot of questions in my mind. I would have preferred to have a blazing argument, but what could he say to me when he had no words?

'I was so angry with you and wasn't prepared to put up with your selfish behaviour any more. You'd pushed me too far this time, to the stage where I felt like giving up on you.'

My eyes welled up with tears. But rather than put his arms around me, Nathan moved away. He put his guard up and retreated behind the emotional wall he'd built up over the years. I don't know why I was so surprised. What did I expect? I'd just broken my husband's heart.

'I'm ashamed to admit this, but I couldn't see a future for us. The tension between us was at breaking point. I thought my only option was to let you go.' My tears rolled silently down my cheeks as we stood staring at each other.

'I had no idea you felt like that.' Disbelief was written all over Nathan's face, and he began to shake his head.

'This is going to sound awful, but Alfie and I ended up together after we'd spent a drunken night in the bar.' I looked up at Nathan with guilty eyes. He stared back at me, but his face was expressionless. I took a deep breath and inhaled slowly while I plucked up the courage to continue. 'You'd hurt me, and I wanted to get back at you.'

Nathan looked at me with empty eyes, and when he spoke, his words had a cold edge to them. 'So that's why you slept with Alfie, is it?'

'I made a stupid mistake, and it haunts me every time I think about what I've done. I wasn't thinking straight; I don't know what got into me. I've let you down in the worst way possible.'

'When I picture the two of you together, it turns my stomach.' Nathan's lips thinned as he clenched his jaw.

'I don't blame you for hating me. I hate myself for what I've done to you.' I wiped my tears away with the back of my hand; I had no right to cry.

'I don't hate you, Gemma.'

But did he still love me? The question was on my lips, but I was too scared to ask it. I wasn't sure I wanted to hear Nathan's answer. How could I have ever doubted my feelings for him? He'd shown me what it was like to be loved unconditionally. He was my rock.

Nathan took my hands in his, just when I expected him to turn his back on me. He was the most loyal man you could ever meet. That was one of the reasons I couldn't picture my life without him.

'I brought this on myself. I shouldn't have pushed you away.' Nathan squeezed my fingertips.

I drew in a deep breath and faced Nathan with the biggest smile I could manage. 'So where do we go from here?'

Not many men would be bothered to stick around if they found out their wife had been unfaithful to them. I'm not sure it's something I could forgive if it was the other way around. That's hypocritical of me to say, I know.

'I want to put this behind us, but I don't know if I can. You know what I'm like, Gemma, I'm jealous and insecure at the best of times, even when I've got no reason to be.'

Tears filled my eyes. The trust had gone from our relationship, and it would be difficult to get that back. Why had I been so stupid? I didn't want to lose the most important person in my life, but if I did, I had nobody to blame but myself.

My mouth began trembling as I went to speak. 'I promise you, Nathan, if we stay together, I'll never hurt you again. I love you more than anything.'

'I want to believe you… but something tells me I shouldn't.'

It was going to take time for my husband to learn to trust me again. Nathan's insecurity stemmed from his childhood and the fact that his father wasn't part of his life. He always had trouble letting people in. Only a select few were close to him.

'I don't want to lose you. You're the love of my life.'

Nathan reached for my hand and squeezed it. 'If we can rebuild the trust, we might be able to get through this.'

I could feel my marriage slipping through my fingers. Everything was based on trust, and without it, we'd have nothing. I should never have betrayed my husband. He was bound to be wary of me now. That was a perfectly natural reaction. Nathan needed to heal from the pain I'd caused him, and that wouldn't happen overnight. I'd have to be patient with him and take things one day at a time. When I looked into his haunted eyes, I knew I loved him more than ever. To say I was ashamed of myself was an understatement. I couldn't bear to look at the shell of a man in front of me, so I cast my eyes towards the floor.

'I still can't believe this has happened to us. I thought our marriage was solid.' Nathan let out a long breath.

I looked up at him with tears in my eyes. We used to be so happy, and now I felt like I was trapped in a nightmare that I couldn't wake up from.

'If I hadn't kept pushing you away, you would never have slept with…' Nathan couldn't bring himself to say Alfie's name.

'I hope one day you'll be able to forgive me. Otherwise, we won't have another option but to go our separate ways.' I didn't want Nathan to give up on us and had to put my trembling hand over my mouth to stop myself from crying. I knew if I didn't, out-of-control sobs were going to escape from my lips.

'I don't want our lives to go on different paths.' Nathan looked into my eyes. 'It won't be easy, but let's do whatever it takes to get back on track.'

73

Alfie had earned his position as an underworld boss using a combination of violence, intimidation and control. He was feared and respected in equal measures. If something didn't go his way, he'd think nothing of pulling a gun on you. It wasn't in his character to back down.

Before we'd got dragged into this, Nathan and I were happily married. Over the course of a few short months, Alfie had exploited Nathan so he could trap us into working for him. As a result, he'd turned us against each other, and caused so many arguments between us, he'd almost succeeded in splitting us up. We realised now, we needed to stick together if we were going to make it through this, and that's what we intended to do.

As Nathan and I walked into the deserted bar that evening, Alfie called us over to his table. I felt the hairs stand up on the back of my neck when we approached the dark corner he was sitting in.

'Aah, isn't that sweet. You two look happy,' Alfie said.

He gave me a smug smile and then stared at our intertwined fingers. Seeing us putting on a united front obviously infuriated him, but he was doing his best not to show it.

'Any reason why we wouldn't be?' I asked. When we locked eyes, butterflies fluttered around in my stomach and made me feel sick.

Alfie grinned. Why had I been so stupid? I should never have got involved with him in the first place. I must have been out of my mind.

'Take a seat. I've ordered you both a drink.'

Alfie handed me a Pink Lady, the bar's signature cocktail. After I took the glass from his hand, I felt like chucking my drink over him, but then thought better of it. He'd be delighted if he knew he was getting under my skin, so I wasn't going to give him the satisfaction.

'Cheers,' Alfie said, and his face broke into a slow smile. He nodded towards Nathan before clinking my glass.

Alfie leant backwards in his chair and began undressing me with his eyes. I felt the colour rush to my cheeks.

'You look a little flushed, Gemma.' Alfie laughed.

'It's hot in here,' I replied.

Nathan sat in silence next to me, watching Alfie's pathetic attempt at male courtship. I could see he was getting a great power buzz from Nathan's unease. This was a game to Alfie, and he wasn't going to stop until he'd won. My heart bled for Nathan. It was bad enough having to come to terms with my infidelity, without having his nose constantly rubbed in it.

I threw Alfie a filthy look in the hope that he might stop torturing Nathan. But if anything, it just encouraged him. Alfie held eye contact with me for longer than it felt comfortable, and although I was desperate to look away, I didn't dare, in case he read that as a sign of weakness. Spurred on by my embarrassment, Alfie continued giving me the once-over.

'Let's get out of here, Gemma,' Nathan said, knocking back his cocktail and getting to his feet.

Leaving my drink untouched, I pushed my chair back from the table and stood next to my husband.

Alfie checked the time on his Rolex. 'Aren't you going to stay for another drink?'

'No, thanks,' Nathan said. He took hold of my hand, and as we went to leave, Alfie stood up.

'Hey, Nathan, I've just had an idea, why don't you go, and Gemma can stay here with me? Or better still, she could come back to my room. The bed's still warm.'

After that, everything seemed to happen in slow motion. Alfie knew his comment would provoke a reaction.

Up until now, Nathan had kept a lid on things, but overcome with jealousy, he couldn't help himself and lunged towards Alfie. Without any hesitation, I threw my arms between them, slamming a palm into each of their chests to keep them apart. I couldn't stand by and do nothing. I didn't want Nathan to get into a fight.

'Do you want me to blow your fucking head off?' Alfie said.

He didn't need to take the gun from his inside pocket and threaten my husband with it. His words were enough. Alfie wasn't just flexing his muscles. As far as he was concerned, Nathan had overstepped the mark and now we were at his mercy.

'Alfie, please calm down.' My voice sounded tense because I knew exactly what he was capable of.

I fixed him with my eyes, and he studied my face. He could see how scared I was, but he showed no emotion. Silence hung heavy in the air for what seemed like an eternity while we waited to see what Alfie would do next. He didn't need to have a good reason to kill somebody; it was just another display of his status and dominance. Taking someone's life meant nothing to him, and he'd told me before that things would be a lot easier with Nathan out of the picture. I hoped for our sake, he didn't really mean that.

I tried to stay strong, but my body began to shake as the cold, hard reality of the situation seeped into my brain. My head was spinning. The speed at which this had all kicked off caught me off balance. The worrying thing was, even though he wasn't holding the gun, I knew we were still in danger. I could feel it in the air around us.

I couldn't blame Nathan for this. I should have put a stop to the chain of events that had led me into the arms of another man. I wished I'd never been unfaithful to my husband; it haunted me every time I thought about it. It was torture seeing the pleasure Alfie got from Nathan's pain.

I wondered what Alfie was thinking about as he stood in silence, watching me without blinking. As far as I was concerned, what happened between Alfie and me was well and truly over. But by the way he was behaving, it was clear he wasn't going to let me walk away that easily.

Our lives were now entangled together, and no matter how much I wanted to break free, he wasn't going to let me. I knew if I didn't make a stand, we'd always be trapped. Without saying a word, I took hold of Nathan's hand, turned away from Alfie and began walking out of the bar.

'Where do you think you're going, Gemma? Get back here right now,' Alfie shouted as we disappeared out of the door.

74

Alfie

When something was predictable, it bored me. I couldn't work Gemma out. She was completely unpredictable, and that was exciting. She fascinated me and brought out the best in me, whereas Nathan brought out the worst. Just being in the same room as him made me see red.

For Gemma to have strayed outside their relationship, something must have changed. She was looking for something Nathan wasn't giving her. Even though they were putting on a united front to the outside world, behind closed doors, there was trouble in paradise. That was an encouraging sign. I'd played my part by stirring things up between them. Sleeping with Gemma had rocked the foundations of their marriage to the core. It was good to know my efforts to split them up hadn't been in vain.

Gemma's patience was finally starting to wear thin. Nathan's behaviour was pushing her straight into my arms. I was more than happy to be a shoulder to cry on. She could rely on me. I couldn't understand why she chose to stay with Nathan. I suppose it was the safe thing to do. Surely she knew she had other options. We bounced off each other, so I fully intended to take her off his hands. When Gemma was mine, I'd make sure she felt loved, happy, safe and secure. She would be so content, she would never feel the need to stray from me.

Nathan didn't appreciate how lucky he was. It was hard for me to sit back and watch him treat Gemma badly. But she needed to work out for herself that it was time to give up on her marriage. I had to let their relationship run its course. Gemma had put up with his behaviour for so long he'd never see it coming. That would make it harder for him to accept. He wouldn't know what had hit him when he ended up alone. Nathan would be lost without Gemma. She was the strong one in the partnership. She was the type of woman who made a stand and held her ground in a situation, and that impressed me.

I loved being around Gemma, so I was prepared to give up the single life to have a relationship with her. I never thought that day would come. I'd always embraced my status as a bachelor and enjoyed the company of beautiful women. Living the playboy lifestyle wasn't exactly a hardship.

There were lots of benefits to not being part of a couple. I liked being the sole decision-maker and not having to compromise with anyone. I controlled my own schedule. I was a free agent and used to doing what I wanted when I wanted. Although the thought of being in a relationship with Gemma was a bit daunting, I was ready to change. What had come over me? I was going soft over a woman. If I wasn't careful, Gemma would ruin my street cred.

75

Gemma

I lay in the darkness, with my head on my husband's smooth bare chest, and stared at the Eiffel Tower. It looked amazing lit up against the night sky. Feeling his warm body close to mine made me ache for his touch. I wanted him to make love to me, so I ran my hand up his arm, then reached up and kissed him.

Nathan pulled away. 'I'm sorry, Gemma, I can't.' He turned his face away so that I could only see his profile.

My tears fell silently on my pillow. His rejection stung and filled me with doubt. I'd hurt him so badly, and I hated myself for that. Nathan's wounds needed time to heal; I'd have to be patient and respect that. All I could hope is that one day, he'd stop being tormented by my betrayal, and it wouldn't occupy his mind like it does now.

In the early hours of the morning, my phone buzzed on the bedside cabinet. A text had come through from Alfie.

Are you bored of playing games yet?

I let out a sigh. Alfie thought he was in control again. I wasn't playing games.

'Are you awake?' I asked, looking over my shoulder at Nathan. His eyes were closed, but I knew he wasn't asleep.

As I lay staring up at the ceiling, I thought about whether I should ignore the text, but decided I wouldn't. There was so much I wanted to say. Before I had a chance to type a reply, another message came through from him.

The bed feels too big without you.

Reading his latest text made me panic. There was no way I was going to reply to that. My fingers fumbled with the keys, and I quickly deleted his message. I didn't want Nathan to see it. Then I switched off the phone, so I wouldn't have to interact with Alfie. How could I convince him it was over between us if he refused to believe it?

The sound of knocking on our door woke Nathan and me from a fretful sleep.

'I'll get it,' Nathan said.

Lying very still, I strained to hear what the muffled voices were saying, but I couldn't figure it out.

'Who was at the door?'

'Tommy.'

'What did he want?' It was four o'clock in the morning.

'He came to tell us to get ready.'

'Couldn't he have waited until later?' I yawned.

'No, we're leaving in an hour.' Nathan stood by the side of the bed, staring at me with haunted eyes.

'What's the matter?'

'He had a message for you from Alfie.'

My heart sank. 'What was it?' I could hear the blood pumping around my head while I waited for Nathan to speak.

'He wants to know why you didn't reply to his texts.'

76

Nathan

Why had Gemma started keeping things from me? I needed her to be as honest as possible at the moment, because if she lied to me, or withheld information, no matter how trivial she thought it was, then we would never be able to rebuild the trust that had been broken. Her behaviour was making me paranoid, and my old insecurities had returned with a vengeance.

I had a gut feeling that something was still going on between her and Alfie. You should always trust your instincts, shouldn't you? Maybe I was being overly suspicious, but I couldn't seem to help myself. No matter how much Gemma tried to reassure me that they had only had a one-night stand, I wasn't sure I could trust what she said any more. Alfie's version of events was so different. I didn't know who to believe. Up until now, I'd had no reason to doubt Gemma would always be faithful to me. How could I have been so wrong about her? I couldn't understand how I'd missed the warning signs. It had happened right under my nose.

I had a tendency to be jealous, so I hated having to watch Alfie openly flirt with my wife. Especially under the present circumstances. He could see it was winding me up. That was precisely why he was doing it. I had to learn not to react and not let him push my buttons. But that was easier said than done. He was getting so much pleasure out of my discomfort. I wasn't very good at hiding my feelings.

Knowing that Alfie had slept with the most important person in my life was eating away at me. I still couldn't get my head around the fact that it had happened. Even if I'd wanted to put it out of my mind, he was never going to let me forget it. I never thought anything or anyone would come between Gemma and me. Our marriage was rock solid or at least it used to be before Alfie came on the scene. What more did the bastard want from me? I had nothing else to give him.

Alfie was behaving like we were competing for Gemma's affection. That made it hard for me to keep a lid on my temper. But if I lost it with him, who knew what would happen? It wouldn't be a fair fight. Alfie didn't venture far without one of his suited thugs.

I was in turmoil. My brain was trying to talk me into giving up on Gemma to protect myself from the pain I was going through. Maintaining a relationship that was causing me so much distress would do more harm than good in the long run. It would be best for my mental and emotional health to get out now.

I knew that was the sensible thing to do. But sometimes it was hard to let go of a relationship. Gemma and I had been a couple for years. We had so much history. Part of me thought, no matter what she had done, I didn't want to accept we weren't meant to be together.

77

Gemma

The atmosphere inside the car was as frosty as the weather this morning. Alfie, Nathan and me sat side by side in silence in the back of the Audi, staring straight ahead like the three wise monkeys. When we drove over a bridge spanning the River Seine, I looked out of the window and saw the soft, subtle colours of the sky reflected in the water. Once again, we were saying goodbye to the city of Paris.

About an hour into our journey, my curiosity got the better of me. 'Where are we going this time?' I asked.

'Antwerp,' Alfie replied without making eye contact with me.

I looked out the window and managed to hold in the groan that tried to escape from my lips. The prospect of sitting next to Alfie for the next three hours filled me with dread. I hoped he wouldn't mention the texts on the long car journey. So far he hadn't. He seemed content with giving me the cold shoulder instead.

*

Finally, my ordeal was over. The Audi stopped outside the ultra-modern Hyllit Hotel, situated in the centre of the Diamond Quarter.

'Meet me in the rooftop restaurant in twenty minutes,' Alfie said after we'd checked in.

In contrast to everywhere else we'd stayed, I was surprised to find our room was compact and quite basic this time. It was very different from the sprawling, luxurious suites we'd become accustomed to.

A smile spread across my face when I put my bag down on the nearest of two single beds. Alfie was so transparent; it was so obvious that this was his way of punishing me for not leaving Nathan. The funny thing was, the downgrade didn't bother me in the slightest. I'm pretty easy to please.

When Nathan and I entered the rooftop restaurant, we could see Alfie was talking to a man of Middle Eastern appearance. He had greying hair and a large, prominent nose. We made our way across the solid wood flooring to where they were sitting. Breaking eye contact with him, Alfie looked up at us, swirled his drink around the glass then downed it.

'Glad you could join us. Sit next to me, Gemma.' Alfie patted the chair to the side of him.

I felt myself inwardly groan before I pulled out the cream leather chair and reluctantly took a seat. Alfie gestured with a wordless wave of the hand to the waiter, who quickly approached our table.

'Bring us another round,' Alfie said. He didn't bother to ask any of us what we'd like to drink. That was just another way for him to exercise the power he had over us.

Alfie's companion stood up and reached a hairy arm across the table towards me. 'I'm Avraham. Pleased to meet you.' The dark skin on his face crinkled and his mouth stretched into a broad smile when he offered me his hand.

'I'm Gemma.'

Avraham's hand was covered with thick black fuzz, and when I shook it, I couldn't help noticing how each of his knuckles had little islands of black hair springing up from them. They almost camouflaged the large, gold ring he was wearing on his little finger.

The short, stocky man sat back down next to Nathan but didn't bother to introduce himself. Instead, his dark beady eyes fixed on me, as he began slowly rubbing his hands together. His interrogating stare had me fidgeting in my seat. That made him smile, and when he did, he exposed his small, stained teeth. I'd only just met this man, but within seconds, I'd formed an opinion of him. I didn't like him. He made me uncomfortable; mistrust seemed to ooze out of him.

'I thought it was about time I introduced you to my good friend, Terry,' Alfie said, clinking glasses with him.

Nathan and I looked at each other. Avraham, or Terry as Alfie liked to call him, was the fence, the dodgy jeweller who'd been making the replicas we'd used in the robberies.

78

Gemma

Nathan and I were exhausted and were just about to go to bed when a text came through from Alfie.

Both of you need to come to my room straight away.

Alfie's tone was abrupt, no please or thank you, I noted.

Tommy, Johno and Terry were already sitting around an enormous table, studying a drawing, when we arrived at Alfie's spacious suite. I was glad to see he wasn't being affected by the same budget cut as us. The level of his childish behaviour brought a smile to my face.

'What's so funny?' Alfie asked. He was clearly annoyed by my cheerful disposition.

'Nothing,' I said, breezing past him. 'I'm just admiring your room.'

I cast my eye over the luxurious interior before I took a seat at the end of the table. Alfie walked behind me and ran his fingers through my hair. His touch made me jump and then I felt myself stiffen. I scanned the room for Nathan. He was looking out of the full-length windows, so he had his back to me. Thankfully, he hadn't seen what was going on. Alfie began stroking my arm; I couldn't stifle my body's involuntary shudder. If he thought it was acceptable to paw me like I was a piece of meat, he could think again. I wanted to confront him over it, but it wasn't the right time. For Nathan's sake, I let it go. Alfie sat down next to me and leant into my face. For a horrible moment, I thought he was going to kiss me in front of everyone. Panic attempted to rise inside me, but I knew I had to stay calm.

'So I take it you're not satisfied with your accommodation. Perhaps you'd prefer to see what the inside of a prison cell looks like?'

How the hell was I going to answer his question without making the situation worse? Nathan turned to face us. I caught his eye. Without saying a word, my gaze intensified. He realised I was warning him to watch his step.

'You're not so lippy now, are you, Gemma?' Alfie said, moving his face to within inches of mine. He was so close to me; I could almost taste the Jack Daniel's on his lips. Then to my relief, he straightened up and turned his attention away from me. 'Gentlemen, tomorrow we are going to carry out our biggest job to date. Terry will be assisting us.'

With his rat-toothed smile planted firmly on his face, Terry put his hand up and waved at each of us in turn, like he was an A-list celebrity.

'This will go down in history as the biggest heist of all time,' Terry bragged in his thick accent.

'It certainly will, my friend.' Alfie squeezed the top of

Terry's shoulder. 'After we pull this off, we'll have enough money to last us a lifetime and Gemma will be able to afford to upgrade her room.'

Peals of laughter erupted around the table. Only Nathan and I stayed silent. I looked up at Alfie, and our eyes met.

'In the morning, we're going to strip the Antwerp Diamond Centre of its contents.' Alfie flashed me a confident smile.

My eyes widened. But there was so much security, how were they going to manage that?

'We have inside information,' Alfie continued.

Surely they would need more than that to pull off a robbery of this size and get away with it.

'This drawing shows the layout of the building,' Alfie said.

'I've been passing myself off as a jewellery dealer at the Diamond Centre for a long time now, so everyone trusts me.' Terry beamed.

Maybe I was being cynical, but I highly doubted that. I knew you shouldn't judge a book by its cover, but Terry's beady eyes were shifty, and I hated the way he kept rubbing his hands together like the evil villain in a pantomime. Everything about him seemed untrustworthy. It suddenly occurred to me that people tended to remember dishonest-looking faces, didn't they? That probably wasn't ideal if he was going to be involved in the job.

'There's also one other thing, but I'll let you in on the secret tomorrow.' Alfie smirked.

I hated it when Alfie held back details to keep us in suspense. 'Can't you tell us tonight?' I asked, trying to keep my tone light and the irritation out of my voice.

'You need to learn to be patient, Gemma.' Alfie moved behind my chair and began slowly massaging my shoulders.

The feeling of his hands on my skin made me shudder and made my muscles tense more. I had a sudden urge to jump up and slap him around the face. But instead, I stared straight ahead, and my eyes met Nathan's. He stared back at me with a haunted expression. I found it unbearable to see him like this, but Alfie was enjoying every minute of his suffering. When he moved his hands from my shoulders and began running his fingers through the length of my hair again, like he was stroking a cat, I couldn't take any more.

'I'm going to call it a night.' I stood up from the table and began walking towards the door. If Alfie was surprised by my sudden departure, he didn't show it.

I wanted to forget about this evening and go to sleep, but my mind was too active. So instead, I spent the night tossing and turning, worrying about the latest job. I was just dropping off when the screen on my phone lit up as a new message came through from Alfie.

The two of you need to come to my room now.

Getting up, I walked over to the other bed where Nathan was asleep on his side, facing the window. Reaching towards him, I traced my fingers across the five o'clock shadow covering his strong jawline, and he stirred. Opening his dark brown eyes, he smiled at me.

'Sorry to wake you, but Alfie's summoned us.'

'What time is it?' Nathan groaned and stretched out his neck.

'Six-thirty.'

★

A make-up artist was inside Alfie's suite when we arrived ten minutes later. Having already undergone his transformation, Tommy opened the door. I couldn't believe what I was seeing. He was unrecognisable. Prosthetics had been applied to his face to alter the shape, and his skin tone had changed.

We took a seat and watched Céline add the finishing touches to Johno's disguise.

'Don't get too comfortable, you're next, Nathan,' Alfie said.

'OK, I'm ready for you now,' Céline said.

'I want you to add a distinctive tattoo to the side of his neck. The collar of his shirt needs to partially cover it,' Alfie said.

'No problem.' When Céline had finished, she fitted Nathan with a professional wig and added a bushy moustache to his face.

'I hope the photoshoot goes well,' Céline said, placing her things back into her silver trolley case.

I locked eyes with Nathan. He looked as confused as I was.

'Thanks for everything – you've done a great job,' Alfie said, paying her with a wad of cash before showing her out.

Just as Céline was leaving, Terry arrived. 'You guys look fantastic.' Rubbing his hands together, he nodded his approval.

'Did you get the uniforms?' Alfie asked.

'Yes, they're in here.' Terry gestured to the suit carrier he was holding.

When was Alfie going to tell us what was going on?

None of this made any sense. I didn't want to have to ask, but couldn't think of a feasible explanation. 'Why are they doing a photoshoot?'

'They're not.' Alfie rolled his eyes at me. 'But I had to tell Céline something, didn't I? I could hardly say, do us a favour, love, make them look extra convincing because they're going to be robbing the Diamond Centre in broad daylight, could I?'

'Their disguises don't fit the stereotypical ones you usually go for. There's not a balaclava in sight.'

'That's because we want witnesses to give the police descriptions of the robbers, which will be inaccurate. That way they'll end up searching for the wrong suspects. Johno and Tommy are going to dress as women to throw the cops off the trail, and some beady-eyed member of the public is bound to notice Nathan's tattoo. It looks good on him, don't you think?' Alfie grinned.

Now I understood why Johno had a blond ponytail and Tommy had a brown plait. But I wasn't so sure the police would be fooled that easily. Although both the brothers had slight builds, neither of them were remotely feminine, and if you asked me, Nathan's bushy moustache was ridiculously over the top. He looked like a Colombian drug baron or one of the Village People. I made a mental note never to let him grow facial hair; it did absolutely nothing for him.

'You guys should go and get changed,' Alfie said, passing them each a suit carrier.

When Nathan, Tommy and Johno returned from the dressing room, they looked much more convincing. It was amazing what a uniform, hat and badge could do for a person.

'Let's get started,' Alfie said. 'We'll do a quick run-through of the plan before you leave. As soon as you arrive at the centre, make your way over to Terry. He'll be in the lobby waiting for you.'

'Won't people wonder what's going on when three officers walk in off the street?' Nathan asked.

'They won't give you a second glance as long as you act with confidence. But if you're nervous, you'll give the game away,' Alfie said.

'The police come into the centre all the time, so nobody will take any notice of you,' Terry agreed. 'Anyway, as it's Saturday, the place will be almost deserted, and only skeleton staff will be on duty.'

'Nathan, you'll have to do the talking. You two keep quiet,' Alfie said, turning to face Tommy and Johno. 'Otherwise, your voices will blow your cover. There's no point dressing like a woman if you sound like a man.' Alfie laughed, then turned back to Nathan. 'Speak to the security guard in the foyer and tell him that you're responding to a call. Then find out how many others are on duty. Don't mess that up.'

'I won't.'

'It's important that all the guards are accounted for. Round them up and get them to follow you. Then separate them and handcuff them in the basement. Do you understand?'

'Yes.'

'Terry's going to escort you through the building, to where the vault's located. Remember the whole place is rigged with heat and pressure sensors, and high-spec cameras will be filming from every angle.' Alfie looked at Nathan, Johno and Tommy, in turn, to make sure they were paying attention. 'Once you've emptied the vault, get out as quick as you can. Gemma and I will be waiting in the car.'

'What if somebody tries to stop us?' Nathan asked.

'Nobody's going to challenge you. You're police officers. But if someone does get in your way, threaten the fucker with violence. That should be enough to make them stop in their tracks, and if it doesn't, give them a slap. Then they'll know you mean business.'

'Are you OK?' I mouthed to Nathan.

Nathan fixed me with his eyes but didn't answer. His silence said it all.

Alfie made everything sound so simple, but I knew stealing the contents of the Antwerp Diamond Centre was going to be almost impossible. I tried not to think about what would happen if something went wrong. For Nathan's sake, I'd have to keep my concerns to myself; it wouldn't be fair to air them now.

Terry looked at his watch. 'It's time we got going. Give me ten minutes to get into position.'

79

Gemma

Alfie and I got into the Audi. We couldn't park immediately outside the Diamond Centre because metal barricades prevent unauthorised vehicles from entering the area, so we got as close as we could and waited. The atmosphere in the car was tense as we sat inches apart, staring through the windscreen.

'My dad's a patient man. He knew he'd get her back at some stage,' Alfie said, breaking the silence.

I hadn't got a clue what he meant. He was talking in riddles again. I arched an eyebrow and eyed him suspiciously. Alfie had a habit of half telling you something. It was infuriating. When he turned to look at me, he could see from the look on my face, I wasn't impressed.

'I wonder what Rosa would think if she knew Nathan was about to rob the Antwerp Diamond Centre.' Alfie smiled. 'Like father, like son.'

Alfie's words turned my stomach. Even though I knew I shouldn't, I couldn't help myself: I was going to kick off. Alfie Watson was about to get a piece of my mind. 'So everything you've put us through was to get back at Rosa, was it?' I couldn't control the anger in my voice; it was rising up inside me.

'Nathan offered himself to the firm on a plate. We couldn't say no, could we?' Alfie ran his fingers through his blond hair while giving me a smug grin.

I let out a slow breath and willed myself to sound steady. 'I think Jethro will be very proud of you, taking one for the team is a noble act,' I said through gritted teeth.

Alfie looked at me as if he had no idea what I was talking about.

The pulse was pounding in my temple. 'You used me to get revenge on Nathan's family.' I should have realised that was why he was so desperate to sleep with me. I couldn't believe I'd fallen for it. I turned my face away. I was so angry with myself; I was about to explode with rage.

'You've got it all wrong, Gemma; I didn't sleep with you to get back at Nathan or his family.' Reaching towards me, Alfie turned me to face him. He stared at me while he ran his tobacco-scented finger across my lips. I could feel his breath on my skin, but I couldn't bring myself to meet his searching blue eyes. 'From the moment I saw you, I knew I had to be with you.'

I didn't want to hear another word.

Alfie placed two fingers under my chin and tilted my face towards his, before he swept my long brown hair over my shoulder and planted a kiss on my cheek. I wiped it away with the back of my hand. Then he put his hand behind my neck, pulled my face towards his, and tried to kiss me. I put my hands on his chest to make some distance between us. I didn't want him to touch me. He made me feel dirty.

Clearing my throat, I composed myself and prepared to give him a dose of the truth. 'Find yourself a new plaything. I've resigned from the position.'

Alfie threw back his head and roared with laughter. But when I continued to tear a strip off him, it wiped the smile off his face.

'You're pathetic, Alfie. Being hit on by you has become an unfortunate part of the daily grind. But I've had enough of it, so I'm going to spell this out for you. Stop pestering me for sex. The thought of sleeping with you makes bile rise in my stomach.'

Alfie stared at me. 'Have you finished giving me a bollocking now?'

'No, I haven't. Just because you spend your life intimidating other people, it doesn't make you a tough guy. I'm not scared of you.'

I wanted to rip his head off, but it would have been impossible in the confined space I was in, so I'd had to settle for giving him a tongue lashing instead. A vein in Alfie's neck began pulsating. I probably shouldn't have said what I did, but at this stage, I didn't care what happened to me. He was getting pleasure out of making me feel uncomfortable, toying with me like a cat does with a terrified mouse.

Alfie unbuttoned his suit jacket and settled back in the leather seat. When he lifted his arm to smooth back his blond hair, I got a glimpse of his holster. It reminded me that he had ways of silencing people. Riling him up was a stupid thing to do. I should take a step back and be on my best behaviour.

80

Gemma

Dressed in their uniforms, Nathan, Johno and Tommy left the hotel one by one to avoid raising suspicion. My heart began pounding in my chest as we watched them walk the short distance to the fourteen-storey building and disappear inside. At least their appearance had given Alfie and me something else to focus on after our argument.

'It's ten past nine,' Alfie said, checking his limited edition matt black Rolex watch.

Nathan, Tommy and Johno walked through the metal turnstiles, flashed their police ID at the guards, and breezed through the lobby.

Following Alfie's instructions, Nathan insisted that all the guards on duty accompanied them to the basement so that nobody would be patrolling the interior. While Nathan pointed a gun at the four men, Tommy and Johno wrapped duct tape around their hands and legs and placed it across their mouths. Then they cuffed their wrists and ankles to metal structures within the basement. Before blindfolding the men, Johno took their wallets from their pockets and handed them to Nathan.

'We know who you are and we'll find out where you live if you start blabbing to the cops. If you want to stay safe, keep your mouths shut,' Nathan said, giving them a warning.

Immobilising the detectors as they went, Terry led the way to the underground safe, hidden deep within the fabric of the building. The door in front of the vault was left open during business hours, so they wouldn't need to disable the pair of plates that formed a magnetic field around it. Now just a reinforced steel grate stood between them and the contents.

As it was a Saturday, all the cameras housed within the fourteen-floor building were monitored by just one man. Terry pressed the nearby buzzer and stared at the screen. The guard in the control room recognised him, and remotely unlocked the vault. Terry, Nathan, Johno and Tommy stepped inside.

The vault was fitted with cameras, motion, heat, and light sensors and surrounded by thick concrete walls. Tommy pushed back a panel in the ceiling and located the wires for the detectors. He installed a sensor bypass so they could move around without triggering the alarms and covered the cameras with black plastic bags.

'We'll have to move quickly before the guard realises there's a problem with the security cameras. But be careful, if we set off one of the alarms, steel shutters will drop down to protect the entrance to the vault, and we'll be trapped inside,' Tommy said.

'Grab as much as you can,' Johno said, popping the lock on a safety deposit box.

'Don't forget the paperwork. You'll need it if you want to be able to sell the diamonds legitimately.' Terry grinned.

Fifteen minutes had passed since they entered the safe and they'd already managed to fill their rucksacks with cash, gold bars, loose diamonds, jewellery and other valuables. They'd need to spend hours in the vault to be able to empty all the boxes stored within it, and time was something they didn't have.

'Let's get out of here,' Tommy said, having checked the time on his watch.

Once outside the vault, Terry paced ahead, dialling Alfie's mobile as he went. 'Start the car,' was all he said before hanging up.

When Terry stepped into the foyer, he immediately noticed two police officers coming through the turnstile. Looking over his shoulder at the others, he put out his hand, gesturing for them to stop. 'Drop the bags and stay here. Make sure you're out of sight. I'll see what's going on.'

Terry walked towards the officers. 'Good morning, gentlemen, can I assist you with something?'

'We're responding to a call from the surveillance room,' one of the officers replied. 'We need to check the intruder alarm in the vault. It appears to have been triggered.'

'Don't worry I'll get the in-house security team to deal with that,' Terry said, thinking on his feet.

'The operator has already tried to contact them. When he got no response, it made him suspicious. That's why he called us.'

'It does seem a bit strange that nobody replied, but there aren't many guards on duty on a Saturday. I'm sure everything is fine, they're probably just having a break.' Terry smiled.

'Can you show us where the vault is located?'

'Certainly.'

Terry turned around and led the officers across the foyer. When Nathan, Johno and Tommy saw them coming towards where they were hiding, the tension in the stairwell became palpable. Terry stopped next to the half-glass door and called the lift. As soon as they stepped inside, the three men picked up their rucksacks and calmly exited through the main entrance, walking across to where the Audi was parked.

'What was all that about?' Alfie asked.

'The surveillance operator thought there might be an intruder. He wants the police to check the vault,' Nathan said.

'It must have been another false alarm. This happens all the time.' Terry's face broke into its untrustworthy smile as he ran his hand over the closed door of the vault. 'The detectors are so sensitive to movement. Last time they were triggered an insect was responsible.'

Alfie sat behind the wheel smirking before he pulled the car out into the traffic. 'Security's so tight around the Diamond District anyone would think they're scared of being robbed.' Alfie started laughing as we drove past the guards patrolling the narrow streets surrounding the centre.

As usual, we were reacting completely differently to the same situation. He was grinning like the cat that got the cream, whereas I sat next to him in the front seat, gripping the sides of the leather chair so tightly my knuckles had turned white. I held my breath and stared straight ahead until we were well away from the area.

'So how did it go?' Alfie asked, looking at Tommy in the rear-view mirror.

'Really well, no hitches at all, but I can't wait to get this lot off,' Tommy replied, making exaggerated movements with the lower half of his face.

How could Tommy say the job had no hitches? They'd almost been caught red-handed. But the bigger the risk, the bigger the thrill they seemed to get from it.

Alfie's mobile rang. 'Hello,' he said, steering the car with one hand. 'That's great news, Terry. We'll see you in a couple of days.' Alfie put the phone down. 'Those dopey bastards examined the area around the vault and decided that it was secure. Terry said he was shitting himself, but he didn't need to worry. They left without going inside.'

Alfie joined the dual carriageway and headed out of Antwerp. We were going back to Boulogne where Knuckles and Frankie were waiting for us on the yacht. Alfie had only been driving for a couple of miles when he pulled off the road and turned onto a dirt track that led into a wooded area.

'Why are we stopping?' I asked when he slowed the car down, wondering if Nathan and I were about to become victims of a gangland execution.

'They need to get changed, and this place isn't visible from the road. I left some bin liners on the parcel shelf, put the prosthetics, wigs and uniforms in one, and we'll burn it. We can't afford to leave any evidence behind,' Alfie said.

A thought flashed through my head as I watched them removing the elaborate disguises. 'Wouldn't it have been easier to break in at night?'

'The guys would never have been able to get in. The building's too secure after dark. It was easier just to walk straight through the front door!' Alfie smiled.

'All the props are in here,' Tommy said, holding up the bin liner.

'Get rid of it,' Alfie replied, slipping his hands into the pockets of his suit trousers.

Tommy lit a match and threw it onto the bag. We stood in silence, watching the acrid smoke and flames rise until there was no trace of the bin liner's contents. Only ash and scorched undergrowth were left behind.

'Gemma, see if you can tune the radio into an English-speaking station,' Alfie said, keeping his eyes on the road.

I leant forward and started scanning through the channels, stopping when I got to Radio X.

'The specialist police force, the Diamond Squad, has called for a nationwide alert following the heist at the Antwerp Diamond Centre earlier today,' the presenter announced.

'Turn the volume up,' Alfie said, looking over at me.

'The commissioner in charge of investigating the case said a team of three had executed the robbery. A man and two women, dressed in police uniforms, brazenly entered the building in broad daylight. They emptied the contents of a large number of safety deposit boxes and calmly left the building one hundred million dollars richer,' the presenter continued.

'Did you hear that? You guys got away with one hundred million dollars. What a result,' Alfie said before leaning forward and turning the volume up some more.

'The investigating team have been left with more than a lingering suspicion that this was an inside job, given that the robbers got past the radar of twenty-four-hour surveillance, and sixty video cameras that constantly monitor Antwerp's Diamond District,' the presenter said.

'Terry's covered his tracks well if all they have is a lingering suspicion that it was an inside job.' Alfie smiled with pride like he was a father watching his son score the winning goal at a football match. 'Notice how they haven't mentioned that two of their officers were called to check the vault for intruders. If they hadn't sent Inspector Clouseau and his equally incompetent buddy along they might have caught the people responsible.' Alfie laughed.

'The commissioner said the elite force would do everything possible to recover the stolen items, but when thieves do a job of this nature, everything is meticulously planned to leave no clues behind. This was not the work of amateurs. The people we are looking for are armed and dangerous career criminals. Interpol have been alerted, as the hunt for the suspects continues.'

'Armed and dangerous career criminals,' Alfie said, and a huge grin spread across his face. 'I like that. I might have it printed on some business cards.'

Tommy leant forward in his seat. 'Do you want me to give Knuckles an update?'

'Yes, tell him to get some champagne on ice, we should be in Boulogne around two o'clock.'

Knuckles and Frankie were waiting on the deck of the *Lady Nora* when we approached from the harbour car park.

'It's good to see you,' Knuckles said. Grabbing Alfie's hand, he leant towards him, and they exchanged a shoulder-bump greeting.

'It's good to see you too, mate,' Alfie said, slapping him firmly on his broad back.

'Welcome back.' Frankie shook Alfie by the hand. 'Do you want me to phone La Plage and ask them to reserve a table for you?'

'No, we'll eat on board tonight. We need to keep a low profile while the cops are sniffing around.'

'How did it go?' Knuckles asked.

Alfie gestured towards the stairwell. He was reluctant to go into details while they were on deck.

'The champagne is on ice as requested. Do you want me to pour it?' Knuckles asked.

'What do you think?' Alfie replied, arching his eyebrows as he made his way below deck.

'Did everything go smoothly?' Knuckles handed Alfie a glass.

'Yeah, it was one of those dream jobs, payback for the months we'd spent planning it.' Alfie held his champagne flute in the air. 'You guys should be proud of yourselves. Cheers,' he continued, clinking glasses with each of us in turn.

81

Gemma

The argument I'd had earlier with Alfie was playing on my mind. Up until now, I'd thought Nathan had just been unlucky when he'd got involved with a gangster. Admittedly, borrowing money from Alfie was a stupid thing to do. But Nathan couldn't have foreseen the spiralling debt that would follow and the stress it would cause. That was part of the plan. Alfie wanted revenge, so he was never going to allow us to clear the debt.

The Watsons had been biding their time until the opportunity to retaliate presented itself. Jethro and Alfie were both gunning for Rosa, but they had different reasons for wanting to get even with her. Exploiting her son and daughter-in-law was the perfect way to pay her back. She was powerless to stop them.

Although Alfie had denied it, I was more certain than ever that he'd used me as a form of twisted revenge. Alfie still felt incredibly bitter about the fact that Jethro was in love with Rosa. He adored his mum and hated the way she'd been treated. It made perfect sense that the long-held grudge he had with Nathan's family drove him to sleep with me.

I'd been a complete idiot, and now Alfie was having the last laugh. I'd allowed him to manipulate me into doing something that had jeopardised my marriage. I had broken Nathan's trust after I'd spent so long building it up. It would take time to repair the damage I'd caused, and there was no guarantee we'd be able to get through this. Only time would tell if we were strong enough to make it.

When I met Nathan, we couldn't keep our hands off each other. The first throes of passion lasted a long time. I never thought the honeymoon period would come to an end, but over time, our desire gradually cooled as we fell into the rut of day-to-day living. I wasn't concerned about it though. That happened when couples had been together for a long time. Instead, we became so finely tuned that we could predict each other's actions and words. That made me feel safe and secure and reassured me that we were extremely compatible.

Right at the beginning of our relationship, I felt Nathan and I were destined to be together. Why had I risked throwing my marriage away? I couldn't answer that. I wasn't sure I'd ever fully understand the reasons I'd allowed my head to be turned. I wasn't usually gullible enough to fall for a smooth talker like Alfie. I used to be able to spot a man like him a mile off and give them a wide berth. I had an extremely low tolerance for a man spouting bullshit. I must have been losing my touch at detecting a silver tongue to have fallen prey so easily. I'd embarrassed myself. I wasn't a seventeen-year-old girl, I was a thirty-year-old woman. Why had I been so blinkered? What the hell was the matter with me?

If Nathan and I were going to save our marriage, we needed to get as far away from Alfie as possible. He was toxic. Tempting as it was to try and get even with him, nothing good would come of it. But I also wasn't going to stand by and let him come between us. If I did that, he'd have won, and Alfie didn't like to lose.

82

Gemma

Under cover of darkness, Knuckles and Frankie went to unload the boot of the Audi. They brought the bags on board the yacht, and with a glass of Jack Daniel's in his hand, Alfie took a seat at the head of the table and began examining the contents. He lifted a gold bar out of the rucksack and kissed it. Then he scattered the rest of the items across the shiny surface. Rough and polished diamonds, precious stones, watches, necklaces and other jewellery were strewn everywhere. His smile grew wide at the sight of it all.

'Sort this lot into similar pieces and bag them,' Alfie said, slicking back his immaculate blond hair with his fingertips.

'Is Terry going to sell the jewellery?' Nathan asked.

'Yeah, he'll come and get it in a couple of days when the dust has settled,' Alfie replied.

'Isn't that a bit risky? I always thought diamonds had serial numbers engraved on them to prevent them from being stolen,' Nathan said.

I raised my eyebrow and had to stop myself from smiling. Nathan had a valid point. Time seemed to stand still while we waited for Alfie to respond. I wondered how he was going to overcome that problem.

'Expensive stones are inscribed with a code to make them easy to identify, but the engraving can be polished off. Terry can remove the inscriptions. Anyway, why are you asking so many questions? You're beginning to piss me off.' Alfie drained his glass, suddenly irritated by Nathan's thirst for knowledge. 'Do yourself a favour and pipe down, or fuck off somewhere else,' Alfie said, throwing Nathan a look.

Alfie assured us that Terry knew what he was doing. But the police were looking for the jewellery. 'What if he gets caught trying to sell it?' I interlaced my fingers to stop myself from biting my nails.

Alfie shrugged. 'Terry will probably strip the jewellery apart. He'll hold on to the big stones for the moment, it's too soon to try and sell those, but he'll shift the small ones straight away.'

'Won't it look suspicious if Terry suddenly has a surplus of diamonds for sale following the burglary at the Diamond Centre?' I questioned.

'It won't be a problem as long as he releases them into the market in a slow trickle.'

Terry would sell the stones cheaply to make them attractive to the dealers, so he would be able to shift them quickly. I thought it was too much of a coincidence. Somebody was bound to realise the diamonds came from the robbery. I was unconvinced by what Alfie had been saying. I found it hard to believe that nobody would ask questions.

'The first dealers that Terry sells the stones to will

probably realise they're stolen, but by the time they've changed hands for the tenth time, nobody will care where they came from.' Alfie lit a cigarette and inhaled deeply. 'Diamonds trade over and over again. That's the nature of the business, and luckily for us that makes them extremely difficult to trace. That's why it's so easy for us to travel across Europe. Thanks to the soft borders, it makes it almost impossible for the police to keep tabs on us or the diamonds. I bet that's music to your ears, Gemma.' Alfie smiled and raised his glass at me.

I let out a long breath. I supposed I was going to have to take his word for that.

Alfie picked up a diamond and sapphire necklace. 'Terry's a true craftsman. Once he gets his hands on this, he'll take it apart and remount the stones in different settings. What's the betting that within weeks Terry will have set those diamonds in somebody's engagement ring? You never know, Gemma, if you play your cards right, I might ask him to make one for you.' Alfie laughed as he locked eyes with Nathan.

Pushing back his chair, Nathan got up from the table and stormed out of the saloon. Fury rose up inside of me when a huge grin swept across Alfie's face. I was fed up with his snide comments and stood glaring at him with my arms crossed over my chest. How could Alfie humiliate Nathan by saying that in front of everyone? I wanted to lash out at him. But instead, I let silent judgement seep from my pores, and fill the air in the room until I was unable to bite my tongue any longer.

'What the hell's the matter with you?' I said, pointing an accusatory finger at Alfie.

I waited impatiently for his reply, aware that all eyes were on me. Tears attempted to cloud my vision, but I wouldn't give Alfie the satisfaction of seeing me cry, so I blinked them away.

'Nothing's the matter with me, in fact, I couldn't be better.' Alfie got up from the table and stood in front of me. 'You, on the other hand, have got a face like a slapped arse.' Alfie ran his fingertips down the side of my face.

'Don't touch me,' I said, looking him straight in the eye.

'What's got into you, Gemma? You used to like it when I touched you.' Alfie smirked. Stepping into my personal space, he slid his hand around my waist and pulled me towards him.

I had to stop myself from slapping him around the face after I pushed him away. There was no doubt the others knew about us, but I didn't want to have this conversation in front of an audience. They weren't going to hear the sordid details from my lips.

The idea of being with Alfie again made me feel sick. It haunted me every time I thought about the night we'd spent together. I needed to put some space between us, so I went on deck to find my husband.

Nathan didn't acknowledge me when I stood next to him. He continued to lean against the railings and stare out to sea, while the material of his T-shirt billowed around him in the cold December air. If the circumstances had been different, this would have been a very romantic moment, just the two of us and the lights from the nearby yachts punctuating the darkness. But I could tell holding hands and stargazing was the last thing on Nathan's mind. He was distant, lost in thought.

'You must be freezing.' I ran my hand up his back to get his attention. 'Are you OK?'

'I can't take much more of this,' Nathan finally replied. 'It's bad enough trying to come to terms with what happened, without Alfie rubbing my nose in it every few seconds.'

'I'm so sorry, Nathan – do you think we'll ever be able to come back from this?' I couldn't bear to think about the future without him.

'I want to put this behind us, but Alfie's never going to let us, is he?' Nathan's words were bitter.

My guilt was eating away at me. No matter how hard Nathan tried to overlook my infidelity, the pain contorting his face confirmed just how much I'd hurt him. I hated to see him like this. I realised at that moment, I wasn't prepared to stand by and let Alfie torment Nathan like this any more. He was playing with his feelings, and it was tearing him apart. My brow wrinkled in concern. I wished I could turn back the clock and make all his suffering go away.

'We need to get away so that we can make a fresh start. Why don't we leave tonight when everyone goes to bed?' I whispered, having looked over my shoulder to check we were alone.

'How can we? Alfie's a psycho, and he knows where we live. What if he goes after my mum? He might kill her if we try to run.'

What a sobering thought. But Nathan was right, Alfie was a control freak, and if we tried to cross him, he'd make us pay one way or the other. I suddenly thought of Rosa; she would be worried sick about us. Nathan is the centre of her universe, and she treats me like the precious daughter she never had. I wished we could try to get in touch with her, but it was too dangerous. Alfie constantly checked the mobile he gave me to make sure I hadn't used it apart from to contact him.

While Nathan and I stood side by side on deck, listening to the sound of the sea, I tried to think of a solution. Right now, we were stuck in a never-ending cycle, but there had to be a way out. We just hadn't found it yet. I wasn't going to lose hope. I was convinced in time an opportunity would present itself.

As we waited for the right moment to come our way, I'd focus on the most important thing: my marriage. Nathan and I were staying together. We still loved each other, so I knew we were going to get through this and whatever else life decided to throw at us.

83

Gemma

Midnight came and went, and I was still wide awake, lying in the double bed next to Nathan. Our cabin was dark, and the only sound I could hear was the water lapping on the hull. I tried to drift off to sleep, but all I could think about was my husband. He often hid from his demons and shut down when I tried to discuss something difficult with him. My infidelity had made him retreat within himself. But if it took me the rest of my life, I would make it up to him and put things right between us. Nobody was perfect, but Nathan and I were perfect for each other.

As I stared at the ceiling, I considered our options and kept coming back to the same conclusion. We'd have to get as far away from Alfie as possible if we were going to save our marriage.

Thanks to Alfie, Nathan and I already had quite a collection of bogus passports: French, Spanish, Italian and German to be exact. We'd been travelling across Europe on those for months now without encountering any problems. What was to stop us using them if we went on the run? The more I thought about it, the more the idea of vanishing into the night was beginning to appeal to me. But if we did disappear, could we escape without leaving a trail behind us?

Where would we go? The language barrier would definitely be our biggest hurdle. I supposed we could head to an English-speaking country, but that would narrow our choices considerably. But what else could we do? If we couldn't speak the language, we wouldn't be able to get jobs easily. As I lay in the stillness of the cabin, tossing and turning, I suddenly remembered that we wouldn't have any employment or credit history either, which would make starting over incredibly difficult.

Every time I thought doing a vanishing act was a viable option, another problem arose, making the whole idea seem impossible. But there had to be a way. I wasn't going to give up that easily. I couldn't spend the rest of my life living in a hotel room being controlled by Alfie. He was the puppet master, and he manipulated us for his entertainment.

We'd learnt a lot from Alfie during the time we'd spent together, so we should make use of it. He told me before that if somebody wanted to successfully disappear off-grid all they needed was to have one decent piece of ID. Once you had that, you could get hold of anything else you needed apparently.

I reached forward and touched Nathan's shoulder. 'Are you awake?' I whispered in his ear.

'Yeah, I can't sleep either.'

Nathan rolled onto his front. He shoved his hands under

the pillow as he tilted his head to the side and looked at me. How could I have ever cheated on him? Every time I looked at his gorgeous face, I was racked with guilt. I'd caused him a lot of unnecessary suffering. But then I reminded myself, if we were going to move on from this, we needed to put it behind us.

'I've had an idea,' I said, turning onto my side so that I could see Nathan's reaction.

'About what?'

'I've been thinking about how we can get away from Alfie.' I edged along the pillow until our faces were inches apart.

'Oh, not that again. I thought we'd agreed, it wasn't safe to do that.' Nathan flipped onto his back and stared into the darkness.

I collapsed back onto the pillows and let out an exaggerated sigh. 'Don't dismiss me before you've heard me out.'

Nathan turned back to face me. 'If we try and double-cross Alfie, we'll be signing our own death warrants, Gemma.'

'But if Alfie kills us, he won't get his money back, will he?'

Nathan shifted onto his side and put his elbow on the pillow. 'He won't care about the money if we shoot through. He'll want to get even with us.' Nathan rested his head in the palm of his hand.

Did Nathan know about the long-standing grudge between his and Alfie's families? Silence hung heavy between us. Maybe he was right. We'd more than paid back what we owed him, and he was still forcing us to work for him. I took in a deep breath and let it out slowly before replying.

'He's never going to let us go, Nathan.'

'He might at some stage. But if we leave before he says we can, he'll come after us. Is that what you want?'

'No.' I couldn't help throwing Nathan a sulky glance. 'But if we pick the right moment...' I broke off when I saw the look on Nathan's face. He was having none of it. Alfie was a dangerous man and a respected figure in the underworld, so Nathan didn't want to cross him. 'Think about this for a minute, there's so much money on board this yacht; we could take some and disappear. I'm not talking about all of it, but you took part in the robbery, so you're entitled to a share.' Keeping the frustration out of my voice was difficult.

'I'm not sure Alfie would agree with you. If we steal his money, he'll come after us. That's the way it works in his world. It's an unspoken rule.'

Nathan and I were at loggerheads over this. We both had a stubborn streak, so neither of us was going to back down easily. Alfie had shown us how easy it was to change our appearance. I wanted us to disguise ourselves and leave in the middle of the night. But Nathan was adamant that if we did that, we would always be looking over our shoulders.

'You need to get this idea out of your head. I'm telling you now if we run, he'll find us, and if he can't find us, he'll go after my mum. I guarantee it.' Nathan's brown eyes were troubled.

Although Nathan had a point, I'd decided I'd had enough of this no-win situation. I couldn't stand it any more. I knew we couldn't risk going home or making contact with Rosa. We'd have to stay away from her. I didn't want to put her in danger. But I'd made up my mind, I had to get out of here. Staying was no longer an option. There was only one problem: how was I going to convince Nathan to come with me? After everything we'd been through, I couldn't contemplate going without him. There must be something I could do to make him change his mind.

I didn't want to spend the rest of my life on the run either, but I was convinced things would settle down after a while. The way I saw it, we didn't have an alternative. If we stayed, it was only a matter of time until we got caught by the police. What did we have to lose? I wished Nathan would push himself out of his comfort zone for a minute. 'Do me a favour and at least consider my suggestion.'

'I have, and I still don't think it's a good idea. What do you want me to say?' Nathan tilted his head to one side and studied me. 'Why won't you listen to me? If we disappear, we'll put my mum in danger. That's the way these things work.'

I understood what Nathan was saying, and the last thing I wanted was for Alfie to hurt Rosa, but if we didn't make a break for it, there would be no end to this. He was never going to let us go.

'If I could guarantee my mum would be safe, I'd be up for it. But Alfie knows where to find her so I can't take the risk.' Nathan shrugged his shoulders. 'I still have no idea how he knows her, but he does, so it's not an option.'

I knew the reason, but Nathan wasn't going to like it. I paused and drew in a deep breath as I considered how to tell him. 'Alfie knows your mum from the restaurant.'

Nathan looked at me with a puzzled expression on his face.

'He told me Jethro owns Mamma Donatella's.'

Nathan shook his head. 'Alfie's full of shit. Donatella and Bernardo own it; the clue's in the name.'

'When Alfie was young, Jethro used to make him sit in the restaurant for hours so he could be near your mum,' I continued, undeterred by the fact that my husband didn't believe me.

Nathan raised his eyebrows. I knew he was sceptical. 'You shouldn't believe everything he tells you. If that was true, how come I don't remember it?'

I shrugged my shoulders. I couldn't answer that. 'Did you know your dad served a prison sentence?'

Nathan's mouth fell open. I could see by the look on his face that he knew nothing about this. I wished I didn't have to be the one to tell my husband that there was more to his past than he realised, but somebody had to.

'Jethro set your dad up. He wanted Gareth behind bars so he could make a move on your mum, but his plan backfired. Rosa wasn't interested in him.'

Nathan's nostrils flared. He threw back the covers and got to his feet. 'I'm going to fucking kill him.'

'Nathan, wait. Let me finish.' I jumped out of bed and blocked his path.

'If that's true, what Jethro did changed the whole course of my life. I grew up thinking that somehow I was responsible for my dad's absence. I can't let the Watsons get away with that.'

Nathan had found it hard to accept his father's abandonment and had struggled with commitment issues and insecurities all his life. By his own admission, he was a needy child and a moody teenager. But Rosa was an amazing mother; she'd tried hard to fill the gap Gareth had left. It was no wonder they were so close.

'You need to hear this. I think Alfie only slept with me to get back at you. He's still bitter about the fact that Jethro never cared about his mum because he was in love with Rosa.' My mouth trembled as I struggled to get the words out. Overcome with emotion, I began to cry. Nathan didn't comfort me but stood staring at me, so I wiped my tears away on the back of my hand.

'He's bitter... How do you think I feel?' Nathan glared at me; his face was like thunder.

'I know it's an instinctive reaction, but please don't confront him about it tonight. Wait until you calm down.'

84

Nathan

My head was spinning. I'd been completely blindsided by what Gemma had told me. She'd dropped a massive bombshell, and I didn't want to believe it, but I had a horrible feeling she was right about my dad. It wasn't just Alfie trying to stir up trouble again.

If this was true, it would have devastating consequences. My relationship with my mum would never be the same again. I wasn't sure I'd be able to forgive her for keeping something this important from me. But why would she do that? There wasn't a logical explanation. I knew I shouldn't jump to conclusions. I should wait until I'd spoken to her first.

Things were going from bad to worse. None of this seemed real. This had become a nightmare of a different kind, one that was too painful for me to comprehend. My throat tightened as I tried to hold in the sadness. No wonder my mum had refused to talk about my dad, and got distressed every time his name was mentioned. She must have been scared of getting caught out if she answered the questions my inquisitive young mind occasionally raised.

I wasn't sure with whom I was more angry, Alfie or my mum. The morning couldn't come soon enough for my liking. I needed to confront both of them. If Alfie's version of events was correct, I'd grown up believing a lie. That was unforgivable. My mum would have some explaining to do. I deserved to know the truth.

I'd only ever heard my mum's side of the story, and there was a good chance that wasn't accurate. So now I didn't know what to think. I'd grown up believing my dad was a bad man and spent most of my childhood completely hating him for abandoning me and not being part of my life. The more I thought about it, the more it made sense. If my dad had been behind bars during my childhood, that would explain why he didn't keep in contact with me. Why hadn't my mum let me go and visit him? His absence had affected my whole life.

Now I was convinced my mum had been lying to me. The issues I had been holding on to for all those years were her fault. I stopped asking about my dad because she'd get upset if I mentioned him. Mum had made it clear she didn't want to rake over painful memories. The experience had been so awful, she wanted to forget it. Out of loyalty to her, I respected that.

Anger was building up inside me. I wasn't sure how I would react when I spoke to my mum. I needed to hear her out, but it was going to be hard to keep a lid on my temper if I found out she'd lied to me.

Even if Alfie's account turned out not to be true, I was suddenly curious to find out about the father I never knew.

I wanted to contact him and hear his side of the story. I hoped it wasn't too late for us to start building bridges.

As I lay in the dark staring at the ceiling, my thoughts turned to Alfie and his family. The Watsons had taken my dad away, they had almost put an end to my marriage, and now they were going to destroy my relationship with my mum. What else did they want from me? When would their grudge be settled?

85

Gemma

It was barely seven o'clock in the morning when Nathan began hammering on Alfie's cabin door with his fist. He still had his hand clenched when Alfie opened it.

'What the fuck do you want?' Alfie said, getting up in Nathan's face.

'Is it true?' Nathan asked. His eyes blazed with fury.

Alfie beamed from ear to ear.

I stood behind them in the corridor, watching the drama unfold.

'I need to phone my mum.'

'Feeling homesick, are you?' To taunt Nathan, Alfie began sucking his thumb.

Nathan flew into a rage and pushed Alfie backwards into his cabin. By the time I made it into the room, they were taking it in turns to shove each other in the chest. No words were spoken, but their rivalry had reached a new height. I got between the two of them so I could stop the fight before it started. Turning my back on Alfie, I put my hands on Nathan's forearms and looked up into his face.

'Please calm down.'

Nathan couldn't disguise the look of fury on his face. His eyes burned with hatred for the man in front of him.

I turned back to face Alfie. I was well aware that if I asked a favour, it was going to come at a price, but I'd have to worry about that later. I needed to help my husband. 'Please let Nathan make a call. He needs to speak to his mum urgently.'

I looked Alfie straight in the eye while I waited for his reply. There was something about the way he stared at me that set an alarm off in my head, but I pushed my unease to the back of my mind. Finally, he broke eye contact, walked over to the far side of the cabin and after entering the combination on the safe, he opened the door to it. Alfie took out Nathan's mobile. He stood with his back to us while he considered whether to give it to him.

'You can phone Rosa as long as you put her on speakerphone. Go out to the saloon,' Alfie said as he crossed the room.

Nathan took the phone out of Alfie's hand, but when he took a seat at the table, he realised his phone was out of charge. It hadn't been used for months. He rolled his eyes and let out a loud sigh. Tossing the mobile in front of him, he put his head in his hands. Alfie went to get a charger, and while he waited, Nathan drummed his fingers on the polished wood. I sat down next to my husband and covered his hand with mine. Nathan pulled away and placed his hands behind his head to stretch out his neck. It seemed to take an eternity for the phone to boot. As soon as it came to life, he selected WhatsApp, scrolled down to Rosa's entry, hit the video symbol and called her number.

'Put her on speakerphone, Nathan,' Alfie said, taking a seat opposite him.

Rosa picked up after a couple of rings, and her face appeared on the phone's screen.

'I've been so worried about you. Are you OK?' Rosa asked.

'Why didn't you tell me Dad had been sent to prison?' Nathan's tone was so frosty it had a Siberian winter's edge to it.

Colour rushed to Rosa's face before she adopted a deadpan expression. Then she took a deep breath to compose herself. 'It happened a long time ago when you were a baby.'

Nathan crossed his arms and glared at his mother. Her admission confirmed that Alfie was telling the truth. 'So, Dad didn't leave us to set up home with another woman then.'

Rosa looked away as a wave of embarrassment swept over her.

'Why did you tell me that?' Nathan asked through clenched teeth.

'I didn't want you to know the truth. I thought it would be easier for you to accept.'

'Easier for you, maybe. I've got no time for Dad because I grew up thinking he'd abandoned us.'

'He had.' Rosa threw her hands in the air.

'Why was he sent to prison?'

'I'm sorry, but I don't feel comfortable talking about it.' Rosa looked sheepish.

Nathan locked eyes with his mother. 'I think I have a right to know.'

I glanced over at Alfie when I heard him crack his knuckles. He was relaxing back in his chair with a smile on his face.

Rosa let out a long sigh.

'Please tell me what happened. It's not fair to keep this from me.'

'Your father attempted to rob a Securicor van while it delivered cash to the bank. He punched the guard so hard it knocked his helmet off.' Rosa's eyes glazed over as she spoke.

Rosa's words appeared to hit Nathan like a steam train. He shook his head as if he couldn't believe what he'd just heard. 'You accused me of keeping secrets from you, and then you drop a bombshell like that. I think it's about time you told me the rest,' Nathan replied, struggling to keep his tone calm.

'Gareth and his partner pointed a loaded, sawn-off shotgun at the poor man. They demanded money and threatened to blow his head off if he refused to hand it over,' Rosa sobbed.

It was horrible to see Rosa break down. I wished I'd been able to comfort her. Nathan clearly knew their conversation was distressing her, but he needed to know the truth.

'When the guard told them there wasn't any money, Gareth shot him.' Rosa began to tremble.

'Did he survive?'

'Yes, the bullet went through his hand and into his thigh, but they could have killed him.'

Nathan shook his head. He didn't know what to say. 'Did Dad get sent away for a long time?'

'Yes, following his trial at the Old Bailey, he was sentenced to twenty-four years.' Rosa let out a long breath as she finished her sentence, clearly relieved that her confession was over.

'I wish you'd told me the truth about Dad instead of letting me grow up believing a lie.' Nathan crossed his arms in front of his chest.

'I was trying to protect you.' Rosa looked into her son's eyes.

'By letting me think Dad had deserted us?' Nathan's brows knitted together in a frown.

'He had, twenty-four years is a lifetime. Your father wasn't going to be part of your life. Does it matter that I didn't tell you the real reason?' A flash of anger crossed Rosa's face as she spat out the words.

'Of course it matters. You lied to me; you said Dad left you for another woman.'

There was a tense atmosphere between mother and son. Nathan's nostrils flared. I knew he was close to flying into a rage, but instead, he clenched his jaw to stop himself from saying any more. Rosa's body stiffened as she glared back at him.

'In some ways, it would have been easier if he had. I had to raise you on my own, Nathan. You'll never understand how hard that was.' Rosa spoke after a lengthy pause. 'I don't like talking about this. It brings back lots of painful memories.' She hesitated. 'I wouldn't have got through it without Donatella and Bernardo. They've been a fantastic help over the years, both financially and emotionally.'

Although he was inwardly seething, Nathan didn't want his silent anger to build up because he might say something he'd regret. 'I feel gutted that I never had the chance to get to know Dad.'

'You were better off without him.' Rosa's words had a bitter edge to them.

'How can you say that?' Nathan suddenly stood up. The anger he'd been trying to contain was now at boiling point. Without a proper release valve, he looked like he was about to explode. 'I spent my whole life thinking he wanted nothing to do with me. That's not fair, Mum. Why didn't you take me to see him?'

'I couldn't.' Rosa's face appeared drawn, and the colour drained from it. 'I wanted no part of the life he'd chosen for himself.'

'So you made the decision to cut him out of my life, without stopping to consider how that would make me feel.' Nathan narrowed his eyes, unable and unwilling to hide his fury.

Rosa looked at her son with sad, hollow eyes. 'What Gareth did made me sick to my stomach. I couldn't condone his behaviour, and I didn't want you to spend your childhood visiting him behind bars. We never saw him again once he went to prison. I divorced him while he was serving his sentence.' When she finished speaking, she lowered her face to the floor.

Nathan stared at his mother, and when she glanced up, they exchanged dark looks. He had always adored Rosa and found her a constant source of inspiration. He knew she'd struggled to bring him up alone and for that he respected her. But she should have told him the real reason his father wasn't part of his life. Instead of letting him believe a lie. Nathan searched his mother's face.

'I know you found it hard to accept that Gareth wasn't around, but you were never going to be able to have a normal relationship with him. He was behind bars the whole time you were growing up.' Rosa's lip twitched, and she tried to blink back tears.

'Even though he was locked up, he was still my father. He always will be. Stopping me from having contact with him won't change that.'

Rosa had tried to be both a mother and a father to Nathan so he wouldn't feel like he was missing out on anything. But it was inevitable he'd find his father's absence painful. She couldn't shield him from that.

'Maybe I shouldn't have cut him out of our lives without consulting you, but you were only a baby. At the time, I thought I was doing the right thing.' Rosa had an anguished look on her face that made her appear vulnerable.

'When I was a kid, I resented you for letting him leave.' Nathan saw his mother shed a silent tear and realised there was no point arguing with her. They were never going to agree on this. He put his hands behind his head and stared into the middle distance as he tried to come to terms with Rosa's confession.

'I've had many sleepless nights trying to work out why Gareth would do this to us. It took me a long time to come to terms with what he'd done. Even after all these years, I'm still angry with him. He let us both down.' Rosa's fragility dissipated as she spoke about her ex-husband. She regained her fighting spark when she talked about the situation that caused her so much pain.

'Is he still in prison?' Nathan asked in an emotionless voice.

'I don't know, and I don't care.' Rosa straightened her posture, and her barrier went back up as she retreated behind the emotional wall she'd built up over the years. 'After what your father did, I had to start my life again without him.'

'I wish you'd told me this sooner,' Nathan said with disappointment written all over his face.

'I intended to, but it never seemed to be the right time. I hope one day you'll be able to forgive me.'

Rosa stared at her son on the screen. She wrapped one arm around herself while she waited for him to respond. But Nathan had no words, so he ended the call without replying. His mother had just broken his heart.

86

Nathan

Mixed emotions were coursing through my body, so I retreated to the cabin. I needed some privacy. So much had changed as a result of that phone call. I was having trouble processing it all.

My upbringing had undoubtedly left its mark on me. Growing up thinking one of your parents has abandoned you has a powerful effect on a person. It filled me with insecurity. I'd battled my demons all my life. Couples get divorced all the time, but that doesn't mean the father stops seeing their kids. I'd never understood why mine had deserted me. Now I knew the truth.

I felt cheated. I'd been denied a relationship with my dad because of a decision my mum made when I was a baby. I realise that she couldn't have consulted me at the time, but as soon as I was old enough, she should have told me what happened. The fact that everyone else found out before me only added to my pain. It felt like somebody had just poured salt on my open wound.

I couldn't believe she'd bottled this up for all these years. I never had a clue she was keeping something so important from me. I could feel anger building up inside me when I thought about it. Then a pang of guilt pricked my conscience when I remembered my mum's tortured face. Her brown eyes filled with tears when she finally came clean.

But upsetting her was unavoidable. If I hadn't made her relive the experience and revisit the past she'd battled so hard to leave behind, she might never have told me about it. If she'd shared this with me, it might have helped her come to terms with it. I knew it hadn't been easy for her either. My mum had lost her husband because of the Watsons.

My biggest regret was that Mum didn't tell me the truth before I heard it from someone else. Keeping this a secret had damaged our relationship and, I'm sorry to say, I wasn't sure we'd ever recover from it.

87

Gemma

The next few days passed by with as much excitement as watching paint dry. To say the atmosphere on the yacht was tense was an understatement. Nathan had withdrawn into himself, which was understandable given the size of his mother's betrayal. I wanted to help him through the pain, but he needed to come to terms with the news on his own. So the best thing I could do was be patient and give him some space.

While we waited for Terry to collect the jewellery, we tried to kill time, but with nothing to do, it was testing everyone's patience. Even though I hated staying in hotels, at least there was plenty to keep me occupied. I could feel my stress levels rising, now that I didn't have a fully equipped gym and an Olympic-sized swimming pool at my disposal.

'I've had enough of this shit,' Alfie said.

Nathan and I glanced at each other, but nobody said a word.

'Tommy, get Terry on the phone and tell him that if he

doesn't get his arse over here today, the deal's off.' Alfie moved his cigarette to the corner of his mouth as he paced up and down the saloon, frustrated by the delay.

'Consider it done,' Tommy replied. Pulling out his mobile, he went on deck to make the call.

'Do you want me to get the yacht ready to sail, boss?' Knuckles asked.

'Yes, fill her up with fuel and get some supplies in. We'll leave Boulogne tonight.'

'Tonight?' I questioned. Alfie's words sent a shiver down my spine.

'Yes, Gemma. Is that a problem?' Alfie glared at me.

'No,' I replied, biting the side of my lip. I was shocked by his response. He never usually spoke to me like that. The stress was obviously getting to him.

I put my elbows on the table and locked eyes with Nathan. We knew what that meant. The time had come to put our plan into action. Nathan had come around to my idea of jumping ship. As it was already mid-afternoon, we'd need to get a move on. We had to be ready before the *Lady Nora* departed.

Tommy came back down the stairs, walked across the saloon and went to stand next to Alfie.

'So what did the slimy little fucker have to say for himself then?' Alfie asked before taking a long drag on his cigarette.

'He said he'd be here around six.'

Alfie checked his watch. 'That's hours away.'

Nathan and I stared at each other. No words were needed. We knew we had to bag as much cash and jewellery as we could carry before Terry arrived so that when the opportunity presented itself, we could make a run for it. The idea sounded simple on paper, but it was full of pitfalls. Getting off the yacht without anyone noticing was going to be easier said than done. I pushed that thought to the back of my mind and forced myself to focus. We couldn't afford to mess this up; we'd waited too long for this moment.

Alfie took another cigarette out of the packet and lit it with the butt of the one he was smoking, then he continued to pace backwards and forwards like a caged animal.

'You look so stressed. Why don't you try and relax?' I said, turning around to face him.

'If I wanted your opinion, I'd have asked for it,' Alfie replied.

Narrowing his eyes, he glared at me, and I straightened my posture in response. When he got into my personal space, I suddenly wished I hadn't said anything. Now would be a good time to learn to keep my mouth shut, I thought. Alfie looked like he was about to explode with anger and suggesting he should try and calm down had obviously had the reverse effect. Even though my intentions had been good, he was spoiling for an argument.

I was determined to stay strong, but my breathing became rapid, and I struggled to keep my emotions in check. This wasn't the right time to show weakness. Alfie was a predator and thrived on overpowering his prey. On the verge of tears, I took a few deep breaths to calm myself down before I replied. 'I'm sorry, I didn't mean to annoy you. I was just stating a fact.'

I'd fully expected to endure another outburst, but for whatever reason, Alfie decided to abandon intimidating me and paced down the corridor towards his suite. After the door slammed behind him, I turned to Nathan and exhaled. I hadn't realised I'd been holding my breath until then.

Nathan and I were sitting opposite each other on the white leather chairs while Tommy, Frankie and Knuckles prepared the yacht for departure.

'I'm going to pack our bags, so we're ready to go,' I said when they were out of earshot.

'Only bring the essentials – we don't want to carry too much,' Nathan replied under his breath.

Once inside the privacy of our room, I placed some spare clothes and our forged documents in the bottom of our rucksacks, then put them back in the cupboard with our jackets over them. Before I went back outside to join Nathan, I changed into my trainers and warm black clothing, so I was ready to make a quick getaway when the time was right.

'You should get changed while nobody's around,' I said when I returned to the saloon and found Nathan sitting alone. 'Wear something black; we'll be harder to spot in the dark.'

Nathan nodded. 'OK, I'll be back in a minute.'

While I was waiting, Alfie reappeared from his room, carrying a rucksack. I summoned every bit of strength I had and looked him in the eye. Without saying a word, he put the bag down on the polished table next to me, walked over to the bar and fixed himself a neat Jack Daniel's.

'Listen, Gemma, I'm sorry about earlier,' he said, fixing me with his intense blue stare.

Relieved that his mood had improved, I took a deep breath and hoped my voice stayed steady. I didn't want to give away how scared I was feeling. I hoped Nathan would come back soon, so I didn't have to be alone with Alfie. I didn't feel safe around him. He was far too unpredictable when he was stressed.

'It's fine. Don't worry about it,' I replied after a lengthy pause.

Alfie sat down next to me and started taking the plastic bags out of the rucksack, placing them all over the table. 'These are the most valuable assets you can have. You wouldn't think something so small would be worth so much money, would you?' Alfie grinned.

'No.' I smiled politely and tried my best to appear relaxed. I didn't want Alfie to know a knot had formed in the pit of my stomach.

'And they're much harder to trace than cash. You could easily hide a stone worth a million pounds in your pocket, and nobody would know it was there.' Alfie's face broke into a huge smile.

That's good to know, I thought. Information like that might come in handy in the future.

Alfie stretched out his long legs and examined a bag of diamonds. He took out a handful and held them up to the light. 'Look at the way they sparkle. They're beautiful, aren't they?'

'Yes.' I nodded and gave him a half-smile. If I didn't know better, I'd think Alfie was turning soft.

'No two diamonds have exactly the same characteristics. Did you know that?' Alfie tilted his head to one side and looked at me.

'No,' I replied before taking a stone out of his hand and studying it.

'Each one is totally unique. They're just like snowflakes.'

'Or fingerprints,' I slipped in.

Alfie raised an eyebrow. In an attempt to suppress the panic that was beginning to rise in me, I swept my hair over one shoulder, hoping to appear casual. Fingers crossed, he wouldn't read too much into my stupid comment.

'Why did you say that?' Alfie glared at me.

'I keep wondering what will happen to us when we get caught.'

'We're not going to get caught.'

I had to hold in a sigh. I should have known that would be his response. Alfie thought he was above the law. He considered himself bulletproof.

'Terry will be here soon to pick this lot up, and then we'll be on our way. We've got cargo to deliver.'

I'd completely forgotten about the hundreds of packages of cocaine that were stashed on board.

'But how are you going to get away with smuggling the drugs into another country?'

'I can assure you, it's easy enough – we've done it loads of times before.' Alfie laughed. Nothing fazed him.

Alfie peered out the window, so we stopped talking. I turned around when I heard footsteps on deck and saw Terry heading towards us.

'Sorry, I'm late.'

I glanced at my watch; it was quarter past six.

'What took you so fucking long?'

'The traffic was heavy.'

'It must have been some tailback. We've been waiting for you for days.'

Nathan came back into the saloon and took a seat at the table. I got up and went to stand behind his chair. We watched while Terry ran his beady black eyes over the jewellery before Alfie put it back in the rucksack.

What happened next was surreal. The sound of machine-gun fire spraying outside caused panic to rip through the room. Shaking with fear, I dropped to my knees and crouched down behind Nathan's chair. Listening to the fast-firing weapons sent terrifying thoughts coursing through my mind. Nathan had to drag me from where I'd become rooted to the spot and force me under the table. Then he covered my head with his arms.

'The cops have got us surrounded,' Tommy shouted down the stairwell.

'For fuck's sake, Terry, you've led them straight to us. You dopey bastard.' Pulling out a handgun, Alfie pointed it at Terry. Then he pushed the jeweller in front of him, using him as a human shield. 'You two stay there,' Alfie said, looking over his shoulder to where Nathan and I were huddled under the table. He stepped out on deck, and disappeared from sight.

The moment I'd been dreading for months had finally arrived. As Nathan and I held each other close, I suddenly became aware of my heartbeat pounding in my ears. This must have been how Bonnie and Clyde felt when they were ambushed by the police, I thought. Their dramatic and untimely end made them into glorified legends, the same wouldn't be said for us. Being detained at Her Majesty's pleasure wasn't something to be proud of. To think, Alfie always used to brag that he'd never get caught. Looks like he was wrong about that.

'Now's our chance,' Nathan said as the gun battle began.

The sound of his voice made me put everything else out of my mind. Nathan held my hand and pulled me out from under the table. Grabbing Alfie's rucksack, he swung it over his shoulder.

'Let's go, Gemma.'

We'd had everything crossed that an opportunity would present itself to allow us to jump ship. But now that it had, I wasn't sure I was ready to disappear into the night. I never imagined our lives would lead us down this path. I just hoped we weren't going to spend the rest of our days living in fear.

'We need to get going.' Nathan squeezed my hand to get my attention.

'OK.' I heard myself answer, but my mind was elsewhere.

'We haven't got much time.'

I tried to focus, but the noise of the gunfire was deafening. We were only going to have one chance to escape, so everything needed to be perfect. We couldn't afford to forget anything, but there was so much to remember.

'Wait, Nathan, we haven't got the passports. You get our bags and jackets from the cabin, and I'll get the cash.'

Luckily for us, Alfie hadn't locked the safe after he'd taken the jewellery out. He'd left the door wide open, and bundles of notes just lay there stacked in piles. Using both hands, I placed all the money in an empty rucksack, leaving only the gold bars behind. They'd be too heavy for us to carry. Our confiscated mobile phones were also there, so I took those along with the charger on his bedside cabinet.

'Are you ready?' Nathan said from the doorway.

All of a sudden, the shots ceased, and everything fell silent. Nathan came across to where I was standing and took the rucksack from me.

'Gemma, we need to get out of here.'

Who would have thought it? After all the months we'd spent following Alfie's orders, just like that our time together had come to an end.

'Torch the yacht,' we heard Alfie shout.

'Oh my God,' I gasped as I tried to process Alfie's words.

He knew we were still on board, but he was prepared to set the yacht ablaze to destroy any evidence it contained. Even though I knew he was capable of cold-blooded murder, I was shocked that he'd go that far. Alfie was willing to burn us alive to stop himself from being linked to his crimes. I'd always known Alfie had an unpredictable nature and was difficult to read. But now that he was cornered, he was showing his true colours, and that made me feel sick to my stomach.

Nathan and I listened to the drama unfolding out on deck. It wasn't long before we heard the sound of the fire crackling as it started to take hold. Then a car's tyres screeched before it sped away. Police cars followed, their sirens wailing loudly before they trailed off.

Harbour staff fought to control the blaze as thick black smoke filled the air above the marina, but the back of the yacht was quickly engulfed in flames.

'This could explode any minute. Let's get out of here,' Nathan said. Swinging the rucksack full of cash onto his back, he took me by the hand.

Stepping out of Alfie's cabin, we could see there was

no way to get out on deck from the stairs as flames were licking the rear of the yacht. I turned to look at Nathan. My breathing became rapid as the reality of our situation hit home. I tried to remain calm, but it was like fighting a losing battle. I was a complete bundle of nerves.

'Don't be scared,' Nathan said. He pulled me towards him and kissed the top of my head. 'It's going to be OK, Gem.' Nathan spoke to me the way a parent would when they were reassuring a frightened child. 'We're going to get out of here now.'

'How are we going to do that? The stairs are on fire.' I had to summon every bit of strength I had to hold back my tears.

'We're not going to use the stairs.' Nathan took me by the hand and led me back into Alfie's suite. Then holding on to my shoulders, he looked into my eyes. 'Nobody knows we're on board and we want to keep it like that. If we can get to the dinghy, we can use it to get away.'

'But how are we going to get to it?' I reached forward and grabbed onto his hands.

Nathan's brown eyes swept across the room. 'We'll have to use this hatch.' Letting go of me, he opened the vent in Alfie's cabin. 'Are you ready?'

'Yes.'

I drew in a deep breath, and Nathan helped me climb out. He signalled to me to crouch down and keep quiet. Covering my mouth with my trembling hands, I sat in silence, for what seemed like an eternity until he joined me.

Paying no attention to the chaos going on around us, we crawled along the deck, hoping nobody would spot us. Thankfully the smoke provided us with cover, but it was difficult to breathe as the toxic air filled our lungs. Edging our way to the far end of the yacht where the dinghy was moored, we lowered ourselves onto it. Nathan untied the inflatable and pushed it away from the burning vessel with the oar.

Looking out into the darkness, we sat side by side on the bottom of the boat. Even though we were off the yacht, my pulse was still racing. Nathan grazed his thumb along the side of my mouth and stared at me from beneath his dark lashes.

'So far, so good,' he said.

Nathan got on to his stomach, crawled to the front of the dinghy and lent over the edge. Gripping one of the oars with both hands, he plunged it into the inky water, first on one side, then the other, like he was paddling a canoe. After a few moments, he stopped, and staying low, he looked over his shoulder towards the burning yacht. A muscle twitched in his jaw as he waited to see if anyone had noticed the dinghy slipping away into the night.

'We're almost there,' Nathan said.

I managed a weak smile, but a feeling of unease swept over me as he inched the dinghy further away from the jetty. Despite Nathan's encouraging words, we still had a long way to go before we'd be out of sight.

As I sat huddled in the dark, I could hear police sirens all around me, and that made panic rise up within me. I needed to block out the sound, so I closed my eyes and listened to the water gently lapping on the side of the dinghy. If I focused on that, I might be able to slow my breathing down. I had to get a grip and stay strong, but that was easier said than done. A voice in my head kept telling me this wasn't going to end well. Alfie would never surrender. That wasn't his style.

'Have we got much further to go?' I asked, peering out into the darkness as my pulse pounded in my ears. This was pure torture.

'No, we're nearly there.' Nathan turned and looked over his shoulder at me, then flashed me a bright smile.

I wasn't sure I believed him, but I smiled back anyway.

The frantic car chase continued through the busy streets of Boulogne while we battled to make it to safety. The sound of wailing police sirens carried out to sea, on the cold December breeze, and gave Nathan and me an eerie reminder that Alfie was still at large.

'Where are we heading to?' I asked, realising we hadn't discussed this part of the plan.

'I'm going to moor up in the next marina.'

Nathan continued lying on his stomach, paddling the dinghy with gentle strokes to avoid drawing attention to us.

'We're nearly there now. Are you OK?' Nathan asked, pausing to stretch out his shoulders.

I could see his breath in the cold night air, but had to strain to hear what he was saying over the fire engines' sirens. 'Yes, I'm fine.'

I hoped I sounded more convincing than I felt. I was terrified, and to think, running away from Alfie was all my idea. No wonder Nathan had been reluctant. If I'd known it was going to be like this, I would have been as well.

'How adventurous are you feeling?' Nathan asked, looking at me over his shoulder.

'Why?' I asked, studying his profile.

Amused by my question, Nathan smiled. His white teeth

shone out like a beacon in the darkness. When he turned around to face me, I narrowed my eyes, dreading his reply.

'I've just had an idea,' Nathan began, having adopted a neutral expression. 'How would you feel about crossing the English Channel?'

'In this? Please tell me you're joking.' I searched his eyes for reassurance.

'You want to go back to England, don't you?'

'Yes, but we'd never make it. It's miles away, Nathan.'

'Before you dismiss the idea, just think about it. Alfie would never expect us to do something like that.'

'Even so, it's a terrible idea.' I shook my head in disbelief. 'We'll never be able to cross a busy shipping lane in a flimsy little dinghy in the pitch black.'

'I just thought it might be worth a try. Boulogne is swarming with police.'

'I know it is, but we'll have to think of something else. It's too risky.'

'It was just a suggestion.' Nathan shrugged his shoulders before plunging the lightweight oar back into the icy water.

'Anyway, we'd probably die of hypothermia on the way. It's absolutely freezing tonight.'

'You don't need to tell me that. The water's so cold, it's made my hands go numb.' Nathan put down the oar and rubbed his fingers together to try and get the feeling back into them.

I wished we could get away from here. The air was thick with the smell of burning fibreglass. Hopefully, Nathan would manage to navigate us out of this marina soon. Then we could continue on foot.

We were making slow progress. The flashing lights of

the fire engines had attracted quite a crowd to the marina. People had gathered along the jetty to watch the crew attempting to put out the blaze. With hundreds of pairs of eyes trained on the yacht, we couldn't afford to draw attention to ourselves. But once we were far enough away from the *Lady Nora* not to be spotted, Nathan put both the oars into the water and started to row the short distance to Le bassin Napoléon.

We'd made it out of the harbour undetected, and luckily this marina was deserted. Taking advantage of the fact that nobody witnessed our arrival, we moored up and began walking in the opposite direction as quickly as our frozen limbs would allow.

'We need to get as far away from here as possible,' Nathan said, intertwining his fingers in mine.

'Where are we going?'

'I'm not sure, but let's keep moving.'

'We could go somewhere on the train,' I suggested, knowing how lax the security was.

'That's a good idea. We'll head to the station and get on the first train out of here.' Nathan stopped and looked at me.

'What's the matter?'

'We should put our hats on. They'll be security cameras at the station, maybe even police. We don't want to risk being spotted.'

'I'm scared, Nathan.'

'Don't be. Even if the police are at the station, they aren't going to take any notice of us, they'll be too busy looking for Alfie.'

For our sake, I hoped they'd already caught him. A

shiver shot down my spine at the thought of Alfie being on the run. When the firefighters put out the blaze on the *Lady Nora*, he'd know we'd escaped. I wondered how far he'd be prepared to go to find us. We'd have to make sure we covered our tracks and left him no leads if we wanted to vanish into thin air, or we'd spend the rest of our lives running scared.

In some ways, Alfie had done us a favour when he'd made us leave home with little more than the clothes on our backs. We had nothing personal with us that connected us to our old lives, and that would make us harder to identify if we did get caught.

88

Gemma

To avoid walking right past all the activity at the marina, we took the long way round to the station. Pacing along the pavements with our hearts pounding, we didn't have time to admire the glittering festive displays and Christmas lights; we were too busy trying to keep our heads down.

It took us almost half an hour to walk to Boulogne-sur-Mer Ville. Luckily we didn't pass many late-night shoppers; the streets were empty. People had swarmed to the marina. They were fascinated by the swirling flames and the burning wreckage of the *Lady Nora*. They were proving to be quite a crowd puller.

'We made it,' Nathan said, squeezing my hand as we walked up the stone steps to the entrance.

When we stepped out of the elements and into the warmth of the station, I instantly felt myself calm down. But my relief was short-lived when I noticed armed police patrolling the forecourt. My heartbeat increased, and anxiety filled me again. An image of Alfie swaggering into a room oozing confidence suddenly came into my head. If I followed his example and believed in myself, maybe I'd be able to walk past them without raising suspicions.

The track number, arrival and departure times of all the trains were listed on the illuminated boards in the main entrance. Looking up at them, we studied the information. The sooner we got away from Boulogne, the better. If we could get to Paris, we could get out of France.

'The 19:07 to Paris is on time. That seems like a good option,' Nathan said.

'But it's boarding. Do you think we've still got time to buy tickets?' I asked, knowing we'd be cutting it fine.

'If you don't relax, you're going to draw attention to us,' Nathan whispered in my ear when we got in the queue.

'But we're going to miss it,' I replied, fidgeting with my hands while we waited to be served.

Nathan smiled, then leant towards me and planted a lingering kiss on my mouth in an attempt to distract me. His stubble scraped my skin as his lips touched mine, and for a moment, I completely forgot where we were. The feeling of his warm mouth did exactly what he'd intended it to, and now my pulse was racing for an entirely different reason. 'Can I have two tickets for the 19:07 to Paris and the overnight train to the Pyreneesplease? Nathan asked.

'Would you like a couchette-inclusive fare for the overnight service?"

"Yes, please, but I'd like to pay extra and book a four-berth compartment."

When the assistant handed over the tickets and

couchette voucher, Nathan looked at me and the corners of his mouth lifted.

'We'll have to hurry if we're going to catch it,' I said.

Clasping our tickets in one hand, Nathan intertwined the fingers on his free hand in mine. He pulled me through the sea of people gathered in front of the information boards, as we quickly made our way towards platform five.

'Here goes.' Nathan let go of my hand and confidently walked past the armed officers.

Having plastered the best smile I could manage on my face, I followed my husband through the metal turnstile to where the 19:07 to Paris waited patiently for us to board.

'Let's get on here,' Nathan said, realising the train was about to depart.

I hoped the police wouldn't notice the nervous vibes radiating from me as I walked past them and climbed on board. We weren't exactly law-abiding citizens any more.

'Do you want to sit here?' Nathan asked, stopping next to some empty chairs at the back of the carriage.

I slumped down in the seat next to the window and turned away from it. When the wheels started to move on the tracks, as the train pulled out of the station, I let out a long breath.

'My God, that was nerve-racking,' I said, leaning over the table towards Nathan.

My husband sat in silence, watching me, paying no attention to the conversations going on around us. Catching hold of his hand, I squeezed his fingers. The words he hadn't spoken were powerful. He didn't need to say a thing; I could see relief was written all over his face.

★

We didn't have a moment to lose when we arrived at Gare du Nord station, two hours and twenty-eight minutes later. We had to get to the other side of Paris to catch the overnight train to the Pyrenees, and we only had half an hour to do it. Pulling me after him, Nathan ploughed his way through the crowd to get to the exit. Although we risked the driver recognising us, we had no choice but to jump into a taxi outside the station.

'*Gare d'Austerlitz, s'il vous plaît,*' Nathan said, as we bundled into the back of the cab for the twenty-five-minute drive.

While the cab crawled through the heavy traffic, I gazed out of the window at the impressive limestone buildings. They looked stunning lit up against the night sky. Paris was even more beautiful at night, I thought, as my eyes were drawn to the tiny white fairy lights twinkling high up in the trees lining the pavement.

The window displays of the Parisian department stores were incredible. But instead of making me feel happy, the animated figures, festive decorations and gift-wrapped presents tugged at my heartstrings and reminded me how close it was to Christmas. For the first time in years, we wouldn't be spending it at home with Rosa.

As our taxi drove over the Seine, the reflection of the lights along the water's edge was mesmerising. They glowed like fireflies on the surface. I wish we could have stayed here, but under the circumstances, that was impossible.

Nathan squeezed my hand and brought me out of my daydream. 'When we get there, you go ahead, and I'll catch you up. We're going to be cutting it fine,' he said, glancing at his watch.

When the cab came to a stop outside Gare d'Austerlitz, I got out while Nathan paid the driver. I was scared to go without him, but we only had a couple of minutes to find the right platform before the train left. I was still scanning the departure board when Nathan appeared at my side.

'The train's leaving from platform eight, but that's at the other end of the station,' I said, turning to face him.

'Oh shit,' Nathan replied.

Our footsteps echoed as we attempted to run through the packed forecourt, dodging the crowd of people trailing trolley cases after them. We could see platform eight in the distance, but we were having trouble forcing our way through the masses, milling about with what seemed like no other purpose than to delay us. Nathan weaved us along the concourse, changing direction frequently, to avoid the slow-moving pedestrians until finally, we made it.

'That was close,' Nathan said. He'd barely closed the door behind him when the train pulled away from the station.

'I didn't think we were going to make it.' Panting, I slumped against the side of the carriage while I tried to catch my breath.

'Do you have a couchette voucher?' an attendant asked.

'Yes,' Nathan replied, handing over the ticket.

'I'll take you to your accommodation. It's on the left-hand side at the very end,' the young man said. He led us down a narrow, carpeted corridor. Taking out his key-card, he unlocked the door of the first-class couchette for us.

We'd reserved the whole four-berth compartment because we wanted to have some privacy. I didn't like the idea of sharing with strangers. I couldn't get my head around the thought of being asleep with someone I didn't know two feet away from me, especially as our luggage was so valuable. I'd end up staying awake all night in case they tried to rob us.

I looked around our compartment. I had to say, I was impressed. I was surprised how comfortable it was. The couchette was much nicer than I was expecting it to be. There were four bunks, a toilet, shower and sink, everything we needed for the overnight train journey. I was so glad we decided to do this instead of lying low in a room somewhere. We definitely made the right decision. It made sense for us to travel through the night. The train was effectively a hotel on rails anyway. It had a restaurant and a bar and better still, when we woke up tomorrow morning, we'd be a long way from Boulogne. The thought of that made me smile.

I was fully expecting to toss and turn on the overnight service to the Pyrenees. I thought I'd be disturbed by the unfamiliar noises going on around me. But instead, the rolling motion of the train on the tracks was surprisingly soothing, and I soon drifted into uninterrupted sleep.

I woke to find the sun flooding through the thin curtains. Glancing over at the bunk opposite, I could see Nathan was still asleep. I wanted to see where we were, so I got up and gently pulled back the fabric, and when I did, the breathtaking sight of the mountainous landscape greeted me.

I didn't want to disturb Nathan. He looked so peaceful,

but I knew we'd be arriving soon, so I had to wake him. When I stroked the side of his face, he opened his eyes.

'What time is it?' he asked, clearing his throat.

'It's nine-thirty,' I replied, checking my watch. 'We'd better get ready; we're due to arrive in twenty minutes.'

A gust of icy air took my breath away when we stepped onto the platform of the remote mountainside town. The beautiful snow-capped Pyrenees stood high above Latour-de-Carol. If we hadn't been waiting here for our connecting train, we'd probably never have come to this small village at the end of the line. It was in the middle of nowhere, but the scenery alone made it worth the visit.

'My God, it's freezing,' I said, zipping my jacket up under my chin.

'Let's go and see if we can get some breakfast while we wait for our connection,' Nathan said, pointing to a chalet-style café.

Nathan and I walked the short distance to the Bistro de la Gare on the station forecourt. I was chilled to the bone by the time we stepped out of the cold, into the warm. We were welcomed inside by a French lady who stood behind the counter. A large set of antlers hung above it. The café's interior was spotlessly clean, and its half-timbered walls and beams reminded me of a cosy ski lodge. I could imagine curling up and hibernating here for the winter, cocooned away from the elements.

Nathan carried our tray of croissants and coffees, and we sat side by side at a corner table near the television, away from the only other customer, an elderly gentleman. The news was on, and luckily for us, it had subtitles. I felt my pulse quicken as I read the words on the screen in front of us.

Acting on their suspicion that the robbery at the Antwerp Diamond Centre had been an inside job, investigators began closely monitoring Avraham Cohen's movements. Having kept him under twenty-four-hour surveillance for several days, their hunch paid off, and Cohen led them to a luxury yacht moored in Boulogne Harbour.

As the police closed in, the thieves, described as armed and dangerous, panicked and set fire to the vessel before attempting to flee in a stolen Audi. Officers arrested the men, after a lengthy chase, when the car they were driving collided with stationary vehicles in the centre of Boulogne.

I could hardly believe what I was hearing. Nathan and I looked at each other over our coffee cups before we continued to watch the report in silence.

Firefighters battled for hours to put out the blaze on board the yacht before an examination of the vessel could take place. During an initial search of the remains, police discovered thirty fake passports belonging to the gang members hidden inside a safe. Further inspection of the craft revealed hundreds of packages of cocaine stashed inside two holding tanks. The drugs had an estimated street value of fifty thousand pounds a kilo.

Interpol have named Alfie Watson as the gang leader and high-profile member of an international drug-smuggling ring that they have been trying to infiltrate for years. Along with the distribution of tonnes of illegal substances, the cartel's members are wanted in connection with money laundering, arms sales and the trafficking of stolen vehicles amongst other criminal activities.

The chief in charge of the case confirmed that although the police hadn't recovered the jewellery and cash taken in the heist, they were confident they had caught the men responsible for the robbery and were not looking for anyone else in connection with the theft.

'That's a relief,' Nathan said, looking away from the TV. He'd tried his best to sound convincing, but he still looked stressed.

89

Gemma

When I climbed on board the 10:48 train to Barcelona and found the carriage was empty, I picked a seat by the window.

'What are we going to do when we get to Spain?' I asked, tearing my eyes away from the view of the Pyrenees.

'We'll take another train somewhere else,' Nathan replied, and a broad smile spread across his face. 'As long as we don't go anywhere near Switzerland, we'll be able to cross the borders easily. You know how lax the security is.'

I had to stop myself from groaning out loud. 'Surely now the police have caught Alfie, we can relax a bit. I was hoping we might be able to stay in one place for a little while.' I fixed Nathan with my best pleading gaze.

His eyes met mine, and he reached for my hands. 'I think we need to keep moving for the time being.' He gave me a weak smile.

I smiled back, but after a few seconds, I felt it fade. I wasn't able to hide my disappointment.

Nathan let go of my hands and looked over his shoulder to check whether anybody was listening in. The only thing he saw were rows of unoccupied seats. 'The police might not be looking for us, but that doesn't mean Alfie isn't. We shouldn't underestimate him; Gemma, he's still a threat to us.'

Nathan was right. Even though he was behind bars, Alfie still had plenty of people on the outside working for him. The thought of what he might do to us made my head spin. He'd know by now that we'd got off the yacht alive and he wouldn't be impressed that we'd double-crossed him. With that thought planted firmly in my brain, I let out a long sigh. I'd imagined once we were free of Alfie it would feel liberating, but it didn't. In some ways, it was worse. We still had to watch our backs. Living with a sense that something terrible was about to happen at any moment was awful. I constantly felt on edge.

'We took Alfie's money, and now he'll want to get even with us. I'm scared he'll go after my mum,' Nathan said, his dark eyes full of sadness. After a moment, he turned away so I could only see his profile.

Reaching across the table, I covered his hand with mine to try and comfort him. I hoped Nathan was worrying unnecessarily, but he had a point. Alfie had a reputation to maintain.

To take Nathan's mind off things, I opened my rucksack and got out a map of Europe. Unfolding it, I spread it out on the table between us. 'We're due to arrive at 14:02 as long as the train's on time. We've got a couple of hours to kill. Why don't we decide where to go next?'

'I don't mind where we go. I'll let you choose.'

'Come on, Nathan, give me some input.'

Nathan stretched back in his chair. 'We can go anywhere we want. The world is our oyster.'

Nathan was right. The options were endless, but that was only going to make the decision harder.

Nathan looked at me for a second before he spoke. 'I would love to go back to Italy.'

Nathan and I both speak Italian, but we're not fluent. We only know enough to get by. I love Italy too, and although it's a tempting option, I think it might be a bit too predictable. If we didn't want Alfie to find us, we'd need to think outside the box and go somewhere we didn't have any connections. I scanned the map, discounting any country we'd previously been to on holiday. Where else could we head to? We needed to bear in mind that flying was out of the question. We'd never get through the security checks.

Travelling by train had to be the way forward. We could make long-distance journeys without going anywhere near an airport. Anyway, I preferred it, and we could travel overnight if we wanted to. My eyes were drawn out of the window as the train followed the rail through a deep valley, passing beneath a ring of snowy peaks. The only disadvantage of travelling at night was that we missed the beautiful scenery.

We were only at the beginning of our three-hour trip, and so far, the train had taken us along a track that weaved in and out of the mountain tops. As it hugged the sides of the gorge's rocky walls, the views of the forests, streams and rushing waterfalls were spectacular.

Forcing my eyes away from the window and the hillside church in the distance, I went back to studying the map. If we wanted to stay ahead of the game, we'd need to introduce an element of surprise. I suddenly had a brainwave.

'What about Majorca? It looks like there's a ferry from Barcelona,' I said, tracing the route on the map with my finger. We hadn't travelled by boat before, so hopefully, Alfie wouldn't be expecting that.

Nathan's face broke into a huge grin. He leant towards me, cupped my face in his hands and kissed me. 'Majorca it is then. I've always fancied spending Christmas on the beach.'

The train pulled into Barcelona Sants station right on time. When we stepped onto the sun-drenched platform, it struck me how warm it was. Not quite the beach weather Nathan had been hoping for, but it was certainly much milder than it had been in the mountains.

As Nathan and I made our way through the crowd of people towards the exit, I noticed a tourist information desk in the centre of the station.

'Let's go and ask about the ferry,' I said.

Armed with a map and directions to the port, Nathan and I jumped in a taxi waiting outside. Trasmediterránea's offices, located near the World Trade Center and the Christopher Columbus monument at Port Vell, were a short drive away.

We purchased two tickets for the 23:00 ferry from the booking office. As it was such a beautiful day, instead of getting a taxi back, we decided to walk along La Rambla, a tree-lined pedestrian boulevard that stretched from Port Vell to the Plaça de Catalunya in the centre of Barcelona.

Being so close to Christmas, Barcelona was a hive of activity. Its beautiful old buildings and plazas were jammed with shoppers browsing the festive windows and stalls that lined the narrow streets.

I stopped on the pavement outside Zara. 'Let's go in here; we need to buy some new clothes.'

Nathan pulled a face, protesting in the manner of a petulant child. 'Ugh, do we have to?'

'Yes, we do. All we've got with us are the clothes on our backs.' I rolled my eyes. 'And make sure you pick things you wouldn't normally wear.'

Nathan let out a long sigh. 'I'll meet you back here in fifteen minutes,' he said, checking the time on his watch before he stomped off with his shoulders hunched towards the back of the shop.

I didn't have time to worry about my manners, I only had a quarter of an hour to get everything I needed. So I barged my way through the packed aisles, grabbing as much as I could before heading for the tills. While I waited to be served, I could see Nathan standing by the entrance, and he didn't look happy.

'How did you get on?' I asked, smiling at the tiny shopping bag Nathan was holding. 'Is that all you got?'

'We won't need a lot of clothes in Majorca.'

After our fleeting trip to Zara, we made our way along the pavement towards El Corte Inglès, Barcelona's equivalent to Selfridges. I pulled a reluctant Nathan by the hand, past the giant Christmas tree in front of the main entrance.

'They're bound to sell suitcases in here.'

After purchasing two identical black trolley cases, I laid them on their sides in a quiet corner of the department store and placed our rucksacks and shopping in them. We left the shop and began making our way through the throng of people again, trying to kill time while we waited for the ferry.

Nathan stopped outside a phone shop and stared at me for a moment. 'I'm just going to pop in here and buy us both pay-as-you-go mobiles. Then we'll be able to make untraceable calls.'

Nathan looked like a broken man as he stood staring into space on the pavement while crowds of Christmas shoppers dashed past him. I squeezed his hand, and the touch of my fingers brought him back to reality, but when he looked at me, he couldn't hide the sadness in his eyes. 'Are you OK?'

'I was just thinking about my mum. I hate being on bad terms with her. Having a close family means everything to me. Without them I'd have nothing.'

Now it was my turn to be sad. Nathan had hit a nerve, but I didn't want him to know that he'd upset me. It wasn't intentional. He was lucky to have a good network around him. His family were lovely. Most of the time, it didn't bother me that I wasn't close to mine. But right now, I found myself longing for something I'd never had.

Knowing you're not your parents' favourite is difficult to accept at any age. Everything I did was judged, and every time my parents judged me, they made me feel like a failure. What gave them the right to do that?

Growing up competing against the golden child, in a game of sibling rivalry, was a huge challenge. At times, it was impossible not to feel inadequate. It gnawed at my very core. If I ever became a mother, I'd never treat my children unequally and pit them against each other.

Nathan taught me a long time ago not to invest my energy in situations that I couldn't change, and for that, I'd be forever grateful. That piece of advice altered my whole outlook.

'Why don't we go and get something to eat?' The sound of Nathan's voice broke my train of thought. 'Food always cheers me up.' He smiled, then linked my arm and steered me back towards Plaça de Catalunya.

We were carried along the busy streets by the masses before we turned into a narrow cobblestoned alleyway so that we could get away from the crowd. Almost immediately, we stopped outside a restaurant with a quaint exterior, bathed in the glow of coloured lights. The authentic Spanish tapas bar, offering a vast choice of local dishes, was tucked away, hidden from the hustle and bustle, in the maze of the Gothic quarter of the city.

'What about this place?' I peered in the window. We'd picked a good time. It was empty unlike the more touristy places a few doors away in the plaza that were packed to the rafters.

El Portalón had a welcoming, romantically lit interior with soothing background music that created a tranquil atmosphere. Exposed brick vaulted ceilings, dark wood panelling and wooden barrels added rustic charm and gave the restaurant a cosy and traditional feel.

We chose a corner booth, furthest away from the distraction of the street, and took a seat at a table laid with simple white crockery, rose gold cutlery, and handmade wine glasses.

Having looked at the menu, we ordered a selection of tapas and the house red. Within a short space of time, a large wooden platter piled high with food arrived at our table along with a terracotta jug full of wine.

'We need to decide on a backstory in case people start asking us questions,' I said, taking advantage of the fact that nobody was around to overhear us. 'It can't be anything too elaborate, or we'll end up forgetting what we've said.'

'We've taken a year off to go travelling,' Nathan replied without any hesitation.

'That's a good idea.' It would be an easy story to stick to.

'Anyway, we should be treating this time as a holiday. We deserve to relax and have some fun after what we've been through,' Nathan said, before loading up his plate with traditional potato tortilla, melon wrapped in Serrano ham, apple and Manchego crostinis and marinated olives.

'How long do you think it will be before we can go home?' I took a sip of the smooth red wine.

Nathan looked up from his plate, wearing his poker face. When he finished chewing his mouthful of food, he put down his knife and fork and rubbed the back of his neck with one hand.

'It's impossible to say. Let's take each day as it comes, but we'll have to be prepared to stay away for as long as it takes, more than a year if necessary.'

My eyes widened at the prospect of having to accept that. 'I thought we'd only have to lie low for a couple of weeks, a month at the most.'

'Don't get stressed about it.' Nathan leant forward and took my hand in his. 'We've always wanted to go travelling, so let's enjoy it.'

'I suppose you're right, but don't you think we should make a long-term plan?' I didn't want to resign myself to the fact that we'd never be able to go back to England.

'Why? It will only complicate things. We've got enough cash to last ages, so at least we won't have to worry about money for once.' Nathan knocked back the wine in his glass before smiling at me. 'I have a confession to make. I've been keeping a secret from you.'

My heartbeat quickened in response to his words. While I waited for Nathan to carry on, I found myself becoming overwhelmed by the claustrophobic silence.

'I had noticed your not so subtle hints about starting a family. The reason I kept making excuses was I'm scared I won't make a good dad. I haven't exactly had a great role model, have I?'

At first, I said nothing; I was too shocked to speak. Then I reached for Nathan's hand. I wish he'd told me this before. He was worried about nothing. 'You'll make a brilliant dad.'

Nathan's face broke into a huge smile.

El Portalón had been empty when we got there, but by eight o'clock it was starting to fill up. As we couldn't talk in private any more, we decided to make our way back to the centre of Barcelona to soak up the festive atmosphere. Even though the shops were closed, Plaça de Catalunya was still packed with locals and tourists. The temperature had dropped sharply, so we decided to take refuge from the cold in one of the many cafés that overlooked the square and its illuminated trees and fountains.

'This is the best hot chocolate I've tasted in ages. It's delicious.' I grinned, dunking a cinnamon-covered churro.

The rich, creamy, bittersweet chocolate was served in a small glass, and was so thick you could stand a spoon in it. It was only just thin enough to drink, but it was the perfect consistency for coating the churros.

Nathan smiled at me. 'You look like you're enjoying that. You've got it all over your face.' Leaning towards me, Nathan wiped the chocolate away with the pad of his thumb before checking the time on his watch. 'If you still want to walk, we'd better get going. We've got to be at Sant Bertrand terminal by ten-thirty at the latest.'

I thought about everything we'd discussed tonight as Nathan and I strolled hand in hand along La Rambla. We walked in silence towards the marina, admiring the twinkling lights that hung in the trees high above us. While I breathed in the crisp evening air, a sense of calm washed over me.

We'd agreed it wasn't going to be easy to start over in another country, but we both knew going home wasn't an option at this stage. If it meant keeping Nathan's family safe, we might have to accept that we would never be able to go back. That was a consequence of double-crossing Alfie and something we'd have to learn to live with. But that was a small price to pay for our freedom.

I was going to handle our finances from now on. Having access to all the cash would be too tempting for Nathan. He had a history of being reckless with money, but he'd given me his word he wouldn't gamble again. Even though I desperately wanted to believe him, I knew it had a powerful hold over him. There was a big difference between saying you're going to do something and actually doing it. He wanted to keep his promise; only time would tell if he managed to. I wasn't going to worry about that now, so I pushed that thought from my mind.

Almost splitting up had taught us a valuable lesson: we'd never take each other for granted again. We were both guilty of making mistakes, but it was time to draw a line under them and move on. Everyone deserved a second chance, didn't they? No matter how good a relationship was, sometimes they caused us pain. It was unavoidable. All marriages have their share of problems. Life would be dull without them.

90

Gemma

'Let's go and check in,' Nathan said, squeezing my hand as we arrived at Trasmediterránea's terminal shortly before ten o'clock.

We made our way to the pre-boarding area and handed our tickets and fake British passports to the lady behind the counter. She looked at the photo of Emma Jones then looked me in the eye. I tried to keep my rapidly increasing heartbeat under control. When she studied the picture of Ethan Jones, Nathan flashed her a bright smile.

'You are booked to travel on the overnight ferry to Majorca,' the lady said, checking the tickets. 'The crossing leaves at 23:00, Saturday, December 23. You will arrive in Palma on Sunday, December 24 at 07:00.'

'That's correct,' I replied.

'Here is your boarding card. Please make your way to gate number three. Boarding will commence shortly.'

'Thank you.' I smiled, taking the card from her.

Nathan and I joined the back of the queue at gate number

three. Before we could board the ship for the eight-hour crossing, an immigration officer rechecked our boarding passes and passports. Nathan rested his head on top of mine while the Spanish official looked at our documents.

The dark-haired, dark-eyed man handed my passport back to me. My forged papers didn't raise any suspicion, and I was waved through with no questions asked. But Nathan wasn't so lucky. The young official peered at his photo, then began examining the passport in great detail.

Almost instantly, beads of sweat broke out on my upper lip. I hoped nobody would realise I was nervous, but it was a cold December evening, so I could hardly pretend I was hot, could I?

Removing a tissue from my bag, I pretended to blow my nose so I could dry the skin above my top lip. It was torture having to watch the scene unfold from the other side of the gate. Why was this happening now? We were only moments away from boarding the ferry and had travelled on these passports numerous times before, without encountering any problems.

'Wait here for a moment please, sir,' the official said to Nathan.

The young man went across to speak to one of his colleagues, a bearded, grey-haired more senior-looking officer. He looked like he'd racked up many years of service, and the scowl he was wearing so naturally made me think Nathan was in for a tough time.

As the officers approached the counter, the older one began studying Nathan's passport. He flicked through the pages, feeling the paper quality between his thumb and forefinger before scrutinising the photo. Nathan held his nerve and waited for the officer to finish.

The senior officer spoke to the other official in Spanish. Then without saying a word to Nathan, the two men took his passport into a private room. Nathan looked at me out of the corner of his eye as he waited patiently at the counter. After what seemed like an eternity, the officers returned.

'What is the purpose of your visit?' the senior official asked. His Spanish accent was so strong I'm surprised Nathan didn't need an interpreter to understand what he was saying.

'A much-needed holiday,' Nathan replied, still managing to appear calm and relaxed.

'How long do you intend to stay in Majorca?'

'I'm not sure yet.'

'Why have you only got a one-way ticket?' the official asked, putting Nathan on the spot.

My stomach flipped. We'd made a stupid mistake. We should have realised that would look suspicious. Why hadn't we just bought a return? But if the officers were so concerned about that, why hadn't they asked me the same question? There must be more to it.

I couldn't ignore the signals my body was sending to my brain. My insides were churning, and cold sweat raced out of my pores. I knew I needed to compose myself, but I couldn't seem to control my racing heartbeat. It was human nature to panic when you feel like you've been cornered, wasn't it?

'I decided to get a one-way ticket because I'm not sure if I'll be coming back this way yet. I want to do a bit of island

hopping and travel between the Balearics while I'm here.'
Thankfully the words tripped off Nathan's tongue.

The officer ran his fingers along the outline of his beard,
contemplating Nathan's answer. 'Did you pack this bag
yourself, sir?'

Now the contents of my stomach somersaulted, and
I thought I was going to be sick in the middle of the
terminal building. We were aware that immigration officers
sometimes carried out random luggage checks, so our hand
luggage contained only the passports we were travelling on
and some bare essentials. We'd put the other documents,
money and jewellery in our suitcases. The problem was,
we hadn't concealed any of it in the compartments. If they
searched Nathan's case, the game would be up.

'Yes, I did.' Nathan looked the official straight in the eye
as if he had nothing to hide.

'And have you kept your luggage with you at all times?'
The interrogation continued.

'Yes.'

'Do you have anything to declare, Mr Jones?'

I held my breath when he asked the question I'd been
dreading. While my heartbeat pounded against my chest, it
took all my strength to stay rooted to the spot. My instinct
was to run.

'No, nothing to declare,' Nathan replied.

'How on earth did you manage to stay so calm?' I said once
we were in the safety of our cabin.

'I don't know.'

'The whole time the officers were questioning you, I was

shaking like a leaf. But you didn't turn a hair. You looked like you had nothing to hide. You were great.'

'I was shitting myself.' Nathan smiled. 'They knew we were travelling together, but they didn't seem concerned that you only had a one-way ticket.'

'I was thinking the same thing. It doesn't make any sense.'

'Maybe they thought my passport wasn't genuine and needed a reason to stop me.'

Nathan could be right, but we'd used them so many times before and we'd never had any problems. We should be grateful that even though the officers had their suspicions, they couldn't prove his passport was a fake, so they had to let him go. I'd had a horrible feeling we were going to have to make a run for it. Thank God they didn't search his luggage! They probably would have done if the ferry hadn't been about to leave. Hopefully, our luck had started to turn.

Nathan seemed unscathed by the hair-raising experience; he'd taken it all in his stride. I was so glad the officials didn't stop me, or the outcome could have been very different. I'd never have been able to hold my nerve.

In the middle of the night, I jolted awake. Living as a fugitive was playing havoc with my sanity. Getting up, I opened the curtain and stared out the window into the night.

'What's wrong, Gemma?' Nathan asked, rolling onto his side.

'I thought I heard something outside.' I turned around to face Nathan, my eyes wide.

'It's just the ship's engines.' Nathan yawned, lay back down on the pillow and closed his eyes.

I slipped under the covers, but I knew I wouldn't be able to sleep. As I lay in the darkness, tossing and turning, I began thinking about what the future held for Nathan and me. Was this the way things were going to be from now on? Were we going to spend the rest of our lives sleeping with one eye open? I didn't want to be constantly looking over my shoulder.

The vibrations from the engine must have eventually lulled me back to sleep because when I woke again, daylight was creeping into our cabin. Pulling back the curtains, I could see a hazy sun peeping through the clouds, as we approached the island of Majorca. While I stared at the view of the horizon in the distance, a pod of dolphins appeared and swam right by the side of the ship. I didn't want Nathan to miss this. It was a sight tourists would pay good money to see.

'Are you awake?' I called over my shoulder. I was reluctant to leave my front-row seat. When he didn't answer, I knew he was in a deep sleep, but I didn't want to take my eyes off the group, so I called again, louder this time. 'Nathan, wake up.'

Nathan slowly opened one eye. 'What's the matter?'

'Look at this.' I smiled.

Nathan yawned, threw back the sheet and stood by my side. He was just in time to see several of the agile creatures leap out of the water.

'Welcome to Majorca,' Nathan said, slinging his arm over my shoulder before kissing the side of my head.

91

Gemma

'We'd better find somewhere to stay. Otherwise, we're going to be spending Christmas sleeping rough,' Nathan said, as we strolled hand in hand along the promenade next to the empty beach.

'I can't face staying in another hotel. Can we rent an apartment instead?' I rubbed Nathan's arm and batted my eyelashes, trying my best to persuade him as we walked towards the town centre.

Nathan shook his head and gave me a grin. 'It's Christmas Eve, so we'll have to take whatever's available.'

Turning the corners of my mouth down, I let out an exaggerated sigh.

Palma's old town was just as I'd imagined it would be: full of colourful buildings, magnificent architecture and monuments. While we were exploring the ancient passages, in the heart of the district, we almost walked right past the unassuming exterior of a small boutique hotel.

'What about this place?' Nathan said, stopping outside the entrance down a narrow side street.

Although I didn't want to stay in a hotel, the location of this one couldn't be better. It was in a peaceful position, in the shadow of La Seu, the Gothic cathedral, whose gargoyles and spires dominated the skyline. But it was only a short walk from all the major attractions, restaurants and bars.

Our modern, minimal room was on the fourth floor of the renovated nineteenth-century building. I sat on the end of the bed, running my hand along the pure white linen, admiring the view from our window. High above the rooftops, I could see a glimpse of the Mediterranean Sea in the distance.

Suddenly the mobile Alfie had given me started to ring in my bag. The sound of it made me jump. With fumbling fingers, I retrieved it from my backpack and stared at the unknown number on the screen in front of me.

'What should I do?'

'I think you'd better answer it,' Nathan said.

'Hello.'

'Hello, Gemma.'

I didn't recognise the man's voice on the end of the line. 'Who is this?' I asked once I had swallowed the lump in my throat.

'I've got a message for you from Alfie.'

My heart began pounding as I waited for him to continue, but he didn't. After a lengthy pause, the mobile went dead.

My hands were clammy, and all sorts of thoughts started swimming around in my head. What was the man implying by ending the call without saying anything? I didn't understand what his silence meant. Why hadn't he just told me Alfie's message instead of making me suffer like this?

'Who was it?' Nathan's voice pulled me out of my thoughts.

'I don't know. He said he had a message from Alfie and then he put the phone down.' I knew it would be a huge mistake to let this man get inside my head. But by staying quiet, he'd sent my imagination into overdrive.

My phone buzzed. At first, I was reluctant to open the text. I was scared of what it might say, but then curiosity got the better of me.

Just for the record, you were wrong about me. I didn't sleep with you out of revenge. I love you, Gemma. You mean the world to me and that's why I'm going to let you go. Keep the money; you earned it. I hope it will make you happy. You deserve to be. Love always, Alfie.

As far as I was concerned, the night we'd spent together was a mistake, and something I regretted. It was clear he didn't feel the same way. I turned off the phone and threw it onto the bed next to me. Nathan crossed the room and squeezed the tops of my shoulders.

'What did it say?' Nathan crouched down so that we were on eye level with each other.

'Alfie said he's going to let us go. Do you think we can believe that? It seems too good to be true, doesn't it?'

'Maybe.' Nathan shrugged his shoulders.

I decided not to tell Nathan the details of the text. What was the point? It would only upset him, and the last thing I needed right now was to go on another guilt trip. So instead, I chose to keep Alfie's confession to myself. Nothing good would come of Nathan knowing what he'd said. It would fill him with insecurity. I knew it was wrong to keep the contents of the text a secret but justified my actions because I wanted to protect Nathan from getting hurt again. Surely under the circumstances, I needed to edit out the part that would distress him, didn't I?

'So Alfie knows we're still alive. Is that all he said?'

'Pretty much.'

'I wonder if he knows we've got the money.'

'He does. He said we could keep it.'

Nathan raised his eyebrows. 'Well in that case, why don't we go out and celebrate? You might as well drink some champagne while you still can, Mrs Stone.' Nathan leant forward and planted a kiss on my lips.

The thought of being pregnant brought a smile to my face, and as I stared into my husband's eyes, I knew I'd made the right decision keeping the contents of Alfie's text to myself. I couldn't risk losing Nathan.

We'd let each other down in the past, but now it was time to put that behind us. I'd been broody for years, whereas up until now, Nathan hadn't wanted to start a family. Finally, it looked like we were on the same page.

Acknowledgements

Thank you to Hannah Smith, my wonderful editor, for giving me this opportunity and for holding my hand through the entire process. You've made my dreams come true.

Thank you to my husband Barry and children, Sarah and James, for your constant support and encouragement. I couldn't have done it without you!

Thank you to my parents, my brother, Keith, my sister, Katharine and the rest of my family and friends there are too many to mention individually, but you know who you are!

Thank you, Sinéad Goulding, my cousin and lifelong friend for suggesting I write a book in the first place. I'm glad I listened to you!

Thank you to my dear friend Bruna Aylieff for your tireless enthusiasm and the good times we've shared being the ladies who lunch!

Thank you to the members of the Romantic Novelists' Association for their invaluable advice on the road to publication, especially Imogen Howsen.

Thank you to everyone at Aria Fiction for working so hard behind the scenes.

Finally, thank you to the readers, reviewers and bloggers.

About the Author

STEPHANIE HARTE was born and raised in North West London.

She was educated at St Michael's Catholic Grammar school in Finchley. After leaving school she trained in Hairdressing and Beauty Therapy at London College of Fashion.

She worked for many years as a Pharmaceutical Buyer for the NHS. Her career path led her to work for an international export company whose markets included The Cayman Islands and Bermuda.

For ten years, Stephanie taught regular beauty therapy workshops at a London based specialist residential clinic that treated children with severe eating disorders.

Stephanie took up writing as a hobby and self-published two novels and two novellas before signing a contract in March 2019 with Aria Fiction.

Hello from Aria

We hope you enjoyed this book! If you did let us know, we'd love to hear from you.

We are Aria, a dynamic digital-first fiction imprint from award-winning independent publishers Head of Zeus. At heart, we're committed to publishing fantastic commercial fiction – from romance and sagas to crime, thrillers and historical fiction. Visit us online and discover a community of like-minded fiction fans!

We're also on the look out for tomorrow's superstar authors. So, if you're a budding writer looking for a publisher, we'd love to hear from you. You can submit your book online at ariafiction.com/we-want-read-your-book

You can find us at:
Email: aria@headofzeus.com
Website: www.ariafiction.com
Submissions: www.ariafiction.com/we-want-read-your-book

 @ariafiction
 @Aria_Fiction
 @ariafiction

Printed in Great Britain
by Amazon

37278610R00248